P9-CAO-030

We are pleased to send you this advance reading copy for review. Please send any mention or review to:

Dorchester Publishing
Publicity Department
200 Madison Ave., Suite 2000
New York, NY 10016

Title: **Tempted Tigress**
Author: **Jade Lee**
Publication Date: **5/29/07**
Price: **$6.99 U.S. / $8.99 Canada**
Pages: **368**
ISBN: **0978-0-8439-5690-0**

PLEASE NOTE:
This is an uncorrected proof and not the final edition.

In Xanadu did Kubla Khan
A stately pleasure-dome decree:
Where Alph, the sacred river, ran
Through caverns measureless to man
Down to a sunless sea.
                    —*Samuel Taylor Coleridge*

This fragment with a good deal more, not recoverable, composed, in a sort of Reverie brought on by two grains of Opium taken to check a dysentery.
                    —*Samuel Taylor Coleridge, 1797*

PROLOGUE

The best thing about an opium high was that one could make the most mundane observation and think it an amazing stroke of brilliance. Right now, Anna Marie Thompson thought the following conclusion was the height of genius: Dying would be unfortunate. And poor Governor Wan was about to experience a very, very unfortunate death at the hands of the Imperial Enforcer.

"Come away, Sister Marie. Do not look out the window. He will see you."

Anna nodded, but she could not make her body move. She reclined on a silk couch right next to the window, and she really had no interest in budging. Especially as she had just come to another brilliant conclusion: Though dying would be unfortunate, the moments before death—the time when one knew one was about to die but couldn't do anything about it—those would be worse.

They were obviously the worst for poor Governor Wan. He was kneeling in his luxurious garden—one filled

with stunning ornamental plants and exotic flowers—
and gibbering like an idiot. Spittle flew from his mouth in
his passion. He alternated between pleading for his life
and cursing the Imperial Enforcer's family. He begged, he
screamed, he cried . . . and he completely failed to save
his life. Nothing touched the emperor's assassin.

Anna stared at the man who towered over the sobbing
governor. Here was the man all drug-runners feared. He
had many names among her set, but they all boiled down
to one thing: he killed. Without mercy or any show of
emotion, he systematically murdered the people who
smuggled opium into China. The users might be shown
mercy, but carriers were gutted like fish.

The Enforcer couldn't be bribed or threatened. Those
had been the first things Governor Wan had tried. And
worst of all: the Enforcer always destroyed the merchandise.

Crowding around Anna, the governor's wives moaned
in horror as they watched the Enforcer pour kerosene on
fourteen pounds of opium. He'd tossed it all into the fire
pit, and now grabbed Wife Number Four's favorite
lantern. With a flat expression on his dark face, he cast
the lamp into the pit. The whoosh of fire sent the women
recoiling in horror.

Anna didn't move. That too was a benefit of an
opium high. It allowed her to watch simply because she
couldn't move away. And right now she stared fascinated
as the blaze reflected off the chiseled features of the evil
man's face.

Surprisingly young, the Emperor's Enforcer had the
typical features of a Chinese man in his prime: smooth
skin, angular bones, and dark eyebrows like brushstrokes
up the planes of his face. But his eyes were larger than
normal, as if he could see farther and more clearly than

anyone. Then he narrowed them, making them appear like his eyebrows: precise slashes made by the finest artist's brush.

How odd, that he didn't appear emotionless to her. That was his reputation, but what Anna saw was a deep-seated rage, as if the man saw everything and hated with a passion beyond anger, beyond fury; hated until it became a kind of madness.

"Come away, Sister Marie," urged Madame Wan again. "We must hide you before the murderer comes here."

Anna blinked and smiled weakly at her hostess. "But he already said he won't hurt you. He comes for your husband."

She turned back to the window as the Enforcer brandished two deer-horn knives. Shaped like crescent moons, the two sharp slivers glinted red in the blaze of the burning opium. Anna smiled, temporarily mesmerized by the flash of light in his hands. It barely registered when the red became blood and not reflected flame: Governor Wan was no more.

And that too barely filtered through her mind, except as another flash of brilliant thought: the province's leading opium distributor was dead.

"Come away, Sister Marie," whispered Madame Wan, a third time, forcing Anna to stand. "We must get you to safety."

"But why?" Anna asked.

"Without you, who will get us more opium?"

Anna nodded as another flash of perception blazed through her fogged mind. Governor Wan wasn't the province's best opium provider.

She was.

". . . not only prison guards and common soldiers, but every official from mandarin and high military commanders down was apparently an opium smoker; capricious and neglectful of duty, sometimes cruel."
—*Jack Beeching*

CHAPTER ONE

Anna Marie Thompson hunched her shoulders to sink deeper into her heavy mandarin tunic. The air was chilled here along China's Grand Canal, but it was the sand that hurt the most. Black and rocky, it cut through her useless straw sandals to slice deep gashes into her feet. She winced with every step but dared not slow her shuffling progress.

Besides, where could she go? To the right was a rocky embankment. To her left strained the long line of coolies, each with a rope wrapped around his thin, nearly naked body. Hundreds of them trudged there, dragging wupan and sanpan boats through the canal, while their low *chor-chor* song ground against her like the heartbeat of an enormous monster.

Anna closed her eyes, feeling trapped deep in the arteries of the beast named China. Soon, soon she could be gone. Out on the open sea, the wind fresh on her skin, the creak of the sails a loving accent to the rush of water beneath her feet. She didn't think beyond the boat, about where she would go after that. Her whole goal was to escape China.

She clutched her bundle of clothing tight to her chest and sidled up to a family of five, keeping beside a little girl with short black braids. She wanted to smile at the girl, but didn't dare expose more of her face. So she settled for a depressed shuffle near enough that an outsider would think she was one of their party—an aunt, probably.

Rubbing her chin lightly on her raised collar, she immediately regretted it. She didn't dare scrape the mud off her skin no matter how uncomfortable it felt. She'd long since learned to ignore any itch along her scalp. Under no circumstances could she reveal her hair. Skin could be darkened, clothing could hide large breasts and sturdy bones, but no amount of mud or dye could make curly brown hair look straight, Chinese black. Fortunately, most imperial soldiers grew bored after the first half hour of searching, and it was now well into the afternoon. The men would scan the crowd for a lone white woman, but they wouldn't look deeper. As long as she acted just like everyone else, she had a chance. No one would check her pockets for the pouch that hung heavy and hard against her sweating thigh. No one but she would smell the sickly sweet scent that she feared clung to her skin and stained her soul.

The little girl stumbled on a rock, and Anna instinctively reached down to catch her. But her back muscles were stiff from days of clenched terror, and her knees had swollen almost as much as her feet. She was too slow to prevent the worst of the fall. The girl dropped her doll and scraped both knees before Anna caught the child's coat. At least she could use her own body to block the continuing line of humanity that trudged doggedly forward. A man sidestepped around them, then planted one big fat foot right on the doll's stomach as he tromped forward. The child screamed in outrage, drawing the attention of both Mama and Papa, plus both brothers.

"Aie-yah!" gasped Mama as she quickly rushed forward. Anna stretched out and rescued the doll, but was unable to wipe the black footprint from the torn cotton dress. The little girl snatched the toy out of her hand and began wailing in earnest while Mama chided the child in rough Mandarin.

Then Anna made her mistake. She met Mama's eyes.

The gesture was what any stranger would do when passing off a distraught child. Women throughout the world smiled at each other, sharing understanding and sympathy in the shortest of glances. But just as nothing could hide the Caucasian nature of Anna's hair, nothing would make her light brown eyes black or shape them into lifted almonds beneath smooth black eyebrows. She was cursed with the thick brown eyebrows of her English ancestors, and the round, tending-to-wrinkles shape of her eyes.

Mama recoiled in horror, and her gasp caught Papa's attention as well. How much longer before the soldiers noticed the commotion?

Anna quickly dropped her gaze, already knowing it was too late. Moving with the quick reaction of long practice, she grabbed the woman's hand and dropped coins—God only knew how many—into the palm. Then she spoke rapidly in low Mandarin, mimicking the woman's accent as closely as possible.

"I am just a woman who is leaving your country. I go home. Let me please leave in peace. Please."

The woman was terrified. She grabbed her child and yanked her firmly backwards, away from Anna. The girl let out a louder squawk of alarm at the rough treatment while Anna closed her eyes and prayed.

Dear Jesus, sweet Mother Mary, help me!

"What's the matter?" Papa's rough voice cut in, his tone hard with accusation.

Anna kept her eyes closed and her head down, her thoughts still spinning with prayer. *Please, please let me go.* Then, without daring to breathe, she hunched a shoulder past the little family and tried to walk by. But the quarters were too tight, especially as the father grew suspicious. His hand was rough, his reach long as he grabbed Anna's arm. The cheap fabric tore where his fingers wrapped tight, and Anna clenched her jaw tight against a cry.

Mother Mary, Christ Jesus my savior . . .

The mother made her decision. She snapped out an angry retort, not to the white devil woman, but to her husband. "Carry this worthless daughter," she ordered her husband. "She dropped her doll."

Anna could feel the husband hesitate, but she didn't dare turn her face to him. She kept her head down, her body hunched in real terror.

Christ Jesus . . .

Clearly impatient, the mother lifted her still-sobbing child and roughly shoved the girl at her husband. Papa was forced to release his hold on Anna while the child wrapped skinny arms around her father's neck. Anna wasted no time, moving ahead with as much speed as possible—which is to say she got nowhere. Only a few steps ahead, and then she was trapped again, moving with slow, dragging steps while her back prickled with awareness. She knew both Mama and Papa were looking at her with undisguised curiosity. Mama perhaps with greed, too.

Anna's danger increased the longer she remained

within eyesight of the little family, and yet there was nothing she could do. She couldn't move ahead, but if she slowed enough to let others pass, the parents would begin to whisper. Then they would turn their heads around, constantly searching behind them for her. Who wouldn't notice that?

No, it was less conspicuous if Anna stayed ahead and let them stare at her back. Meanwhile, she kept up her silent prayers.

Tau Zhi-Gang felt his entire body thrum to the beat of the coolie chant. The words were simple—"put your shoulder to it"—but the *chor-chor* sound rose and fell with such power that Zhi-Gang's spirit ran after it in joy. Here was China, breathing with great lungs, its qi power soaring through the air while thousands of people toiled beneath its mighty demands. Sitting on a tilted sedan chair along the Grand Canal's bank, Zhi-Gang felt both humbled and enlightened. But most of all, he felt a dark, raw fury.

All through this canal, carried by boat, by human, by the very air, floated the poison of China: opium. Everyone from the highest imperial to the lowest peasant lusted after the gray-brown poison from the west. It hid in packed wads that looked like bad dirt and tasted even worse, but one by one, China's people succumbed to its false allure. Zhi-Gang sighed, his gaze wandering over the vague wash of color and shadow—all that his damaged eyes could discern. He couldn't see the white man's curse on China, but he knew it was there. He felt its presence as surely as he felt his own pulse. And as Enforcer, it was imperative that he find and end it—or it would be his own pulse that was abruptly ended. So said the emperor of China.

The guard beside him stiffened, and Zhi-Gang's atten-

9

tion sharpened. What did the man see? It was probably nothing. The guards were being especially vigilant as a way to impress Zhi-Gang. They did not know that Zhi-Gang's status with the Imperial Court had slipped somewhat of late. It did not matter. Appearances were important because appearance was all they had. In truth, not even the most clear-sighted of Chinese enforcers could see all the wads of brown dung opium that traveled the Grand Canal.

Zhi-Gang canted his gaze to his "servant," who was hovering just to his left. Feng Jing-Li stood close enough to be seen as more than a vague form. In truth, his body had color and definition, enough to read his closest friend's expression. "What do you see?" Zhi-Gang asked, as if he were testing the man.

Jing-Li responded in a low mutter: "A woman who looks . . . different."

"How?"

"She walks hunched as a woman ought, and yet her steps have purpose. Her clothing is worn, not tattered; the style old but well cared for." He paused, and Zhi-Gang felt a tightening in his friend's focus. "I do not see a companion."

"Is she fleeing?"

"Perhaps. A husband and wife quarrel over her while she presses ahead."

"Interesting."

His friend nodded, then pitched his voice louder and in a tone appropriate to a servant. "Honored sir, our boat is ready. They are prepared for your esteemed presence."

Zhi-Gang flashed a grimace at his friend. Jing-Li's warning was well placed. They were not truly here on an inspection tour for the empress dowager. Certain appearances were important, such as standing high upon an embankment to frown at the crowd beneath. China's rulers liked it when the masses saw their enforcers. Certain other appearances—such as performing an actual investigation—were not only unnecessary but counterproductive as well. Sitting on the Grand Canal was not really an effective way of finding opium.

Zhi-Gang sighed, then impulsively reached for the secret pouch on the inside of his jacket. Beside him, Jing-Li visibly paled.

"Honored sir, I fear the air is inconvenient to your health." His voice took on a more alarmed tone. "You appear faint!" Jing-Li lurched forward, one hand placed strongly upon Zhi-Gang's back while the other gripped his arm.

Zhi-Gang froze, his hand wrapped around the heavy wood case that always rested against his chest. "Really . . . ," he began, but Jing-Li's grip tightened even further. The message was clear: do not use the secret object. Not in so open a location.

"It is harmless," Zhi-Gang whispered.

"Nothing from the West is harmless," his friend snapped.

True enough. Zhi-Gang relented with a sigh. They were, after all, on an embankment overlooking thousands of Chinese peasants. He had no wish to start a riot by using a Western implement.

He returned the case to its hiding place. "I feel much better," he said coldly to his servant. Jing-Li had no choice but to bow and withdraw. Then Zhi-Gang turned his attention to the guard. "Bring me the unusual woman," he snapped.

The guard was startled; his attention long since slipped to something else, but he leapt forward to do as he was bid anyway. Of course, he had no idea which unusual woman the Imperial Enforcer meant. And so Zhi-Gang waited, his attention and his sense of humor focused on Jing-Li. Would his friend relent and help the guard? Or would he remain stiffly remote and allow the guard to suffer and probably bring in whichever hapless woman first crossed his path?

Jing-Li cursed just loud enough for Zhi-Gang to hear. Something about obscenely swollen testicles, then he pointed angrily at the crowd. The guard nodded and dashed away. Zhi-Gang barely restrained his smirk. Then he relaxed back against his hard bamboo seat and enjoyed his friend's annoyance. He'd almost forgotten the woman by the time the guard returned, dragging the poor thing forward and throwing her down at his feet.

He leaned forward. She was at the edge of his vision. He could see a dark tunic and bowed head. Her hands were long and unusually large where they landed on the rocky ground, but he really couldn't see much more than that. With an internal curse, he drew on his other senses. He heard her breath as it rushed in and out in frightened gasps. He smelled her scent—both sweet and sour. Most of all, he felt her qi: the intangible force of energy that invested all life. He touched it with his mind, allowing himself to steep in her crystalline light. He felt the sweetness of a woman with a flexible strength beneath, that skeleton of will that was softer than a man's and yet so much more alive. He smiled to know that she was one who would survive where others would fall.

But then the energy shifted. His intent had been to *know* her, and he believed he had. And yet, the moment he touched her energy it shivered away from him, it covered itself in layers of coldlike dirty snow and then turned on him. He felt his own energy change. He had no understanding of what or how; it happened too fast. He only comprehended that the transformation was core-deep and had the echo of immortality within it.

Zhi-Gang reared back in horror, certain truths imbedding themselves in his thoughts. He knew then that this woman—this shaking, terrified thing at his feet—had the power to change everything at the most fundamental level. He didn't understand how he knew this, only that it was true. She could change his life.

And she was white.

He couldn't see her face, didn't know anything beyond what Jing-Li had said. But wise men did not question qi knowledge. And so he responded without thought.

"Kill her," he snapped. Then he remained stone-faced while beside him, Jing-Li gasped in shock. The guard nodded once, then drew his sword. But his attention remained on the woman as her head reared up in shocked horror. He saw her lips open on a cry, and her eyes shimmered with tears.

"Why?" she cried in Mandarin. She scrambled forward on her knees only to have the guard grab her tunic and hold her fast with a knee pressed hard into her back. She was pinned to the ground. Her face hit the rocky dirt and something cut her chin. Zhi-Gang saw the faintest edge of red well up as her blood began to soak into the ground. And still she spoke, her eyes desperate with shock and confusion. "Why?" she repeated. "I have done nothing!"

There were other sounds, too. Jing-Li was speaking in a low urgent tone. Zhi-Gang did not hear the words, but he knew the meaning. The emperor had just been incarcerated by his mother. Zhi-Gang was the emperor's Enforcer and therefore someone fully allied with the son and not the mother. Jing-Li was reminding him they could not afford any extra attention.

Yes, a murder along the Grand Canal would certainly create attention. Even if they pretended her death was an official punishment, they had hundreds of witnesses within a quarter li. The local magistrate would need a report, the body would need to be disposed of and Zhi-Gang's trip would be delayed by a day at least.

Zhi-Gang ignored it all. His attention remained on the woman's angry expression. He'd been prepared for sobs and pleas, for all the tricks that women played on men. What he saw instead was confusion, horror, and a growing fury.

He could not see her white eyes clearly, but he knew their shape. Hers would be round and ugly, their color light and insubstantial. And yet in his mind he saw a different woman—his sister, so many years ago. She had been a young girl with dark almond eyes and a fury that defied her captor. Zhi-Gang had been too young to stop the man. His sister had fought with all the strength in her tiny body. All the while, she screamed two words: *No!* And . . . *Why?*

Before him, the white woman rasped the same words over and over while the guard raised his sword, point down. At least the man knew how to kill a prisoner. He did not lift his sword like an ax, but raised it with the hilt high, the point aimed between her shoulder blades. She would be pinned like an animal to the rocky ground, her life blood seeping into the black dirt. The clouds parted enough for a flash of reflected sunlight to arc across the dull sky. A lesser scholar would claim that Heaven blessed the hard metal, approving of the kill. Zhi-Gang prayed it was true.

"Why?" Her final gasp coiled deep into his spirit, souring his stomach and poisoning his qi. Still, Zhi-Gang forced himself to watch. He would not turn away as the sword descended. He would see the white woman die.

The guard's muscles bunched and the sword descended. *Thud.* Hard and clean. Zhi-Gang felt the impact in the earth from his feet all the way through his entire body. It was done. She was dead. Her sobs had stopped on a kind of gurgle, and now silence filled their tiny circle of rocky ground.

Only now did he realize he'd shut his eyes. Silly that, since he could barely see anyway. He opened his eyes, steeling himself for the spreading stain of dark blood from a prone body. He saw the guard straightening from the right, tensing to pull his sword from the dirt. But when he looked down, he saw Jing-Li crouched above the woman, body vibrating with fury.

Zhi-Gang looked lower. The woman was still alive. Her breath was silenced on a gasp, her eyes were still wide with terror, but she spoke not a word. He doubted she even breathed.

"What is the meaning of this?" Zhi-Gang demanded of his friend.

Jing-Li dropped into a kowtow, his forehead pressed almost but not quite into the dirt. When he spoke, his tone was nearly—but not quite—subservient. "Honored sir, your anger is justified, your righteous fury reaches to Heaven. Of course this whore should be killed, her blood is yours by law. But stay your hand, I beg you. Your concubine must confess her deceit so that we may know how deep her lies have soiled the ears of your friends and family." Then Jing-Li raised his head, and his eyes held a desperate warning. "Kill her later, great sir, at your leisure. I will see it is done painfully. You need not poison all those around with the stench of her soiled spirit."

Zhi-Gang didn't answer: his throat was closed tight. Revulsion boiled in his blood, but his mind was separate enough to recognize his own irrationality. He had no cause to kill this woman, and no reason to hate the very air she breathed. And yet, he did.

It was his sister, he realized. It was the Chinese girl who begged and pleaded in his memory. *She* was the one he wanted to kill. Or more exactly: the memory of her, of what had been done to her. Anything that reminded him of her—even this innocent white woman—would always be ruthlessly suppressed. Especially since this white woman was *not* innocent. That, too, he knew to his core.

He straightened from his chair, his footing unstable on the shifting ground as he stalked forward. The guard had managed to recover his sword. Zhi-Gang saw now that the blade had struck just to the side of the woman's neck. Jing-Li must have blocked the downward stroke. Grabbing the sword from the startled guard, Zhi-Gang kicked his friend aside.

"Please," Jing-Li gasped, even as he struggled to recapture his breath. "Your concubine—"

"My concubine?" Zhi-Gang bellowed. It was a lie, but an effective one. If others thought this woman his lawful wife, then he could do whatever he wanted—including killing her—without fear of reprisal. "My concubine!" he agreed.

His hands twisted on the heavy sword. The heat made his hands slick with sweat and the hilt would not settle securely in his scholarly hands. The damn thing was much too heavy compared to his deer-horn knives. So he tightened his grip and raised the blade high. The woman tried to scramble backwards, her voice still silenced by shock, but a guard—a new one—caught her with his boot. Two more appeared beside the newcomer, adding their boots to her body. All had come to see the show.

What am I doing? The thought slid through his mind, repeated over and over. But like ink mixed too thin, it had no substance. He would kill this woman. Had he not felt the truth in her qi? She would be the death of him. She would change his world irrevocably, and he could not afford another such life-shattering change.

Jing-Li found his breath and this time banged his head for real against the dirt. "Master Tau! Master Tau! Where is your reason?"

Gone, he thought. And he did not know why. The sword was slipping in his hands. All too soon it would descend whether he willed it or not. He tensed his stomach, intending to kill her with a single stroke. Nausea rolled in his belly, but he fought it down. Then he met her eyes. He was close enough to see them clearly: round, light brown, and rimmed red from her tears. He saw the streaks of wet on her cheeks that revealed the pale white color of her skin. And he saw her rough lips, chapped and swollen from the sun, now swelling where she had bit down, her blood welling thick and dark across her white teeth. Nothing appealing about her at all, and yet he knew she was beautiful. Something about her fired his blood, and that made him all the more angry.

"I curse you," she hissed in clear Chinese. "I curse you to taste forever the tears of all women, to feel the aches of their broken feet and taste the blood of their lost virginity. I curse *you* out of all men in China to know what you have done to me." Then she spit her blood at his feet and stretched her neck to wait for the sword.

As one, the guards leaped backwards. Curses were no

small thing, and the curse of a dying woman carried the ugliest taint. None wished to share in this damnation.

"So be it," Zhi-Gang acknowledged, accepting the punishment. Then he pulled the sword down with all his might.

The blow never landed. Though smaller of stature, Jing-Li had always been faster. There had been no time to leap from the ground to stop the sword, and yet, there his friend was, his hands gripped around the sword, desperation lending strength to his arms. They grappled for a moment, sword twisting awkwardly between them—two scholars unused to such a weapon. But in the end, Jing-Li won. He knocked the sword to the ground such that it clattered loudly against the bamboo chair.

"You cannot take such a curse upon yourself!" Jing-Li cried. "You will kill us all!" Then he glared at the guards, mobilizing them into action. "Take her to our boat. Chain her. I will kill her there."

All was accomplished with amazing speed. The woman was dragged off, the sword sheathed and gone. Even his chair disappeared, taken by his true servants. All that remained was himself and Jing-Li, locked one against another.

"Where is your mind?" Jing-Li rasped, his breath sour with fear.

Zhi-Gang acted without thought. He threw his friend off him with a curse. In raw strength, he had always been mightier. Then he stood over Jing-Li, his breath hot on his lips and in his lungs. He had no answer for his friend, and that made his blood boil even hotter.

"You will not touch her," Zhi-Gang rasped. "I will kill her with my own hands. I will drain the blood from her body and have her heart for my dinner." Then he twisted, leaning forward until his forehead nearly touched the smear of compressed dirt on Jing-Li's. "Interfere again, and *you* will be the one in chains sent as a special gift to the Empress Dowager."

He waited while his words spread into Jing-Li's spirit. Then, with a last curse, he spun and stalked away. His heels ground into the rocks with every step and his hands itched where he'd clenched them into fists. As he walked, he narrowed his eyes and prayed he didn't trip.

It wasn't just that his poor vision washed the world in fuzzy gray. It was that his spirit seemed covered in an oily blackness. It coated his thoughts, polluted his moods, and ate at his reason. How could a man chart a clear course when his every action, his every thought was haunted by fury? By moods so black that they caused him to threaten a woman just because she was white. Just because she was on the Grand Canal where no white was allowed. Just because she reminded him of another woman who begged and pleaded and received no mercy. Why should a white woman receive pity when his sister had not?

He stopped his angry progress across the shifting dirt, closing his eyes as he tried to steady his qi. He was the Emperor's Enforcer. He'd been charged by the Son of Heaven to eradicate the poison that threatened China. And yet, how could he purify China when he could not even steady his own spirit? And what was he going to do with a lone white woman who traveled in a place no white was allowed?

Questions spun in his thoughts, distracting his focus and muddying his spirit. But even as they cluttered his mind, he knew they were completely unimportant. The real problem had come as a whisper. These questions were merely his attempt to drown out the tiny ripple that continued to roll through everything he did.

He had touched her qi and knew she would change his life. She would change everything about him, starting at the deepest foundation of his spirit. A white woman would change his life.

No. No! A thousand times *no!* He would kill her before he allowed such a thing. Of that he was absolutely certain.

January 4, 1876
Dear Mr. Thompson,

It is with great sadness that I write to inform you that your wife and infant daughter did not survive childbirth. Without other direction, we have interred them in the mission graveyard, giving them all the necessary Christian services.

I am also given to understand that there is another girl, Anna by name, who stayed with a neighbor during your wife's labor. Though I am sure that the home is all that a God-fearing woman would expect, your wife did express some fear for Anna in that the neighbor already has four children of her own. If you wish for additional supervision of a Christian nature, please know that we at the mission stand ready to assist you.

With sincerest regret,
And in Christ's name,
Mother Francis
St. Agatha Mission
Shanghai, China

So twice five miles of fertile ground
With walls and towers were girdled round:
And there were gardens bright with sinuous rills,
Where blossomed many an incense-bearing tree;
And here were forests ancient as the hills,
Enfolding sunny spots of greenery.

—Samuel Taylor Coleridge
from "Kubla Khan: or, A Vision in a Dream. A
Fragment"

CHAPTER TWO

Anna closed her eyes, her soul too drained for even tears. At least she was off her swollen feet. And with her eyes shut, she could feel the sway of the boat and pretend she was on the ocean speeding away from this horrible country.

She sighed and opened her eyes. Her gaze landed immediately on the iron shackles about her wrists. There was also a rope wrapped around her left ankle that tied her to the bamboo skeleton of the Chinese junk. Wupan or sanpan or whatever-pan, she didn't know except that the boat was double-tiered and designed for beauty. Anna was on the topmost level beneath bamboo mats that served as a ceiling. On the floor opposite her lay a nest of silk cushions beside a small stack of Chinese books. She guessed she'd been imprisoned in the mandarin's bedroom for a very unsavory reason. He either wanted to slit her throat in private or he had other activities in mind. Or both.

And yet, she found it hard to care. Her earlier fury had drifted away. Even her prayers were gone. Now she knew nothing but the hot still air and the heavy weight of the opium sack still tied around her waist. That more than anything depressed her spirit and silenced her prayers. That sack doomed her, and she was hard-pressed to quarrel with the punishment.

The only whites allowed in the interior of China were missionaries. And yes, she had preached the Gospel, yes, she had daily labored in the hospital bringing relief to the sick and dying. She had even considered going through the motions of marrying Christ Jesus. But the truth was that she carried opium under the guise of being a missionary. Jesus had done nothing for her, and why should He? She was a liar and a fraud. She was a opium smuggler, a runner who carried the drug into China under the lie of religion. The punishment for such a crime was death. Quick or slow, brutal or not, her death was a just and lawful punishment. At this moment, she wished for only one thing: to smoke that which she carried.

She licked her dry lips, imagining the hot caress of opium across her tongue. It would fill her mouth and lighten her mood. Her body would relax and float away into the beautiful blue sky. She wouldn't notice . . . so many things. And in this way, she could die—if not in peace, at least in ignorance.

Time passed without conscious reckoning. Pretend bliss wasn't nearly complete, but it let her mind drift to where it always went: the dark eyes of the Enforcer and his bloody knives. He was relentless in his pursuit of her. And she . . . she wasn't running this time. She stopped and turned to him. She slowly, erotically, she undressed before him. Then they were kissing, touching, joining in the most basic of ways. Her body began to soar, her skin tingled with his caress, and then all ended as a sound woke her from her doze. A man entered the little cave-like chamber, lifting the silk tapestry from the opening such that a fresh breeze stroked the top of her head. It was gone before she could raise her face to it, but the memory lingered, as did the dream.

She opened her eyes without planning to, blinking to bring the dark figure into focus. It was the mandarin, looking as austere as before. He wore dark clothing, loose pants, and an embroidered jacket that sagged open across another richly decorated tunic. She knew who he was, recognized him from her memory fragments and night-mares. It was rather disconcerting to know that her opium dreams had become truth. The Emperor's Enforcer was indeed going to be the one who executed her. She knew his piercing black eyes and his long elegant fingers, for they had haunted her dreams since the night three months ago when she watched him kill Governor Wan.

What she didn't see was his weapon of choice: two deer-horn knives that he usually carried strapped to his hips. That meant he probably wouldn't kill her right away.

Relief slipped into her body, releasing some of the tightness in her chest. Surprise came second as she realized she cared. She was actually thankful that she wasn't going to die right then. And as her fear lessened, passion returned. It made no sense to lust after the man who would kill you, and yet she could not shake her dream of sweet caresses and slow lovemaking.

The Enforcer said nothing as he stood before her. His feet were spread wide on the deck, and his hands rested firmly on his hips as he glared at her. With a curse of dis-gust, he reached under a fold in his shirt. She tensed in reaction, knowing many men who kept pistols hidden there. But before she could do more than gasp, he drew out a thin wooden case. Not bamboo, but smooth polished mahogany. With a snort that sounded almost like defiance, the Enforcer flicked open the case and drew out a pair of gold wire glasses. He set them carefully on his nose, adjusting the ear hooks with practiced ease, then carefully tucked the case back into his breast pocket.

Only then did he peer at her, clearly frowning. "You stink," he snapped in English.

"You're cruel," she replied, before she thought better of it.

He reared back as if struck. "Prisoners are to stay silent," he roared in Chinese. Then he clapped his hands twice.

On cue, the silk tapestry doorway pulled open and servants poured in. One carried a chair, another a small table. Yet more brought in a rolled scroll and a scholar's desk set. All was arranged with speed before the servants bowed to the ground and backed out of the chamber. Only one servant remained: the tall one with the familiar manner. The one who had stopped his master from killing her by the canal.

That servant rolled open the scroll and waited patiently while his master wrote a series of characters with clean, deft movements. Anna found herself mesmerized by the sight. This man was the Enforcer, the Emperor's killer, and yet his hands were elegant, his fingers long and precise. She knew without looking that his calligraphy would be a work of art. This was no brute of a killer. This man was a poet who killed, and the dichotomy fascinated her. How nice that her executioner would look beautiful as he killed her.

* * *

He did not glance up when he asked—in English—for her name.

She didn't answer. She was dead anyway. She would take what little joy was left to her in annoying this arrogant mandarin.

He looked up, the long strokes of his eyebrows drawn together in disapproval. "Name!" he snapped.

She lifted her chin and did not answer. Before she completed the motion, the servant crossed the room and brutally backhanded her. "You will answer!" he boomed in Chinese.

"He said prisoners do not speak!" she cried, furious to realize that her eyes watered from pain and humiliation.

"You are not a prisoner," the Enforcer responded evenly.

She blinked, completely thrown. "I'm—"

"Name!" bellowed the servant.

"Sister Marie," she answered in truth. Except, of course, it wasn't the full truth. Marie was her religious name, and the one she had been given the day she began swabbing the floors of the Shanghai mission when she was eight.

"Missionary?" the servant demanded. She blinked, thrown by his demand when all of her attention centered on the Enforcer. It was almost as if the servant weren't even in the room. Except that, when she didn't answer his question, the man began to dig at the blouse covering her chest. She tried to shove him away—finally forcing her gaze from the mandarin—but she had no leverage, especially as he backhanded her across the face. The blow pounded through her skull and her head snapped backwards to crack against a bamboo slat. Her breath felt choked off at the source but she could still smell the ginger that clung to his thick, clumsy fingers as he pulled open her collar.

He hooked a finger beneath the coarse twine about her neck and lifted out her large wooden cross. The heavy wood scraped roughly against the inside of her breast as he dragged it out, and tears stung her eyes from pain. The twine cut harshly into the back of her neck as he hauled the cross forward, tilting the polished wood to his master. "Missionary," he repeated with a sneer. Then, with a snap of his wrist, he jerked it off her head.

She swallowed and let her gaze slip back to the mandarin. Internally, her soul quieted despite the servant's abuse. It felt right that the cross be removed: She shouldn't die with a lie around her neck. Meanwhile, the Enforcer dismissed everything with a flick of a single tapered finger.

"Surname?" he inquired in English.

Anna shook her head, her lips firmly compressed. But then the servant raised his arm to strike and she shouted at him, "It's just Sister Marie! I don't have a surname!" she lied. "I'm an orphan!"

The servant's arm remained poised to strike, but no blow fell. Instead, he glanced at his master, who stared at her with quiet eyes and a blank expression. In the end he grunted, then calmly dipped his brush in the ink. "Marie Smith," he spoke aloud, stroking characters on the paper.

She frowned, startled that he knew enough about the English to guess at common surnames. It had been remarkable to hear him speak in barely accented English, but that was not too uncommon among the Chinese elite. That he would assign her the name Smith was . . . interesting.

"Why aren't I a prisoner?" she asked. Then she frowned and rephrased in Chinese. "People who are not prisoners should not be shackled." Then she held out her arms as if expecting the chains to be removed.

The Enforcer didn't respond; he simply finished what he was writing and carefully rinsed and stowed his brush. That strange fascination with his movements overtook Anna again. She barely even noticed when the servant left her side to stand silently by his master. With great ceremony, he opened a distinctly Chinese box and pulled out a long ivory chop. The mandarin lifted the identifying seal, then carefully pressed the square stone into the red paste used as ink. With equal pomp, he set the chop on the scroll.

It was tantamount to signing an official document, and Anna could not help craning her neck to see what was written. She couldn't see much, and worse, her command of written Chinese was sketchy at best. She saw long lines of Chinese characters, and—shocking—two words in beautiful English letters: Marie Smith.

She gasped. "You can write English?"

Servant and master exchanged an alarmed glance. Then the servant abruptly rolled up the scroll and tucked it into a bamboo case. He did not even look at her as he turned to back out of the little hut. He did, however, pause just before the threshold to whisper urgently to his master.

"Kill her soon," he said. Then he backed out.

A shiver of terror slid down Anna's spine, but she ignored it. She had been in fear for her life for so long that she easily hid it with bravado. She straightened her spine and reextended her hands. "I am not a prisoner," she pressed. "Release my chains."

The Enforcer made no move toward her. Instead, he leaned back in his chair and inspected her in a long, leisurely fashion, a grim smile on his face. "You are not a prisoner," he said coldly. "You are my concubine. By both our laws, I can legally do much worse than shackle you."

He spoke in Chinese, so it took some moments for his meaning to sink in. When it did, her body stiffened in horror. "Married?" she gasped. "We aren't married!"

"Of course we are. Have I not just made it so?" He gestured negligently at his desk before him.

"That scroll?" she whispered. "That was our wedding?"

He nodded.

"But the priest? The vows? The . . . the . . ." She clamped her mouth shut. She was being ridiculous. The Chinese were heathens. Women were bartered and sold with complete impunity. First wife or concubine made no difference. It was merely a matter of timing since all were bought or disposed like old clothes. A wealthy Chinaman could record on a scroll their false wedding and then with complete legality kill his new woman. And no doubt he thought the entire procedure completely civilized.

"You can't marry a white. Your Chinese friends will be appalled. You will be thrown out of court. You . . ." She was babbling, scrambling for anything that might end this farce. But he simply shrugged.

"White women are sometimes gifted to us. Prostitutes, usually, but beautiful like you. They all die in the end without any man—Chinese or English—making a complaint."

She stared at him, knowing what he said was true. "I am no whore," she murmured.

"Of course not," he returned, his tone bland. "You are my concubine."

"Until you kill me."

He smiled, the expression bizarrely friendly. "Exactly."

She had no idea what to make of this man. Was he the terrifying Emperor's Enforcer or a madman? Or both? She had no idea, so she focused on what she could control. She held out her bound wrists.

"Your new wife shouldn't be in shackles," she said. "It isn't fitting for your station." She was being stupid. She had no hope of escape. Trapped on a boat with servants and soldiers loitering on every spare inch of the deck, she couldn't run with or without chains. And yet some tiny spark within her refused to die. She had better odds without her chains, therefore she would try to get them removed however she could.

"It isn't fitting that she stink either," he drawled.

"Then allow me to bathe."

He didn't respond, just continued to stare at her. It wasn't an intense gaze, more of an abstract look in her direction while he thought of other things, and yet she felt the weight of it as a physical pressure. And worse, because of that dream, her body tightened in passionate hunger. She twisted awkwardly against the wall, wishing for a more comfortable—more dignified—position. She wished for something to do with her hands or perhaps . . . yes: a hot bath. Anything to take her mind off—

"Do you not know how to sit quietly?"

She abruptly stilled, her thoughts awhirl. She stared at the Enforcer and felt her interest sharpen. After a decade of living in this country, she thought she understood the Chinese better than anyone. But this man seemed different. Murderous one moment, then calm and deliberate the next. In a country where serenity was prized, he had allowed his fury to flow, and yet . . . She narrowed her eyes. His quiet now told her his earlier display might have been just that: a display. But why?

And more important, why did she care? What did it matter if he had an agenda? In her experience, high-ranking Chinese were always plotting something. What would it gain her to figure out his motives, to match wits with a man raised on stratagems?

She jingled her chains. "Why should a doomed concubine sit still?" she challenged.

"To prepare for death?"

Her life, then. The prize was her life.

"And if I am already prepared for death?" she asked, secretly fearing she was not nearly prepared.

"Then you should be at peace, your body and your mind quiet in acceptance of final judgment."

"How very Christian of you," she drawled. It was not the statement a missionary would make, and yet she found herself unable to stay silent. A spark had kindled inside her, an interest that she had not felt in a long time.

While she was occupied by her own thoughts, the mandarin began to lean forward. His eyes fired with a dark light and he gripped his small table with a fierceness that made his knuckles white. "Do you think the *Christians*"—the word came out as a sneer—"are the only ones who understand damnation? Do you not think the Chinese believe in judgment after death? How arrogant you are, even in chains! I despise your vanity!"

She drew back, her eyebrows rising even as her soul remained quiet. The spark of interest flared hotter as she mulled over his reaction. She had touched on something in him, something painful. Something primal.

Without conscious thought, she found herself on her feet despite the rope around her ankles. She stood before him as straight as possible, one shoulder braced against the wall, and said nothing. She faced him as she would face a firing squad. And in that moment, she made a decision.

She wanted to live. Against all odds, despite the darkness that already tainted her soul, she wanted to live. And to that end, she would do anything—anything at all—to attain that final freedom away from China. Lying, cheating, thieving—these were the smallest prices she would pay. After all, she had already done these things. But now, with conscious thought, she decided any of the cardinal sins were available to her hand. She would kill, she would whore, she would do whatever it took to escape this accursed country. And when she at last boarded the boat away from China, she would begin a new life of atonement. At that point she would beg forgiveness for her sins. She might even become a nun. But first she had to get to that boat. She had to find a way around this man and out of China.

It was a hard decision to make, perhaps the hardest of her life, to know that no depravity was beyond her so long as it furthered her goal. Yet it was made in an instant. And once made, the chains of morality slipped from her soul. A giddy weightlessness filled her heart— black though it was—and she began to smile.

The Enforcer's anger cooled. Only a few moments in his presence, and she saw that he was a man of mercurial moods. His anger was fierce, but it quickly faded. He frowned at her, obviously startled by her smile. And so she deepened it, made her stance less confrontational, more mysterious. More womanly? Was he a man to be tempted by a woman's appearance?

He sneered and turned his face away.

Not sex then. What else could she sell? The answer was obvious. The weight of the opium beneath her skirt was a constant drag upon her thoughts and energies. She knew the Enforcer wouldn't take it. As far as she could tell, he was incorruptible. But his servants? The sailors and his soldiers? Maybe they could be bribed. She would have to be careful. If any knew what she carried, they could simply take it and leave her with nothing. If the Enforcer found it, she would likely die before she could draw her next breath.

No, she would have to barter something else now, reserving the opium for later. But what? She tilted her head in thought, her words light and conversational when she spoke.

"You have kept me alive for a purpose. What is it that you want?"

The mandarin shrugged. "Entertainment? To relieve the tedium of a long trip."

As if on cue, the boat crew began a low chant. They had been calling to one another in their own boatman's cant for some time. But now the chanting began. The junk was moving, and Anna's smile became genuine. The boat moved smoothly, didn't jerk roughly, every inch dragged from a hundred coolies pulling against the flow of the water. That meant they were traveling south; nearer and nearer to Shanghai and the boat that would take her away.

"Arabian Nights, then," she said. "I accept."

He clearly did not understand the reference. She explained.

"There is a book. It tells the story of a woman trapped by a wealthy man. She is tasked with entertaining him every night. If her stories bored him, she would be killed in the morning."

"How long does she live?"

"A thousand nights—until she is set free," she lied.

"After telling stories?"

She nodded.

He leaned back in his chair and folded his arms. "I will not be amused by stories."

She had not expected he would, but it was a place to begin. "Are you so sure?" she challenged.

His smile was slow in coming, but it spread evenly and thoroughly across his face. "I am very sure. But you are welcome to try."

"Then you must leave now and allow me to bathe. Send fresh clothing and a trunk for my effects."

He arched a brow. "Why would I do that?"

"Because an entertainer must have her props. I must be allowed to present my tales in the most pleasing manner possible, and use what meager things I have in secret." She swallowed, knowing she had to force this issue. "My trunk of clothing must be inviolate. How else could I surprise you?"

He stared at her, his eyes like dark ink pools: completely black, completely indecipherable. She waited in silence, forcing herself to remain still.

"Very well," he said, his tone laced with . . . disappointment? "It will be done." He pushed up from his chair. "And I will tell Jing-Li to sharpen my knives for your execution."

September 18, 1876
Dear Mr. Thompson,

Nine months have passed since your sweet wife Cassie breathed her last. During that time, I have cared for Anna as if she were my own. She has eaten at our table, slept in the same bed with my Beth, and even attended Sunday services with us.

But my Sam is not a wealthy man and we have another child on the way. Without word or money from you, we cannot keep her any longer.

Were she a different child—a calmer child—perhaps we could reconsider. My boys adore her, you know, but she frightens Beth with her loud voice and her boyish ways. You perhaps have not noticed since you are at sea so much and home so rarely, but your Anna has a temper. Angry at times, sulky the next. We never know what moves her from smiles to fury, all in an instant.

Therefore, I have left her with Mother Francis at the Benedictine mission. I have told her all that I relay to you. Perhaps after a spell with the nuns, the wildness will be ironed out of her. Then perhaps, with appropriate compensation, of course, I could bring her back to my home. As it is, she simply eats too much.

Mother Francis was most understanding.

In Christ's love,
Mrs. Susan Miller

The use of opium in not a curse but a comfort and benefit to the hard-working Chinese.

> —1858 press release from the British firm of
> Jardin, Matheson & Co., China's biggest
> opium importer

CHAPTER THREE

Zhi-Gang allowed the white woman the illusion of privacy. He called for a bath and even had Jing-Li empty out a small trunk for her. But he was no fool; he knew she was a drug-runner posing as a missionary. He had seen enough of them—killed enough of them—to recognize the look. And yet there was something truly uncommon about this woman. Something that drew him even as it enraged him.

He gave her false security so that she could hide her opium or her money. Or perhaps it was something worse. It didn't matter. Jing-Li would discover it, and in truth, Zhi-Gang was loath to learn of it. He wanted his mysterious white woman to be something special, someone to justify his fascination, even though he knew she was nothing more than a despicable drug-runner who deserved an ugly, brutal death. He knew, and yet he did not kill her. He hated her, and yet he respected her privacy and allowed her a place to store her secrets.

He was an inconstant man plagued by irrational fits and moods, and he hated himself for it. That too was nothing new. So he chose to sit quietly beneath the second sail. The breeze was strongest there, and the beat of the drum for the coolie trackers not so overwhelming. Best of all, he could read if he chose. That was the one activity where he did not long for his glasses, and so he doubly cherished those moments of serenity.

By now, all the boatmen knew he wore glasses and no longer warded themselves from evil whenever they saw. But Jing-Li worried—with good reason—at the appearance of anything western. Now was a dangerous time to be seen as someone who sympathized with—or used anything created by—the ghost barbarians.

Zhi-Gang smiled. If Jing-Li feared a display of western glasses, how did he feel about a white concubine? It had been Jing-Li's idea, of course, but only to keep the murder out of the public eye. He would not have imagined that Zhi-Gang might keep the woman alive. He'd probably be terrified enough to kill the woman himself, no matter what his orders were.

Zhi-Gang abruptly straightened from his seat against the mast, his unfocused gaze searching through the increasingly vague shapes at the back end of the boat. He saw nothing useful, and he heard . . . nothing unusual. No female screams or curses. But no slosh of water, either.

He was on his feet, moving quickly through the coils of bamboo rope littered about. He walked by touch and memory, having spent long hours learning the pathways along the deck. By the time he made it to the rear, his entire spirit felt like a disordered brush.

"Jing-Li!" he bellowed, heedless of how such an unseemly display would reflect upon his dignity. "Jing-Li!"

"Here!" His friend rushed forward, dropping onto his knees then flat onto the deck in a kowtow. The action was completely appropriate for a servant, but the look of annoyance was not.

"What have you been doing?" Zhi-Gang demanded.

"What you ordered, master! Water for the bath. Silks for a gown." He dared lift his head then. He didn't speak, but his face clearly showed confusion.

Zhi-Gang squinted, trying to discern the details of his friend's face. He dropped his voice to a near whisper. "What were you doing?"

Jing-Li straightened his arms, lifting his torso off the deck. "What I do best." When Zhi-Gang didn't speak, he finally confessed the truth. "Watching," he hissed.

Zhi-Gang frowned, trying to understand. When he did, he felt a total fool. Of course there were peepholes in the tiny hut at the top of the boat; the walls were made of bamboo mats! Of course Jing-Li would find the gaps and peer into Zhi-Gang's bedchamber. That's what Jing-Li did: He spied. And thanks to that talent, they were now on this mission to a southern port and not dead or imprisoned with the Emperor in the Summer Palace. Still, Zhi-Gang couldn't suppress a surge of anger.

"Where?" he demanded. He gripped Jing-Li's arm, pulling him to his feet. "Show me."

"You are the master," Jing-Li hissed. "It's not fitting . . ." His voice trailed away. He obviously knew Zhi-Gang would not be deterred. And so, with a sigh, he led the way.

They wove as silently as possible around the bamboo slats supporting the mat walls. At the edge of the boat, braced on both sides by barrels of water, a small hidey-hole appeared. Jing-Li had even managed a worn blanket set as a cushion to allow a spy to sit more comfortably.

Zhi-Gang frowned. "How often do you look in on me? Do you watch me as I shit?"

Jing-Li shrugged, straightening. "My life rests in your hands. I do not take your safety lightly." Then he grabbed hold of a barrel and began to shift it for more room.

Zhi-Gang's hand shot out, gripping his friend's arm. "Go find out when we will arrive in Jiangsu province."

Jing-Li's face held genuine surprise. "But . . . why?"

He couldn't answer. His friend had reason to be startled. How many times had they spied together on the lesser women in their quarters at the Forbidden City? From the ages of thirteen to fifteen, Jing-Li's aunt's home had been a particular favorite, with excellent peepholes into the women's area.

And yet, this woman was different. This time was different. Zhi-Gang had no tolerance for his friend's prurient lusts. It sullied the white woman in some indefinable way. That he did not understand his attitude bothered him, but it did not change his mind. "You will not spy on this woman."

Jing-Li's face darkened, and his fists tightened. "Enjoy her if you must, Zhi-Gang, but do not grow attached," he warned. "She must die before we reach Jiangsu."

Zhi-Gang knew it was true, and yet he could not stop the surge of fury that boiled through him. "Do not seek to instruct me!" he snapped. "Without me, you would be dead alongside the Emperor's guard!" For all Jing-Li's spying, it had taken his own Enforcer's blades to make their escape. And even then, they had been unable to save the Emperor.

Jing-Li did not answer, though he obviously struggled with the desire to speak. In the end, he bowed and backed away even as he threw in a final suggestion: "Use her roughly, my friend, and loudly. I will make sure her death looks like rigorous enthusiasm." Then he slipped around the barrel and disappeared.

Zhi-Gang forcibly restrained himself from bellowing after his friend. He had never enjoyed violent bed sport like many others of his age and status. The sight of bruised and bloodied women disquieted his qi to the point of illness. The process of strangulation during bed play was another barbarian import that appealed to only the most corrupt of his countrymen. And yet, it would be a ready excuse for a concubine's demise.

A noise from within his chamber drew his attention: a soft, feminine gasp and a large splash. He struggled with his conscience but could not stop himself. He wanted to see the white woman. He needed to understand what about her drew him so strongly. His discussion with Jing-Li forgotten, he settled quickly down on the blanket and pressed his eye to the peephole. Two peepholes, in fact, perfect for relaxed spying. But he saw nothing. With a silent curse, he drew back and put on his glasses. Then, at last, the chamber grew distinct, the muted light became bright enough to see.

No one. He could see the outlines of the wood tub, but . . . A leg. One long leg lifted out of the water, barely discernable before the view was cut off by his desk. Whatever had possessed him to leave his desk there?

A sudden eruption of noise and form: the woman rising up from where she'd been submerged beneath the water. He had not realized how every sound carried so clearly. He could hear the splash of droplets on the deck, her gasp of breath as she stretched upward, and the rush of water that streamed from her hair back into the tub.

She was . . . bouncy. That was his first thought. Given his youthful pursuits and his current age and status, he had seen and enjoyed many a Chinese female. They were, as a rule, small with crippled feet, tiny hands, and little breasts. Not this woman. She dwarfed the round wood tub in which she sat. Her legs—what he could see of them—were sturdy. Her hands were large by comparison and her shoulders broad. But what riveted his gaze were her breasts. Big breasts. Large bouncing breasts that jiggled as she wrung out her hair.

He was fascinated. She was arched over, her back a long, beautiful line on which he detected the shadow of ribs on a body deprived of rich foods. And yet, even as she revealed her thin body, her breasts dangled like ripe honey pomelos. Would her skin be resistant like their rinds? His hands itched to touch, his mouth watered just thinking of their sweet taste. Her flesh would fill his hands to overflowing, and still there would be more to suckle.

She finished twisting the water from her hair, and she straightened and wound the thick mass on top of her head. With her arms raised, her breasts lifted even higher and he at last caught his first sight of a white woman's nipple. He had thought they would be pale like the rest of her skin, but now he saw it wasn't true. Her nipples were dark, like ink made from tea leaves. They were puckered from the chill air and shaped differently than he expected—flatter, more round, and yet no less pleasing. Indeed, he spent much time watching, trying to decide on the best flower analogy for those lifted brown tips. None came to mind, though his mouth and tongue grew restless imagining their shape and texture.

Blood pounded in his ears, and his legs spread naturally to give his sex more room. He longed to touch himself, to relieve the ache inspired by this woman, but he held himself back. It was not dignified for a man such as himself to sit on a boat deck, hidden though he was, and fondle himself.

Yet, he did not stop watching. The woman leaned over the side of the tub, reaching with long fingers for something on the floor. Soap. It was Chinese cake soap such as any fishwife might use. For the first time since fleeing Peking, he mourned the loss of his western rose soap. How sweet she would smell with the scent of flowers upon her skin.

She applied the soap vigorously. He had heard the whites were fastidious in their bathing, but he had not expected such furor. Every curve, every dimple, every inch was rubbed until he could see a fine pink cast even from this distance. Her face, her long neck, her white shoulders, and the full length of each arm grew flushed from her ministration. And his cock throbbed thick and heavy against his thigh.

Her breasts came next, and he was disappointed that she spent no more time there than anywhere else. And yet, there was still excitement in the tantalizing way she lifted and moved them. And when she squeezed the sponge, sluicing water down her chest, he nearly released his seed right there. His mind seemed to fixate on that rapid gush of water. It flowed over her breasts, sluicing across her nipples, only to cling there, hovering, beading.

In truth, he couldn't see these tiny details, but his mind created them. And in his thoughts, he was inside, licking each sparkling drop.

He must have made a sound. He must have done something to alert her, because she abruptly froze. He saw her straighten. She tucked her knees beneath her such that she was kneeling in the water, her hands tight on the tub rim. Then she turned, slowly rotating so that she could see every darkened shadow in the room.

The sight made Zhi-Gang's blood heat even further. The way she turned, shifting slowly as she craned her neck one way or another—it gave him a full and glorious view of her. He saw her breasts from all angles, watched them bounce with her movements, and yes, he imagined those sweet drops of water slicking her body with the most bewitching perfume.

But then she stopped. She must have again believed herself alone, because she leaned back against the tub wall. Her knees tucked momentarily against her chest, compressing her breasts into fat pillows, then she slowly extended her legs.

To Zhi-Gang's great delight, she pushed each leg high in the air—probably to keep any drops of water and soap inside the tub. *Tien*, she had long, long legs. He had not thought her so tall, but of course she'd hunched to hide her white woman's height.

The desk that blocked his view was no problem at this angle; her limbs extended above the plane of its hard surface. And she moved with such languid care that he could watch the way her thigh and calf muscles flexed beneath the smooth expanses of her porcelain skin. She allowed one leg to dangle over the tub edge, bouncing slightly against the side. The other foot was drawn close in as she began to soap it. He noted the high arch and tiny toes on her large, healthy feet. He had never liked the Han Chinese tradition of binding, and he smiled as she took her time slipping her fingers between each of her tiny toes.

How beautiful a full foot was! He vividly remembered his sister's screams during the binding process, and ever since then, the sight of crippled golden lotuses had always nauseated him. But this woman was whole, this woman's body strong in its full perfection.

She moved to soap her ankle and calf, flexing and arching her foot as she slowly thrust her leg through the circle of her hands. Up, up, up her leg went, while her hands slipped from around her ankle to underneath her calf, then she rounded the slight bend in her knee before drawing high on the inside of her thigh.

Zhi-Gang's breath caught, his mouth dropping open as she paused—leg still raised—to soak the sponge with water. Then, to his absolute delight, she drew her leg back in, raised her arms high—which also lifted her breasts—and squeezed the sponge. The deluge felt like a release to him; water sluiced down and he sighed in delight.

A single large bubble perched on her ankle. As the water hit, it popped and disappeared, but not in his imagination. In his mind's eye he saw that bubble slide up her leg, coiling around beneath her calf and knee until it settled into the dark hair that was hidden from his view. The thought was so compelling that he had to stifle a groan, his momentary release gone as he imagined his hands and organ plunging deep inside her. His dragon was no longer quiet against his thigh, but reared up full, proud, and very hungry. He would pierce that bubble between her thighs. He would lift her hips so that her long legs gripped him tightly behind his lower back. He would use the sponge to trail spicy perfume across her breasts and into her cinnabar cave.

All these things he imagined over and over while she applied herself to her other leg, cleaning and rubbing in a way no Chinese woman would unless she prepared herself for . . . His thoughts stumbled. Could it be? Did this white woman prepare to sacrifice herself to him for her freedom? The thought was titillating, to be sure. She was a beautiful woman, and he was already bursting through his underclothes.

Then the unthinkable happened. The woman glanced around. He could not tell if she was nervous or angry or simply curious, but he thought perhaps she was afraid and checking the shadows one last time. How very much like a woman to believe that she could have any privacy in a situation such as hers. But according to his English teacher, white women were extraordinarily secluded in their childhood. Perhaps this woman really was a nun. Perhaps Sister Marie had been cloistered in a Christian temple at a very young age. That would explain why she had little understanding of the ways of the world.

What she did next was all the more enthralling. She allowed both her legs to relax against the side of the tub, then lolled her head back as if she wished to rest. But her hands were not still. One traced a path from her neck down between her breasts, and then—rather abruptly—straight to her left breast. She cupped it, squeezing her hand tighter and tighter until her thumb rolled over her nipple.

He could see that the motion was not practiced, not a motion like that of a slave trying to entice her master. There was no subtle offering of the breast to an onlooker, or even a coy glance from beneath hooded eyes; Sister Marie's eyes were kept tightly closed as if this act were for herself alone.

And then her right hand moved as well. He watched it

slip off the lip of the tub to land on her thigh. He could only barely see her long fingers above the wooden edge. And then they disappeared altogether.

She couldn't possibly be about to . . . She *was*. He could see her skin flush with her exertions, heard the water splash in the tub, and—most telling of all—watch her arch her neck back as she pushed against her hand.

He pressed his face forward, and his glasses pushed hard against the bridge of his nose. He saw that she kept her mouth tightly closed—no doubt to stifle any sound—but he heard her anyway, his imagination more than able to supply extra details. Her hips would be lifting and lowering against her long fingers, the water splashing chaotically with her increasing rhythm. He watched her throat constrict as she swallowed, and he imagined himself kissing the hollow between jaw and throat. He loved to press his ear against a woman's cheek while his lips stroked the pulse point of her neck. He loved the sound of her shortened gasps and feeling her trembling heartbeat against his tongue.

Her left hand abruptly released her breast and flung sideways to grip the wood slats. He saw her fingertips whiten as she lifted her hips in passion and her mouth gaped slightly open from her exertions.

Then suddenly it was upon her. She stretched hard against the restrictions of the tub. He prayed she would lift her belly above the water line, high enough for him to glimpse the tiniest flash of her yin center. Anything would do—her quivering white belly, her long and nimble fingers buried deep inside her, or best of all, the red and puckered lotus petals that welcomed him in his imagination.

She didn't, of course. But he saw all in his mind's eye, and with the hard grip of his hand as on aid, he plunged himself into her over and over until he too joined her in glorious release. The roar in his ears and the darkening of his vision ripped her from his senses, but in his heart, he remained inside her throughout. He flickered his fingers, playing upon his dragon like he would a flute—as her body's contractions would. And he kissed her shy lips, giving reverence to her sweet spirit and beautiful body.

By the time his heartbeat slowed, she had finished her bath. Suddenly, as if ashamed of her actions, she grabbed a towel, wrapped it fully around herself and stood. He saw nothing of *her*, none of what his imagination had just kissed and spread and impaled. And yet, he cherished her even more for this new modesty. And he held his breath, pressing his glasses as hard as he dared against the mat as he prayed for another glimpse of flesh.

There was none, though she dressed right before his eyes. The angle of her body and the dark outline of his damned desk prevented any. Fortunately, it didn't matter. Her spirit was already imprinted upon his mind and he would cherish this afternoon for many years to come: the afternoon when he first saw his Wife Number Four.

The lightness of spirit held for over an hour. Long enough for the white woman to finish dressing and combing out her hair. Long enough for the sway of the boat to lull him into a gentle doze despite his cramped location. He was so content that he barely opened his eyes when Jing-Li pressed a knife to his wife's throat.

From Anna Marie Thompson's journal:
February 22, 1880
Sister Mary wants me to write down my sins. She wants me to confess all to merciful Jesus on paper. Here are my sins:

I hate Susanna. She acts superior because she has a mom who visits her. She's not an orphan. Well, I have a parent too. My mom may be buried by the chapel, but my father gave me a pearl ring when he was last in port. And a doll from India. The most beautiful doll in the world. I have a father, and he is not, not, not dead. So I hate Susanna.

I hate Bible study. I don't care that Jesus healed the sick and made cripples walk some time long ago and far from China. He isn't helping anyone here, and I still have to clean up vomit and piss and worse whether I pray or not. So why should I study someone dead who isn't helping anyone?

I hate being white. The Chinese girls come and sit with their mothers. They get to stir the laundry pots and play with their brothers and sisters. They are not dirty heathens like Sister Mole-face says. They're happy and healthy and in their own country. I wish I were Chinese.

My dad has been gone four months, two weeks, and four days. That means one month, one week, and three days until I start watching the road for him. He said he'd bring me a new doll all the way from England. He's the best dad in the world. Much better than that stupid Susanna's mother who smells like flowers but looks like dung.

But oh ! that deep romantic chasm which slanted
Down the green hill athwart a cedarn cover!
A savage place! as holy and enchanted
As e'er beneath a waning moon was haunted
By woman wailing for her demon-lover!
                              —*Samuel Taylor Coleridge*
                    from "Kubla Khan: or, A Vision in a Dream. A
                                                  Fragment"

CHAPTER FOUR

Anna looked at her hands, gently clasped on her lap, the
rich feel of silk a sweetness on her freshly scrubbed body.
She had never worn anything so fine as the yellow gown
now wrapping her body. She certainly hadn't enjoyed the
luxury of a long bath or a quiet afternoon in over a year.
She should feel pampered and clean—most especially
clean. Instead, she felt unsettled. Not exactly sullied, but
not even remotely virtuous.

Fortunately, she was no stranger to guilt and quite
adept at ignoring it. She even had the added excuse that
she had vowed to do everything possible to survive.
What was a little show for the Chinese against her life? If
pleasuring herself made her all the more interesting to
the voyeuristic Enforcer, then so be it. No guilt. Simple
survival.

Except, she hadn't just done it to tantalize the mandarin, who had surely been watching. Why *had* she done
it? Why had she slipped her fingers between her legs and

done what every priest had preached against since the church began?

Why had she done it? Because she was about to die. What a fool she was. She should be thinking of a way to survive, to live to tomorrow, no matter what the cost. But in her last hours of life, she had needed to give herself a little pleasure, a moment of ecstasy to savor before it all ended. It made no sense, and yet she hadn't been able to stop herself. She had needed release. She had wanted to feel—if only by her own hand—why life could be so very good. And if her erotic dream had replayed in her mind as she touched herself, then it was only to give form and detail to her last moments of delight.

And now that it was done, she could face death. She didn't even flinch when a cold blade slid across her shoulder, aiming for her throat. She'd felt the breeze when her assailant lifted the tapestry flap to enter the room. She had absolutely heard his harsh breath as he hefted his blade. Someone had come to kill her. And perhaps this was God's punishment for her debauchery.

Or perhaps not. Without conscious thought, she slammed her elbow hard into her attacker's ribs. The knife hadn't quite made it to her neck. And besides, the man—Jing-li, she now saw—was obviously not used to slitting throats. He didn't have a good grip on her or the knife. She was able to knock the blade away with ease, then twist out of his floundering grip and punch him hard in the chest.

He went reeling back, banged into the tub and fell down. He didn't land flat, which might have been better. At least it would have ended it quickly. Unfortunately, he tried to catch himself. One arm went deep into the water, and his chin banged on the hard wood. His feet were still scrambling for purchase on the wet deck, and he naturally lost his footing. Without his feet to support him, his upper body dropped. His neck caught hard on the edge of the tub and he gurgled in real pain.

She might have helped him. She had not planned to murder the man, simply to disarm him. But his feet were flailing and she could not get close. Within moments, he'd toppled the desk. At least the smooth wood had been empty of ink or brush, but the hard bamboo edge caught her skirt as it overset. Amidst the clatter of the desk and the servant's garbled curses, she heard the ominous sound of fabric ripping. Looking down, she stifled her own curse.

Her skirt was ripped in a long inverted V shape where the edge of the desk had gouged a hole. Now her entire left leg was completely exposed and scraped raw. She wasn't sure which bothered her more.

Light flooded the tiny room as the silk hanging on the door was ripped away. The Enforcer rushed in like an avenging god. She glimpsed his face contorted in fury, his long black queue whipping behind him as he bolted forward. And then he was gone.

He'd fallen flat. In his haste to get to her side, he slipped on the very wet deck and dropped forward. But unlike his servant, he'd gone down neatly, catching himself on his hands in a kind of push-up. He was clearly coordinated, as he held himself there for a moment, reestablishing his poise, then abruptly flipped onto his side and tucked in his knees. Within moments, he had settled his legs beneath him and was completely composed, though his silks were darkening with water.

Then he did the most amazing thing of all. He burst out in laughter, catching his breath only to burst out again. "It is a good thing that you are not an assassin, Jing-Li. I am sure you would starve!" Then he settled back into another hearty laugh.

The servant glared at his master, dark fury tightening his wet features as he managed—finally—to lift his neck off the tub. His throat was red, but his face was more so. Anna had not realized how large his hands were until she saw them tighten into fists. Would he lunge at his master? She very much feared so, especially as the servant whipped his dripping queue away from his face only to have it wrap wetly around his opposite arm. This was a man who lost all coordination when angry. A lumbering bull who would cause indiscriminate damage.

All the while, the Enforcer laughed and laughed, seemingly oblivious to the danger. Anna glanced hurriedly around, searching for the lost knife. She saw it underneath one of the cushions, and she stepped quickly to it, tucking it tightly to her side until such time as she might need it.

The Enforcer noticed, of course. He pointed. "See, Jing-Li," he continued in Chinese. "She is armed now. We are such blunderers that a white nun can overpower us both!"

The servant narrowed his eyes in her direction. He was no longer dripping wet, but his skin remained dark with fury. Anna tightened her grip on the knife, slowly raising it before her. She doubted it would save her life, but it would allow her to cause some damage before other servants came in to overpower her.

She widened her stance and prepared to fight while the Enforcer sobered. The growing quiet seemed to finally affect Jing-Li. He turned to his master and his color began to recede. His lips trembled as if he hovered halfway between mirth and fury. Then the mandarin tipped the scales, leaning forward in a conspiratorial whisper.

"What would your aunt say if she saw us now?"

The servant shook his head. "She would say nothing. We would simply be whipped and sent to bed."

"Ah, but what would she say to her ladies?"

Jing-Li grinned. "Every detail."

"With exaggeration."

"I would have nearly drowned—"

"I would have fallen atop you, holding you underwater by accident."

"And the nun would be a blind old woman who couldn't hold a knife with her two palsied hands."

The two descended into mutual laughter that had Anna slowly drawing the knife down into the folds of her skirt. Meanwhile, the servant pushed to his feet then leaned forward to help his master stand.

"You only got what you deserved," the Enforcer commented. "I will not allow you to kill her."

The servant grimaced as he hauled his master up. "You cannot keep her alive. She draws too much attention."

"We can hide her in a palanquin. No one need see her face."

The servant threw up his hands in disgust. "Have you lost your reason? We cannot be saddled with a white woman!" He stepped forward, and his boot was loud on the deck. "Lust has thickened your brain. You can have a dozen women such as her! Han women, white women. Ones with fatter breasts or smaller feet. Whatever you want, but not until Shanghai!"

His tirade ended on an loud exhale. The two men stood face to face, the Enforcer slightly taller, his friend and servant shorter but more powerful. Or at least so it seemed. Except, the more the servant blustered, the taller and more composed the mandarin appeared. His face remained placid, his stance almost casual, but there was no mistaking his power when he finally spoke.

"Have you forgotten that you pose as my servant? Compose your tone."

They spoke in court Chinese—similar to the Mandarin she knew, but more stylized. Clearly they did not think she understood, and she did not enlighten them. But she could not stop her internal start of surprise. She knew the Chinese, like the British, often kept servant families. Children would often grow up together, and therefore by nature would have excessively familiar attitudes toward one another, even servant and master. But what the mandarin said meant "pose." The friend posed as his servant, which meant things here were not as they appeared.

Meanwhile, the "servant" grimaced, and though his body and tone took on a more servile expression, his face did not. "It is too dangerous to keep her alive,"

"She is my wife, and you will not touch her unless I bid it."

"You have other wives," the servant groused.

Anna had to fight to keep from reacting. Of course she was a concubine—a third wife, fourth, maybe hundredth wife. It didn't really matter. And yet, this blackened her thoughts nonetheless even after the Enforcer dismissed his past spouses with a casual wave of his hand.

"Two dead and the third gone." He frowned. "Where is she now?"

"Companion to my mother in Canton. She still curses

your testicles and swears she will cut them off if ever you come for her again."

The mandarin gave a mock shudder. "As if that would ever happen." He glanced back at Anna. "So I have an adequate number of wives, and may now indulge in the women I want." His voice continued in that conversational tone as he addressed her. "Do you comprehend, wife? Your life depends wholly on me."

She did not respond, pretending to not understand his words. She doubted she fooled the mandarin, but his friend dismissed her with a shrug. "Why do you play with death? She is a ghost woman. Her kind will only bring ill fortune."

"That is your aunt speaking, not your brain. How will you fare among the whites of Shanghai if that is your attitude?"

Jing-Li sighed dramatically. "Most ill, I am afraid. I will likely die within a year." Then he frowned at Anna. "Less, if you continue in your ignorant lusts." He leaned forward, his entire body urging the Enforcer to listen. "We cannot take her to Jiangsu. The place is too small to hide her."

The mandarin stared back, his body rigid. But moments later, he slumped. "I know," he finally said.

Everything in Anna urged her to step forward and demand an explanation. How far away was Jiangsu? How long did she have before she died? But what was the point? They wouldn't answer her, and she would give away that she understood their court dialect. She bit her lip and considering fleeing right then and there, but there was nowhere for her to go. Not on a boat filled with the Enforcer's servants. So she decided to bide her time and pray for an opportunity.

"Leave us, Jing-Li," the Enforcer snapped. "I have made a bargain with her. Entertainment for her life."

The friend rolled his eyes. "She will bore you with white God stories, then slit your throat while you sleep."

"Then you should not be so careless with your knife." And he held out his hand to Anna, obviously demanding the blade.

She pretended ignorance, shaking her head in confusion. "I only speak Jin dialect of the north," she said in that language.

Though she knew the man was the Emperor's Enforcer, his attitude these last hours had been of a scholar and an official. She had seen him give in to his friend and servant. She had not been thinking of him as the Emperor's killer, so she was not prepared for his next action. He moved with startling speed. Before she could do more than cringe, he was beside her, one arm wrapped across her chest—near to her throat—and the other gripping her hand just above the knife hilt. His thumb was sharp and painful where it dug into her wrist at the base of her palm.

She had no choice but to release the blade. It clattered to the floor where Jing-Li snatched it up. Then she waited in absolute stillness for him to release her. He did not. Instead, he whispered harshly into her ear.

"Isn't lying against your religion, Sister Marie?" Except for her name, he spoke in court Mandarin. "Lie to me again, and I will kill you for breaking your vow to your white god."

She swallowed, unsure what to do. And as she hesitated, his arm crept higher on her body, brushing past her breast up to tighten ever so slowly around her neck. She made a noise of distress, but it did not stop him. His arm was implacable as he began to cut off her breathing.

"Confess, little nun. Beg forgiveness for your sin."

She need only stay silent. She knew that. The best lies were adhered to against all odds. In time, she could even convince herself that what she spoke was the truth. Stay silent! she ordered herself.

But she couldn't do it. Not with the breath trapped tighter and tighter in her body. Not with Zhi-Gang's free hand now slipping around her arm to press against her belly. She was flush against his body, his erection a hot presence against her hip. She felt him everywhere— against her back, wrapped around her belly and throat, even against her ear and cheek as his hot breath coiled around her face.

"Yes!" she cursed in his Mandarin dialect. Then she twisted abruptly, shoving him away with all her strength. He went nowhere. "Yes, I understand your lying speech. I know you will kill me despite your promise. So do not curse me for lying when you have no honor of your own."

He released her then. Not because she had begun to fight him in earnest, but for some quixotic reason of his own. He even had the gall to smile at her as he clapped his hands.

"Excellent!" he cried, though she had no idea what he thought was so good. "We shall let Jing-Li clean up this mess, and then our evening can begin." His eyes grew darker, his lids slipping to a sensuous pose. "I trust you will not bore me with 'white God tales'?"

She swallowed, unsure how to respond. "No," she finally whispered. "No morality plays. My stories are . . . of a different kind."

He grinned. "I look forward to them."

She bit her lip, knowing she should remain silent. But she was frightened and off balance. She could not stop herself from trying for some type of security. And if not security, then at least foreknowledge of what he expected.

"They are just tales, you know. Nuns are . . . Nuns do not . . ." She swallowed, knowing how ridiculous this was, given what she had been doing in her bath moments ago. But some men might be content with that—with simple viewing. It was a vain hope, but she clung to it nonetheless. "If I am to keep my vow of honesty, then I must keep my vow of chastity as well." She lifted her chin. "Do you accept that? Will you honor that?"

He wouldn't, of course. She knew. Hadn't she just felt his erection hot and hard against her bottom? And yet she still waited in anxious silence as he studied her. Jing-Li watched as well, his brows contracted in thought as he obviously plotted something of his own. She wanted to look at him, to discover some clue as to what the servant/friend intended, but she couldn't tear her eyes away from the Enforcer. His presence—even in silence—trapped her somehow. It was that powerful and that terrifying as she waited for his response.

In the end, he simply nodded and bent his head and upper body in a slight bow. "Of course I will honor the vows of any cleric, male or female. To disrespect that would taint my qi."

She snapped back, startled by her own daring: "What happens to your qi when you kill a cleric?"

He grimaced. "Feng-Du punishes such crimes most severely."

She frowned, not understanding.

"Feng-Du is where spirits are judged and punished after death. Demons torture those who commit evil crimes."

"Hell," she supplied. "We call it Hell."

His smile seemed twisted somehow, but it was hard to

tell as he gave another slight bow. "Exactly." Then he turned, gesturing negligently to Jing-Li. "Clean up this mess, servant." He grinned, obviously enjoying forcing his friend to wait upon him. "I believe I shall rest."

Jing-Li tensed. His shoulders lifted and his face took on a dark, angry flush. "You push this ruse too far," he growled. "You are no better than me. Less, by birth."

The mandarin arched a finely sculpted brow. "And how much does your birth help you now? You hide from the Empress on the Enforcer's boat." He grinned. "You must act like what you pretend."

"We are friends!" hissed Jing-Li.

The mandarin sobered, obviously answering a question neither had voiced. "We will find you a new place, Jing-Li," he said softly. "Away from the Empress, you will be able to live freely again. Just not right now." Then he stripped off his wet silk pants and tossed them at his friend.

Pretending to a modesty she didn't want, Anna forced herself to turn away from this interesting conversation. No nun would allow herself to see the mandarin's finely sculpted legs, and so she turned her back, but she kept listening closely, hoping for more clues about the man who held her captive. She heard nothing of use. Only his chuckle as he settled upon the cushions.

She heard his soft sigh as he stretched out and probably reclined, his hands behind his head as he quietly laughed at his friend's work. And then she imagined that his gaze drifted to her, wandering over her body clad in this tight Chinese silk. She felt uncomfortable awareness prickle between her shoulder blades, tighten her breasts, and heat her belly. She pulled her exposed leg in close to her body, knowing it made no difference. The fabric was too torn. He could see all of her leg from the knee down.

Such exposure was not so uncommon, really. Though the cool temperature in the north made for heavy fabrics that covered everything, the southern provinces were vastly different. In Shanghai, for example, tight skirts were often slit way up the thigh, especially among a certain sort of woman. The sight of Anna's knee and calf could hardly compete. Still, she felt his gaze burn there with erotic intensity. And yet, she dared not move away for fear that everything she imagined was simply that— her imagination—and moving away would bring on the attention she feared.

This made no sense. She knew that. And so, giving a muttered curse of disgust with herself, she stomped past Jing-Li to the toppled desk. She righted it quickly, then sat on the stool behind it. Once she was settled, she allowed herself to look at the Enforcer, this man who had haunted her dreams and now tormented her reality.

His eyes were closed, his chest shifting in the slow breathing of a man deeply asleep.

He slept like a man without fear: deeply and with total relaxation. He lay sprawled across the cushions, completely insensate, while Jing-Li finished cleaning and departed. Meanwhile, Anna sat on the stool, her thoughts weaving in and out as she longed for her own rest. After so many days of running, she was in sore need of sleep. In the end, she could not resist. She slipped off the stool to curl up on the hard deck. She did, of course, manage to quietly steal one of his pillows to tuck under her head.

She was asleep in moments, no doubt as deeply as he because when she next became aware of anything, her body ached from long inactivity and someone was singing badly nearby. It was loud singing, in that nasal baritone so loved by the Chinese. Much more interesting was the smell of dumplings sizzling in a pan.

She opened her eyes. She saw the tub again, dead center of the room, and the Enforcer's long queue undone down his back. Indeed, at first she thought she viewed a woman, so beautiful was his dark curtain of hair. But then he began another chorus of whatever Chinese opera he was singing, and there was no mistaking his male voice. Neither could she mistake the broad expanse of his shoulders as he straightened in the tub.

"Did I wake you, little missionary? Are you awake yet?" The words were sung, and it took some moments for her to realize that he was singing his questions to her rather than intoning some operatic refrain.

She twisted and attempted to straighten her legs, grimacing at the stiffness of her body. Had she truly been sleeping with her hands clenched about her knees? Apparently so, since it took real effort to untangle her arms before she could even contemplate straightening.

"I thought nuns slept on hard boards all the time," he sang. "Do you tell me that your body is unused—misused—not used—unused to such things?" He was clearly adding his own rhythms to a traditional melody.

She grimaced, wondering how he could know she was awake when all she could see of him was his back. Meanwhile, she managed to shift her legs and slowly roll to her knees. Her muscles protested the movement, but the change in blood flow was welcome if painful. Then she rolled her head a bit on her neck to remove a crick, only to stop halfway.

He had a mirror. Probably not a large one by his stan-

dards. It rested on another stool and was held in place by
two hands—Jing-Li's, no doubt. That mirror was angled
perfectly so that he could watch her and she . . . She sat
back on her heels. She could see him in all his naked
glory. Well, everything from the waist up, that is.

He grinned at her, his eyes sparkling. Then he lifted a
sponge high above his face and squeezed. Water gushed
from his hand in an audible splat upon his chest. It was a
broad chest, she realized, smooth and surprisingly muscled. His body didn't bunch like so many of the brutes in
her adopted father's employ. Instead, the Enforcer seemed
to have a lean strength, his tone and form much too . . .
too . . . interesting for her tastes. Especially as it made
him an effective killing machine.

She dropped her eyes to maneuver her feet underneath
her. Her hip was tingling with renewed blood and her left
foot still had little control, but she managed nonetheless.
The sting from the scrape along her thigh helped focus
her thoughts. Finally, she was able to force her body upright. She stood with little grace, but at least she didn't
knock anything over.

The Enforcer made a gesture, and Jing-Li tilted the
mirror back so that she had a fuller view of his naked
torso. He—presumably—had a better view of her, too.
She bit her lip, wondering what game he was playing.
From this angle she could see all of his muscled chest in
front of the sleek curtain of his black hair. His skin was
golden in color and absolutely smooth as it rippled across
his broad form and narrowed in at his waist.

Then he grinned and reclined backwards in the tub,
stretching his arms high above his head. "My goodness,
Jing-Li, I do believe that I have tired of singing."

"Praise Heaven," his friend intoned from behind the mirror.

"I wonder, then, what else I might do to pass the time. What else could one do in a bath?"

Anna's gaze snapped back to his face. His eyes were alight with mischief, and his expression challenged her to . . . to do something. Obviously he knew what she'd done before in her own bath. Given his expression, she knew she'd guessed correctly. He had indeed been watching her. Strange, how that thought didn't bother her as much as it should. She ought to feel humiliated by his not-so-private teasing. And she did—a bit. She also felt a strange exhilaration building inside her, another affirmation of life in this game she played with the mandarin.

One of the things she'd learned about the Chinese is that they were as circumspect about sexual activities as the English—in public. More so, in fact. But in private— between a husband and his wives—a great deal of exploration took place, especially among the wealthy elite. The most scandalous things were whispered among the married ladies when she wasn't supposed to hear. Obviously, the Enforcer was indeed of the elite. Of the frankly sexual elite.

While she tried not to stare, he was making exaggerated motions with his arm. She couldn't see if he actually stroked himself; the edge of the tub blocked her view. But his motions were meant to be explicit.

She continued to chew on her lip, wondering what to do. It was not as if she had never seen a naked male organ before. Her work at the hospital, for one, had stripped all of that modesty long ago. But she was supposed to be a nun who—presumably—was innocent. Except, she was obviously not nearly as innocent as appeared, given what her bath had been like.

She pulled her lip out of her teeth and firmed her jaw. Her own dithering was beginning to irritate her. The Enforcer obviously delighted in tormenting his victims. This was just a different method of torture. But it also told her something about him. He enjoyed the unusual. He was obviously delighted by her bath-time activity. And now, he teased her about it to see if she would give him another unconventional reaction. Very well. She would work on being peculiar. She was, after all, supposed to entertain him tonight. Besides, she had never been the kind of person to look away.

She stepped out from behind the desk, her eyes trained on the Enforcer's reflection. "Good evening, great sir," she began formally. "I thank you for allowing me to sleep. It was most kind of you."

She remained behind the tub, but her angle of view in the mirror increased the further she walked into the room. One more step and . . . yes, she could see past the lip of the tub to his most private part. Or would have if his hand and the sponge were not blocking her view.

Her gaze canted up to meet his eyes in the mirror, and she arched a brow, silently challenging his modesty. His smile widened as he obviously enjoyed her game. "You looked so sweet sleeping—like a child curled around a treat. I could not bear to wake you."

"Most kind of you," she murmured, shifting her weight to the side as she moved around the desk. He shifted the sponge accordingly. Her lips curved into a smile. "Was Jing-Li born higher than you?"

She'd succeeded in startling him, as his hand and expression froze. Jing-Li was not so affected. He leaned around the mirror and smirked.

"I only ask because you are so kind to me—a concubine wife whom you are about to kill—and yet so cruel to your friend whom you have known since . . . childhood?" She was guessing, but from their earlier conversation she knew she was right. She took another step forward. "Was it hard, great sir, being the one always thought lower in status, less worthy because of a simple accident of birth?"

The mandarin's eyes narrowed and his gaze slipped to Jing-Li. "Yes," he answered simply, but there was a wealth of understatement in the one word.

"A good thing you were not born a woman," Anna drawled. "I do not think you would have tolerated it well. The smarter female always has a difficult time."

"Pah!" he responded, sloshing the bathwater in his vehemence. "There are no smart women."

She had sidled closer to the tub. Her angle now allowed her to look down directly, but he still kept the sponge carefully resting so that she could not see anything of importance. "Do you think so?" she mused. "Then you must think that we women couldn't possibly be as brave or bold as one such as you—a male in the prime of his life, and a scholar as well."

The mandarin shrugged. "It is so."

She arched a brow at Jing-Li and the man's arrogance, but Jing-Li merely shrugged. Obviously, he thought so as well. She carefully adjusted her skirts and knelt down beside the tub. The mandarin shifted position so that he looked directly at her. That suited her purpose just fine. It only brought her target that much closer.

"You have not found any woman more clever than you?" she asked.

He sneered.

"More brave? Perhaps your mother. She did brave childbirth for you."

"Very true, but children are a woman's purpose. To avoid it out of fear would mean to be completely useless."

"My, that is certainly a male perspective." Anna reached down as fast as she could and snatched the sponge from its resting place. His sex lay thick and heavy against his thigh. She openly stared at its shape and length. "And this is certainly another perspective."

He said nothing and so she slowly, reluctantly lifted her gaze to see his face. He was grinning, his eyes sparkling. "And now you see what you wished. And I have delighted myself in allowing you to do as you secretly desired."

She nodded, as if she'd known all along that he would allow her to reveal himself fully to her. And perhaps she had. Only a man comfortable with himself would bathe in front of a woman. So she tossed aside the sponge, then carefully maneuvered her legs in her tight Chinese gown. It took some work, but in the end, she sat on the ground, her arms folded atop the edge of the tub, her chin resting on her hands.

"Oh," she murmured in mock defeat. "Well, then go ahead."

He frowned, clearly not understanding. She had fooled him! Glee bubbled up inside her, but she kept it carefully hidden as she straightened in dismay. "I thought you said you planned for this."

"Of course!" He leaned back, silently offering his organ. He apparently expected that she would try to buy her freedom.

This time she couldn't stop a small smile. "Well then, prove me wrong. Prove that I was not more daring and more clever than you."

He folded his arms across his chest. "Woman, you are illogical and stupid. Do you not understand what you are to now do?"

She shrugged in pretend confusion. "I'm not sure," she said. "I knew you were watching me this afternoon. And yet I acted in the full knowledge that I did so for your entertainment. Do you say that you are not equally brave, equally capable?"

He blinked, then his eyes widened. "You do not intend to . . . ?"

She pulled back. "*I* did not have help. Do you say you are incapable of doing it yourself? Tsk tsk." She shook her head. "And yet you claim you are more skilled, more clever than women."

His expression darkened, but not so Jing-Li. The man burst out in barely restrained laughter. "He is capable, woman. As a child, it was the only way—"

"Get out!" roared the mandarin.

With perfect ease, Jing-Li set the mirror aside, then bowed. "Of course, Zhi-Gang," he said in an undertone to the floor. "It is a brave and clever thing you do," he taunted. "I understand you want no witnesses should you fail."

"Out!"

Jing-Li was still laughing as he skipped quickly out of the room. But that left just Anna beside the tub and the mandarin jutting proud and hard out of the water. She looked at his face, trying to gauge his mood. His expression was no longer angry. Perhaps it was more thoughtful, more curious, as he seemed to inspect her carefully. Thoroughly. And with a frank sexuality that unnerved her. Or perhaps not. Her nipples tightened under his dark regard, and she felt her tongue wet her suddenly dry lips.

"You wish to see a show?" he challenged.

She canted her glance away. "I wish merely to entertain, honored sir. I—" Her words were cut off with a surprised squeak as he suddenly gripped her chin and slowly, inevitably, turned her head to face him.

"Do you seek to hide now, clever woman?"

She swallowed. In for a penny, in for a pound. "I would never hide from any sight you chose to show me."

He grunted in pleasure, as if she had just promised more than she'd intended. But before she could do more than wonder, he began to pull her head down. His grip wasn't brutal, merely firm as he tugged her chin back to its place on her forearms atop the edge of the tub.

"You wish to see? Then watch." Then he wrapped his hand around his organ and began to stroke.

From Anna Marie Thompson's journal:
December 14, 1881
A man came today. His name is Samuel Fitzpatrick, and he has a nice smile. He said he did business with my father, so he knew that Father had a daughter. He said Father

　　He told me
　　He was very sorry
　　I can't write it! He can't be! But Samuel brought me a doll. It wasn't from England. He said it was Italian, and that my father would have bought it for me if he could. But he couldn't because

Samuel said it was yellow fever. That lots of sailors died from it. Samuel said Father loved me very much and he heard from the captain that his last thoughts were of me and how much he loves me.

I told him he was lying. I threw the doll at him and ran from the room. He must have left the doll behind when he left because Susanna has it now. Says it was a gift from her mother. Except I know it wasn't. She's a filthy liar. And my father is not dead. He is NOT dead!

Samuel told me something else though. He told me the name of Father's ship. I'm going to go to the ship tomorrow. I'm going to leave right after evening prayers. I know how to get to the dock. I'll find his ship and my father. He isn't dead. He'll give me a real doll from England like he promised.

I am not an orphan! I have a father!

[We] shall teach such a lesson to these perfidious hordes that the name of European will hereafter be a passport of fear, if it cannot be of love, throughout their land.

—*The Times of London*

CHAPTER FIVE

Zhi-Gang wrapped one hand around his dragon while the other stretched across the edge of the tub to touch Sister Marie's shoulder. He pretended to hold her down but in truth he simply wanted to touch her skin, to feel her heat, and to know as precisely as possible her reactions to all he did.

Her eyes were huge as she perched her chin on her forearms. And only because he had his hand on her shoulder did he know that tiny tremors shook her. She was not nearly as sanguine as she appeared, and he smiled in real delight.

How unusual was this little fake nun. She had probably seen a man's dragon before; her reaction when snatching away the sponge had been one of mild curiosity, not a virgin's terror. And yet she was not nearly as hardened as the usual opium runner, male or female.

"Did you work in a mission hospital?" he asked abruptly.

She jerked at his question, her gaze rising to his face. "What— I—" She swallowed then flushed at his smirk. "Yes, I did." Then he felt her straighten her shoulders and pretend to a disaffected shrug. "I saw many male organs there. Many much larger than yours."

He nodded, believing her. "Of course you did. But it is like seeing a sword in an armory. You can see them lined up in a row, care for them, even compare length of the blades, the girth of the hilts, and measure the sharpness of the tips. But until you see one in the hands of a master, wielded by one who knows it as intimately as his lover—well, then, you know nothing about swords at all, do you?"

She blinked as she thought about his words. With understanding came a sweet blush to her features—a virgin's innocence, despite extensive hospital experience and a somewhat bold nature.

A *very* bold nature, he corrected. Her gaze had already returned to where he massaged his dragon with long, slow strokes. When she spoke, her tone was mocking. "And you claim to be a master, of course."

"Oh, no," he returned with false modesty. "I am much too young to have attained that status. I am more of an apprentice in the bedroom arts." Then he slowed his stroke, pinching the mouth of his dragon so that a yang pearl seeped out. She stilled in surprise and curiosity, and he leaned forward to push his advantage. "But I learn quickly," he drawled.

He reached down and lifted the pearl onto his forefinger. "Here," he whispered as he held the sacred substance before her lips. "My gift of yang to you."

She did not know what to do, but she was smart: She

understood his implication. And yet, even without touching her, he could feel the war within her. Yang emissions were not typically appealing to a virgin. But she was pretending to be world-weary, and he was enjoying discovering the edges of her experience.

She frowned at his finger, and her nostrils expanded as she quietly sniffed. Then she extended the tip of her tongue. It protruded slowly, as if she had to force herself. She clearly had no idea how erotic the sight was to any man: a woman's shy, questing tongue, nearly touching him. Nearly . . .

He could not resist pulling his finger away, just out of her reach. How beautiful was the sight of her open mouth! He could see the white of her teeth and the soft darkness beyond.

Then, while he was lost in the recesses of her sweet mouth, she lifted up on her knees and abruptly snatched away the pearl. She did not touch it with a quietly questing tongue; she abruptly surged forward and wrapped her entire mouth around his lifted finger.

Wet heat surrounded him, her swirling tongue. She added suction as she drew back, pulling at his finger. He felt as if his entire spirit went with the yang pearl, drawn into her body as swiftly and as inevitably.

Heat exploded through his body, shocking both him and her. Without his conscious intent, his dragon disgorged its yang fire. Zhi-Gang gasped in release, his mind overwhelmed by all that he felt as it and his qi spilled onto his chest and into the water. Wasted! Yang power and male seed spilled uselessly.

Except, it did not feel as if his energy fell away. He sensed it entered her, drawn in by some white magic. His awareness, too, seemed to connect with her. He flashed briefly upon this woman's heart—her trembling confusion and deep sweetness. He also knew for one brief instant an overwhelming darkness. She was angry, and bitterness stained her spirit.

So like his own. Her spirit and his—both were angry, both were stained. Both of them were acquiescing to darkness like ink spilled on parchment. He felt a bizarre kinship with this white woman, and his spirit shivered in alarm. His body though still disgorged its essence. It could not stop. He could not stop.

Never before had he felt the flow of qi as he did with this woman. Never before had he felt himself merge—even for the briefest instant—with anyone. He stared at her in open shock, but deep inside he knew a link had been forged. Two people lost in a black fog were now connected at their deepest core.

The thoughts were ridiculous, and yet they were also divine. Any idea that appeared in that moment of release—when qi flowed at its strongest—was deemed Heaven-sent. He believed that now, and the horrifying concept—that this woman might be the only way out of his darkness—made him push away from her in panic.

He reared out of the bath, splashing water every which way. His legs were not capable of sustaining him, and he stumbled. Without conscious decision, he steadied himself by gripping her shoulders, thereby continuing their unnatural connection. The fullest strength of it was gone, but there was still an echo, a whisper of knowledge—spirit to spirit—that made him rear backward again.

"Jing-Li!" he bellowed. "Jing-Li!"

He made it out of the bath and wrapped a thick towel

about his hips. He did not look at her, but kept his back resolutely turned. He heard her move, though. And what he couldn't hear, he imagined. She would stand in maidenly shock and confusion, her eyes wide with fright. Or she would slowly stand, a secret smile on her traitorous lips. She would know that she had taken his manly energy into herself. That she had connected their qi, linking them together forever. He couldn't kill her now. It would be killing himself, slaying his own spirit, because once linked, they were joined forever.

He had bound his spirit to a white woman! Did she know what she had done?

He didn't know, and so he spun around to discern her true nature: Was she a demon sent to ensnare him, or an angel sent to guide him out of the fog? He didn't know. And he couldn't see. She was gone.

He spun around, rapidly scanning every shadow in the room. She was nowhere. He scrambled for his glasses, pulling them on too quickly so that they perched awkwardly on his head. He searched every corner, every shadow. Empty. She was gone.

"Jing-Li!"

How long had his back been turned? Not long. But still long enough for her to make an escape. Long enough to for Jing-Li to slip inside and grab her? Perhaps. He wasn't sure.

"Jing-Li!' he bellowed again. Then when his friend still did not appear, he rushed outside still clad in his towel.

The boat crew said nothing, of course. They merely averted their eyes at his unorthodox clothing. He didn't care. Where was she?

"Jing-Li!" Still there was no sign of the people he

wanted, and that horrible dread expanded inside him. Could his friend have decided to help him? Could Jing-Li be right now killing her?

He grabbed the nearest worker—the man who beat the drums for the trackers. "The woman," he demanded. "Where is the woman? My wife!"

The drummer merely shook his head. It took a moment for Zhi-Gang to realize the man shook his head because he didn't understand Mandarin. The boat people had their own dialect, which Jing-Li spoke.

Spinning away from the drummer, Zhi-Gang scanned the deck and the rocky ground nearby. They had moored for the night, the sanpan tucked tightly against the bank and held in place by a half dozen thick ropes. Any young boy could run along those cords and make the bank. Then it would be an easy matter to hide amidst the shadows and rocks.

Not so much more difficult to drag an unwilling woman ashore—or better yet, carry an unconscious woman like a sack of rice. Was that the rope ladder unrolled off the side of the boat? Yes! Someone had definitely gone ashore! Could Jing-Li have carried her off, dropped her behind a large rock, then slit her throat? His friend would think it a kindness to take such an unpleasant task away from Zhi-Gang.

"Jing-Li!"

In his rational mind, he knew there hadn't been enough time for such a thing. Zhi-Gang would have heard if Sister Marie had been dragged off or hit on the head. He would have heard something! But where was she? And where was Jing-Li?

What if she attempted to escape? That would be most definitely in her character. And if Jing-Li saw, then he would follow her, wait until the perfect moment to leap upon her. He could be skillful with his knife. The whole thing would be quick and quiet.

"Jing—"

"You bellow like a trapped water buffalo!" his friend groused, popping his head above deck. Zhi-Gang rushed to the edge of the boat where the man was nimbly climbing the rope ladder. "What are you doing out here? Dressed like that?"

"The woman—Sister Marie—she is gone!"

Jing-Li grinned, then spoke in an undertone. "Yes, I know." He hopped the last step onto the deck. "I made most sure of it."

Anna felt her ankle roll beneath her and heard the telltale sound of fabric ripping as she slid sideways into the knee-deep mud of a lotus field. She'd been on the run for most of the night now, and her once-beautiful yellow silk gown was now filthy and torn despite her efforts to keep it clean. It was the only sellable item she owned, and so she had hoped to keep it in decent condition. Looking at the caked mud that blackened the delicate flying cranes, she groaned in real distress. What would she sell if not this gown?

She grimaced as she hauled her leg out of the sucking mud, but her eyes lingered on the open lotus leaves floating on the dirty water. Her foot had just fallen afoul of one of the thick below-water vines, so she knew they were there. She knew too, that there were probably edible roots down there. She had eaten lotus many times over the last decade, and her stomach cramped in hunger at the memory.

Unfortunately, she had no idea how to harvest or cook

the food, and she had no knife to aid in the process. She didn't even know if the plants were mature enough yet to eat. In truth, for someone who had lived and worked in this country her whole life, she was woefully ignorant of how to survive. Though she had treated lotus farmers with cracked and brutalized feet, with sores on their skin or infections in their bodies, she had no understanding of what they did, when or how. And knowing how to treat bites from waterborne insects was of no help now.

She grimaced, well-used to her own private litany of uselessness. Her stomach tightened again, and she blocked it from her thoughts. She should have grabbed some of the Enforcer's sizzling dumplings when they'd been right in front of her, but she'd been too afraid. Too slow. Too stupid. . . .

She thought again of the opium sack still on the boat. How sweet it would be to just lie back, her feet cooling in the water while she smoked a pipe. How sweet . . .

But she had left without thinking of the drug, her mind too scattered to remember her only other means of coin beside this dress. And besides, she did not want the dark powder. She didn't smoke anymore.

Forcing the memories away, she managed to pull herself back to her feet and continue doggedly along the raised ridge between lotus fields. She had no idea where she was going—and that too was added to her list of stupid things she had done—but she knew she had to keep walking.

When the mandarin had turned his back, she had seized her opportunity and bolted. She still could not quite believe no one had seen her scramble overboard. True, it had been dark, but . . . She shook her head, only able to thank God that He had managed to engineer her escape.

The moment she had hit the shore, she had run as far and as fast as possible. She had not slowed to see if anyone followed. She had hugged the shadows and skirted tiny groups of trackers huddled together in sleeping lumps. She had run and prayed that no one would stop her.

Now it was nearly dawn. She was wandering through farmland well away from the Grand Canal, and it was time to start thinking of finding a place to rest. If God were indeed merciful, she'd stumble upon a Christian mission or even a Chinese monastery. But nothing appeared except muddy lake after muddy lake of lotus or rice.

Then she saw it, rising out of the semidark like the Hand of God: a building. Tall and thin, it perched in the center between four fields. She narrowed her eyes, judging the structure. She knew it was a shed to store tools—they were a common sight out among Chinese fields. But this one was unusually tall, high enough to have an upper-story perch to look out over the fields. Few were built that tall or that sturdy, especially when it was barely large enough for one person to stand inside. But this one had a kind of upper story that would be a perfect place to rest. She could do a lot worse. Especially since she was falling down from exhaustion.

She would have to pray that no one was working in these fields today. Or if they were, that they wouldn't look closely into the shed.

She fumbled her way inside, grateful that the lock was not a heavy western iron one, but a simple Chinese *suaw*. It looked like a tiny metal carpenter's box with two pieces fitting inside and against one another. A metal key—or a well-shaped stick—fit inside both pieces and pushed them apart.

It took too long for her to force the lock open, and she

was nervously looking around long before she was done. But she eventually succeeded and half walked, half fell inside. Then she had to maneuver the door shut before climbing up the bamboo ladder. She finally managed it all and leaned awkwardly against the window frame.

The situation wasn't ideal. Looking down, she saw a thin stream of light on the floor, which meant the door hadn't fully closed. Worse, anyone looking closely at the window would see her sitting here like Rapunzel in the tower. But there was little she could do about it. She closed her eyes and thought about the mandarin and his sizzling dumplings. But as she turned to the delectable food, they changed into smoking bags of opium. She extended her hand, wondering which she preferred . . .

She woke to screeching women and children with sticks.

"Ghost! Ghost!"

She blinked into the sunlight, her fuddled mind slow to grasp anything beyond the fact that her legs and back ached like the very devil. She looked down to see children and women screeching. One woman banged a wok with a stick, making a racket that added to the pounding in her head. Another girl and her mother had made it to the building and began beating at the walls.

Anna's head pounded, and her mouth was dry. Grimacing, she pushed the hair out of her eyes and groaned.

"She is in pain!"

The noise redoubled. A woman grabbed hold of the building and began shaking it while emitting the most unholy shriek. The building began to creak, the tiny floor pitching and twisting in an alarming fashion. Anna abruptly grabbed hold of the walls, trying to stabilize her position. She couldn't, of course; the place was made of bamboo and would tumble down at any moment.

"Stop that!" she bellowed in Chinese. Except, it was the Chinese language of the north, and not at all their dialect, which she was beginning to realize was similar to Shanghainese. Had she come so far south?

The women gasped in shock. A couple girls screamed in horror and ran. But the boys—three little boys of the hellion age—were undeterred. They roared and bellowed even louder. Then the oldest of them picked up a rock and threw it at her.

He missed, hitting the side of the building with a frightening thud, and Anna recoiled from the impact. That was enough to give the rest of the boys encouragement. They picked up stones, sticks, even clumps of mud, and began hurling them at her.

"Stop it! Stop it!" Anna screeched in Shanghai dialect. It had no effect. The women, emboldened by their sons, began shaking the building again in earnest. And even the little girls came back, banging on their woks hard enough to dent the metal.

Then a clump of mud sailed true. It came right at her face. Reflexes she hadn't used since childhood came roaring back. She ducked down, hearing it clatter behind her. She had already pushed to her feet, intending to climb down the ladder. At least inside she'd be safe from rocks.

But the last mud ball hit just above her shoulder, splattering wet dirt all over her face and dress. The dress she wanted so to keep clean. With a muffled curse, she rose from her crouch and watched for the next missile. Fortunately, the boys weren't strong enough to hurl heavy stones.

She saw another rock fly at her, at just the right height and speed. She waited then reached out, snatching the stone out of the air. Then, with another curse, again in Shanghai dialect, she hurled it right back. It hit a boy flat in the belly. Not hard enough to hurt him, just sting a bit. The boy gasped in shock. The mothers and sisters too were startled enough to stop what they were doing and stare.

The silence wouldn't last long. Five seconds at most before the peasants realized she wasn't a ghost but some-one who would fight back. Anna didn't give them that long. She began speaking as clearly and forcefully as pos-sible, though in a dialect she hadn't used for over a year. Fortunately, it came back quickly enough.

"Shame upon you, bringing dishonor upon your fathers and husbands! Should I curse your name? By the Son of Heaven, I could bring guards here to destroy every field for tens of *li*. Do you dare throw mud and rocks at me? Do you not see the fine silk I wear? Do you not know—"

"Ghost demon! She will kill us all!" screeched a young woman, who then grabbed her children—two little girls—and ran for all she was worth.

Anna watched in satisfaction, hoping that the others would follow. But they apparently were made of sterner stuff. The women were now picking up stones. After all, Anna had just threatened both their children and their livelihoods. She quickly changed her tone.

"I am prepared to forgive you," she said more softly. "And my husband will reward you richly for aiding me." She narrowed her eyes, trying to judge the crowd. She knew from her father that people always needed someone to blame. It was all a matter of shifting the blame away from oneself. She singled out the eldest boy, the one who had first thrown a rock. "He will have to work hard for my gifts. But you others . . ." She straightened her spine and opened her hands in a gesture of beneficence. "If you help me, you will be richly rewarded." She looked at the woman who wore the poorest clothing, whose frame was the most thin and weak. "You. Will you aid a lost wife to find her mandarin?"

The woman hesitated, her fear palpable, but she was clearly tempted. A moment more, maybe a well-phrased promise, and she would help. But Anna didn't have a moment. Two men—one with a hoe, the other wielding an old and rusty sword—topped the rise. They were led by a boy, who pointed at her. The men came forward with a roar.

Predictably, the women turned to wait for the men to sort it out. Damn, damn, damn! There were only two ways to handle men—sex or tears. Anna wasn't going for the first, and she'd never been great at the latter, but she would have to try.

Rushing down the ladder as fast as her aching body could manage, Anna came out of the shed with a gasp.

Stumbling toward the poorest woman, Anna began to sob. Well, she mimicked the motions well enough. True tears were harder to dredge up, but they would come in a moment. Meanwhile she spoke whatever nonsense came into her head. She whimpered about losing her favorite ivory fan when she and her servants had gone for a respite from the awful boat. She stuttered out that she'd gone to look for it, but mean Number-One Wife had refused to allow her even a servant to help. And then—the real tears had finally begun—she'd gotten lost and fallen down and ripped her dress. And now there was mud on it. She was so frightened she was trembling. But oh, she has the most handsome jade earrings that would look lovely on this girl who had such beautiful earlobes. And her husband had a pocket watch that he had given to her. They were the most amazing things, an invention from the West. In truth, she'd been sent to carry the mandarin the pocket watch as a gift so many years ago, but he had wanted her instead. So she had been given in marriage to the mandarin and now her husband and her father were in business together . . .

One of the men's eyes flickered in interest. He obviously understood what kind of business a mandarin and a white man would be in. How much opium was in a countryside village between the Grand Canal and Shanghai? Not enough, she'd wager. She smiled at him, and he lowered his sword. "My father," she added in a soft tone, "always considered me his favorite. He will reward anyone who helps me."

The sword dropped to the ground as the man's face split into a broad grin. "Silly women," he laughed heartily. "Mistaking a lost woman for a ghost."

"But, but . . ." stammered the boy. "She is—"

"A foreign barbarian," Anna supplied. "Yes, I am. But I am no ghost and certainly not a demon. Here . . ." She extended her arm. "Touch my skin. You will see I am warm and whole just like you."

The boy wasn't so bold. Or he wouldn't have been without practically the whole village staring at him. So with a shaking hand, he slowly, awkwardly poked a finger into her arm, drawing it back with a gasp.

"She's soft!" he exclaimed. He poked her again, this time lingering a bit longer. "And warm!"

The men boomed with laughter, clapping the child on the back. "Of course a woman is soft and warm. What else would she be?"

The other children crowded around, all wanting to touch her in some way. The women eyed her curiously now, studying her hair and clothing before corralling their children. They all turned the same direction—presumably the main village—and there was talk of food. Anna's stomach cramped in response. She began moving in the direction they pointed. But the children kept tight to her side, hampering her progress. She leaned down and picked up the smallest so that they could move faster.

The fear was broken. She was nothing more to them now than a potential windfall and a way to break up the monotony of a hard existence. Anna breathed a sigh of relief, though she kept the tears ready and her smile wobbly.

Then there came a shout from the distance as some of the children dashed ahead, but Anna could not make out the words. She could follow the language of one person at a time, but a dozen all speaking at once? The words degenerated into a sea of sound in which she struggled to remain afloat.

In time, she gave up. Her thought was for food—only food. Until the sounds began to recede and the children pulled away. At first she was grateful for the room to move without tripping over little bodies. But then the girl in her arms was snatched away and all was abruptly silent.

She looked up in confusion, her thoughts on sizzling dumplings. She saw instead three men. They were different than the peasants. Better weapons—well-oiled swords and heavy fists. Better fed—broad shoulders and thick muscles. And worst of all, better resistance to any manipulation she could find. These were hardened men who responded to two things: force or money, and she had neither.

So she ran. She didn't even stop to think. She simply took off running as fast and as far as she could. But her skirts were tight, her footing unstable, and there was a child in the way.

She swerved. She stumbled.

And she was caught.

From Anna Marie Thompson's journal:
December 16, 1881

I found the ship. I found Father's ship, and they were really nice to me. I'm going to be on bread and water for a month, but it was worth it.

I escaped just like I planned. It was so easy! And then I got a rickshaw and went to the docks. It took a long, long time to find the boat, but it helps that I can speak both English and Chinese. There's always some-one who needs help translating. Even the rickshaw run-ners will give me a free ride if I help them get a rich white customer.

It took a long time to find the right ship. And then they caught me sneaking on board. A couple of the sailors were really mean. They were going to throw me overboard, but the captain stopped them. He was kind, especially when I remembered his name. I told him I was looking for my father, that I had to speak to him. That I was Frank Thompson's daughter and I had to find him. Then he asked me into his quarters to talk, even gave me some hard biscuits to eat.

That's when he told me about my father. I didn't be-lieve him at first. Everybody lies. But he showed me his records. People lie with their mouths, but records are more honest. And this captain had a book that listed everyone on the boat and what they were paid.

Father was paid a year ago, and then he didn't come back. He didn't get on the boat again. I didn't know what to do. If he wasn't sailing, then where was he? I started crying—big English men always help when a little girl cries.

Except, the captain couldn't help. He didn't know where my father went or why. He said that a lot of bad things happen in Shanghai and that I should contact my family back in England. That was my only hope. Then he gave me a whole guinea, plus took me all the way back to the mission. I told him I could take a rickshaw. Even told him how I could get a free ride, but he insisted.

I should have run away then. I should have just escaped to crawl back into bed so no one would notice. But he wanted the nuns to know I had slipped out. Mother Francis was very polite to him, very thankful. She even promised him I wouldn't be punished. Ha! Like I said, everybody lies, even Mother Superiors.

But it was still worth it. I know my father's somewhere in Shanghai. Or at least he was. I think I'll go find Samuel Fitzpatrick on Tuesday when Sister Christine starts leading matins. She'll go to bed really early and fall right to sleep by seven. It'll be easier to slip away then.

And from this chasm, with ceaseless turmoil
   seething,
As if this earth in fast thick pants were breathing,
A mighty fountain momently was forced:
Amid whose swift half-intermitted burst
Huge fragments vaulted like rebounding hail,
Or chaffy grain beneath the thresher's flail:
And 'mid these dancing rocks at once and ever
It flung up momently the sacred river.
           — *Samuel Taylor Coleridge*
      from "Kubla Khan: or, A Vision in a Dream. A
                        Fragment"

CHAPTER SIX

The stench of opium filled the captain's quarters be-
lowdecks. Zhi-Gang curled his lip against the smell even
as his tongue noted the sweet taste of the smoke in a
room unused to such things. Slamming the door shut behind him, he didn't need his glasses to see. He already
knew what he would find: the captain, his wife, and their
baby, all dozing in drugged sleep on the bed. Nearby, Jing-
Li would be lounging across cushions, a silly grin on his
smug face, a long thin opium pipe clutched in his hand.

"Where did you get it?" Zhi-Gang hissed as he stomped
forward. With each step, his friend's dark form resolved
into exactly what Zhi-Gang expected: a rich boy smoking
in luxury. "Where did you find the opium?"

Jing-Li shrugged. "Payment. Bad luck to cheat boat
people. They will curse our journey."

Zhi-Gang abruptly reached down and hauled his childhood friend up by the collar. Nose to nose, Zhi-Gang
could see a sharpness in Jing-Li's red eyes that proved the

man wasn't nearly as far gone as he pretended. "Where did you get it?"

"Do you have money for the captain?" Jing-Li challenged.

Zhi-Gang didn't answer. They both knew they had little money left. "We are on a mission! I am the Emperor's Enforcer! I kill people who commerce in this poison. You cannot go about *using* it!"

Jing-Li bared his teeth in response. Zhi-Gang dropped him back to the floor in disgust. He heard the opium pipe clatter to the floor and he whirled about to find it. There! He stomped forward, slamming his foot down on the bamboo and breaking it in two. He wanted to grind the shards against his heel, but the wood was too strong and his boot too soft. Instead, he felt a sharp piece stab into his skin and he drew back with a curse.

He had to twist his foot up so he could pull the sliver out while Jing-Li watched and laughed. It was a long, carefree giggle, filled with simple goodwill, and Zhi-Gang stopped what he was doing to squint at his friend. When was the last time the man had laughed like that? When had either of them felt happy and open, able to lounge upon the floor in simple pleasure? Months? Years?

"There is more if you want," said Jing-Li, his voice thicker and infinitely tempting. Then with a soft curse, the man leaned forward and abruptly jerked Zhi-Gang's foot forward. Unbalanced, Zhi-Gang half hopped, half stumbled to the bed, then waited in resigned silence as his friend pulled the sliver out of his foot.

"Jing-Li," Zhi-Gang pressed when the procedure was finished. "Where is the opium?"

His friend ignored him, choosing instead to twist sideways and grab another pipe, one that had fallen beside

the bed, obviously used by the captain. Some of the powder still smoked at the far end. Zhi-Gang would have
snatched the pipe away and smashed it as well, but Jing-
Li's nimble fingers twirled it out of reach before he
popped the end into his mouth.

"More for me," he said, then closed his eyes and inhaled deeply.

Zhi-Gang felt his hands clench into fists. He could demand the truth. Even under normal circumstances, Zhi-
Gang could beat his friend in a fight. But what would be
the point? Jing-Li had been smoking for at least an hour
now. Even half-blind, Zhi-Gang could pin his friend in
seconds; but to what end? The opium numbed Jing-Li's
sensation to pain. Even a broken bone might not be
enough to force Jing-Li to give up the location of his
stash.

Fortunately, there were less direct ways of getting what
he wanted. And besides, who could blame the man for
taking one night's escape from reality? With the Emperor's incarceration, Jing-Li had lost everything—his
good friend, his money, even his family. All of that had
been abandoned on this flight to the south. At least Zhi-
Gang had been poor as a child. He was used to privations
and the endless pressure to succeed. Not so the wealthy,
titled, and pampered Jing-Li.

With a sigh, Zhi-Gang turned his back on his friend
and slipped out of the captain's chamber. He shouldn't
have allowed Jing-Li to hide from his enemies as a servant. The Enforcer could have traveled with a friend or
companion. Except that Zhi-Gang had never traveled
with anyone but his servants, and often not even them.
He worked alone, judged and executed the guilty alone.
A companion would have been noticed by the Dowager

Empress's spies. Jing-Li would have been discovered and killed.

So Jing-Li had become just another servant, while his friend the Enforcer continued searching for opium dealers, this time in Jiangsu. It was all perfectly normal, all perfectly hidden from their enemies. And truthfully, Zhi-Gang enjoyed the companionship. Well, he enjoyed his companion when Jing-Li was sober.

With a vehement curse, Zhi-Gang put on his glasses and began a slow, laborious search of the boat. He would find his friend's stash and he would destroy it. And then Jing-Li would return to the careful, intelligent scholar he once was. Away from temptation, starting in a new life outside of the Peking pleasure palaces, Jing-Li would become the man he was meant to be.

It took hours, but Zhi-Gang discovered the opium stash. It was in Sister Marie's tiny private locker. He should have looked there first, but he hadn't wanted to accept the truth. He had searched the rest of the boat, through the crew quarters and every nook and cranny imaginable. But in the end, he had surrendered to the inevitable.

He pulled out the runner's bag, seeing that it was only half full. Lifting it to his nose, he closed his eyes and inhaled deeply. He smelled the sweet stench of opium, wet hemp from the coarse fabric, and overlaying it all, Sister Marie's unique scent. All hope that she was truly a nun died at that moment. She was a drug-runner and therefore doomed to death.

Moving wearily through the boat, he made his way to the back and the deepest part of the river. He stood at the railing, staring into the black night, but in his mind's eye, he saw Sister Marie. He remembered every moment of their time together, reliving her defiance, her bold sensuality, and even that time when he watched her curled tightly in sleep. She was a beauty, he realized, and the kind of woman he had searched through all of China to find.

Then he threw the bag of opium overboard. It hit the water and began to sink to the bottom of the Grand Canal. As Zhi-Gang slowly pulled off his glasses, he visualized the fascinating Sister Marie. And he watched her drown beside her illegal bag of opium.

"You lived here?" Jing-Li sneered. "What a pig's bottom!"

The two servants trailing behind them on this ox-track road nodded in agreement, but Zhi-Gang said nothing. Jing-Li was finally coming out of his post-opium stupor, which meant he would be critical and irritating for at least a day. As they were supposedly on an official government visit to the village of Huai'an in the province of Jiangsu, the man's disdain only backed up their story. It did nothing to alleviate Zhi-Gang's particularly black mood.

Huai'an *was* a pig's bottom of a village. Even without his glasses, Zhi-Gang could see the truth. It was muddy, shaped like a flea, and smelled of manure. The dirty-faced villagers gaped, expressions showing broken and foul teeth. Their minds were dull and their children naked. That he had been born in such a place revolted him. That he might still be here if his father hadn't committed a heinous sin twisted his thoughts into darker and darker veins.

"So, where did you live?"

He gestured vaguely to the north. There had been wealth in this village once, long ago. In his grandfather's time, or perhaps before. Before the rivers shifted and the favor of Heaven turned from the people here. Now it was nothing more than a pig-bottom village to Jing-Li and a place of nightmares to Zhi-Gang.

"The teahouse is that way." He gestured vaguely around a cluster of huts. In his mind, he remembered a palace of beauty and mystery: two stories tall, built of gleaming wood with painted designs, filled with the scents of fine cooking. It was a palace before he had seen what real majesty looked like. A place of glory before he had seen the Forbidden City.

And it was also where he had imagined his glorious return home. He was now a wealthy mandarin, the Emperor's Enforcer, a man feared and revered throughout China. And he intended to gloat about it in front of all who had ever tormented him as a boy.

"Pig-bottom," Jing-Li muttered as they rounded a corner and saw the inn. Zhi-Gang had to agree. How had he ever imagined this a palace? The wood was cracked, the painted dragon laughably childish. He thought it would look better as they came closer, but he was sorely disappointed. The stench reached him long before he could see clearly. He smelled cheap oil, rancid tea, and piss—animal or human, he couldn't tell. What was that thing on the floor? He squinted as he entered the tiny building. A hen, escaped from its pen and wandering about the main floor. He kicked it aside and forced himself to tromp through, careful of his footing on the slick floor.

"You can't be serious," Jing-Li muttered from beside him.

Zhi-Gang didn't answer. He moved by memory to the stairs, climbing quickly as he headed for the most elegant seat in the house. His childhood mind had magnified the chair on the second story to something that equaled the Dragon Throne. He had now seen the Dragon Throne with his own eyes, even touched it in a moment of true boyish daring. This overly large, badly carved wooden contraption in the exalted eastern corner was a joke.

He curled his lip as he kicked the wormy footstool aside and dropped into the chair. He knew he shouldn't be so disdainful of his surroundings. This was the best these poor people could afford, and they all thought it magnificent. And if a Tao Master were to point out the biggest fraud in this ugly place, it would not be the tea-house owner, but Zhi-Gang himself, who had built his entire life upon a crime. And if someone were to count riches, Zhi-Gang didn't even have an ox or a horse on which to travel, so that made the farmers far more wealthy.

Still, this was his moment of glorious return. He would live it to its fullest no matter the reality of the situation. So he dropped down on the chair, sitting with his legs braced wide apart like a warrior. His infamous deer-horn knives were clipped to his waist, reinforcing his image as Enforcer. Jing-Li also carried a weapon—his father's sword—which banged against the wall when he slipped into position behind Zhi-Gang. The two servants he'd brought through the mud with him took places nearby, as if they were real bodyguards rather than thick-armed boat people. And then Zhi-Gang waited and wondered where all the peasants could possibly be. He had seen almost no one on the tedious trek here.

A form bustled upstairs. Zhi-Gang waited until the fuzzy image resolved itself into a large-busted woman with missing teeth. She had made an attempt to scrub her face and smooth her hair, but had done too hurried a job. A long streak of mud smeared her left cheek, and a thin glob of pork fat glistened in her hair where she had not combed it away.

"Great sir, great sir! What an honor to have you here!" she wheezed.

Jing-Li nodded in response, then turned to whisper into his supposed master's ear. "I thought you said all the women were beautiful here."

Zhi-Gang shrugged. "To an eight-year-old boy, all breasts are beautiful."

Jing-Li shuddered in horror. "Not true. Not true at all." But then he turned to address the woman. "Tea for the mandarin!"

"Tea for the mandarin!" she echoed in a loud, shrill voice.

"Tea for the mandarin!" someone repeated below, and then kept doing so. "Tea for the mandarin! Tea for . . ."

"And dumplings? Excellent dumplings, your honor, better than in the Forbidden City."

Zhi-Gang doubted that. And truthfully, his mouth was watering for something else—something plainer and re-membered from his impoverished youth. He glanced at Jing-Li and murmured his request. His friend's eyes widened in horror, but he knew better than to object. Jing-Li put on an air of much suffering and turned to the woman.

"The mandarin requests *congee* . . ." He had to take a breath before finally voicing it. "Fermented bean curd in . . ." He sighed. "Watered rice."

The woman gasped in horror. "No! No! Such a thing is not fit for your honor! We have good dumplings! Steamed if you prefer—"

Zhi-Gang smiled, knowing it was time to reveal himself. "But Madame Sui, I remember your porridge. I have told Jing-Li of your excellent cooking. He is most anxious to taste it." Then he paused. "Do you not remember little Tau Zhi-Gang who used to steal your dumplings?"

Madame Sui frowned, her ample face scrunching tight as she stared at him. She even dared a step closer as she inspected him. Zhi-Gang waited, his breath held, as an oft-dreamed-of moment hovered tantalizingly close: his glorious return.

She frowned and laughed at the same time, the sound completely uncertain. "Of course, of course," she murmured in confusion. "Little Zhou."

"Zhi-Gang. I had two brothers and . . . a sister. We lived just north of here."

"There is nothing north of here but ruins and—"

"Yes, yes. Ruins. My home. We sold it when I was ten."

"A storm destroyed it. It is all ruins now." She abruptly grinned, clapping her hands. "But I will bring you dumplings fit for the Son of Heaven himself! Steamed dumplings for the mandarin!" she cried as she hustled away.

"Steamed dumplings for the mandarin!" the voice downstairs echoed.

Zhi-Gang glared at her retreating back, his stomach souring in fury while Jing-Li's laughter grated in his ears.

"She doesn't even remember you!" he chortled. "How long have you dreamed of this? How long have you talked of returning home to your little village and being—"

"Silence!" Zhi-Gang bellowed. And when his friend did not react except to arch a disdainful eyebrow, he grabbed the man by his collar and shook him. "Find the slaver," he hissed. "And speak no more of homecomings."

Jing-Li sobered, but his eyes still sparkled with merriment. "You said everyone comes to this teahouse."

Zhi-Gang released him with a restrained shove. "Yes." He settled back into the ridiculous throne. "This is his chair."

"Then he will come to you."

"I wish you to find him," Zhi-Gang growled. Then he cut his gaze across the room. "All three of you, go!"

Jing-Li hesitated. "But you will be alone. Unprotected . . ."

And half blind. But Zhi-Gang threw away the warning. "Do you think me incompetent against a bunch of half-starved peasants? Go!"

His friend had no choice but to obey. Jing-Li nodded, his expression pinched now with worry as he and the other two trudged off. Zhi-Gang ignored their nervousness. Even without his glasses, he was more than capable of handling himself in the village of his birth. The place where no one remembered him. The dirty ox-track between the Grand Canal and the city of Jiangsu.

Madame Sui brought up his dumplings and a tea that smelled like pig shit. He passed over them both to gaze out at the muddy landscape. "Where are all the villagers? Surely someone will remember me."

"I remember you, honored sir!" she lied. "You were most respectful and had a bright intelligence—"

"The people, Madame Sui. Where are they?"

She frowned and looked around. "I am not sure," she responded. "A ghost, they say. Someone found a ghost near Huang's lotus fields."

He almost brushed it off. His thoughts were on the slaver and his purpose here. But always Sister Marie was in the back of his mind. Where had she gone? How would she survive without money or opium? And . . . His thoughts slid into focus. And what else would these peasants call a white woman on the run but a ghost found in a lotus field?

He was on his feet in an instant, shoving aside the table as he grabbed Madame Sui. "Show me! Show me this ghost!"

"But . . . But . . ." she babbled. "I cannot! I don't know . . ."

"I will protect you from the white demon. We know of these things in Peking." He tightened his grip. "It is most urgent, and you will be rewarded handsomely."

She bobbed her head. "Of course, of course." Then she bustled away, bellowing as she went. "Make way! Make way for the mandarin!"

He hurried to keep her ample form before him, his eyes squinting as he tried to scan the horizon for Sister Marie.

"Make way!" Madame Sui continued to bellow. "Make way for the manda—"

"Stop it!" he abruptly snapped. "I do not need such pomp. It is annoying."

She turned, her pinched eyes blinking at him stupidly. "But noise frightens away the ghost," she said. "I am keeping it away."

He stared at her, his thoughts spinning even darker as he realized here was the true reason behind her earlier bellows. She wasn't trying to honor him. She was scaring away a ghost.

"We are going *to* the demon," he finally growled. "I do not wish to frighten it away!"

"Oh." She blinked at him then eventually shrugged.

"Very well. This way." She obviously thought him insane, but intended to humor him in hopes of a rich reward. He did not care so long as she showed him the way. She did. She led him down the stairs, through the main floor (he had to kick the chicken aside again), and then around the building before meandering through a field.

"Madame Sui! Can you not move faster?"

"Aie, no, honored sir. I am an old woman and my joints are stiff!" A lie if there ever was one. The woman was obviously afraid of the ghost and did not trust Zhi-Gang to protect her. Worse, there was nothing he could say or do to get her to move any faster. So he had to stick with her tedious pace while frustration had him growling in the back of his throat.

So far, nothing of his trip had gone as planned. His wondrous reunion with the place of his birth, his glorious return to avenge his sister's death, even the simple trip down the Grand Canal had been marked by mishaps and delays. But all would be counted as unimportant if . . .

He saw her—or what he guessed was her: a screaming, dirty lump of yellow silk and brown hair pinned beneath a heaving, sweating hulk of a man. Nearby, two other large men stood guard. People moved on the edge of Zhi-Gang's vision: women hustling children away or men not wanting to watch. He couldn't really tell nor did he care. He reacted without thought, his actions—even half blind—still precise movements from years of training.

With a roar of fury, he pulled out both his deer-horn knives and attacked. The men tensed as they fumbled to draw their swords. They had obviously not expected any resistance. Zhi-Gang barely noticed them except as obstacles to his real quarry: the man on top of Sister Marie. With a flick of his wrist, Zhi-Gang slashed sideways at the first guard. He felt his blade cut through heavy leather, then tasted the ugly scent of blood in the air.

Madame Sui began jumping up and down, screaming the most helpful words he'd ever heard. "No, no!" she bellowed at the guards. "He comes to kill the demon! Don't hurt him!"

The second guard paused, sword half raised as he looked between his bloody companion and Madame Sui. That hesitation saved his life. Zhi-Gang dropped his shoulder and shoved the man aside, then descended upon his target.

The man was an easy mark. He was much too occupied in restraining Marie. One hand held her wrists, the other rooted around between her belly and his legs. With a leap, Zhi-Gang straddled the man. He didn't even slow as he converted his forward momentum into a reach and grab. Even holding the deer-horn daggers, he had enough finger strength to haul back on the bastard's queue, easily lifting the man's head and exposing his neck. His other blade closed the distance and, with a quick pull, he sliced straight through to the spine.

Blood gushed out—hot, sticky, and with a brutality that would become nightmares later; he knew that from experience. But for now, he was tossing the body aside—kicking it with his foot when it was too heavy to lift—before dropping down beside Sister Marie. She was gasping in horror, her eyes wide with shock and fear, her face a bloody mess, but not from her own injuries.

Then, out of the corner of his eye, Zhi-Gang caught a shadow of movement. He instinctively raised his daggers to block an attack, but none came. It was his own men—Jing-Li and the other two—taking up positions around him. To the side, the uninjured guard was gaping at his master's body.

"Leave and never come back," Zhi-Gang hissed. Then, as an added threat, he shifted his grip on his daggers. "I can throw these very well, too," he lied.

The man didn't wait. He took off without a backward glance. The second did too, although he moved with a staggering half stumble, holding his hand against the bloody gash on his side. Zhi-Gang dismissed them from his thoughts and returned to the woman on the ground.

"Did he hurt you? Can you breathe?"

She was wiping away the thick, sticky blood with muddy hands. He caught her wrists, startled by how much she trembled. She still hadn't spoken, and he doubted she had breath. He could hear the air move through her throat in shallow, choking pants. He glanced up at Jing-Li.

"Give me your sash," he ordered. His own clothing was already bloodstained.

Jing-Li's face paled as he looked down at his finely embroidered clothing. "But . . ." His words trailed off at Zhi-Gang's glare. Then with a heavy sigh, he began to untie the fabric that helped hold up his pants.

Zhi-Gang returned his attention to Sister Marie, slipping his fingers beneath her as he pulled her upright. It was easy work, she weighed little, but he was worried by her lax state. She had no more strength than a doll. He opened his mouth to say something to her—what, he hadn't a clue—but at that moment, Madame Sui found her voice.

Actually, the woman had been screaming for a while, but not words. At least, not since Zhi-Gang killed. Now she abruptly stepped forward and slapped him across the face as one would a naughty child. She began to berate him.

"Are you crazy? Why do you kill him? He was restraining the demon! And my best customer, too! Why you do this to me? Aie, aie!"

Zhi-Gang felt his features tighten in fury. Rage still simmered in his blood, so it was fortunate that he had Sister Marie in his arms. As it was, Jing-Li stepped forward, both handing over his sash and pushing Madame Sui backward. "Do not interfere with the mandarin," he growled.

The woman was not to be put off so easily, but Jing-Li had a great deal of experience with subduing servants. "You deserve to be beaten, woman!" he snapped. "Get water for the concubine. And sweet tea! Lead the way back! Now!"

Zhi-Gang worked both hands beneath Sister Marie. He made it to his feet, lifting her easily in his arms. Looking down, he could see her pale face clearly, even beneath the gore. Her eyes were open, her breath steady, but she showed no urge to fight him and he doubted her legs would support her. As he watched, she lifted Jing-Li's sash with shaking hands and managed to wipe her face. It didn't help much as gore smeared everywhere, but she obviously felt better for the task. Meanwhile, he adjusted her in his arms and began the long trek back to the teahouse. He didn't even look at the dead body he left behind except to step carefully around it.

"We will clean ourselves at the teahouse," he instructed Jing-Li, his thoughts churning. There was something important that he had forgotten, but the knowledge eluded him. "Then you will bring the slaver to me. I still have questions for him."

Just ahead, Madame Sui spun around, her eyes narrowing even further. "Slaver?"

"Gan. He called himself Mr. Gan."

She grimaced then released a short blast of noise he guessed to be laughter. "You will get no answers from Mr. Gan," she snapped.

Jing-Li stepped forward, his hand raised to strike. "Do not mock the mandarin!" he bellowed.

"Why?" Zhi-Gang interrupted. "Has he left the area? Does he ply his trade elsewhere? I tell you he can hide in any corner of China and still I will find him. He will tell me what I want to know." He spoke with all the strength of his vow, made not far from here so many years ago. He spoke with power and fury, but inside his anxiety grew. Madame Sui would not be so bold without a reason.

"Then go, mandarin," she sneered as she pointed behind him at the dead body. "He is there. See if you can get answers from him now."

He spun around, his anxiety blossoming into dread. It was a hard thing to stare at the face of the man he had just executed. Harder still to peer through the blood and gore to match it with a two-decade-old memory. But he did, and the realization made his knees weaken.

He had just killed the only lead he had to his sister.

From Anna Marie Thompson's journal:
December 21, 1881

I couldn't find Samuel. I haunted the docks, asked every bawd or drunk I could find. They all knew who he was. Apparently, he's an important man on the docks. But no one knew where to find him. I left messages. Said Frank's daughter wanted to see him.

It won't work. He won't care, but I had to try.

I am glad to say that our Chief Superintendent
seems completely weaned off his hostility to the
drug traffic.

—*Opium trader William Jardine on Britain's
highest-ranking official in China.*

CHAPTER SEVEN

A warm gush of fluid, sticky and thick across her face.
The stench of bile. The taste of copper. Anna squeezed
her eyes shut and tried to focus on the present sensations,
not her memories. The warm fluid was not blood, but
tepid water washing the filth away. She smelled cooking
oil and greasy dumplings. And no one was screaming in
horror, least of all herself. It was kitchen chatter on the
other side of the wall. She sat on a rough bench behind a
teahouse, cleaning herself with cheap fabric rinsed in a
bucket of dirty water.

She swished the cloth around in the dark red water,
wondering if her hand would be stained red as well. She
knew it would not, and yet she could not help but wonder. Besides, what else did she have to look at? One of the
mandarin's guards standing nearby? His eyes were dark
and hostile. At the mud-encrusted huts of this tiny village where children ran from her in terror and women

shut their doors? No, there was no help from them. More likely another stoning.

So she focused on the bloody water and the feel of wetness that was not sticky, of tepid water that was not body temperature. In truth, she had washed away gore many times behind the mission hospital, so the sensations were familiar, the process done almost by rote. Many times she had felt bathed in blood or human filth. Many times . . .

Never. Never had a man been murdered while lying on top of her. And yet, she was not sorry. What he'd been doing . . . What he'd been about to do . . .

She squeezed her eyes shut, trying to block out all thoughts. *Opium.* That's what she wanted: the hot curl of smoke, the sensation of floating; the quiet, blissful rest of mind and body: She hungered for it with mind-eating obsession. It consumed her entire focus until her body shook with need. At that moment, she would have sold anything, done anything, been anyone if only it meant a pipe at the end of the day.

"Are you clean, honored lady?" Mrs. Sui's voice was harsh, but Anna latched onto it like a lifeline. She turned quickly, her fevered imagination already seeing a pipe in the woman's hand.

But the woman carried sour, greasy dumplings, not powdered bliss. It was probably the best the woman had to offer, and Anna tried to be gracious. She forced herself to take the tray while in her mind she calculated how best to ingratiate herself. She would find the opium supplier in this dirty little village, and then she would . . .

"I have brought clothing, honored lady. My daughter's. Not fine silk, but it is clean. Just washed last week."

Last month, more likely, and worn often since then. Though nicely folded, the rough cotton tunic had dark oil stains and smelled of sour soy sauce. Still, Anna set aside the food tray to give overflowing compliments as to the style of dress, that it wouldn't look nearly so pretty on herself as on the lovely Miss Sui, wherever the girl was.

The woman understood the compliments as lies, especially given the large size of the tunic and skirt. Young Miss Sui appeared to be a good ten inches larger around the waist than Anna. And yet, the mama warmed nonetheless.

"But you are not eating!" Mrs. Sui admonished. "Quick! Take some before they grow cold!"

The dumplings were not what she wanted, yet Anna pushed herself to pick up a single greasy crescent. They looked like fat larva to her, but she blocked the thought. She also tried to erase the idea that dumplings like these had probably been the murdered man's last meal. All the village appeared to gather in this sad little teahouse. She could hear them clearly jabbering behind her.

"Eat! Eat!" Mrs. Sui urged.

Anna did. It was the only way to the opium. A teahouse owner would know everything that went on in the entire province, so Anna chewed and swallowed, then declared it the best dumpling in all of China. And then she began to cry. Tiny little drops at first, but growing steadily larger until fat streams slid down her face.

In truth, she hadn't intended to sob. Ladies were supposed to have tiny tears that misted their faces and subtly revealed the deep ache inside. Ladies were not supposed to have great big, gulping sobs that tore through them like a hurricane. Anna's body shook, her stomach cramped, and the only reason she didn't scream was because she hadn't the breath. Mrs. Sui looked horrified. Even the guard backed up a step. Anna had to stop. She could not frighten these people with a fit. But the heaving gasps would not end, and the tears kept coming.

She buried her face in her skirt, mortified by her actions but more ashamed that she had such little control of herself. But then, that had always been her problem, hadn't it? No control.

Madame Sui hovered uncertainly. "Honored lady . . . Honored lady . . ."

Anna fought for breath, struggling to regain calm. She had none. None at all as she looked up with desperation, her heart and her soul revealed for all to see. "Opium," she whispered. "Please . . ."

Madame Sui slumped, her eyes softened and her entire stance filled with understanding. Anna straightened slightly, hope growing with every breath. She clutched the woman's arms.

"Do you have any? Can you get—"

"Well, that's better!" a hearty voice interrupted. It was *him*—the Enforcer—stepping through the back door to find her. Her thoughts had been growing warmer toward him, especially when he had carried her here. When he had stopped that other man. When . . . But that brought the other memories—the warm gush, the smell—and she suddenly wished him to Hell for eternity.

She didn't look at him. She kept her eyes on Mrs. Sui, who was going to say something, who was going to offer her opium. But Mrs. Sui immediately dropped her gaze and shuffled backward, deferring to the mandarin.

Hell. Yes, she wished him to Hell. She shot him a malevolent glare that drew him up short for a moment.

His eyes widened and his steps faltered, but he quickly recovered, moving to stand before her. And then maybe he would stare down at her, curl his lip in disdain at the filth she'd been unable to remove, then spin on his heel and leave. Then she could try again with Mrs. Sui.

But he didn't. He dropped down into a squat before her—just like any coolie—with knees in the air, bottom dropped almost to the ground between his legs. He and she were nearly eye to eye. If anything, his head was lower than hers as he touched her chin and lifted.

"This has been very difficult for you," he said softly, staring into her eyes.

To her horror, tears came. She almost said it—she was so desperate she almost begged the Enforcer for opium, but at the last moment she shifted her words to something more prudent. "Are we returning to the boat then?" she asked in a small voice. Her stash was there. She didn't care that it was her only means to buy her way out of this godforsaken country. If it were at hand, she'd smoke it.

But he shook his head as his thumb stroked her cheek. "Not yet. We wait to speak with the governor."

Mrs. Sui stepped forward, her eyes alight. "The governor! Here!" Then she spun and spoke over her shoulder in rapid Chinese that was too fast and too accented for Anna to understand. Something about more dumplings, more wine. Anna looked away, uninterested.

But that brought her eyes back to the Enforcer, whose thumb continued to scrub at her cheek. He looked at the bucket of water and grimaced. "Mrs. Sui!" he snapped. "Fresh water. This is disgusting!"

"Yes, yes, your honor. Of course!" She bustled forward, squatting to grab the bucket. Anna thought she was merely responding to orders, but at the last second the woman caught her gaze. "You wait for the governor, honored lady. He will help you." She waited a moment, obviously trying to deliver a message.

Anna frowned, trying to understand. Would the governor give her opium? She straightened, her thoughts whirling. Of course. How stupid she was! The supply lines *always* went through the local government. How else could an illegal trade thrive but by buying off the authorities?

Hope sparked within her, but questions came equally fast. Did this governor know that the mandarin was really the Emperor's Enforcer? Would the governor be as righteous as the Enforcer? Or would he be corrupt enough to be grateful for the forewarning? She returned her gaze to the mandarin and tried to probe for answers.

"Is he a friend of yours, this governor?"

Anna knew that China was ruled in a strange combination of feudal and democratic principles. The Emperor ruled the land, but he administered it through governors who managed huge provinces. It was all very feudal, with taxes flowing up the line from villager to mayor to governor to Emperor.

Except, each governor was appointed by the Emperor from the list of scholars who had passed the Civil Service Exam. Therefore, anyone who could pass the exam could become a governor. Which was very democratic. Except, in reality only the wealthy could afford the education and the price of the exam. Which meant that most governors came from the same set of rich elite, and most knew one another.

The question was: Did the governor belong to the Enforcer's moral, lawful sect? Or to the larger, opium-addicted, corrupt group of rulers?

The mandarin shook his head, and she caught a glitter of something in his expression. Cunning? "No, the governor is not my friend," he answered. "But wouldn't you come to see me if I suddenly showed up in your village?"

She took a breath, clearing her thoughts. She focused on his face, using him as an anchor to ground herself. It was an unusual moment for her. Usually she wished to escape, to flee. But at this moment, with him squatting before her, she wanted nothing more than to look at him, to focus on the long thin angles of his face. His eyebrows were like elegant dark strokes of an ink brush, his eyes the bright accent beneath. Long nose, curving mouth, he was like a subtle work of Chinese ink brush: elegant, understated and . . .

What was she missing? Something hovered beneath his expression. Something in his eyes, his stance, his . . . what?

"You ran from me," he murmured, his voice low enough for only her to hear.

She blinked and forced herself to follow his words and not the mystery of his face. "I have done nothing wrong," she lied. "You had no cause to hold me."

"You are my wife. I can do whatever I wish with you."

She narrowed her eyes. She squinted them to slits so that all she saw of his face were the dark wings of his eyebrows and the bright pupils beneath. "You would never marry a white woman. You are a Chinese official, a mandarin and an advisor to the Dragon Throne. You would be chased out of the Forbidden City by eunuchs with very big swords."

He flinched and, when his body steadied, the mysterious "something" was gone. In its stead she saw hardness, perhaps even anger. "Long ago I loved a woman. She was to be the first wife of my heart, but she was an opium addict and died. She was also the Empress Dowager's niece." His voice remained clipped and hard as he spoke, but his touch stayed gentle on her face. "Since that moment, I have had one goal, one purpose in life: to end the opium traffic in my country. I have been so charged by both the Son of Heaven and his mother, the Dowager. As long as I remain faithful to my task, as along as I find and destroy that evil commerce, then I can do whatever I wish. I can kill whomever I wish." He paused as his hand dropped away and he regarded her with dark intent. "I can even take a white wife."

She swallowed, seeing the absolute purpose in his eyes: an unswerving faith to this task and his freedom to act without consequence. She had no response except false bravado. "I don't believe you," she lied. "No one in the Forbidden City would accept a man with a white wife."

"We are not in the Forbidden City," he said.

He straightened, his long black queue whipping around in the air behind him. "Make yourself presentable, wife. We meet a governor."

Then he left, and the reality of her situation came crashing down on her. She was completely dependent on this man. Her life, her safety and her future lay in the hands of the Enforcer. In the wilds of China, this man was the law—whether for good or ill.

Odd, how the thought was not as terrifying as before. He was a killer, but with a purpose: to end the drug trade. She could not fault him for that. She knew first-hand the evils of this unholy trade that bartered not only drugs but little girls, too.

Very well, she decided, feeling herself grow stronger now that she had accepted her situation. She was de-

pendent on the Enforcer to live. Therefore, she would do
what she could to aid his goals while waiting for an opportunity of her own. So she put all her effort into cleaning herself as much as possible, to tying and pinning and
adjusting Mrs. Sui's poor cotton tunic into something
that would garner the attention of a governor. And then,
when she was done, she allowed the guard to escort her to
the upper floor and her pretend mandarin husband. He
was talking to his friend/servant as she approached. Jing-
Li looked tired, his normally haughty stance now droop-
ing with fatigue.

"Both gone," Jing-Li reported to the Enforcer. "And
with the slaver dead . . ." He shook his head.

Anna's steps slowed. A slaver? The man who had attacked her, whose blood still stained her skin was a
slaver. She would have been beaten, raped, then sold to
the brothels for more of the same. Her gaze went immediately to the Enforcer. It unsettled her to realize that
her jailor was the man who rescued her from that horrible fate. It bothered her even more that when she
thought of that awful moment, her mind skipped over
the worst to focus on the best—the way he had held her.
His arms had surrounded her, cradling her in warmth
and comfort. He had said things to her too, things she
did not recalled exactly, but the memory comforted her
nonetheless.

It was all so confusing. She just wanted to leave,
wanted to be in England where things made sense. That's
what everyone at the mission said. That in England people acted like people and life made sense. She had no idea
what that meant, but she wanted to find out. She wanted
to know what was so different, so perfect, in England.
And failing that, she wanted an opium pipe. What she

had instead was an enigmatic husband who was growing more . . . intriguing by the second.

Meanwhile, Jing-Li continued to drone on. "There is no point in remaining. No one will talk to us. We should leave now for Shanghai."

The Enforcer rolled his eyes, then gestured vaguely at his friend. "Wait over there. Have some *congee*."

Jing-Li's horror was palpable, and Anna might have laughed. The mandarin certainly did. But then his gaze caught hers and her breath stopped. The flow of her air ended, her mouth went dry, and even the beat of her heart seemed to still. She had no explanation for her body's bizarre reaction, but the way his eyes touched her made her insides still as if frozen.

He abruptly laughed even harder. "You look like a drowned crane trapped in a sack!" he chortled.

She stiffened, feeling the insult even though she completely agreed with him. Her hair was wet and flat as it clung in dirty brown strands to her head. She'd done what she could with the coarse tunic, using a rope as a belt to give her body some shape. But looking down, yes, perhaps it did look like a sack tied about her body. But she had tried to look pretty. She had . . .

"And yet, your beauty shines through," he continued. "I have never met a white woman who could rob me of breath so well as you."

She forcibly exhaled. She had no understanding of how to react to this man. He laughed at the oddest moments and said exactly what was on his mind. He appeared to be shallow and mercurial, with no subtlety at all. And yet, there was something beneath his surface, something clever and cunning and dark. Very dark. It drew her. *He* drew her, and she found herself gliding forward without conscious thought.

"I did my humble best," she demurred.

His laughter faded into a warm smile. "How are you feeling?" he asked.

She swallowed, her mind lost in the storms of conflicting thoughts. "I want to leave China," she answered honestly. Then she clapped her mouth shut, stunned that she had revealed herself so totally. What was wrong with her? Why could she not think?

The humor faded from his eyes and his entire body sagged. "China holds many dangers. Stay with me a little while, and I will see what I can do."

She smiled, her lips trembling with the effort. He was lying. They both knew it, and yet gazing into his eyes she could almost believe. "You are a very good businessman," she murmured. The actual word was "conman," but she only knew that word in English. Besides, her adopted father had always called himself a businessman whenever he lied to the officials.

The mandarin reeled back as if struck. "Do you purposely insult one who offers you assistance?"

She blinked, genuinely startled. In her father's world, she would have given the highest compliment possible. But clearly to the Enforcer, she had not. "But . . . but . . ." she stammered.

"I am a scholar, white woman! I have studied Huang Di Jing and Xun Zi. I have debated morality with the Emperor himself! I am a Confucian disciple and a follower of . . ." He continued on for quite a while, his voice growing louder and more passionate as he listed names she did not know and ideas she could not follow. All she could do is stare at him in shock, forgetting even to dip her head in apology.

And when he had punctuated his last statement with a fist on the table, she blinked and said the first thing that came to mind: "No wonder we developed gunboats first."

The silence that greeted her words pounded against her temples. Eventually, it became so overwhelming that she dipped her chin in a show of true humility. Who was she to tell this man how to run his country? She needed him to survive. She was being worse than stupid to challenge him in this way.

Too late. She had said the words and they continued to hover in the air. Out of the corner of her eye, she saw Jing-Li step forward, his hand upraised to strike. She closed her eyes, bracing for the blow. But she did not brace too much. After all, she deserved it for being so stupid.

No blow fell. Instead, she heard the Enforcer speak—a single word that echoed in the room like thunder. "Explain!"

She looked up, completely confused. She had already lost the thread of the conversation. Her words were not important. She had challenged the mandarin in his own country. No good could come of that. Except, apparently, her words *were* important.

"Explain!" he commanded again. "About your gunboats."

She scrambled to answer and came up with nothing but the honest truth. "You are a leader of this country." *The Emperor's Enforcer.* "And yet you insist you're an academic and you spit on tradesmen. You think and you study and you debate, but the rest of us need things— food, machines . . ." *Opium.* "The whites have scholars, too. But our countries are run by businessmen who understand engineering, crop yields, and weaponry." And opium—the best cash crop in the world, according to Samuel.

"Barbarians!" spat Jing-Li from the side. She glanced at him long enough to see that his hand still quivered with the need to strike. She quickly looked back to the mandarin. How odd that the servant seemed more violent than the Enforcer.

"I am a woman and know little of men's affairs," she lied. "But if you lead only by moral example, then how do you understand the immoral? The barbaric? You cannot. And so . . ." She shrugged. "The barbarians develop better weapons and overrun your poor country."

"It is not the gunboats that overwhelm China," the mandarin said. From the side, Jing-Li released a loud snort. The Enforcer sighed and shot his friend a dark look. "The gunboats helped, but it is the other that destroys us, woman. It is your opium."

She couldn't stop herself from salivating at the word. She barely restrained herself from leaping forward, so great was her hunger at the moment. But she focused on debating with the mandarin instead. She pushed away her need and looked into his eyes. "Scholarship is a great thing. As a woman, I have little education." True enough, though she had a great deal more learning than any Chinese woman. "But that only means I see what you cannot—the needs of the ignorant and the impoverished." She sighed and admitted the truth: "If one cannot have food, she will buy a drug to forget her hunger. If one cannot have hope, she will pay for sleep before she faces another useless day. If there is nothing more than unending horror, why not lose oneself in smoke?"

She looked away, wondering if she had revealed too

much. Did he know that she spoke of her own life? Did he realize that she felt more kinship with the lowest Chinese peasant than the men of her own race?

"Come here, wife," he said. His tone was gentle, his face even more so. He gestured to a bench beside his thronelike chair. She complied without demur, not because he ordered it but because his expression promised understanding. It was a lie, of course. What else could it be? She tried to steel herself against it, but the illusion was too beautiful to resist.

She walked to his side, but before she could rest on the bench, Jing-Li pulled it away. He hauled the rough wood back and stared at her with dark, angry eyes. "A wife should sit at your feet," he said to the mandarin.

The mandarin sighed and turned to her. "Forgive him, wife. He is ever aware of my consequence."

She bowed her head and stepped to his side. She tried to look completely demure, especially since another person had just topped the stairs. She had not noticed him at first; she had been too focused. But now as she turned to sit, she saw a man surrounded by four guards enter the room with great dignity. The governor, she guessed. So in order to enhance the mandarin's status, she chose to act as a good Chinese concubine.

She tucked her legs beneath her and began to fold herself at the mandarin's feet. But he was there before her, cupping her elbow before she could drop all the way down. "It is filthy in here," he murmured. "And the floor is very hard."

He shucked his jacket, revealing an ornately embroidered tunic beneath. But it was the jacket that commanded attention as he shook it out, his official emblem flashing in the sun. Then he carefully folded it into a cushion that he lay beneath her knees. In the background, Anna could hear Jing-Li sputter in shock, but the mandarin merely shrugged.

"It has bloodstains on it. What is a little dirt compared to that?"

Jing-Li apparently had no comment, though he managed to look severely disapproving as the mandarin helped her to settle. She was excruciatingly aware of his hand on her elbow, warmly cupping her arm. Like the burn of a brand, even when he released her arm, she still felt the outline of his fingers where they had touched her through the thin cotton fabric.

She tried to close her senses to him, but he sat so close and his presence was so strong. She could not be in a room with him without feeling his personal power. How much more potent was it here, right beside him, as he turned to face a governor? Potent enough to unseat her craving for opium. Potent enough that she could focus on him and not think of sweet, drugging smoke. Potent enough that she knew nothing but him beside her.

"Greetings, Governor Bai," he said. "I appear to have removed a rat in your garden."

The governor bowed in greeting, then seated himself across from the mandarin. His position neatly echoed the mandarin's in that he sat with his legs apart, his weapon—a long ugly sword—dangling from his hip. "Greetings, greetings," he boomed, though his voice was higher and more nasal than the mandarin's. "Yes, that rat was newly come to my home. I had not yet found the time to root him out."

"Of course, of course. Though I am afraid he has been here a great deal longer than you think."

The governor's eyebrows rose in surprise. Anna was

startled as well. It was not politic to challenge a man on his own land, but the mandarin did not seem to care. He continued to speak blithely on.

"Ten years, I believe, or more." He leaned forward. "There was a young girl taken from here ten years ago. The youngest daughter of an impoverished scholar. Taken and sold to . . ." He let his voice trail away. The implication was clear: the mandarin wished to know where this girl had been sold. What brothel did the slaver supply?

Anna repressed a sigh. Though obviously smart, the mandarin was no negotiator. This kind of information was best obtained over good food and wine. What he had just done was reveal exactly what he wanted most—information on this girl—without any pretense or subtlety. And from the canny look on the governor's face, he would pay a high price for such information.

Nevertheless, he was committed now, so all waited in silence to see what governor Bai would do. While he waited, the mandarin casually reached out and stroked Anna's cheek. It was an unconscious gesture, as if she were a favored pet, and Anna stiffened instinctively at the insult. But she did not draw away. To do so would only weaken the mandarin's position.

All the while, the governor watched, his black eyes narrowing in thought. "An unusual . . . companion," he finally said.

The mandarin shifted, as if surprised. "Oh! Yes, of course. My concubine."

"A white ghost? Do you not fear for your health?"

"A gift I could not refuse." He shrugged, a slow smile curving his lips. "And I have no fear of the whites."

Anna did her best not to react. She wanted to turn and stare hard at the mandarin who had suddenly become the coldest, cruelest businessmen she had ever known. His every word held double meaning, his every caress was a statement that he and whites were as thick as thieves. But what did he mean? What did he want?

Whatever it was, the governor wanted it too. With an abrupt clap of his hands, he shoved to his feet. "Come, come! We cannot talk like this: in the heat of the day with dust in our tea! We will go to my home and discuss the matter like civilized men. I can even arrange for a palanquin for your lovely consort!"

"Aie," the mandarin sighed, in what Anna recognized as a clear ploy. "Unfortunately, your rat has caused us some discomfort. The woman is distraught, and our clothing . . ." He shook his head in dismay.

"But all that can be mended at my compound!" the governor boomed. "Silk gowns and jade to soothe her rattled nerves. Peking tea, gifted to me from the Emperor's chief eunuch himself." The man was bragging about his connection to the Son of Heaven.

"Yes, Lie-Zi is most generous with the Emperor's tea. I myself prefer the Dowager's special blend." Zhi-Gang meant that he was more closely aligned with the Empress.

"Of course, of course. But I thought I had seen you with the Emperor the last time I was in Peking. In fact," the governor said, his voice slowing with threat, "I am sure of it."

Anna frowned. She recognized the governor's words as a kind of menace. She felt the mandarin's fingers stiffen against her cheek; but she could not understand why. Then she remembered. Not more than a month ago the Emperor had taken ill and now resided in the Summer

Palace under the care of numerous doctors. In truth, it was rumored that he had been poisoned by his own mother—the Empress Dowager—who now ruled in her son's name. And every day that passed, another one of the Emperor's modernizing edicts was being countermanded by his mother.

In short, the Empress Dowager had staged a coup d'etat. China's modernizing movement was dead, and now being replaced by a steady push back toward closed borders and an end to all white influence. Anna hardly cared since she wanted out of China anyway. But to these men, allegiance to either the ousted Emperor or the winning Empress made a great deal of difference.

So it was no surprise when the mandarin eventually conceded. In truth, Anna suspected that it was in his head all along to go to this man's compound. After all, where else would he get free new clothes, good food, and a soft bed? But there was more in his mind beyond that, she was sure.

"Very well," the mandarin finally said. "But only for one night. I have an urgent mission for the Empress Dowager."

"Then let me make arrangements with all speed," Governor Bai said as he pushed to his feet. But he paused a moment, his gaze returning to Anna, and she felt his inspection spread like a slow coat of oil across her body. "I will make you most comfortable, honored lady," he murmured. "Most comfortable, indeed." Then he bowed to the mandarin and left.

And at that moment, Anna understood the bargain. The knowledge burst through her consciousness like a crossbow bolt through her chest. She had just been sold. The Enforcer would get all the information he wanted about the slaver and the missing girl. In return, he would allow the slimy governor to spend the night with her.

She twisted her head to stare at the mandarin. It couldn't be true. He wouldn't sell her like that. He had just killed the slaver who intended to do the exact same thing. And yet, even as her heart denied the possibility, her mind knew the truth. The Enforcer had no reason to act faithfully to her. Theirs wasn't a true marriage. Most Chinese thought whites no more than animals, barely more intelligent than a monkey. Of course he would sell her for something he wanted. And she, of course, could do nothing about it, not surrounded as she was by guards and frightened peasants.

"No," she whispered, barely even aware that she spoke at all.

"One night," the Enforcer responded with a congenial smile. "And then we shall see about your escape from China."

From Anna Marie Thompson's journal:
December 25, 1881

He came! Samuel came! And he brought me PRE-SENTS!!!!! Much, much more than anyone else got. He brought presents for all the other children too, but he brought the most for me. Dolls. And dresses. And a big ham for everyone to eat.

Mother Francis wasn't very nice to him because she's a shrew. She said he wasn't a God-fearing man. She's stupid because he gave us everything! I got a necklace too. It's a real pearl on a string and I'm never taking it off because Susanna will steal it like she stole my doll.

Best of all, he said I should call him Father. He said because my father and he were such good friends, my father would want him to be my new father and that it was all perfect. I have a real father again! And best of all, he lives in Shanghai! He can come visit me whenever he wants. Mother Francis said she would never allow me to live with that man because he didn't go to church.

I don't care. I'm going to live with him some day. He's going to be my real father! And he said I looked beautiful in my new dress! I have a FATHER!!!!!

Five miles meandering with a mazy motion
Through wood and dale the sacred river ran,
Then reached the caverns measureless to man,
And sank in tumult to a lifeless ocean:
And 'mid this tumult Kubla heard from far
Ancestral voices prophesying war!

—*Samuel Taylor Coleridge*
from "Kubla Khan: Or, a Vision in a Dream. A
Fragment"

CHAPTER EIGHT

Zhi-Gang sipped his tea carefully as he stretched his legs out in Governor Bai's main dining room. The man hadn't lied; this was indeed the Emperor's favorite tea blend. Which meant the Governor had spent time with Lie-Zi. Which meant he might well recognize both Zhi-Gang and Jing-Li as the Emperor's great friends who were now running for their lives. Unless, of course, he knew that Zhi-Gang was the Enforcer, in which case, Bai might just be shaking in his boots. It was hard to tell.

Zhi-Gang smiled up at his host, pretending to savor the special tea. In truth, he barely wet his lips as he tried to plan. He had never excelled at court politics, preferring instead to discuss matters of public policy or Confucian ethics. But some things were simple survival in Peking, and so his actions were rote. He had already enjoyed the good meal, since he was fairly certain none of it would be poisoned. He was still too much an unknown for governor Bai to kill him outright. And while he traded pleasantries and gossip, he took his time inspecting the governor's home.

The man was clearly corrupt, with an eye for opulence and a taste for female flesh. Zhi-Gang had already heard at length about the Governor's five concubines. That alone indicated corruption. No man could afford five women on his official salary. And given the way the man eyed Marie despite her hideous clothing, Zhi-Gang knew Bai was interested in a swap as well.

At one time, Zhi-Gang might actually have considered it. What was a woman but something to barter, made for a man's enjoyment and to be used for his own ends? That was what he'd been taught and how most of the elite behaved. But not Zhi-Gang, and certainly not since the nightmares had returned. His sister should not have been bartered. His "wife" would not either.

He still intended to offer her up for Bai's use. An offer was an enticement, a ploy, a tease. It gave him an excuse to enter the governor's home and look around. Jing-Li would naturally be doing his own investigations among the servants. Between the two of them, they would find ample blackmail material on this corrupt dog. Which meant that his little drug-runner wife would remain his and his alone.

The thought made Zhi-Gang smile in anticipation. Meanwhile, Jing-Li was whistling that ridiculous opera aria he so loved. It was a signal, of course. It meant the man had found something. Wonderful, but unneeded. Zhi-Gang had already learned enough on his own. But at least his friend was now in position by the door. It was finally time to act.

Zhi-Gang delicately pretended to sip from his full

teacup while he leaned back in his cushioned seat. His knives were in easy reach, still on his belt, and his vision was clear enough at this distance—a mere table width— to act effectively.

"You spoke no lie," he drawled, indicating the tea. "This is indeed the Emperor's favorite blend, and you are obviously favored of the Son of Heaven."

The governor preened.

"You are aware, I assume, that the Emperor has taken ill? That his mother, the revered Empress Dowager, is forced to rule in his stead?"

The man nodded. All knew, even governors of a back-water hole such as this.

"Then you know as well that it is a lie."

Governor Bai leaned forward. "Truly? What have you heard?"

Zhi-Gang almost rolled his eyes. Did the man think he was being subtle? With a sudden burst of fury, Zhi-Gang threw his tea in the moron's face. He was then across the room, both his knives pressed hard against the man's fleshy chin before Bai could do more than sputter. Then Zhi-Gang began to release his rancor.

"Do not lie to me, traitor to China! You serve me the Emperor's drugging tea and think I do not know who you are? What you are doing?"

"No! No!" the man gasped. "The tea is pure! I drink it all the time!"

It was a lie; the Governor would only bring this brew out for special guests. He would not waste it unless there was someone to impress. Of course, Zhi-Gang's accusa-tions were also a lie, but that did not stop him from press-ing his blade harder against the man's flesh or making a show of tensing his arms in preparation of a killing stroke.

"Fool! I know it is laced with a white man's poison, one that makes the will weak and the mind open."

Bai's eyes were darting from Zhi-Gang's face to the door. He was wondering where his guards were. But Jing-Li had clearly taken care of them. Lazy bodyguards were easy to distract, and now Jing-Li stepped into the governor's full view.

"Confess all, Governor," Jing-Li said with pretend regret. "It is the only way to save your life."

"C-confess?" the man stammered. "Confess to what?"

"We know the truth. We know that you are in league with the Emperor to poison all of China—"

"No!"

"We know that you buy opium from the whites and sell it to China's poor—those you have sworn to protect!"

"Ahggg . . ." It wasn't clear what the man meant to say, but his expression clearly admitted guilt.

"Slaves, too," Zhi-Gang continued. "China's flowers sold to the whites through the rat I just killed this morning."

The man's eyes were bulging in terror, but his hands gripped Zhi-Gang's arms. "Not me . . ." he whispered.

"Dog! Do you not understand? We have already learned of these things! Do you imagine I would have killed the slaver before learning of these things? We already know of your crimes!" Then he dropped his voice, his posture stiffening as he delivered the final blow. "And as the Emperor's Enforcer, I have the right to execute you for your crimes."

He saw understanding seep into the governor's feeble mind. His eyes narrowed in confusion as he studied Zhi-

Gang's face, and then Bai abruptly paled. "But . . . but . . . But the Enforcer wears glasses!" he gasped. "Lie-Zi told me!"

Zhi-Gang grinned. "I could put them on if you like."

The man sputtered, his gaze darting about the room to no point. His guards were not coming. Zhi-Gang allowed him to stall—for a time—but in the end, he began his interrogation. "Tell me about these girls you have sold."

"But it is nothing!" Bai gasped. "Peasant girls sold by their paren—" His words were cut off on a gasp as Zhi-Gang drew blood. The crimson stain welled on the edge of his blade, shiny in the lantern glow.

"Do not women add value to a man's home? Beauty and song? Sweet nectar for their husband's pleasure, and sons to bless his old age?"

"Peasants and ugly girls," the governor whispered. "No one of value."

Rage darkened Zhi-Gang's thoughts, and his hands trembled with the need to slit this bastard's throat. Bai was a putrid excuse for a governor and part of a system of graft and illicit trade that the Emperor had tried to end. It actually hurt Zhi-Gang to pretend—even for a moment—that this corrupt system was supported by the Son of Heaven. But he claimed allegiance to the Empress Dowager. Therefore, all corruption had to stem from the enemy camp—her son—when the blame lay far more at the eunuchs' feet.

Either way, Bai had important information. But Zhi-Gang felt sullied by the game he had once embraced. So he jerked his head in Jing-Li's direction, signaling that his friend should continue the interrogation. He had already grown weary of it.

Jing-Li crossed the room on silent feet to stand over the quivering governor. "Who bought the girls?"

When the man did not answer, Jing-Li set a firm hand on Zhi-Gang's arm, pressing gently backward. Zhi-Gang hadn't even realized how hard he pushed on the governor's neck. The man didn't dare speak for fear of slitting his own throat. And still, Zhi-Gang found it difficult to pull away. So he leaned forward instead, whispering his words for fear that he might scream them otherwise.

"You kill China, do you know that? Every bribe that warms your body steals food from the people's mouths. Every time you smoke an opium pipe, you open China's doors to the white thieves that kill our country. That you would dare sell our children to the ghost devils makes you worse than a dog. Your life is forfeit, Governor Bai." He would have finished it then. He would have drawn the blades together with relish if it were not for Jing-Li.

His friend eyed him with a dark warning, the words clear though totally unspoken: *Do not push too hard. We are still outnumbered and very far from our friends.*

Zhi-Gang swallowed. Corruption was part of China and had been since long before even the Qing ruled this land. One man could not hope to stand against it, least of all himself, and yet the need burned inside him nonetheless. In the end, necessity stayed his hands. He pushed away with a snort of disgust, turning his back to this dog who had—at a minimum—allowed his sister to be sold.

"Save your life, Governor." Jing-Li spoke in a low undertone, inaudible to any but the three of them. "Tell us of the girls. Where did they go from here? Who purchased them?"

"I . . . I only know of three. Brothels in Shanghai where . . . where I had no need to pay."

"Name them."

He did. With the ease of a steady customer. Zhi-Gang turned to face him. "And when you went there to whore, did you ever look in the girls' eyes? Did you recognize their faces as the children of the servants who draw your water, as the babies of the farmers who grow your food? Did you see them and remember? Even once? As you rutted between their legs?"

The governor stared at him in stupefied confusion. He gaped while Zhi-Gang waited. In the end, the man sputtered the only answer he had. "But they were just peasant girls."

Zhi-Gang reacted without thought. He leaped forward without conscious will and took great satisfaction in slitting the man's throat. For the second time that day, he killed in a white-hot rage. This time the blood spilled onto the floor and not into a woman's face.

"Shit! Diseased monkey shit!" Jing-Li cursed from where he had jumped out of the way. "Must you go about killing every corrupt dog you meet? You will have a larger mountain of dead than General Kang! What now are we to tell his wives?"

Zhi-Gang carefully wiped his blades on the elegant silk that covered Bai's thick legs. He had to bend down nearly to the floor to find fabric clear of gore. "Tell them the truth," he replied in an amazingly calm voice. "That the Enforcer judged their husband a traitor to the Dragon Throne and summarily executed him." He straightened. "And then order me a bath."

Anna dipped her head a bare half inch in thanks to the governor's First Wife. She would have kowtowed to the sour-faced bitch if she thought it would help, but she knew that to do that would be to demean herself in the woman's eyes. Much better to pretend to a status far above the First Wife and allow the shrew to ingratiate herself.

At least that was the plan. She was currently in the First Wife's luxurious quarters, with wives Two through Five hovering in the background. They ranged in age between late fifties to the young teenager Wife Number Five. All were dressed in their finest, sitting or—in the case of the youngest two—standing as they pretended to embroider clothing for the governor's children. In truth, they all were staring at her, memorizing her every word and action for later discussion.

Anna ate as delicately as possible, doing her best to play a haughty aristocrat in a borrowed *chong san* of darkest black—probably the best outfit allotted to the tiny Fourth Wife. Anna's hair had been cleaned, combed and ruthlessly wrapped by a servant around a bamboo board in the style of the Manchu rulers. The delicate butterfly decoration that perched on the left side of the board had been a gift from Wife Number Two.

Now Anna ate sweet rice with pork and hot vegetable soup while the women hovered around her, their dark Chinese eyes studying her every breath as if she were a great mystery. And perhaps she was. A white concubine of a Chinese official? Who had ever heard of such a thing? And so they had hovered when she dressed, whispered behind her back whenever she looked away, and now stared at her when she ate.

Anna pretended to an aristocrat's arrogance, acting as if she were always the focus of such undivided attention. And all the while she studied the women and wondered one thing: Who had the opium?

They had some: that much was obvious. The youngest

wife—Number Five—was clearly an addict. She was waif-thin with sunken eyes and dry lips. Worse, the girl bore the mark of a man's fist on her face and arms. God only knew what her bastard husband had done between her legs. But her eyes were glazed in that half-aware place of a user. She'd probably taken enough opium to make her forget her pain and yet still function as servant and nursemaid to Wife Number One.

Wife Number Four was twitchy, clearly hungering for the drug but abstaining. Anna judged her to be about six months pregnant. Poor woman. Her bruises were gone, but there was a tightness in her shoulders that gave her a hunched and frightened appearance.

Wives Number Two and Three had similar aspects—a shrinking, timid appearance coupled with old bruises. Number Two was the worst, with a leg so crippled that she needed a cane to move about. She was perhaps the thinnest of the wives—even more so than Number Five—and Anna doubted she got enough food to survive.

A primary question, of course, was who had beat them. It would be easy to say the double-damned governor had done it. He certainly allowed the beatings to occur. The physical marks were much too clear to miss. But a First Wife could be equally brutal and ten times more inventive in ways to hurt the lower wives.

Whatever the case, Anna was sure that the First Wife held the bulk of the power in the women's quarters and therefore the main stash of opium. Befriending her would be the first goal. If Anna could not worm some opium out of her, then she would have to focus on finding the other women's hidden stores.

Anna finished off the last of the rice, a little startled that she had eaten everything so fast. She hadn't even re-

alized she was hungry, but had consumed the food—
praising the First Wife's chef to the skies—in the hopes
of making an ally. It had worked. Wife Number One visibly preened, beaming smugly at the lower wives as she
patted her obviously dyed black hair.

Next came praise of the children. Two sons were dutifully trotted out and admired. Apparently Wife Number
Two had a son as well, but he was left in the children's
quarters because—according to First Wife—he had a
weak chest and would likely die soon.

Next came the litany of all of First Wife's pains and
struggles. How life was so cruel. Anna sympathized, encouraging the woman to talk as much as possible, to detail the when and how of each injury and how it affected
her. And thus she got a complete picture of the power
structure in the home.

The governor was a bastard. That much had been clear
early, but only his current favorite wife would experience
the full extent of his cruelty. Though half the First Wife's
complaints were the aches and pains of old age, the other
half stemmed from her time as her husband's only woman.

Which meant the youngest wife got the opium because
she was the governor's newest victim. Which meant all
Anna needed to do was appear pathetic . . .

Anna allowed her mind to drift back to unpleasant
moments—to hot sticky blood coating her face, to the
stench of decay in the hospital's hopeless ward, and worst
of all, to the stench of sex in a smoke-drenched room.
Her eyes teared and her breath choked off.

As expected, every woman in the room abruptly
stopped what she was doing and stared. Anna turned her
face away, burying it in her hands, but her shoulders still
shook with pretend strain.

"Lady. Honored lady? What is it that ails you?" gasped the First Wife.

Anna didn't lie, though she could have created an elaborate fiction on the spot. But the truth was always easier to maintain. "My deepest apologies," she murmured. "It has been so hard. Sometimes I cannot breathe for the pain. The memory . . ."

"But what happened? Why is it so horrible?"

This was what all of them had been waiting for: a story to remember and recount over and over as they passed each day in tedious chores. Anna did not hesitate, though the words came slowly.

"I had a kind life once," she confessed, her eyes misting. "A mother who loved me, or so they told me. Nursemaids who fed me sweets."

All the ladies nodded. All of them had been either wealthy or beautiful children. They had to be in order to marry the governor. Someone in their childhood—either a parent or nursemaid—had to have loved them. And so they understood her beginnings, though she was white and likely not nearly as wealthy.

"My father visited occasionally. He brought gifts that I treasured—a doll from Canton, sweets from England. Until he died."

"Was it a sickness?" asked Wife Number Four.

"Hush! Do not show your ignorance by interrupting!" snapped First Wife.

Anna shook her head, the memories building up in her mind like a wave crashing over her. She fought it, as she always did, but sometimes they were too many to escape. "It was worse than that," she said. "There was a problem. A bad shipment, a gambling debt. I don't know."

"Murdered, then," said First Wife. "For his debts. And you were sold."

Anna stiffened, unable to stop herself from snapping. "Whites do not sell their daughters like that."

First Wife recoiled as if slapped, and so it was left to Wife Number Two to explain their assumption. "But you were given as a gift to the mandarin. How else would you be his wife?"

Anna looked away, stalling for time. How stupid of her to forget the story the mandarin had created. And how impossible to tell the truth of their meeting. "I lived in a mission," she said. "That is where white children go. And I wrote—I write letters to my father's family in England." She lifted her chin. "They want me back. They want me to come to them," she lied.

"But . . . how do you come to be married then? To a Chinese Imperial scholar?" Wife Number Two's eyes betrayed intelligence despite her wasted frame.

"My father's business partner came to the mission. He claimed . . ." She shook her head. "He said I was pretty and that he needed me to help him. He lied to the nuns. He claimed he was my real father and that he wanted to take me home to England." She looked up, real tears brimming in her eyes. "I didn't know any different. And he was so nice to me."

"*He* sold you." Wife Number Five's voice was dark and cold—like a whisper from the grave and equally hopeless.

Anna looked at her, at her battered face and deadened eyes, and she could not bring herself to say the truth. She could not show this girl that there was no hope in this world, though that might be the cruel reality. So she switched to exactly what they wanted to hear: an elaborate fable.

Taking a deep breath, she sighed and shook her head. "Oh no," she whispered. "My new father turned out to be horrible and mean." True enough. "It took me a long, long time to see the truth, but eventually I did. And then . . ." She shrugged. "I ran away."

As one, they gasped in shock. She could tell by their eyes that every one of them had dreamed of such a thing. They had hoped and schemed and prayed, but in the end, they did nothing. Where would they go? How would they survive?

"I ran away," she said firmly. "I stole whatever I could carry and I ran as far and as fast as I could."

"But how?" whispered the youngest wife.

"I walked. And I took rides on carts. And I sold something to pay for passage on a boat down the Grand Canal."

Wife Number Two's eyes narrowed. "You ran from Peking all the way down here?" It was clear she didn't believe.

"No. I was caught quickly enough. By the mandarin himself."

The First Wife's mouth pinched in disapproval. "Your father must be very powerful indeed to send a mandarin to catch you."

Anna shook her head. "Not powerful. Rich. And not every mandarin is as wealthy as they pretend. Besides, the mandarin was not sent to find me. He was sent by the Dowager Empress for another reason. He only discovered me by accident."

"Humph," snorted the First Wife. She didn't really believe the story, and neither would the other ladies either. That wasn't the point. The story was to give hope and to gain sympathy. It didn't matter if it was real.

"But I don't understand," whined Wife Number Three. "How are you with the mandarin now?"

"We fell in love," Anna stated. She hadn't thought she could say the lie without choking, but it came out easily enough. She spoke quickly, not giving the women time to question as she spun a story about a glorious courtship and marriage on the boat. She claimed it had been years ago, and that they lived in Peking now and that she had given the mandarin a son.

They didn't believe her. No one in this country would accept that a rich Chinese official would stoop so low as to marry a white woman. A ghost barbarian? Impossible! And yet they hung on her words, wanting to believe. After all, if someone little better than a monkey could marry a Chinese official for love, then how much easier to write a happy ending for them—Chinese women with access to money and jewels. They wanted to believe, and so they listened to her story as they would drink a dark wine or inhale sweet drugging smoke—with outward reluctance, but an inner desperation.

"You cannot be in love!" exclaimed the First Wife.

Anna nodded, pushing herself to believe it. And the Peking life she created for herself and her husband was so wonderful as to make her ache with the same longing she had for England. It was so beautiful that she nearly forgot her primary purpose—to create sympathy enough to get opium. Fortunately, Wife Number Two recalled her to the purpose.

"If your life is so happy," she challenged, "then why do you cry? Why were you running in a field and sleeping in a tree? The villagers threw stones at you." Then she sniffed. "I heard the story from my husband's guards."

Of course. Wife Two was the smartest of the bunch. Her network of spies would not be large, but it would be accurate. Anna paused as she studied the crippled woman and judged the best way to gain her sympathies. Then she heaved a dramatic sigh and looked down at the floor.

"I . . . I have not told you the full truth," she confessed. "We are very happy together, my husband and I. But even a mandarin could not possibly take me as First Wife." She raised her gaze to the Second Wife. "And my mother-in-law . . ." She shuddered.

"You ran from them?" snapped the First Wife. "The women who are your sisters through your husband? The women who share their food and their home to you, a white—"

"You do not understand!" Anna cried. "You are the kindest and most gentle of wives! You cannot know how cruel some people can be!" She wiped away her pretend tears as she continued to bemoan her fate. "They pinch me and hurt me. They order me to do the most terrible things!" Then she looked up, her eyes pulled dramatically wide. "But I could stand those things! Maybe I deserve them, I don't know." She took a hiccupping breath. "I ran because of my father!"

Wife Number Three frowned, clearly lost. "But I thought he died. Murdered for gambling."

Anna grimaced. "My pretend father. The one who took me from the nuns. He never stopped looking for me. He wants his things back. The things I sold to escape him."

Wife Number Two's eyes narrowed. "What things?"

"He found me a month ago. It is a big story in Peking about the mandarin with a white wife. Everyone talks about it. They don't believe it is possible, that we could fall in love. But then they see me with my fine clothing and the jade in my hair, and they know it is true."

First Wife nodded darkly. "Those who look will always find you. You cannot escape them."

"But I did. For years, I have been so happy! But he found me. Samuel." She whispered his name like the hiss of a snake, and all the women recoiled in horror. Then she continued, her shoulders shaking from a fear more real than she cared to admit. "A month ago, he found me and demanded payment for what he lost."

Again Wife Number Two spoke. "What was it that you sold?"

"I convinced my husband to bring me along when he traveled south. I told him I could make him happy. We could make another son."

First Wife knew the next step. They all did. "Your father pursued you. Everyone would know where you were going. A mission from the Dowager Empress would be known by all. Silly girl, it would be easy to follow you."

Anna nodded. "I gave my father all the jewelry I had. It was worth far more than what I stole, but he was not satisfied."

"Men do not get satisfied," murmured Fifth Wife. "They always return for more."

Anna focused on the young girl and nodded quietly. How many times had she suffered at the hands of her husband? "Yes," Anna confirmed. "He demanded more. And when I had nothing, he hit me." She showed the bruises on her arms, the ones given to her by the villages and the slaver.

Wife Number Four finished the tale then. "He tried to steal you back. He grabbed you and ran but the mandarin pursued. He found you—"

"And he killed your pretend father," said Number Five. "The evil Ssssamuel."

"And then you ended up here?" scoffed Number Two. "I do not believe you. Why would your husband not take you back home then? Why not to your boat to shower gifts upon you?"

"Because it only just happened!" retorted First Wife. "Did you not see the blood on his jacket when he arrived here? Was she not wearing peasant clothing that hung on her like a sack? It was because of the blood, because he only just killed the evil father."

Anna let them squabble, noting who sided with her, who did not. It was Wife Number Two who was most suspicious, most disbelieving of a happy future. And given her crippled form, the woman had cause to be skeptical. So Anna directed her tears to that woman, showing her agony to the one woman who could not believe.

"No, no," she whispered. "That is not at all what happened."

It took a moment for them all to quiet enough to hear her. But when they did, she once again had a rapt audience. She told them, as quickly as she could, of being caught by the villagers, of the slaver who had come to sell her into an unspeakable life, and of her "husband's" dramatic rescue. It wasn't easy, and yet it wasn't hard either. She dwelled on his warmth, on the security she'd felt in his arms and how if he hadn't arrived when he did . . .

And as she spoke, she felt a rightness in her words. The mandarin *had* saved her. He had been very kind to her. The question was why? But that was not something to be answered now. Instead, she turned her tragic gaze back to Wife Number Two.

"He does not know," she whispered. "He does not know my father still pursues us. He does not know that if we return to the boat, my father will be waiting nearby for the next time I am alone." Her voice trembled and she clutched at her skirt, crushing the delicate silk.

"Tell him!" Wife Number Three said. "Tell him and he will protect you."

Anna bit her lip. Chinese wives had a long tradition of keeping secrets from their husbands. They understood the companionship of sisters, the silent hiding of sins from one's husband. And so she closed her eyes and allowed tears to fall.

"He will hate me then. He thinks . . . I never told him the truth of my childhood. I let him believe I was a rich white girl lost in China." She bit her lip. "He has a terrible temper. I fear he will kill me if he learns the truth."

She peeked upward, studying the women's faces. They understood the fear of being killed by one's husband. Then she raised her head, noticing something for the first time. There was a gap in ages between Wives Three and Four. The youngest two might not even be twenty yet, whereas Wife Number Three was mid-thirties at least. That often happened when a man could not afford a new wife. Or . . .

"You know," she whispered. "You know of men who kill their wives, don't you? The governor had other wives, didn't he?"

All five women looked away. In the end it was left to First Wife to answer the question. "There were two others. We do not speak of them. The two here—FuXi and LiBo—should be Wives Number Six and Seven, but we do not speak of the others."

Wife Number Two keep her face averted the longest. She spoke in the softest of whispers, her face turned to the wall. "We do not speak of the others," she repeated.

"So you understand," Anna responded. "You know I cannot tell him. I have to appease my father." She swallowed. It was time to finish this. It was time to get what she needed and disappear, as fast as possible. They would give it to her now. The First Wife was definitely on her side, along with the youngest two. Even if Wife Number Two suspected the lies, she would be silenced by the others. Besides, they all needed to believe in the dream she had created. They all needed a part in making it come true. When she got to England, she would buy them something wonderful—English lace for their clothing and mechanical toys for their children. Something special to make up for what she took from them now. She would do that as soon as she could. But for now . . .

"What does your father demand?" First Wife asked.

Anna raised her eyes, pretending to an innocence she had lost within a week of leaving the mission. "I couldn't ask it of you. You have been too kind."

"Our husband is very rich," put in Wife Number Three. "We have more than enough of everything. Surely we could share. What do you need?"

They were committed now. Whatever she asked for, Number Three had just committed them to supplying it. Anna mentally upgraded what she could ask for. Meanwhile, she blinked back more tears. "You have been so kind . . ."

"Enough!" snapped the First Wife. "We will not sit by and watch you killed. What do you need?"

Anna opened her mouth to answer. The word was simple and eloquent on her tongue, but she never got the chance to voice it. Someone else said the word. Someone who had been listening silently for some time. Someone who might very well kill her for what she had just done.

"Opium," he said from the doorway. "She wants opium."

Anna turned and saw the mandarin standing there, his expression as hard as stone. Anger poured out of him, staining the room like spilled ink.

"My husband!" she cried, hoping to distract him. It didn't work.

His expression remained trained on her, but his words were for the rest of the room. "I am here on a mission from the Dowager Empress. I am to find those that poison China with the white dung powder." He took a step further into the room. "My job—my sworn duty—is to kill any I find possessing opium." His gaze left Anna's face. He slowly inspected each woman, one after the other. Each shrunk from him in terror, bowing and sidling backward if they could.

Anna swallowed, recognizing the speech for what it was. The Enforcer always said such a thing to the wives and the children. He told them who he was, then he threatened to kill them if any were caught with opium. His next words were delivered with a kind of softness, even.

"None of you have such an evil thing, do you?" he asked.

"No, your honor," the women answered, as they always did.

"Of course not, your honor."

"Never."

He released a sigh. A slow one, which held real regret.

"Good," he said in a much softer tone. "Because your husband did deal in such poison. He is dead now by my hand."

Anna pressed a hand to her mouth to repress a cry of shock. Even knowing the end of the Enforcer's speech, she had not expected such a thing at this moment, at this time. He had killed the governor? Moments ago?

The other women were also frozen in shock. They said nothing, only stared.

"My servant will help you deal with matters," he said to the wives. Then he crossed to stand beside Anna. "Now, if you will please excuse me, it is time I spoke with my wife."

January 3, 1882
To Mr. And Mrs. Kent of Oxford, England:

My name is Mother Francis, and I am the Mother Superior of a mission hospital in China. I write to you today with a troubled heart. I believe you are the parents of an Elizabeth Kent who married Frank Thompson, a sailor by trade. I understand that he and your daughter subsequently left England to make their fortune in Shanghai, China.

Did Mr. Thompson write you of your daughter's death some years ago? It is my fervent hope that he did. However, if he neglected this important and Christian act, I must sadly in inform you that your daughter and her infant died shortly after the new year 1876. They were victims of a childbed fever.

However their eldest child—Anna—still survives. She came to us when her father was at sea. He provided for her in the way of all careless men and has ap-

parently met his fate of drink or women or worse, I cannot say.

But the child Anna remains. Surely you wish to know your last surviving grandchild? She is of an age that she could travel home to you should arrangements be made. I pray that you will desire to reunite with your granddaughter in all Christian charity, as she has lately fallen into the company of one of her father's associates, Mr. Samuel Fitzpatrick. I do not like this man or his reputation. Though I keep strict control of the men who visit my charges, Anna can be a willful child and she sees in Mr. Fitzpatrick a substitute father. It would be best for your granddaughter if she were removed from the disturbing atmosphere of China as soon as possible and remanded into your care.

Surely you wish such a thing? Surely you want to know your granddaughter.

However, if my prayers are in vain, perhaps you know of Mr. Thompson's family. Would not his parents be interested in their beautiful granddaughter?

> *In God is good grace I pray,*
> *Mother Francis*
> *St. Agatha Mission*
> *Shanghai, China*

By the late 1830s, there was no doubt that opium was leading to the destruction of China. By 1836, opium shipments were more than 30,000 chests, enough to supply 12.5 million smokers. The Chinese imperial army lost a battle against local rebels because the army was addicted to opium. The financial drain on China was disrupting the entire economy.

—*Robert Trout, The Chinese Opium Wars*

CHAPTER NINE

Zhi-Gang waited until the governor's wives left the room. The wailing started soon afterwards, about five steps into the hallway. Long enough for the First Wife to remember that she was supposed to grieve for her husband's death, not feel complete and total relief.

That's what he'd seen in the seconds after he'd delivered the news: blatant relief. The youngest wife had even flashed a shaky smile. Even if Zhi-Gang hadn't understood the governor's character before, the wives' expressions—complete with ugly bruises—told him that China was better off without Governor Bai.

Unfortunately, false grief was usually much, much louder than real grief. He closed his eyes as the sobs crested to a head-splitting shriek before beginning again. Tradition demanded forty-nine days of wailing for a husband. He intended to be gone in the morning. As for now, he had an errant wife to interrogate.

She was dressed beautifully in black silk that hugged

her lush breasts but remained too loose around her waist. In Peking he would hire the best seamstress and shower her in gowns that accented her full curves. Except, of course, they were not going to Peking. As the Enforcer, he had full authority in the wilds of China. If he wanted a white woman, no one would dare question him. But in Peking, politics muddied everything. No one could predict how the Empress Dowager or the white ambassadors would react to such a thing. Zhi-Gang might be thought of as progressive, or more likely assassinated as an example to all.

He sighed and settled into the nearest chair. Anna remained seated across from him, her body completely stiff, her eyes wide with anxiety. Though he hated to see the panic in her expression, he could do nothing to alleviate it. He had to know the truth. And for that to happen, she had to fear him.

He sighed. "That was a wonderful story you created. You are a gifted liar."

She swallowed, and he watched her grip her hands together. Probably to stop them from shaking. But when she spoke, her voice was steady and strong enough to be heard over the wives' wailing.

"They needed the fantasy. Women need to believe in love."

He frowned, thrown by her response. "Why?"

"Because there is so little of it in this world."

"So, you do not really believe in it, do you?"

"So, you are not really going to let me leave China alive, are you?"

He blinked, startled. He had not expected her to challenge him. And yet, he found himself smiling at her spirit. "I stand by my word to help you escape China. It makes little difference to me if you get onto a boat or are dead and buried, so long as you disappear."

"Then let me go. I want nothing more than to escape your horrid country."

He shook his head. "But we are desperately in love according to your story. How would it look if you left now?"

She had no answer, so she dropped her gaze to her hands. Odd, how perfectly she appeared a demure Chinese wife. And yet underneath . . .

"You are not really a nun," he said. "And the opium that Jing-Li used was yours."

Her eyes leaped to his at the word *opium*, but then the blood drained from her face.

"Yes," he confirmed. "Jing-Li smoked it with the boat captain and his family. I think I destroyed the rest, but I cannot be sure." He shook his head. "I dare not sail again until any remaining drug is gone. An opium-dazed captain is very likely to sail us straight into the rocks."

He fell silent, watching her closely. He saw her struggle to control her expression, fighting to hide the desperation and longing he had seen too many times.

He sighed, feeling the painful truth deep in his bones. "You are an addict."

She flinched, but did not deny it.

"Now where," he mused, "would a white woman get so much opium?" He looked across the room at his beautiful wife—the liar and cheat. "You are a runner. You pretend to be a missionary, carry the opium into the interior of China, sell it, then travel back to Shanghai for more."

She looked impossibly pale, but once again she surprised him with a steady voice, steady stare. "If that were true, then why would I be running south with the opium?"

He had wondered the same thing, spent most of the walk to Huai'an asking the same question. It was only moments ago as he had listened to her story of love and longing that he realized the truth. The secret that under-lay her story was there for any who chose to listen.

She longed for something, craved it desperately, and when she held it in her hands could not bear to give it up no matter what the cost. She'd labeled it love in her story, but he knew the truth: she wanted opium, craved opium, would die for her opium.

He heard himself laugh, the sound unpleasant. "You are an addict caught in the same snare you set for my people. You ran because you could not bear to sell the drug you crave so desperately." He shook his head, surprised as always by such stupidity. "You must know you will be killed. If not by the buyer who has no opium now, then by the man who supplies you. And what did you intend to do when the poison ran out?" He shook his head. "Stupid, stupid, stupid."

"And how like a woman," she drawled, her voice matching his for dark humor. "To not think beyond the current moment. A smart man would skim little bits off the top. It's probably even expected as the normal price of doing business. Steal a little for myself, sell the rest. That way my supply would remain, I would still have the opium, and no one would be trying to kill me. But because I am a woman, you assume I cannot think that clearly."

Exactly so. But her tone indicated otherwise, so he leaned forward, ashamed of the hope that sparked in his breast. Could she be honest? Impossible, and yet he so wanted to believe in her. "Then tell me the truth. Who are you? Why are you carrying opium?"

She shook her head, confirming exactly what he believed even as she spoke in a completely different way. "Your friend," she said. "Jing-Li. Is he addicted?"

Yes. "We are not speaking of my companions."

Ignoring him completely, she pushed on. "And does he not do stupid things when he smokes? Says too much or too little? Shares things he does not have or own?"

Yes. And yes. And also no. They were alive now because two eunuchs thought Jing-Li was too insensate from opium to understand that the Empress plotted against her own son. But he'd woken from his sleep too late to help the Emperor, and barely soon enough to save Zhi-Gang.

"Why?" he challenged. "Why do you ask?"

"What would you do," she answered, "if you were raised to . . . to run opium? If that was all you knew?"

"Whites have many choices. We did not ask you to come to China. We do not want you here."

She nodded. "And I do not want to be here. But Chinese or English—women have few choices." She abruptly pushed to her feet, anger fueling her movements. Anger, and a raw desperation that set her entire body to quivering. "I. Hate. This. Country. I hate the opium I carried. I hate the men who bought the damned drug, who poisoned the villagers who then destroyed their own lives with craving the evil thing. I saw them, you know. I saw the farmers and the children, the merchants and the leaders—all of them, one by one—after years of smoking, they came to the mission hospital. I saw them wasted and dying, still craving that last breath of dirty smoke. I saw them," she hissed.

"And you became one of them?"

"Yes!" Tears filled her eyes and she spun away.

Oddly enough, he never found her more beautiful than now, when fear and desperation left her with only raw honesty. But that did not change who she was. "So you stole the drug you carried. Why? To smoke it yourself?"

"No. Yes." She threw up her arms in disgust. "I don't know, and it doesn't matter anyway."

But it did matter to him. He wasn't even sure why. She was a confessed opium smuggler. He had the moral right and obligation to kill her for her crimes. The drug traffic had to end. Lenience had never been an option. Certainly not for the man called the Emperor's Enforcer. And yet, he didn't want to kill her. He wanted to understand.

"Where were you going?"

She didn't answer, but he saw her reach toward her neckline. She once wore a tiny Christian cross there, he remembered. Apparently the memory still lingered because she kept her fingers right above her heart, twisting and rubbing though she wore no ornament.

"*Where?*" he abruptly shouted, and he saw her start in surprise, her hand dropping away from her throat.

She whipped around to face him. "England! Or Australia!" There was conviction in her whole body. She truly had meant to leave. But then she looked away. "It doesn't matter. I was leaving. I want to leave."

"With your drug?"

She threw up her hands in disgust. "I could not sell it anymore! It would only be sold to farmers, to mothers, to people who could not afford such a thing. Don't you understand? We sell ourselves, our heirlooms, even our children just for more of the damn stuff! I couldn't do that anymore. I couldn't." Her voice broke on a strangled sob as she turned her back to him.

He pushed to his feet, his instincts urging him forward,

telling him to wrap her in his arms. She was in pain. He could see it in her tight body, hear it in her stuttered breath, even feel it in the air between them. But he was the Enforcer. He had to know the full truth. He had to know exactly who she was and what she did. Only then could he find a way to save her.

"What did you do?" he asked softly. "What did you sell?"

She shook her head, refusing to answer. And so this time he did go to her. He wrapped her in his arms and drew her close to his chest. Despite his intentions, he stroked her arms, surrounding her with his strength as he comforted her. And yet, he still had to know.

"What did you sell?" he pressed.

She trembled beneath his hands. Her entire body shook with the power of her emotions. He need only wait and she would tell him. He knew this, and yet part of him didn't want to know. Part of him wanted to help her hide from what she had done. "Marie—" he began.

"Anna," she whispered. "My name is Anna. And I don't know."

He blinked, confused by her words. "You don't know what?"

Her body stilled beneath his, her shoulders dropping in defeat. "I don't know what I sold. I was drugged already. And when I woke . . ." She swallowed, unable to go on.

He tightened his hold, willing his strength into her. And in time, she stumbled into speech again.

"I woke naked. There was blood where there shouldn't be. And I was sore, so sore." She shook her head. "I remember fighting him. Them. But I was too weak." She took a breath, her tears flowing freely. With a gentle touch, he urged her to turn around. She went easily, burying her face and her tears into his chest. "That was the first time I took opium. The other times . . ." She shook her head. "It was to forget the first."

"Who?" he demanded. "Who did this to you?"

She sighed. "Another runner. The one who taught me the trade." Then she abruptly straightened in his arms. In her eyes, he saw a haunting desperation. "Kill me, please. Do it soon . . . and quick. But first let me smoke a little more. Just a tiny bit. The First Wife has some, I am sure of it. Let her give me a little, then you can . . . you can do what you will, as you will. Take turns with Jing-Li. Whatever you want. Just give me a little to smoke first. Just a tiny bit and I won't fight . . ."

And that was when he knew what had happened to her. He did not know when or how she had become addicted. It probably took years, but sellers often took a smoke in front of the buyers. It proved the opium wasn't poisoned.

And if the runner was a beautiful woman, she could be encouraged to smoke a little more. And a little more. And once addicted, how would she stop? And once lost to opium dreams, how would she stop them? How many times had she been raped? How many men—runners and buyers alike—had used her before she came to this, begging him for her own death?

It would be a mercy to kill her. Indeed, Imperial law demanded that he do so immediately. Runners were given no mercy. With a fluid shift of his wrists, he drew one of his knives. He raised it before her face and even pressed it to her neck.

The blade bobbed as she swallowed convulsively, but his hand did not waver. "What?" he mocked. "You do not curse my ancestry? Doom my balls and my descendants

154

with your last breath? Where is the woman who knelt before me three days ago, terrifying all? Grown men cupped their organs and ran from you. Where is she?"

"Quickly. Please," she whispered.

He couldn't do it. He could not slice open a woman's throat, no matter who she was or what she had done. That is what he told himself, though he knew it was a lie. He had killed women before. Opium smugglers. Whorehouse madames. Cunning women all, surviving off the misery of others. He had killed them without a second thought.

But not this woman. He could not kill this woman, though she deserved and even begged for it. He had no wish to examine his own reasons why.

He would not kill her. But he would not stop her. He abruptly stepped back, spinning the blade in his hand as he grabbed her arm. Then he pressed the handle into her palm and raised it back to her throat. "A single pull backward," he instructed. "Draw your elbow back hard and you will slit your own throat. It will be quick and relatively painless."

Then he released her hand and stepped backward. He waited while she watched him with startled eyes. He had not thought a white woman's eyes could be so dark, but they were. The tiny black pupils seemed to swallow the soft brown that surrounded them, and he imagined he could see into her very core.

Deep inside her, he saw pain and longing, a hunger for more and a fear that life would give so much less. What he saw was himself: his own desperation, his own fears. And yes, his own hopes.

He watched her tense her shoulders. Her eyes grew shuttered and her grip on the hilt became firm. She was going to do it. She was going to kill herself before his very eyes. Without thinking, he dove forward, intending to wrest the blade from her hand.

Too late. With an agonized scream, she twisted her elbow . . . and threw the blade across the room. But he was already diving toward her, unable to stop his forward movement. He tackled her, and they fell, him on top, her contorted awkwardly beneath. She was screaming still, her voice echoing in his head. A woman screaming. A girl. A woman. A girl. Screaming and screaming and screaming until someone had dragged her away.

No; that was not now. That was in his nightmares. This time he could do something about it. He cradled the woman against his chest. He held her tight while sobs wracked her body. He held her until her screams finally faded into stuttered hiccups.

"So," he whispered into her hair. "You do not really wish to die. And you have begun to understand that there will be no more opium."

Her body shuddered, but she made no comment.

"Do you wish to live then? Do you wish to help end the nightmare?"

She could not understand the question, of course. He had not told her enough to comprehend. But that didn't truly matter. What he needed right then from her was a single statement. And he prayed that, once stated out loud, she would not recant later.

But she was not speaking. She buried her head in his chest and remained there, her breath hot against his skin.

"Say it!" he commanded. "Say you want to live."

Another shudder convulsed her body, but he did not release her. He tightened his grip on her shoulders even as he drew back enough to stare into her eyes. "Do you wish to live? Say it!"

"Yes!" she snapped. "Yes, I wish to live!"

"Will you help me then?" he demanded.

Her expression grew wary. The lamplight had dimmed in the time that they had been together, so her face lay half in shadow. But he stayed close enough to track every nuance of her expression. She was afraid, terrified even, but he did not release her.

"I want to follow this trail of opium and sold peasant girls," he said. "I want to trace it from slaver to governor then back to the source."

"Where?"

"Shanghai. That is what the governor said before I killed him. That the girls were sold in Shanghai."

He felt her stiffen, and he tightened his grip. "Was your supplier also in Shanghai?"

She nodded, though slowly.

"Do not think to lie to me."

"I'm not," she whispered. "My . . . he lives in Shanghai."

"Your pretend father?" He had heard enough of the story she had told to the wives.

She nodded.

"Then we will follow this trail back to Shanghai. We will find the girls and maybe even your pretend father. Will you help me with this?"

She nodded, and this time the motion was smoother and more determined.

"If you do this with me, if you help me follow the trail until the very end, then this I swear to you: I will put you on your boat to England or Australia or wherever. I will send you from my accursed shores and think no more of you again."

Hope lit her eyes. "You swear? On your ancestors? And . . . and your balls?"

He grinned. "On both of my young and very healthy balls, I swear." Without truly meaning to, he felt his hips shift forward. When had his dragon hardened? When had her hips cradled him so that he could feel the heat that pulsed between her thighs? He gazed down into her eyes and saw interest flare. Her body was still beneath him, her breath suspended, and then . . . A slight pressure in return? "Anna . . . ?"

"I will tell you all you need to know about my pretend father." She was rushing her speech, but the words still had the resonance of a vow. "I will tell you everything about Samuel Fitzpatrick."

"Excellent," Zhi-Gang said. A slow smile spread across his face. He remained where he was, cradled by her hips, their gazes locked. Heat began to build in the scant space between them. "Do you want opium?" he asked, his voice low and seductive.

She blinked, obviously startled. "Yes," she whispered. "Oh yes."

He rolled to his feet, easily lifting her up with him. "Then come with me."

She hung back, her steps reluctant. "What? Why?"

He smiled at her, seeing her flushed and tear-strained skin, noting the way her breasts still lifted and lowered in unsteady and provocative gasps. She looked a mess, and yet he could not help but think of spreading her thighs while he rested his head upon her ample bosom. It was a depraved thought, but then he had often been labeled a depraved man.

"I am the Emperor's Enforcer. I cannot give you opium. Indeed, if I were to ever find you with even a pipe in your hands, I would be forced to kill you immediately. Do you understand this?"

She nodded, her expression frozen in anxiety.

"You are never, ever to touch a pipe again. Do you understand?"

She swallowed, and her voice came out hard and bitter. "Yes. I understand. Opium equals death. I learned the equation long ago."

His fierceness eased. She did understand. Few addicts ever did. "Excellent. Now that we understand each other, we must now proceed to the next step: how to deal with your cravings."

She blinked, completely lost.

"I will not force you," he continued. "But you are the one who created the fiction."

"What fiction? What are you talking about?"

He lifted his chin. "We are desperately in love. That is what you told the governor's wives. We are desperately in love."

"Yes, but—"

"Don't worry," he said, cutting off her objections. "I know just what to do." He leaned forward, intending to make his kiss swift and sure. But he failed in his intentions. Instead of a quick press of his lips against hers, he lingered, stroking her startled mouth with his tongue. He teased her skin, touching and probing until she widened the tiniest bit. Then he pulled back.

"With me, sweet Anna, you will never ever crave opium again."

She frowned at him, releasing a snort of disbelief. "That is not possible."

He grinned. "I accept your challenge. Now come, my beloved wife. It is time we showed the world our devotion."

* * *

Anna felt her shoulders—her whole body—tighten in fear. "That was fiction," she said softly. "We are not in love." Her heart tightened at the words, but she pushed on. "The wives will be wailing all night long. There is no need for—"

"Don't you crave opium right now?"

Yes. The answer echoed in her body and soul, but she refused to admit it aloud.

"Why?" he pressed.

"What?"

"Why do you want opium? You were not in a drugged stupor when we saw you on the Grand Canal. You have carried opium halfway across China. Did you smoke any of it?"

"No." She had thought about it, dreamed about it, even fondled the drug, but she had not smoked. There had been opportunity, but . . . "It was to be my payment aboard a ship."

He nodded, as if he had expected such a thing. "So why now? Why are you so desperate to smoke *now?*"

Anger shot through her, and she grabbed it with both hands. "Because you meant to kill me. Because you intend to . . ."

"To what?" he challenged.

She swallowed but stiffened her spine. "To rape me," she accused.

His smile came slowly, but not with the veneer of evil she expected. Instead, his eyes were gentle, his touch even more so. He stroked a fingertip across her cheek. "I will do nothing you do not wish. This I swear."

She did not believe him, but she dared not call him a liar to his face. Nor did she wish to admit another thought, another desire: Perhaps she wanted him to touch her: Perhaps she wondered what it would be like to be touched when she was awake, aware, and . . . intrigued?

His hand dropped away from her cheek and he stood quietly facing her. "My friends . . ." He sighed. "Jing-Li turns to opium when he does not wish to think. Without a governorship, he has too much time on his hands, too much wasted talent. Some—the eunuchs most especially—just want relief from the tedium of their days. You understand?"

She nodded. "Forgetfulness," she whispered. "We wish to forget."

He stepped closer and she would have shied backward if it were not for the mischievous light in his eyes. "I know of better ways to forget. Indeed, I have made quite a study of it."

She grimaced. "Men forget during sex. Women do not."

"Are you sure?" he challenged.

No. She kept her mouth pressed firmly shut.

"What if I made a bargain with you? A few minutes, nothing more. Enough to convince the women that what you told them was true. That we are indeed in love."

"This is ridiculous! We do not have to prove anything to them! Besides, they believe you angry with me because my father is coming to blackmail me for opium."

He nodded. "Exactly! And how would a good wife distract me?"

"But it is all a lie!" she screeched. Her hands tightened into fists and she would have beat him if she could. But he grabbed her arms and held her close enough that she could smell his scent: spiced wine. That is what he smelled like to her—a seductive, exotically spiced wine.

They were less than a foot apart, but he had hold of

her forearms. He slowly drew her to him. She turned her face away, not wanting to offer him her lips again, and yet her heart beat triple-time at his nearness and her mouth tingled in anticipation.

Was she attracted to this man? She couldn't be! And yet, she knew deep down that she was. From that first moment on the Grand Canal, he had figured prominently in her thoughts. When she had touched herself in the bath, she had thought of him. When she ran from him, her mind had been consumed with questions about what he was doing: Was he looking for her? How could she avoid him? And when he saved her from . . . It had seemed inevitable, somehow, that he would be the one to rescue her.

Was that love? Certainly not. But perhaps it was attraction. Perhaps it was . . . lust?

"I will teach you how to forget without opium. I will show you that there are ways to know nothing but the caress of a tongue on your nipples, the hot curl of a womb on fire, and the press and pulse of two bodies in ecstasy."

"So, you would replace one sin with another—promiscuity rather than addiction? Is it better to live as a wanton or an addict?"

He shrugged, not offering her an answer. At least not with words. Instead, he leaned down—he was already so close. She thought he meant to whisper to her, but instead she felt his tongue slip around the edge of her ear. It was wet and cool. It should have been repulsive, but it was not. She felt the heat of his breath curl across her skin and every time she inhaled, she relished his scent.

Would it be so awful? Or worse, what if it were wonderful? What if a night with the mandarin was as blissful, as amazing as a night spent in an opium haze? What if she ended up craving the man as much as she hungered for the drug? What then?

"I do not even know your name."

"Zhi-Gang," he answered. "Tau Zhi-Gang."

"The Emperor's Enforcer," she said.

He stilled for a moment against her cheek. She knew anxiety coiled in his belly, though how she could feel such a thing was beyond her.

"Yes," he finally said. "I am a man of violence, a man who kills. You know this."

"And you are a scholar," she said. "A man who studies Confucius and Lao Tzu. The two must be very hard to reconcile—being both scholar and warrior."

He pulled back, a bare inch, so that he could look her in the eye. "Yes," he whispered.

"Yes," she repeated, knowing she was yielding to whatever he wanted. In truth, her surrender was inevitable. Without opium, she was lost. And without direction of her own, his would do. She was that weak and wretched. And yet, when he feathered his lips across her neck to press just beneath the edge of her collar, she did not feel awful or lost or alone. She felt cherished.

It was a lie. She knew it to be one of the greatest—and most common—of men's lies. She knew it, believed it, and yet, when he slid his hands up her forearms to cup her elbows, she could not fight him. She wanted to believe—even for these few moments—that she *was* his beloved wife, cherished and adored, just as she had pretended to the other women.

"I am your adored wife?" she asked, her voice barely

above a whisper. She felt his hands slip to the clasps above her left breast.

"Of course," he responded, his low voice creating a shiver that started at her neck but traveled down her spine until it encompassed her whole body.

"And what will I be in the morning?" she asked.

"Well loved," he answered.

Her heartbeat skittered at the word "loved." Her breasts tingled even as the tight silk began to peel away. Lies, she told herself, and yet what was her alternative? A night spent sweating, mouth dry in hunger for a smoke? If she could not have forgetfulness that way, she would take the other path.

"Then make sure," she challenged, even as she allowed her neck to drop backward, lifting her breasts to him, "make sure I think of nothing but you."

She felt his lips pull into a smile against her skin. She was arched backward, his hands on her elbows. But at her words, he bent down and wrapped his hands around her hips. Before she could do more than open her eyes, she felt him lift her up. He was carrying her, easily shifting his weight so that she fell forward over his shoulder.

She squeaked in surprise, then gasped in shock as he slipped one hand underneath her tight skirt. He could not go far, but his hand felt very hot and very large as it slipped between her thighs. She tightened against him, halting his fingers' progress up her legs. It gave her something to focus on rather than the heavy jostle of movement as he carried her out of the room.

His strides were long and efficient as he moved out of the room. He barely even paused when Wife Number Three—surprised in the hallway—stopped weeping long enough to gaze in shock at him.

"Lead me to my bedchamber," he commanded.

She nodded mutely, then abruptly scurried forward. He followed with his smooth stride, but his attention—and Anna's—remained centered on his hand between her legs. She held his fingers pinned between clenched thighs, but he could still move a little. He twisted his hand, he squeezed her skin, and he wormed the tiniest bit higher. She found herself breathless with the game. Could she keep him out? Where would he touch her if she could not?

He rounded a corner and grunted a quick, "Thank you," to Wife Number Three. Then he was through the door and heading for a large bed in the center of the room.

Anna managed to lift her head enough to see Wife Number Three still staring at them from the doorway, her mouth open. But what startled Anna the most was the need in the woman's huge eyes. As if she drank in the sight of Anna flipped over the mandarin's shoulder and would hold the image close to her heart for all of her days.

Anna might have said something then. She might have screamed out the truth—that this was all an act, that Zhi-Gang was no different than any other man. But at that moment, he flipped her upward and over so that she practically flew from his arms to bounce on the large bed. The only sound that left her mouth was a squeak of surprise and a gasp, because despite her movement, he still kept that one hand between her legs.

Indeed, as she flew through the air, her legs had separated enough for his hand to slide nearly all the way up. Then, while she still bounced on the mattress, he used his knees to separate her further. She felt the silk skirt strain, then rip, as he followed her down to settle heavily against her thighs. She felt his organ, thick and heavy inside his pants, as he settled between her legs.

Then he looked down at her, his eyes glittering in the darkness.

"Shut the door, please," he called to the woman behind them. He didn't move, clearly waiting to hear the door settle into its frame. Wife Number Three took a long time doing as she was told, and so Anna had a long moment to stare at Zhi-Gang, feeling her legs open wider until her sex was fully exposed to the hot press of his belly and the rough abrasion of the fabric between them.

Finally the door shut, and Zhi-Gang smiled at her. "You must remember to scream," he murmured to her. "They will be listening at the door for noises."

Anna blinked in confusion.

He shook his head. "Never mind. I will make sure all is done to their satisfaction."

It was happening too fast. Anna could not think, could not catch her breath. She couldn't even comprehend his words beyond the low tremble of sound that vibrated between his chest and her belly. But that was all to the good, she realized.

He shifted between her thighs, gliding his hot organ upward and across her sex in a way that made her squirm. Then she felt his hand against her thigh. Had it been there all the time? She didn't know. She didn't care. The truth was undeniable now. She wanted this. She wanted *him*.

He lifted slightly off her and she gasped at the sudden caress of cool air. But then his hand replaced his groin as his fingers pushed upward to touch her intimately. She felt her buttocks clench in withdrawal, but then her back arched, pushing herself more fully against him. Sensation shot through her spine all the way up through her brain.

It was fire, it was lightning, it was everything she wanted and more.

In the gloom, she saw him smile. "Excellent," he murmured.

She lifted her head to look him in the eyes. She took a deep breath, realizing in that instant that she wanted him as fiercely as she had once craved opium. She wanted him to touch her, to open her, to overwhelm her. She wanted everything he could give her and more, over and over and over until she dropped exhausted into sleep.

She lifted her chin in challenge. "You will have to work hard, Zhi-Gang Tau. I will not scream easily."

"Yes," he said, his expression smug. "You will."

April 19, 1882
To the Mother Superior of the Shanghai Mission on behalf of the Kent family, England
Dear Mother Francis:

It is with some consternation that I received your letter. It is my sad duty to tell you that Mr. and Mrs. Kent will not help in the matter of Anna Thompson. In truth, if it were not for another soul of my parish, I would not even know that the Kents had a daughter. They steadfastly refuse to speak of the child who ran away so precipitously. When I put your letter into their hands, it was immediately returned to me. They said, "We have no daughter or granddaughter in China."

Though I have tried often to change their minds, their hearts remain closed. Please understand that they were very hurt by their daughter's defection. Though all are precious in God's sight, the Kents have ample grandchil-

dren who visit them often. I fear they will never pay for their missing granddaughter's voyage home.

In short, Anna has no family here.

In sad regret,
Father Stanton

The shadow of the dome of pleasure
Floated midway on the waves;
Where was heard the mingled measure
From the fountain and the caves.
It was a miracle of rare device,
A sunny pleasure-dome with caves of ice!
                                —*Samuel Taylor Coleridge*
                    from "Kubla Khan: or A Vision in a Dream. A
                                                        Fragment"

CHAPTER TEN

Anna closed her eyes and gave herself up to the experience. She didn't want to think at all, so she sought that half-floating, half-mystical feeling of an opium dream. Let him do as he will, she thought. I know nothing. I feel nothing. I am nothing.

She couldn't find it. Without the smoke, she could not float. Without the floating sensation, she could not blunt the other things—the touch of his hands on her thighs as he slowly spread her open, the heat of his breath as it branded the skin just below his hands, or the caress of cool air across her most intimate place.

She shivered, her belly and shoulders shaking first, but then the wave expanded through her whole body. It felt so good and so . . . new. She could feel him smile against her thigh. She thought she remembered what came next. But he wasn't moving, wasn't doing anything, and she frowned in confusion.

"What are you thinking?" he asked, his voice a low murmur near her belly.

She opened her eyes. He had raised up on her body, though he kept her legs spread. "I—I am wondering." He arched an eyebrow in question, and she stammered out an explanation. "I don't . . . I mean, what do you . . . I mean, what happens next?"

He paused. "You have never done this before?"

She shook her head, her eyes blurring with tears of shame. "I have. I just . . . I mean . . ."

"You were smoking and you don't remember. Did you even agree?"

She closed her eyes, wetness slipping down her cheek. How to explain? "I don't remember," she finally confessed. She didn't know why she told him the truth. It was all part of the strange hold he had over her. She wanted to talk to him, to challenge him, to . . . do things with him. Why was he so different?

He twisted, shifting so that he sat beside her, and his gaze was infinitely gentle. Though one of his hands abandoned her, the other slid to the outside of her thigh to rest there, to warm her skin, to remind her of what was to come.

She should have hated his hand there. She was certainly very aware of it. It felt proprietary, as if he would brand her with his large palm high on the outside of her right thigh, fingers spread, gently wrapping around her leg toward her hip bone. She should have hated it, but she didn't. She liked the way he touched her: a simple presence, without pressure or demand. It linked the two of them, created a connection for whatever moments they had together. In truth, it felt . . . loving; and she found herself raising up to look at his hand and her thigh.

"Relax. Enjoy. I promise you will remember tonight."

"I . . ." How to tell him she didn't want to remember? Except, looking at his hand, large and strong on her thigh, perhaps she did. She lifted her gaze until she met his eyes. His expression was gentle. More important, it was steady. His eyes didn't flicker, his hand didn't tremble. He simply looked at her, waiting. For what, she wasn't sure. But within moments, she was smiling at him, anticipating what was to come, not dreading it.

"I do not think of opium when I am with you." She spoke the words with surprise.

He grinned. "That is most excellent." Then he leaned forward to place his mouth on hers.

She met his lips with her own, feeling a tingle of fire spread through her mouth. She inhaled on a gasp, but didn't pull away. He extended his tongue, stroking across her lips in a single long caress.

She remembered other kisses: fumbled, wet, of-center and of little interest. This was different. She felt a shiver of delight and the slow spread of desire. Her belly clenched, her toes curled, and she wanted to know more.

She pressed forward, opening her mouth to his invasion. She felt her lips thin against her teeth and she arched her neck to give him better access. But he did not deepen the kiss. Instead, he simply rubbed his lips across hers.

The tingling was fading, replaced by the heat of friction and her own confusion. Was she doing this wrong? He gave no clue until impatience made her bold. She extended her tongue to touch his lips, to push into his mouth, to . . . To be sucked and tugged on by him. Surprise had her pulling back, and he narrowed his teeth to slightly abrade her tongue as she withdrew.

They separated enough for her to stare at him, her thoughts spinning wildly. He merely grinned and waited, but words would not coalesce. In the end, she merely lifted back to his mouth, wrapping an arm around his shoulders to draw herself higher—closer—to him.

Their mouths met again, and this time she did not hesitate to push her tongue out, to stroke it against his teeth, to thrust and toy. Soon she was sitting upright in her pursuit of him, and found she liked meeting him on an equal plane. Or perhaps not so equal as she pressed even further forward, raising herself higher than him.

He allowed it for a time, playing at submission, teasing her with his tongue even as she plundered him. Then he began working on another front. She felt his free hand working the clasps at her shoulder and neck. He started at the top notch of her collar, slipping a finger beneath the tight silk. She hadn't been aware of the restriction of fabric too small for her white chest, but she was now. She wanted it off, she wanted to breathe fully, she wanted to know if he could set her whole torso to tingling.

With the thought came the result. Her nipples tightened, and the fire in her mouth spread—she was dimly aware—to her breasts. She broke from his mouth to undo the frogs that fastened her *chong san*. Her fingers moved quickly, her hands steady, and she stopped a moment to stare at them. Her hands were steady. She was in complete control of her body and her mind!

She looked up at him. He too had stopped, his gaze intent on her face. This was significant—this total control—but why? She didn't want to answer, but how to stop her thoughts?

He caught her right hand in his and slowly drew it to his mouth. While she watched, he curled his tongue around her finger, straightening it, then sucking it in. He still held her hand, his thumb slipping inside her curved fingers to rub circles across her palm. And all the while he sucked on her finger, pulling it deep into his mouth before using his hand to draw it out. Or nearly out. And then he would suck it back in again.

In and out, in and out.

She knew what he simulated; she understood that much of the sex act. And yet, she felt her whole body tighten with sensation. Her thoughts were gone, lost in the circle of his thumb and the wet slide of her finger.

His hand left her thigh to release the last clasps of her blouse, this one down by her waist. His hand stroked across her belly, opening the fabric to allow air to flow in a narrow channel from her navel up between her breasts all the way to her chin. At last she could breathe. She inhaled deeply, feeling the silk rub against her breasts. Simultaneously, she moved her finger across his tongue, brushing the texture there. He mimicked the action with his free hand as he brushed the blouse open. He widened the channel from her belly upward, fluttering strokes from the center outward as the fabric fell away.

Her belly quivered as she imagined his caress to be the gentle stroke of a Chinese brush. He was writing things on her skin; he was marking her as his, he was . . . Then he pulled his hand upward, between her breasts. His fingers widened as he painted fire across the top of her breast and upward over her shoulder.

The fabric of her clothes peeled away as he moved, but he could not draw it past her bent elbow. He returned to the beginning, at her belly, and touched her other side, pushing away the fabric there.

The tight silk pinned Anna's arms behind her, making her arch her back, lifting her breasts to him. She expected him to look down, but he did not. His gaze remained locked with hers as he sucked her finger deep inside his mouth one last time. Then he slowly pulled it out.

Cold hit her finger, and the wetness glistened in the candlelight. Then he drew her hand down. She broke away from his eyes to watch what he did with her finger. He drew it down to her own breast, pressing it to her taut nipple. He moved her finger to stroke and flick there.

Her breath caught as lightning streaked from her nipple to her womb, but he did not stop. He continued to move her finger across her own nipple, circling, flicking, even pressing the edge of her nail into the tight edge. She stared, mesmerized. He was making her hand a brush, just like his had been. He made her write characters into her skin, her own words, as if he helped her create herself.

"Do you remember when you touched yourself in your bath? I was watching," he said. "Never have I seen anything more—"

He said a word in Chinese that she did not know. She echoed it.

He shook his head. "I do not know the right word in English," he murmured. "Sensuous. Beautiful." Then his other hand lifted to cup her other breast. She felt his fingers extend, support, touch. His thumb drew a line from her breastbone up to her nipple. He rolled his thumb there, flicking, scraping, even pinching against his forefinger while she closed her eyes to better appreciate the sensations he created.

"Tell me what you feel."

"Everything," she answered, awe suffusing her soul. Everything was so . . . present and so different.

"Tell me," he pressed.

"T-the one side is cold," she stammered, struggling to

form words. "The other . . . so full. You make it feel light, and hot. And . . ."

"Good?"

"Great."

"Keep talking," he said. "I love the sound of your voice." Then he bent his head to her right breast to put his mouth on it.

She felt his hair first, the soft brush of black silk. It was tied back in a Manchu queue, but the thick braid fell forward to stroke her shoulder where his breath had not touched. Then that sensation was lost amid the wet of his mouth, the stroke of his tongue, and the gentle pulsing suction on her nipple.

Then he pulled back. "Tell me!"

She shook her head. "There's so much!" But she tried nevertheless. "My chest . . . my breath . . . it's so tight. My heart is beating and beating."

He lifted his lips off her breast to press a kiss against her throat. "Here?" he whispered, and she imagined her pulse trembling against his lips.

"Yes," she whispered. "But my nipple is cold again. My breast feels blank without you." The words made no sense, but he somehow understood. He returned his mouth to her breast and began sucking again.

She spoke without prompting, her thoughts rambling but exciting. They clarified what she felt, narrowed her thoughts to him and her. To what he did.

"The suction . . . it is like the beat of another heart. Your heart. Strong, it draws me in. It takes me to you. All of me. I feel each pull in my breast. In my belly. Even my toes curl with what you're doing."

He lifted up and she saw his grin flash above her.

"Touch yourself," he commanded, once again pressing her hand to her own breast. "Pinch. And pull."

She did as he instructed, seeing his eyes widen and his nostrils flare. His face hovered just above her hand.

"I love seeing you clearly," he murmured. Then he glanced back to her face. "I will reward you if you say something very inventive."

She stilled in surprise. "What?"

He didn't clarify, but she understood nevertheless. And as extra incentive, he flicked her nipple with his tongue—a quick nip to make her gasp and arch her back, begging for more. Then he dropped a kiss on her hand, the one that still cupped her left breast. "Don't stop that either," he said. "I want to see what you do to yourself."

She had no idea what to say, how to respond to him. So she did as he bade her, massaged her own breast, squeezing the nipple, even offering the tip to him. He watched with an avid expression, his breath whispering so lightly across her other breast, his lips barely touching her skin.

"Say something," he ordered.

She let her head drop back, her mind spinning. "I want to stay here," she whispered.

She felt his expression shift, felt the way his eyebrows lifted as he turned more fully to her breast. "Very good," he murmured. And as a reward, he flicked his tongue over her nipple again. She gasped and arched, stunned by how her entire body reacted to him.

"For years now, I have wanted to leave China," she said. "I think that is why I take opium. It is a way of leaving, you know."

He nodded, and she felt the coarse brush of his chin stubble on the edge of her breast. Then he curled his tongue around her nipple and pulled it into his mouth. She waited for him to begin sucking, but he did not.

"Right now, I don't want to leave. I want you to keep . . . to touch . . ." She swallowed. "Please suck on my breasts."

He did. It was a rhythmic pull that had her arching against him. And when her other hand stilled, he tapped it with his fingers, reminding her. Her stomach quivered in response, and her womb tightened. As she began to time her pinches with his pulls, she felt a wetness in her core. She wanted to spread her legs wide open, but her skirt pulled awkwardly at her hip.

"I want my skirt off. It is too tight."

He left her breast to lick tiny strokes down her belly. "Have you ever been fully naked before a man?"

She shook her head, then started to giggle. "I guess I'm a kind of virgin after all." He stopped kissing her then, his body frozen as he considered her words.

She felt her face heat, appalled by her brazen words. She lifted her hands, intending to push him away; she'd had no wish to expose her wretchedness. But he stopped her by pressing a long, almost clumsy kiss into her belly. And when he lifted up, he smiled at her. "That was the best thing you have said to me tonight. And for that, you will be richly rewarded."

So saying, he easily untied the twisted fabric of her skirt, lifting it up and away. He moved so quickly that before she could do more than take a breath, she was completely naked. Her belly quivered from the cool brush of air, which felt wonderful on her overheated skin.

"You are beautiful," he breathed. "Like ivory kissed by candlelight."

She heard the awe in his voice and could hardly believe he meant it. But, one look at his face and she knew it was true. Her vision was washed by tears and she blinked, confused by her reaction. Was this shame? Or gratitude?

"I don't know what I should feel," she whispered. "What *do* I feel?"

Panic echoed through her, building within her chest. And yet, she had no wish to be covered, no interest in ending what they did. She wanted to run, to hide from him, and yet she also wanted to remain right here, fully exposed.

"Do not analyze the animal inside you. We are all human, and as such have human needs. It is possible to satisfy both, you know, to be both human and . . ." He gestured to his head. "And of the mind."

She frowned. "I do not understand anything of what you just said."

His lips twisted into a wry smile. "I am a scholar. We are taught to think, think, think. Ignore the body, because the mind must be honed to perfection." He shrugged, pushing himself off the bed to stand beside her. "But many scholars in China destroy themselves. They take opium to stop thinking. Or they become greedy with drink or food or riches." He pulled off his undertunic with quick motions. "They are often bitter or angry."

The candlelight touched the golden muscles of his chest. How large he was. All Manchu clothing was designed to broaden the shoulders, to give the appearance of breadth in the chest, but now she saw that he needed no such padding. He had wide shoulders and a muscular torso. She stared, fascinated by the play of shadows across it.

"I believe that is because they ignore the body," he continued. "Purifying teas. Celibate life. Bah! Neglecting the body's needs—the animal needs—that is the path of a fool. We are human. Certain things must be attended."

He shucked off his pants with equally swift movements. She raised up on an elbow to watch closer. She was dimly aware of his narrow hips, flexing buttocks, and the corded power in his thighs and legs. But what she saw most was his thick, dark organ as it thrust upward toward her. The hair at its base appeared silky black, like the finest of brushes with his organ as the handle. It was a ridiculous thought, and she smiled at her silliness.

"Why do you smile?" he asked. He looked down at himself.

Her gaze jumped for a moment to his face before falling again to his sex. "I thought of a scholar's brush," she confessed.

"Ahhh," he responded. "You are not afraid anymore."

She blinked, and this time her gaze lingered on his face. "No, I'm not, but . . ." Shame was ever present. And yet, with him, she felt . . .

"Speak your thoughts aloud! I want to know!"

She bit her lip. "I am ashamed. And yet, I am not." She extended her hand toward him but stopped before she had even gone half the distance. "I want to touch you, and yet I should not." She looked down at the bed, unable to hold his gaze. "I want you to suck on my breasts again, and yet I should not." She looked to him. "Tell me what I should feel."

"No." He gently pushed her backward until she lay on her back. "*You* tell *me*."

He took her nipple into his mouth again. She arched upward, wanting it, wanting him. He began that steady suction, the pulse and pull of mouth and breast drawn together. The rhythm fogged her mind and lifted her body. Her legs spread of their own accord.

"Tell me more," he said as he switched to the other breast.

"I feel hot. Everything is hot."

His hand stroked over her belly and she shifted her hips, restless. Then he slipped his hand between her thighs. His finger was large, but she barely felt it, so slick were her folds. She tightened her buttocks, thrusting upward along with the pulse of his mouth. She arched.

"Tell me something more," he urged.

She cried out, wanting his mouth back on her breast.

"Tell me!"

"Touch me!" she gasped. This part, she knew. This part she had done to herself. She could feel the tightening in her belly. Soon. She was ready. If only he would press his finger into her. If only he would push against that place.

"No!" he snapped, then he lifted up and abruptly spread her thighs. She was wide open, with him standing between her legs. He wrapped his hands around her hips and abruptly dragged her down so that her knees were bent in the air, and her most intimate place perched at the edge of the bed.

"Watch and tell me what you see," he ordered.

Then he stepped forward. His organ was large, pushing toward her, its tip reflecting the tiniest bit of light where a drop of liquid trembled.

"It is darker than I remember," she said. "Redder, but still with a hint of gold."

"Do you like how it looks? Are you afraid of it?"

She shook her head. "I don't know. I . . . No." She knew what would happen next, or thought she did. And yet, this was all so new.

He put the tip of himself against her folds. She immediately arched, pushing against it, and was startled when he moaned. Her eyes leaped to his face. "Tell *me* what *you* feel," she demanded.

"My thighs are bunching, but I am holding back. My buttocks push me forward because you are wet and hot. You embrace me, and your acceptance makes me tremble with need." He shifted his hips and slid his organ across her folds from just above her opening to higher—higher! Her legs quivered with need.

"Again!" she cried. "Please. Again!"

He did, and her back arched with sensation, but it wasn't enough. She wrapped her legs around his back, trying to control his movements, but he grabbed hold of her hips and held her—and himself—completely still. She whimpered. His set rested at her opening, neither thrusting in or sliding up.

"Please, Zhi-Gang. Do something."

He did. He slowly slid through her folds again. He thrust once—twice—against her favorite spot. Then he stopped. She tightened her bottom, using the muscles to lift her higher against him, but his hands pushed her back down into the mattress.

"Do you feel how you surround me even here? I want more, too. But the heat, the friction, the exquisite slide—that is best felt at the tip."

So he guided himself down again, then thrust upward. Not inside her, but across, over in the most wondrous way. They moaned as one.

"Watch!" he ordered, and her eyes snapped open. She hadn't even realized she'd closed them. She looked down. She was trembling as she watched, her belly quivering while his sex slid back and lower. She felt him at her

opening and stared in wonder. To see such a thing made it
so . . . conscious. So deliberate. It made her decide here
and now that she wanted it. She wanted him to put himself inside her.

"Please do it," she said. "Go inside me."

He pushed a little way in. She almost didn't feel it, but
then she did: An expansion. A widening. He opened her
as never before.

"What do you see?" he demanded.

"Me," she answered. "My hair. My body. And you, connecting us together. Like a bridge, you link us."

He slid the tiniest bit deeper. "I feel you tight, gripping
me. I want to feel more."

She tightened her inner muscles, trying to draw him
deeper. It didn't work; he remained steadfast in his position, but his breath caught and she smiled.

"You are so large," she said. "I like seeing you there.
Come closer."

He pushed further inside. She felt herself stretch, her
most sensitive place tugging down, stretching open. She
didn't know what exactly he did, but she knew how she
felt: perfect. Everything felt perfect.

She tightened her thighs, drawing her lower on the
mattress, closer to him. He slid further in. Soon they
would meet groin to groin. "I want to see us without the
bridge. I want to see you completely inside me."

He pushed the last few inches in. They hit with the
tiniest of bumps, but the pulse of sensation burst through
her body and mind.

"Do you like this?" he asked. Their hair intermingled,
and she realized that, this close, she could not tell his
from hers. She could see his hips, just beneath her spread
thighs, and the darker skin that nearly touched hers.

She shifted slightly, bringing her hand forward to stroke there. It drifted over his belly, then down between his hips, down to where their hair began. She had no idea of her purpose, just the need to touch his heat, to feel the textures, to know in the most basic of ways that this was happening.

"Touch yourself," he said. "Like you did on the boat."

She looked up into his eyes and saw raw need and a rigid discipline. But it was the need—his hunger—that slipped into her mind and made her smile. He wanted her. And she liked that.

"Pull back halfway," she instructed.

He did, moving slowly enough that she arched in response, instinctively wanting him deep. But then he stopped, and she relaxed enough to ease her lower back down. To open up enough space between them for her to touch.

She stroked downward across his belly, through his hair, to the dark organ between them. It was slick and had thick veins that created an uneven texture. And when she touched him, he sucked in his breath.

"Touch yourself," he ordered again. "Let me see you do it."

She pressed her middle finger down, sliding it along his length until she met her own folds. The she slowly moved her finger upward, between her spread lips, to her own hard pearl. She pressed deep into herself, sensation roaring through her mind. He abruptly released her hips, leaning forward to touch her breasts. He lifted them as if in reverence, pulling them upward before pinching and rolling her nipples. She cried out as sensation leaped between her breasts and womb and pearl.

"What do you feel?" he demanded.

"Everything!" she gasped. Then she lifted her gaze to

him, feeling a boldness grow the more their eyes connected. "Everything," she repeated. "But I want more." And so saying, she tightened her legs. Her grip was fierce and she drove him deep into her. Her hand was compressed between them, pushing hard into her pearl. She cried out, the contractions beginning. Familiar contractions, a familiar response. And yet it was so much more than she'd ever experienced.

He was inside her. He was with her. He was part of her.

His hands abruptly dropped away from her breasts to grab her hips. In one swift motion, he lifted her up, dislodging her hand as she fell backward. Then he drew back and slammed in again. She felt him ram against her pearl, driving deep into her again and again.

Her contractions grew stronger, deeper. She knew without thought that his own climax matched hers, that he pumped with her. That they compressed and expanded as one.

She cried out in her fulfillment and heard him shout. Yet still it went on and on and on.

At last it stopped. Her mind returned to her body and her heart slowed enough that she could breathe. She opened her eyes to see him standing absolutely still between her legs. His eyes were closed in ecstasy, and his chest lifted in rapid breaths that perfectly matched her own.

In time, he also came back to himself. He looked down at her and smiled, and she found it easy to smile back. A thought hovered at the edge of her awareness. An emotion or an idea. She could not stop it. She could not—

He withdrew from her in a rush, and she gasped at the sudden loss. Then, before she could draw her legs together, he dropped to his knees. She looked down her body, seeing his face between her thighs.

He grinned at her, the intention both boyish and almost sweet. "Did you think it was over?" he asked. "No, sweet Anna, there is much, much more."

She had no understanding of his meaning until he did it. He put his mouth to her inner folds and began to kiss her. She felt his tongue stroke everything, everywhere. It even thrust deep inside her before moving upward to surround her pearl. He sucked there as he had sucked on her nipples, and the sensations lifted her off the bed to push her deeper—harder—more fully against his mouth.

He took every part of her. He pulled away all her restraints, all her thoughts, everything that kept her grounded in reality. And as he continued to stoke her contractions into full-body undulations, her mind soared, it flew . . . and then it came right back—to him. To now.

To them.

From Anna Marie Thompson's journal:
March 3, 1882

I'm twelve! I'm twelve! I'm twelve years old today! Father came and took me out to dinner just like a real woman. We ate in the best restaurant in Shanghai and I wore my new dress and my pearl on a string. He said I was the most beautiful girl in the place.

And afterwards, he took me to his home. I'd never been there before. It was HUGE! Plenty of room for me!! But it smelled like the prostitute women, so I know Mother Francis is right about that. He's not a church-going, God-fearing man. But you know what? I don't care! Hear me, God? I DON'T CARE!!! He is my father and I love him. He comes to visit me when no one else does. He gives gifts to me and to all the other chil-

dren. He brought food to the mission. I don't care that he doesn't go to church. He's my father and I love him!

And he gave me something else. Something that he said I shouldn't tell anyone about. He said since I was twelve, I was old enough. I told him I already knew all about opium. That I'd been taking it on and off since I was six.

I think he knew I was lying, but it didn't matter. He's like that. He just gives me this look to tell me that he knows I'm making up a story, but he lets me pretend anyway. Eventually I tell him the truth. I just have to work my way up to it.

So he let me have some. Boiled. It was WONDER-FUL!!!! I've been trying to think of a way to describe it. It's like all the angry frightened pieces fall away. Everything that makes you mean when you don't want to be or makes you stupid because you don't understand—all that goes away. And all that's left is so clear and so happy.

I understood everything and everything understood me. I started to talk to my new father, really talk. And he listened and he understood because everything makes sense on opium. Then a lady came in—as a present to me—and she sang. It was so beautiful I cried. That too is different. I didn't hear her breathing or any of the notes she probably missed or the noise out in the streets. I just heard music the way God intended it—filled with feeling and such perfectness.

I wish I could take some before mass. Imagine hearing a hymn the way it should be, as a celebration to God, not as Sister Christine trying for notes she can't make. But Father said I can only have opium on my birthday. It's not for other times. It's too dangerous.

But oooooohhhhh, I can't wait!!! I can't wait until my next birthday when I can have more.

A war more unjust in its origin, a war calculated in its progress to cover this country with a permanent disgrace, I do not know and I have not read of . . . [Our] flag is become a pirate flag, to protect an infamous traffic.

—*Opposition MP William Gladstone, 1840*

CHAPTER ELEVEN

The morning came with wailing, and Zhi-Gang tried to bury his head against the sound. He ended up burrowing into soft female flesh—a breast? He smelled the familiar musk of a night spent in what he and Jing-Li called physical study. He felt the lift and lowering of the woman's sweet chest, heard the steady beat of her heart, erratic now that she too was waking, and the ever-present wailing from the other room.

It was the widows, making their show as was wholly traditional, proper—and exceedingly tedious. He could not wait to escape this mud pit, and yet he had no wish to cease his current studies.

He rubbed his face against the woman, noting the size and texture of her breast. It was large and full and especially delightful. He smiled and opened his eyes. Morning light shone full on her white skin, the faint rosy tint the effect of his morning beard on her tender flesh.

Anna. Sweet Anna.

He blinked, memory coming back with a flood of mixed delight and horror. The delight was obvious. His body was relaxed with satisfaction, his muscles even sore from their exertions. In truth, they had done nothing he had not experienced before, and yet she had been wonderfully open to everything he did, everything they tried.

What was different was the way she had spoken to him. He grew hard remembering her words: awkward and stuttering, but in time flowing stronger, more articulate. She'd told him what she wanted and how she felt when he touched her.

He had not minded when her speech had splintered into disassociated thoughts, bizarre images, and unusual associations. That made it all the more amazing, all the more erotic, since he knew he was the one who'd sent her mind flying into unforeseen directions. And where she went, he went too. He'd shared every moment of her experience and that made his own all the more explosive.

She was different from any woman he had ever touched, and that made her exceedingly special to him. Especially since he had no expectation that last night's explorations would be any different from tonight or the next night or the night after that. Her mind was a strange and amazing place. He could spend many long nights in exploration of her thoughts and never grow tired, even as he pumped himself into her over and over again.

The thought was so compelling, he found himself catching her rosy nipple in his lips, teasing it into a tight point. She responded immediately, her breath catching on a gasp. His hand had been on her belly. He slid it between her legs where she was wet and slick and ready.

He forgot the horror of the morning's equation. All was lost in the scent of a willing woman. Then she started speaking again, and he could not pretend this was just any woman; she was herself, her words unlike anyone else's, and he wanted to be inside her more than he wanted his next breath.

"Tell me more," he gasped as he shifted his weight between her thighs. It was an awkward movement since he was still stroking her yin pearl, but he managed while she began to arch into his hand.

"Your fingers spread me open," she said. "I can see it in my mind, you opening me up."

"Like spreading apart flower petals; I hunger for the pollen inside."

He felt her chest ripple with humor. "I was thinking more like parting the curtain into Venus's immortal pool."

He plunged himself into her. He had no idea who this Venus was, but he liked the image. "And now?" he pressed. "What do you see now?"

She opened her eyes, looking directly into his. "You," she whispered. "I see you, and I feel you inside."

He began pumping his buttocks, though leisurely, without any great power. Not yet. He wanted to hear more, to know what she felt. "As I slide in and out, I think of you squeezing me, pumping the vital essence of my organ into my blood, my heart, my mind."

"I think of you taking me with you—drawing into you, then being pushed back. Me into you. Then—"

"Then myself into you," he said.

"Yes."

He smiled. "I like that."

"Every time you thrust, you pull more of me around you. And every time you withdraw, more of me follows."

He shook his head. "I am the man who pours into you.

My vital essence heats, it burns, it erupts . . ." *Not yet. Soon, but not yet.* "It will become part of you. I will become part—"

"You dive into Venus's pool." She arched, her inner muscles tightening in preparation. "I am the water that surrounds you."

"Take me." His rhythm was faster now, his body thrusting hard against her pelvis, grinding up and around when he could. "Squeeze me." She did, and his eyes nearly rolled back in his head from the exquisite sensation.

"Fill me," she gasped. Her quivering was beginning, starting at the base of his organ and flowing upward, over and over, each wave more intense, more demanding. "Take. Me."

"Where?" he gasped, trying to hold off. "Where will we go?"

"We'll. Fly!"

"Yes!" He erupted. His body, his mind, all his will poured into her. His vision went dark as it flew with her, and he felt completely weightless, completely empty. He knew nothing but the endless flow of power into her. It was as if she wiped him clean, and he gloried in his newness.

Until it was over. His mind slipped back inside his body, his vision returned, and he could hear his heartbeat as it pounded through his head. He returned to himself, and eventually, he forced himself to open his eyes.

His arms were straight, supporting his weight. She lay beneath him, her face flushed, her lips open, red, and wet. Below, he could still feel her contract weakly around him. Her eyelids fluttered and she looked up, a dazed expression complementing her soft smile. Her breasts shifted with her breath, and her belly still quivered. In his mind's eye, he saw her pulsing feminine flesh as it had been last night, smelled the womanly scent of her, and knew the absolute truth:

He had consorted with a white opium runner. She was a clear link in the chains of drugs and prostitution that bound his country. And rather than cut her out of his life and his homeland, he had taken his ease between her thighs. He was a vile hypocrite!

Anger began to well up inside him. As quickly as the rise of lust, this fury boiled, making his hands clench and his face twist.

He was familiar with this reaction. It often happened in the morning when he looked down at his women, whichever lay beneath him. But like everything else with Anna, his feelings were this time stronger, quicker, more raw. He could not stop them if his life depended on it. Nor how he would lash out at her, cutting her with words for no reason he understood.

"What are you thinking?" she asked, her words jarring the rhythm of his hatred. It threw him off his stride.

In anger—at himself, not at her—he began to roll off her, but she was faster. Her legs wrapped around his and she gripped him in place. He could not even pull out of her, she held him so tightly.

"Don't leave until you answer. What are you thinking?"

"That the widows' wailing is irritating." The sound had been a steady backdrop to last night's and this morning's exercise.

She shook her head. "Why are you lying?"

He had been looking at the sunlight on her white skin—so pale he could see the tracery of blue veins beneath. But now his vision snapped to her eyes, her round brown eyes.

"You are not who I thought you were." The words were confusing and not at all what he meant.

"I am not anyone to you. A white prisoner. A woman who wanted opium but got this instead." There was no anger in her voice, merely . . . confusion. "I have not thought about opium at all until this second." Her expression shifted into a stunned smile. "Not at all." Then she wrinkled her nose. "But I don't suppose Father Thomas would approve of the substitute."

She was a bizarre creature, her mind hopping from one thing to another without any evident logic or reason. A moment before, he had found it charming. Now he found it . . . He groaned and collapsed half on top of her, half to her left side. He still found it completely intriguing. He could not predict anything about her, and that kept him interested.

She shifted with him, keeping him trapped. Except, he did not feel trapped. Even his hatred was distracted. "Will those wailing women ever stop?" he grumbled with a curse.

She did not answer. "You are angry. I am not who you wanted. I was acceptable for a night and a morning, but you are angry because—"

"Do not lecture me, woman!" he bellowed into the mattress.

She fell silent, obviously startled by his anger. He felt her take a breath, shifting her shoulders even more. "You spoke into the sheets. I couldn't understand you."

He lifted his face off the mattress. "Do not lecture me, woman," he said slowly and clearly. But it did not have the same effect. And it was a stupid comment anyway. She hadn't been lecturing him. Only Jing-Li still tried to do that, and his friend took great care in his timing.

"Is this part of your habit, then?" she mused aloud. Her eyes were dark as they flowed over his face and body. "Do you always wake angry?"

"Yes," he snapped. Then he frowned, hearing the truth in his words. "Yes, I always do."

She nodded, as if she had expected such a thing. "I myself wake every morning thinking of opium. And that makes me angry." She frowned. "What woman do you want?"

A tiny face flashed through his mind: sweet and young, it contorted with fury while tears streaked the dirt on her cheeks. He closed his mind to the image, but apparently he forgot to mind his tongue. Words flowed too easily with this woman, and he was speaking before he even realized.

"A girl. My sister."

She pulled back, horror on her face. "You want to do this with your sister?"

"No!" Then he pressed down on her knees, shoving backward and out of her. She was not strong enough to stop him, and he was too unsettled to be delicate. "No!" he repeated firmly. "You . . . this . . ." He rubbed a hand over his morning beard, using the motion to settle his thoughts. "You distract me from my plans. I am trying to find my sister, and this . . . this distracts me from her."

"And here I thought you meant to distract *me* last night." Her voice was dry.

Her accusation was also true. Last night he had thought with his organ. Today brought a new direction. He was headed for Shanghai.

He stepped away from the bed, the morning air chill on his naked body, and he pushed away his thoughts, performing his morning exercises with quick, fluid motions. He followed his daily regime, which was necessary to keep capable with his knives. The patterns were exact, the motions ingrained after years of practice.

Yet, this too felt new. She was watching him. And that

added extra potency to his movements—to the swipe of an arm, the stretch of a leg, even the sudden slash of a pretend blade.

"Where did you learn that?" she asked as he began his second pattern.

"Peking. It is where I learned everything."

"But you were born at that village, weren't you? You stayed there how long?"

He answered easily. Between her questions and his morning exercises, the anger was fading, the moodiness that came after bed games quickly eased. "Until my father could teach me nothing else. I was ten when we left."

"And now you go to Shanghai to find your sister."

"Yes."

"How did you lose her?"

He was spinning on his heel, ducking a shoulder before a complicated twist that he had perfected by the age of fifteen. At her words, his belly tightened, his rhythm shifted, and he lost his footing. It was not a large stumble, and yet it infuriated him. The peace he had gained flew from him, and he found his hands clenching as if he had real blades in his hands.

He rounded on her, raising his hands to slice with his pretend blades. All she saw were fists coming up toward her face. She should have flinched. She should have cried out and run away. She did none of those things. She remained on the bed, calmly watching him. Her eyes barely even blinked as his fists made it to her throat and held a blade's length away.

Her lips quirked in a wry smile. "Last night you saw my darkness," she said. "I told you what I have done, why I want to fly away." She swallowed, her skin impossibly white in the morning sunlight. "Why I eat opium to forget." She reached up and surrounded his fists with her tiny hands. "You have a darkness too, an anger that boils through your moods, staining everything you do. Sometimes you can hide it. When you are thinking, perhaps, or, pursuing a criminal. But mostly, I think, you are as addicted as I—and for the same reason."

"I have no taste for your opium!" he snapped, his fists quivering near her throat. But he did not move, and neither did she.

"Not opium. But you distracted me from it with sex. I believe you distract yourself in the same manner." She sighed and rolled away from him, easily pushing his fists out of the way. He watched her breasts bob as she reached for her skirt. He stood fascinated by the fullness of her bottom as she tried to shake the creases from the silk.

"I do not eat opium!" he repeated, knowing she accused him of something else entirely. Then he stepped forward, rubbing his hand down her behind, feeling the smooth warmth of her skin. Already his organ stretched for her, and without prelude, he slipped himself close to press into her. He was not hard enough to penetrate, but soon he would be.

She did not flee from him, and yet she did not press backward either. "I am not thinking about opium right now," she said softly. "I do not need such distraction." She twisted to look at him over her shoulder. Her dark curls tugged backward with her movement, lifting up over her near breast. He watched the dark strands slide upward, slowly revealing the white globes of her breasts. Unable to stop himself, he reached forward and cupped one, squeezing the nipple with just enough pressure to make her gasp.

"Where is your sister, Zhi-Gang? Why does talking about her make you want to run to the nearest woman?"

He would have discarded her then, perhaps pushed her away with an angry curse, maybe even hurt the breast that he cupped so gently. But again, she covered his hand with her own, holding him still. And below, she arched her pelvis backward, stroking his organ enough that it thickened most delightfully.

"Answer my questions and get a reward," she said lightly, an echo of what he had said to her last night. "What happened to your sister?"

He closed his eyes and leaned into her. He smelled their musky scent, well mixed now, and still heady. He was fully hard, and he wanted to be inside her. To reach for the forgetfulness of release. To be wiped clean once again.

But she pressed him to speak, and he could not refuse her. He had no understanding of why. Perhaps she was the first woman to ask in such a way as to tempt him to answer. It did not matter. He pressed her forward so that she bent over the bed. She did not resist, but she did not help either. And so he began to speak.

"My sister was sold into prostitution when I was ten." He thrust himself fully inside her. She was wet from before, so he went in easily. But she was also tight enough to grip him wonderfully, and excited enough to gasp at his motion.

"There is more," she prompted.

"Oh yes," he agreed, and reached around to cup both her breasts.

She stilled. He felt her inner muscles relax completely. "You are tracking a child sold . . . how long ago?"

"Nearly two decades."

She arched the tiniest bit more, and he was able to move again: sliding out, pressing in.

"So, let me get this straight. You are on a dual

mission—the first, as the Emperor's Enforcer, to destroy the opium routes into China. But the second, you also track your lost sister to Shanghai."

"Yes." He continued to slide back and forth into her. In and out, in a steady tempo that held the anger at bay, that erased the guilt and would soon wipe his mind clean.

"But the Emperor has been imprisoned. His mother rules in his name, and she has begun killing all who were in his inner circle."

He was so close. His release was at the very edge, but he froze at her statement. "How would you know about these things?"

Her laughter rippled through her body into his. "I live in this country. Why wouldn't I know about these things?"

Because she was a woman. Because she was white. Because a thousand different things filtered through the sensations that distracted his mind. He stilled his body to think more clearly. "You should not know these things."

"You should not use women to distract yourself."

"You should not eat opium or sell it to my countrymen."

She fell silent, and he knew she was as unsettled as he. So he reached for the one thing that would calm them both. He slipped a hand down off her breast, across her belly, and into the junction between her thighs. She welcomed this change. Her responses were no longer words but soft gasps that fired his blood.

He began to time his movements, rubbing her yin pearl with his fingers as he pushed his sex deep inside her. His tempo increased, their breaths shortened. And soon she cried out in joy, her body convulsing around him.

He thrust one last time, deep inside, and poured himself into her. Again, he felt his mind wiped clean, his body trembling with release and relief.

They trembled there at the end of the bed, holding themselves in their ecstasy. And then as one they toppled forward. He slipped away as she dropped boneless onto the mattress. He fell beside her, finding barely enough energy to wrap his arm around her and tug her backward against him.

He spooned her and buried his face in her hair. He held her tight, wondering if she would pull away, but she did not. In time, she exhaled a shuddering breath and relaxed completely back against him.

They would have slept them. He felt her breath steady into a slower and deeper rhythm. His own eyes drifted shut, his breath synched to hers. Sweet oblivion awaited, and he rushed headlong toward it.

But then the wailing stopped.

The widows' sobs had been a constant noise, heard, felt, and mostly ignored. Until silence thundered into the room. Anna heard it too, for she stiffened and lifted her head. Zhi-Gang frowned. Something important had happened. Something had stopped the women's wailing.

Then he heard it; distant pounding of feet as someone ran down the hallway. Zhi-Gang raised his head to hear better. Was that Jing-Li? Bellowing something? Finally, the word filtered through the walls enough to be clear.

". . . guns!"

From Anna Marie Thompson's journal:
February 19, 1886

I'm almost sixteen now, and it is time I looked to my future. Most of the orphan girls become nuns, remaining here or in other missions for the rest of their lives. They think it the most holy of vocations and embrace it completely. This, of course, means that they are too ugly or too mean to embrace any man.

Thankfully, I have another choice. Father has shown me another world, another possibility. He says that I have to choose between living for God or living for myself. Living for God is glorious and honorable, but it's not a very fun life. Living for myself doesn't mean I'm bad. It just means that I'm not holy. Most people chose to live in the world and not bank on Heaven later.

It wasn't a hard decision. Some of the nuns are nice, but they're also the meanest people in the world. Just because I don't want to live for God, they say it makes me ungrateful or bad. But that's not true. Samuel isn't bad, and neither are his friends. They're just people who don't always believe in what the nuns do. That's not wrong. It's just not living for God.

So . . . I choose the world. I want to live in the world. And that means I need money. Most women get that through their husbands, but I don't want to marry anyone. Father says I don't have to. That many women live without a man. They just need money. And he has a way for me to earn lots. He said he'd show me on my sixteenth birthday, and then I can decide.

I've already decided. I don't want to be a nun. I'm going to be with Father. And even better, I'll get to smoke five grains of opium this time because I'm a year older!

This is going to be the best birthday ever.

A damsel with a dulcimer
In a vision once I saw:
It was an Abyssinian maid,
And on her dulcimer she played,
Singing of Mount Abora.

> —*Samuel Taylor Coleridge*
> *from "Kubla Khan: Or, a Vision in a Dream. A*
> *Fragment"*

CHAPTER TWELVE

At first Anna could not make out Jing-Li's bellowed words. His accent was too different from what she was used to. Zhi-Gang abruptly leapt from the bed and began dressing with rushed motions.

"Guns?" he said in a low hiss, more to himself than to her. "Whose guns?" He flashed her a frown. "Get dressed." She had already left the bed and was grabbing her silk skirt. "Not in that! Something servantlike."

She looked at that the fabric in her hand, then around the room. She had no other clothing.

He must have understood her confusion because he cursed under his breath. "Whatever you can find." He was nearly dressed. With his undertunic unbuttoned, he strode to the door and hauled it open.

"Who has guns?" he snapped, presumably at Jing-Li, who finally clattered to a stop outside the door.

Anna made quick work of her skirt and shoes, all the while straining to hear.

"White men," gasped Jing-Li. "Speaking Shanghai dialect. They killed the guards at the gate."

A shiver of fear skittered down Anna's back, and her fingers fumbled on the fastenings at her throat. Men from Shanghai? Her father's men? There were many opium dealers in Shanghai, but few penetrated this deep into China. Just Samuel and one or two others.

"How many?" Zhi-Gang demanded.

"Only five at the front gate, but more surround the house. I have seen four at least."

No, Anna thought. *You have seen boys or clothing around straw. Not real men.*

"They have white men guns," Jing-Li continued. "The First Wife speaks to them now, but they don't believe the governor is dead."

"She should show them the body."

Jing-Li growled something under his breath. "She fears—all the wives fear—they will be raped. They demand that we protect them."

"Their fool husband brought this on them. This is his Shanghai supplier. Bai probably stole money from them. They all steal eventually."

True enough, thought Anna. Samuel had once said that was his biggest problem: theft. She shuddered at the memory of exactly what he did to thieves. If Bai had been stealing, then this was a show of strength and retribution. Depending on the extent of the theft, the entire household could be raped, tortured, then burned alive.

"How many?" Zhi-Gang muttered. He abruptly turned so he could face her. "Anna! Find the wives. Tell them to hide the children and to dress as servants . . ." His voice trailed away as he stared at her.

She would have looked directly at him instead of at

the door frame, but she could not seem to move. She was sitting on the bed, her top frog-clasp still unbuttoned. Her body seemed made of stone; she could not move or run or fly. She could not do any of the things that her mind screamed for her to do.

"Anna? What is it?" When she did not answer, he strode forward, grasping her shoulders and shaking her enough that she could look at him. "What do you know?"

She shook her head, her eyes filling with tears. "Nothing. I do not know anything. Not for sure."

His eyes narrowed, and she struggled for words. She struggled to think. "Did you see them move? The men in the trees around the house. Did you see them move?"

She was still looking at Zhi-Gang, so she saw clearly when his expression tightened with suspicion. "We did not say that they were in trees."

She nodded, though the motion was jerky. "Did the bodies move? A hand, an arm, anything?"

Jing-Li stepped around the door to glare at her. "That means nothing. If they seek stealth . . . Warriors are trained to keep still."

"So are straw dummies pretending to be an army when they are not." She looked at her hands. "It is a favorite trick of drug-runners. They . . . we cannot travel through China in large numbers, so when we need a show of strength . . ." She shrugged. "There is enough fear of whites that a straw dummy can be just as effective as a real fighter. Or sometimes we hire local boys for a penny or two. Give them a change of clothes and have them sit in the trees."

Jing-Li frowned and glanced back toward the main house. "I will check." Then he started to leave, but hesitated long enough to touch Zhi-Gang on the arm. "The

First Wife will not be able to hold them off for long." He glanced back at Anna. "Do you think they will kill her?"

Anna shrugged. Some of her father's men would; some would not. Opium runners were an unpredictable lot.

"Go," Zhi-Gang snapped at Jing-Li. "Find out if we are threatened by straw men or children."

"Look for a cart," Anna called abruptly. "Real warriors do not need a farmer's cart to hide their tricks. Find the sharpest eye here and look for grass in the cart."

"A child," Zhi-Gang said, as he reached into his pocket. "They spy the best. Find one who can run fast."

Jing-Li was gone before the last order could fade. Anna had been watching Zhi-Gang the entire time, seeing him shift from tender lover to the Emperor's Enforcer. She wondered what he planned, though already guessing the answer. She steeled her spine for the sight of his deer-horn knives, for blood and gore and the stone-cold killer that he could become. But what he pulled out of his pocket completely reversed everything she expected.

Glasses. He pulled western glasses out of his tunic pocket and set them on his nose. She blinked, startled. She had seen them before, of course, back on the boat. But she had forgotten he used them.

"You are a scholar," she said, more to herself than to him. She thought of him first as the Enforcer—a warrior and a killer. It was startling to see him without his weapons, his spine somewhat stooped, and with wire spectacles perched near the end of his nose.

He grimaced. "This is what I wanted to be." His tone was grim as he carefully slipped his knives inside his jacket. "But I am something else."

The longer he spoke, the more she was able to breathe, to move. To think. "What?" she asked.

He practically growled. He narrowed his eyes at her. "Can you fight?"

"Not like you need," she replied, feelings of worthlessness building inside her.

"At least you are strong. And smart." He glanced at her feet. "And whole."

"You want me to protect the children," she said. It was more a statement than a question.

He shook his head. "The wives. Children in a household like this know how to hide. They will disappear and stay silent, protecting one another. It is the wives who are in the most danger. These are beaten women accustomed to abuse. I want you to keep them from being stupid."

He grabbed hold of her arm and drew her from the room. His grip was not brutal, but it was strong and she had no choice but to follow. She did not mind. Truthfully, she felt safest beside him.

"You will hide behind the women's screen with . . ." He stopped. "Who is the brightest of the wives?"

"First Wife is the strongest, but Two is the canniest. You'll want Two beside you."

He shook his head. "I want you, but you are white and hard to explain."

She didn't respond, but a lightness filled her body and she quickened her step to stay close to him.

"Watch from the women's screen with Two," he continued. Then he frowned at her. "Do you think she will betray us?"

"Not if you bribe her."

He grimaced. "I will say nothing. You must keep her aligned with us."

She nodded, considering how. "And the others?"

"Jing-Li will tell them to stay in the women's room. I

will spare one man to defend them. They will have to keep themselves from panicking."

Anna swallowed, then slowed down. "I will talk to them. They will do better after I can explain what is happening."

He froze, his eyes hard as he looked down on her. Though his grip did not tighten on her arm, she knew that could change in an instant. "What *is* happening, Anna?" He spoke with a deceptive calm. She could see that his anger was very close to the surface.

"I don't know," she answered truthfully. "I don't! It could be bad luck. If the governor was stealing from his supplier, then this is a show of strength to discipline him." She took a deep breath. "Or it is about me."

"You?"

She nodded. "Samuel's men are looking for me. If they tracked me here . . ." She shuddered at the thought of what would be in store for her.

He looked at her, his eyes impossibly dark behind his wire glasses. Then he pulled her to him, slowly, inevitably drawing her fully against his body. "I will not give you to them," he said. "No matter who these people are or what happens. I am not done with you yet."

She should have been afraid of the darkness in his words, the blackness that stained his soul. But she was not. She wasn't even dreaming of a way to escape or her next taste of opium. She was thinking of him and his surprise when her lips curved into a smile. "I will stand by you, too," she vowed. "Just do not let me be taken."

Color leeched from his face, and his gaze grew distant. She knew for a moment that he thought of someone else. His sister perhaps? She didn't have time to wonder as he pressed a swift, abrupt kiss to her mouth. "No one shall have you."

"A fine sentiment," drawled Jing-Li as he rounded a corner. "But we are four against an army."

Zhi-Gang spun around to his friend. "The soldiers are real?"

His friend nodded darkly. "And badly hidden. I think we are meant to see them."

"Then they could be locals—farm boys with no fighting skills." Zhi-Gang released Anna's arm. "See to the women, and bring Wife Two to the screen. First Wife—"

"Has already let them in," interrupted Jing-Li.

Anna did not wait to hear the rest. She ran as fast as she could to the women's room. She winced as she crossed the threshold, mentally counting the number of people. Wives Two through Five were present, huddled together with their children clutched between their knees. Unlike last night, their tears were real.

"Where are your male servants?" Anna asked, turning to Wife Two. She was the only one not dealing with a sobbing child or fighting tears herself. She seemed grimly resigned, with an anger that was part bitterness, part annoyance.

"Gone," Second Wife answered with a sneer. "When your husband killed our husband, they ran, fearing for their lives."

"Cowards," Anna spat. "You are better off without them. They would not help in a fight anyway."

Second Wife blinked in surprise. "That is what I have been saying. But what can we do with no protection?"

"You are not unprotected!" Anna snapped, startled by her anger. "My husband and his men will save us." She had their attention now. Wives and children alike quieted enough to hear her. She lifted her chin and tried to exude a confidence she didn't feel. "But we must also rely on ourselves."

Second Wife cursed and spat. "What can we do?" She gestured to her leg and then the room at large. "Lame, pregnant, with babes in our arms—we are doomed."

Anna took a deep breath, praying that Zhi-Gang would be correct about the children. She turned to them, catching their eyes as best she could. "Can you hide? And be very quiet?"

The eldest boy—a child of about nine—stepped forward. "I am the head of the family. I will not let my mother—"

"You will not endanger your mother or your sisters and brothers," Anna said with a stern tone. But then she allowed her voice to lower with respect. "Will they listen to you?"

He puffed up with pride. "Of course! I am the oldest."

"Do not lie, child. All our lives depend on you answering correctly. Do not die from stupidity like your father."

It was a harsh thing to say to a child, especially one who had just lost his parent. But apparently the child was also smart, and had a realistic view of his parent.

"My father was—"

She didn't understand the words, but his attitude was clear. Especially as he straightened and gestured to Wife Two. "Mother and First Auntie have taught me better." He looked at his siblings. "They will listen to what I say."

Anna glanced at Second Wife. "He can be counted on to protect them?"

Second Wife nodded. "He knows his responsibilities. As does *she*." A second child stepped up. A girl, obviously Second Wife's daughter. She appeared to be the oldest girl child, graceful on her bound feet, and with a spark of honest bravery in her eyes. Better yet, she knew to keep just behind her older brother, where she could be seen as a leader without upsetting his masculine pride.

"Very well," Anna said. "All our lives depend on the next few hours." She turned to the boy, but her gaze encompassed all the children. She was excruciatingly aware of the time she was taking with this. Who knew what was going on in the reception room? But the more she gave the wives the impression that someone was in charge—herself and the two oldest children—the more manageable they would be.

She straightened and put as much force as possible into her voice. "The children must hide and stay silent." She looked at the oldest daughter. Girls tended to be much better than boys at that last part. "You take them and keep them quiet."

The boy spun on his heel and ordered his sister in a sharp voice, "Pretend father has the ugly ghost on him. Go!"

The girl didn't respond. She was already herding the younger ones out, whispering instructions in their ears before they dashed away. She paused to glance back at Anna. "They will stay out of sight," she said.

"And quiet!" the boy added.

The girl ignored her brother, slipping away with two of the youngest. Anna breathed a sigh of relief. The children were in good hands. Now for the harder part. She turned back to the boy. "You must keep your aunties safe. They are frightened and must rely on your strength. Can you do it?"

"Of course!" he said with haughty pride.

Anna dipped her head in respect for his status: head male of the household. "My husband will send a man to guard the door, but he may be called away. If that happens, you must keep all your aunties very, very quiet. Maybe even help them hide if need be."

He opened his mouth to give her what would probably be a very masculine response, but she did not let him speak. Instead, she turned abruptly to Second Wife and held out her hand. "You must come with me. My husband needs your help."

Second Wife's eyes widened in surprise, but she struggled to her feet. And as they hobbled together to the door, she managed to start interrogating Anna with short insightful questions. "Your husband knows everything now?"

"Yes. Everything," Anna said with absolute truth.

"Hmph." Second Wife clearly doubted.

"He will protect us," Anna pressed, startled to realize she believed. Zhi-Gang—the Emperor's Enforcer—would keep them all safe.

"Is it your father who attacks?"

Anna didn't falter. "Yes, I think so." Actually, she had no idea who it was, but people tended to follow direction better if they believed you understood the situation. And who better understood a man than his own daughter?

Second wife paused at a crossway in the hall, and looked hard at Anna. "Do you trust your husband?" She glanced to the left, in the opposite direction. "There is a good place to hide. Back there. We could say we got lost."

Anna hesitated for a moment. She did not pause because she doubted, but out of habit. Running and hiding was what she'd always done.

She shook her head. "I trust my husband."

Second Wife stared at her a long moment, then sighed in envy. "You are a fortunate woman."

Anna nodded, but the movement was uncertain. She had never thought of herself as fortunate—still didn't—and yet, for one moment it was a delight to feel that what she pretended was true: Zhi-Gang loved her and would risk all to protect her.

Still lost in uncertainty, she didn't notice when Second Wife turned down the wrong hallway. The woman was halfway to the door before Anna caught up.

"Where are you going?" she gasped. "My husband needs you in the receiving room."

Second Wife nodded, but her eyes focused on the gaps in the window lattice work. Anna was about to reprimand her again, but something in the woman's narrowed gaze made her stare out the window instead. "What do you see?"

"A boy. In the tree."

Anna nodded. "One of the soldiers. I thought he might be clothes stuffed in straw, but . . ." Even she could see that the soldier swung his leg back and forth in boredom.

Second Wife snorted. "Might as well be straw. That's Tseng's first son, and a more useless boy never lived."

Anna took a step closer to the window, still keeping out of view. She inspected the man. Second Wife was right. He was very young, barely out of his teens, and—more important—without the hardened air of her father's career mercenaries.

An idea began to form. She pushed away the silly romantic feelings of a moment before and began to think for real. "This boy," she pressed. "Will he talk to you? Will he listen to you?"

Second Wife straightened her spine, her face splitting into a grin. "I could get that boy to sell his ancestral shrine."

Anna returned the smile. "Then by all means, let us go this way."

From Anna Marie Thompson's journal:
March 3, 1886

    I saw. I'm sixteen today and I saw what Father had to show me. Another boy went with me. He was a little older—a half white, half Chinese boy they call Halfy. He's the son of a prostitute, and he had large hands and big eyes. He didn't talk much. I think he's shy, but we went together to celebrate my birthday with Father.

    We went to an opium den. Father owns it. He showed us how to measure it, how to boil it— everything. He told us the amount of money that he gets every day, and we watched while a customer lit his pipe. I couldn't wait to taste it. I know how it feels! I knew and I thought we were there to smoke.

    But we watched this man smoke. He was tall and lanky for a Chinese, and his smile lit his entire body. One puff and his eyes began to sparkle, his hands lost their tremble, and all the bad things fell away from him. I could see the smoke work in him, and I remembered.

    Then Father—Samuel—asked him if it was good. "Very good," the man answered. Even his voice had changed. Instead of being high and nasal like before, it had dropped to a lower, sweeter tone. People are so much nicer when they're smoking. I even sat down next to him on the bench because I thought I would get my turn.

    All the while, Samuel kept talking to the man, asking him about his last run. That's what the man did for Samuel. He ran opium into the interior of China, to a governor in a province where white people weren't allowed.

    He answered easily enough. He talked about how

happy the governor was, how much money he paid, and all the details. Father had told me and Halfy to listen carefully, so I was very attentive. He said he'd test us on it afterwards. I listened and I remembered, and then, just when the man was about to talk about the governor's wives, Samuel killed him. Stabbed him. Right through the heart. There wasn't even really a rattle. More of a gasp, and the man was dead.

Samuel pulled out the knife, wiped it on the man's pants, and then ordered me and Halfy to carry the body out to the back. Halfy didn't want to do it. He just stared at the body, his eyes huge and kinda watery. But I've worked in the mission hospital since I was seven. Dead bodies are nothing to me. Still, it was hard. Hear the body was still warm and we had just been talking to him.

He was really heavy. Halfy went to get the wheelbarrow, but he wanted me to lift the body into it. At least I didn't have to strip the body. Halfy did that. And he did it so fast, I'm pretty sure he'd done it before. Not strip a dead body. But a drunk? Probably. It doesn't matter. Halfy did that, and then together we got the body into the wheelbarrow. Samuel walked with us to the river where we dumped it in.

"Just another dead Chinese," *Samuel said.* "There are lots of dead people who float down this river. Women, men, white or yellow or something in between."

I swallowed. I think I would have thrown up if I didn't have a question just bursting to get out. Samuel waited. He knew what I wanted to ask, what both me and Halfy wanted to know. Finally, I just said it.

"Why? Why would you kill your own runner?"

"Because he smoked it," *Samuel said.* "He was late

delivering because he was smoking. He came back with too little money because he'd been smoking."

"But you want us to taste it," I said. I don't know when I got so bold. The runner had seemed like such a nice man and . . . and I don't know. It didn't seem fair. "You want us to celebrate with the customers! You've said so!"

Samuel looked at me hard, and there was no trace of the man I call Father. When he spoke, his voice was cold enough to make me shiver. Even now, remembering it, I am still afraid.

"A good runner can make a fortune," he said. "A bad runner dies."

I understood then what he wanted us to know. Life outside the mission has its own set of rules. Break them and die.

I understood. And more than that, I had already made my decision. "I will take his route," I said.

I know I surprised him. He raised his eyebrows and smiled—slow and sweet, like a man who suddenly sees his child for the first time. I have seen that at the mission, so I know what it looks like. Samuel looked at me just like that, and it was better than opium.

"I will run for you, Father," I said. "And I will be the best runner you've ever had."

But as they have no mode of raising money for the expenses of war unless from the drug sales in China, we think [the British government] cannot avoid giving it some toleration.

—*Memo to associate by opium trader*
James Matheson, 1840

CHAPTER THIRTEEN

Zhi-Gang listened closely for a noise—a shuffle, a whisper, something—coming from behind the women's screen. Nothing. Anna was not there yet. And his belly clenched in fear that she would take this opportunity to escape. She would slip out behind the compound—and be caught by these men.

He swallowed, forcing his thoughts to the present. He could not stop her from choosing a wrong path, a deadly path. And anyway, he would be much better off without a white "wife." Or so he told himself as he slumped his shoulders and tried to look benign. If these bastards recognized him as the Emperor's Enforcer, there would be no hesitation. They would kill him on sight.

First Wife was wailing loud enough to make his eyeballs hurt. Fortunately, that only helped Zhi-Gang appear more sickly. The invading men had bullied themselves inside to look at the governor's body: five thick-armed brutes with short earlobes and scrunched faces. To counteract the evil fortune in their faces, they had obviously become killers for someone even uglier and more brutal than they.

Zhi-Gang shifted his attention to the leader of the little band. The largest of them all, a half-white, half-Chinese bastard, he had stooped shoulders and a dark intelligence in the small eyes below his thick forehead. He carried a sword at his side, but his meaty fists were all that were needed to intimidate Madame Bai. Zhi-Gang cursed himself again for not arriving earlier to the First Wife's side. By the time he'd made it to the front hall, she had opened their only defense against these brutes and led them inside. They claimed, of course, that they merely wished to see the body, then would leave. Only Madame Bai believed the lies.

Now Zhi-Gang waited for the best time to appear, all the while listening for Anna. She still wasn't here. In truth, there was no reason for her to witness these brutes intimidating Madame Bai while they inspected the governor's body; he merely wanted Anna nearby so he could protect her. So he knew she was safe. But she was not here, and he could not delay much longer.

The half-white leader had already taken out a dagger to poke and cut at the body. Abused wife or not, Madame Bai could not allow such desecration.

"Stop it! Stop it!" she screeched. "Curses on you for doing such a thing to my husband! May his ghost—"

Her words were cut off by an abrupt slap across the face that sent her reeling into an incense brazier. Zhi-Gang was through the divider in time to catch her and stomp out the ashes before the entire building burned down around their ears.

"How dare you do such a thing!" he wheezed. "Where is your respect for the dead? Your fear of his ghost?"

First Wife was sniffling, cowering behind him in the most irritating manner. Though she helped present the right image, she was at too great a risk here. One of the brutes would likely kill her just to shut her up, so Zhi-Gang turned to her with a gentle smile. "This is too much for you, Madame Bai. Go rest in the women's rooms. I will dispose of this matter."

First Wife had no need to be told twice. She scurried away before he could think of a way to have her find Anna, too. He grimaced, then turned back to where the half-white thug poked idly at the Governor's body.

"Why do you desecrate him?" Zhi-Gang asked in all honesty. There had been no time last night to do more than get a quick, poorly made casket. Silk cushioned the body and draped to the floor, simultaneously appearing regal and hiding the bloodstains.

Meanwhile, the half-white man lifted the covering off the governor's face and grunted. "Who are *you*?" he asked over his shoulder.

"The new governor here," Zhi-Gang snapped. An easy lie. With the Empress Dowager's corp détat, governors would be changing all over China as she appointed her own people. Meanwhile, he kept his posture weak. With mostly women and children in the compound, he couldn't risk a show of force. It would be too dangerous for the others—and too likely to fail. His plan now was to not challenge the man's authority, but to barter.

The man wrinkled his large nose in disgust. "Then you are responsible for the old governor's debts."

Zhi-Gang laughed. "Do you think to get blood out of a

stone? Why do you think he was killed?" He gestured disdainfully at the dead body. "Debts! All that could be stolen was already taken by his killer."

The half-white straightened. "We will search for more."

"You will make a deal with me," Zhi-Gang countered. "Opium. Girl prostitutes. Even oxen, if you want. These things I can help you market. All at the same terms you had with him. And I will not gamble away the profits, so there will be no need for me to steal from you."

The man sneered. "Pay his debt first."

"No." Zhi-Gang narrowed his eyes. "Unless . . . there is *something* else you want." If they wanted Anna, they would say so now.

The leader drew his sword with an ugly grin. "We want money. Or you die."

Zhi-Gang felt relief spill through him. They weren't looking for Anna. But they were looking for blood, which meant he had no choice. They meant to kill him and ransack the compound unless he stopped them.

Before the man's guards could even reach for their swords, Zhi-Gang threw both his weapons. Two of the men dropped, deer-horn daggers sticking out of their throats. Five opponents abruptly became three, but now Zhi-Gang was unarmed. The others drew their swords.

Zhi-Gang didn't move. He merely shrugged. "I have archers there and there." He pointed to where he had entered, and outside the window. "Think hard before you attack. You will be dead before you can take another step." Then he narrowed his eyes at the half-white leader. "You will die first."

The man hesitated, but he wasn't completely cowed. "I

have men outside, too. What makes you think they have not already killed your archers?"

Zhi-Gang made a show of rolling his eyes. "Because if they had, my men would now be the ones bleeding on the floor. Besides, these boys can't kill a dog much less my men. This was another calculated risk, but he trusted Anna's guess. His sweet little opium addict knew a great deal more about this business than she let on, and if her suggestion caused him to look informed . . .

The half-white narrowed his eyes but did not advance. Zhi-Gang waited, his legs tensed to dive sideways should they attack. But in the end, his opponent waved his men to sheathe their weapons.

"You give us girls, we give you opium. A half pound each."

Zhi-Gang felt the old fury build. Selling China's girls to buy poison. How had such an atrocity ever begun? To cover his anger, he slowly moved toward one of the dead guards. With a show of weakness, he struggled to draw the blade out of the man's neck: the Enforcer had the reputation of wielding his blades with lighting speed, so the less like a warrior he appeared, the better for everyone. Meanwhile, he had a negotiation to manage.

"You think girls go easily into your hands? Ten pounds each." The blade felt good in his hand.

"Ha!" the half-white snorted. "You cannot think—"

Zhi-Gang threw his blade into the neck of the nearest brute. Now there were only two left alive.

"Stop that!" the half-white exclaimed. Then he charged, his last remaining companion only a step behind. But Zhig-Gang was prepared. He side-stepped the leader, then followed up with a disarming strike. The half-white's sword tumbled into Zhi-Gang's waiting hand just in time to fend off the companion. As he suspected, the brutes were not trained fighters. They used intimidation to get their way rather than skilled swordplay. In a few short moments, the companion had fallen—stunned but not dead—and the leader was pinned against the coffin while Zhi-Gang pressed a sword to his neck.

"You tire me," Zhi-Gang drawled." Who is your puppeteer?"

The man frowned. "What?"

A familiar female voice answered: "He means Samuel, you moron."

All turned abruptly as Anna sauntered in. Beside her stood one of the governor's wives—the second, Zhi-Gang guessed—and a mulish adolescent sporting a new bruise on his sulking face. A bruise that looked like it could have come from the Second Wife's cane.

"Why aren't you at your post?" the leader of the things demanded of the boy.

Anna answered. "Because morons hire morons." She stepped further into the room, making a show of inspecting the new bodies. "Yeah, I can see what a good job you're doing here, Halfy." She gestured to the last remaining guard. "You. Get them out of here."

The guard hesitated, and Anna abruptly slapped him hard across the face. "I am giving the orders here! Go or die!"

The man scrambled to obey. Zhi-Gang didn't blame him. Anna said the words so forcefully that Zhi-Gang momentarily wondered whom she had killed before. Then he realized she was probably bluffing, just like him. Or perhaps not.

After all, he didn't really know much about this woman, did he? Especially not the woman who was boldly ordering around . . . what had she called him? Halfy. She was clearly acting like she not only knew the bastard, but was due a great deal of respect and deference. And if that were true, she wasn't just an addict and a runner. This woman he had kissed, bedded, and possibly impregnated last night might very well be a leader in a major opium organization.

The thought nearly made him retch. Instead, he continued the game, pretending to be the newest buyer in the most evil trade. "I am sick of you both," he sneered with absolute truth. "Where is Samuel? I will speak with him."

"Moron," Halfy sneered, apparently unable to think of a different insult. "Samuel can't come inland. He's white."

Zhi-Gang shrugged. "So is she, and she's here."

Anna snorted. "We'll go to him, Governor. Or you can keep your local girls and live without the opium. We got poor whores coming out of our ears in Shanghai."

Halfy stomped his foot in petulant irritation. "Samuel don't meet with buyers. That's for me to do." Then he narrowed his eyes at Anna. "What are you doing here? We've been looking all over China for you."

Second Wife chose that moment to exert herself. Despite her crippled stance, she was able to slap the big half-white man flat across the face. It was so unexpected a move that everyone stood frozen in shock.

"Half-breed ape, we will discuss nothing more with you or her!" Second Wife glared at one and all, her spine growing straighter as she spoke. "This is a house of mourning. Get out, all of you! And take your dung-house business and go!"

Anna arched her light brown eyebrow in a very Chinese expression. "Well, Governor? Do you come with us? Or do you squat here without opium, without income except what an honest leader would take?"

It was a challenge if he'd ever heard one. Did he accept the setup suddenly arrayed before him? With the right bribes, he could be assured an appointment to this very post. He could lead this province where he was born and see that nothing happened again like what had happened to his sister.

Or he could follow his personal obsession, continue as the Enforcer, and see this through to the end. Assuming, of course, that sweet little Anna was being as honest with him as she pretended. Which, of course, was a huge assumption.

"And what will you do?" he asked.

He saw a moment of fear flicker through Anna's eyes, but it was quickly gone as she gestured at Halfy. "You heard him. Samuel has been looking through all of China for me. I will go and explain myself to my adopted father." Then she held his gaze for a long dark moment before she spoke again. "I knew he would find me eventually. It was foolishness to believe something else, even for a night."

Halfy curled his lip into a sneer. "So you were running away! Samuel didn't believe you would be that stupid, but I knew. I knew—"

"Silence!" Zhi-Gang hissed, pressing the sword point deeper. How he wanted to shove it all the way through, but the situation was too complicated right now.

Meanwhile, Anna stepped up until she was eye to eye with Halfy. "I will explain myself to Samuel and no other. You can either be rewarded for taking me to him or die now. That is *your* choice."

Halfy subsided into a sulk. Clearly he wouldn't fight now. If he ever got her alone, though . . . well, that would be entirely different. Meanwhile, Anna touched Zhi-Gang's sword arm, gently pressing it back and down. He could have resisted, but her warmth curled through his entire body. His sword dropped away without him even realizing.

"Stay here, *Governor.* Leave me to negotiate on your behalf."

Was she protecting him, encouraging him to take the easy life of a governor? Or did she simply seek to escape him? Either way made no difference. He was not done with her or with his responsibilities as Enforcer. He would meet this white man who bartered girls and poisoned his country, and he would see the snake dead.

He lifted his chin. "I will meet this Samuel face to face."

She curled her lip in disdain. "You will be gutted like them if you think your arrogance will gain you anything with Samuel," warned Anna. "Think hard, Governor. You have women, land, a good life here. You can begin again. Are you sure you want to traffic with white devils?"

Zhi-Gang narrowed his eyes, trying to read his wife. Odd, how the added vision of his white man's glasses gave him no help. His clues came from her words and her tone. He caught an underlying tension in her voice, a warning that if he followed her to Shanghai, they would probably both die. And yet, when he looked in her eyes, he saw fear and loneliness. An addict's panic, perhaps? Or simply the same yearning he felt: to be with her, to stay by her side, to see that she was protected and cherished. It was a ridiculous emotion to feel for a white woman, and yet he did not deny it. He would not abandon her.

"I go to Shanghai with you," he said firmly.

Anna nodded, her expression blank. But as she turned to go, Second Wife grabbed her by the arm and pointed at Zhi-Gang. "You will leave your men here to protect us," she ordered. "We must be treated as befits our status!"

Zhi-Gang nearly smiled. As the second wife of a dead governor, the woman had no status whatsoever, and no power to order him. And yet, he found he admired her spunk. It was all the more amazing given the life she must have led up until this point.

Rather than crush her in the name of authority, he simply bowed his head. "Jing-Li will remain here. He will administer in my name." Then he straightened, his voice hardening. "And now you will release my wife. She has packing to do."

The words were not lost on Halfy. "Wife!" he screeched, clearly torn between shock and admiration. "Wife! To a governor?"

Anna paled, but not so much that anyone but Zhi-Gang would notice. "As I said," she drawled. "You will take us to Samuel. We will explain to him and no other."

"Ha!" chortled Halfy. "He'll either reward you or kill you. Hard to tell which. Ha!"

Anna looked hard at Zhi-Gang, her expression unreadable. "Isn't it nice to know, *husband*, that you and I will suffer the exact same fate."

Anna's hands were shaking as she finished changing into travel clothes. Stupid really, since all in all she was more secure than ever. Despite their liaison last night, Zhi-Gang was still the Enforcer and might kill her for her crimes. Now her father's men were a few rooms away, and they would at least attempt to defend her if she asked.

She was safe with them until she met with Samuel. They wouldn't risk killing her before her adopted father ordered it.

Of course, with Halfy one could never really know. That was the problem with associating with drug-runners. They were so much less predictable than marks. But perhaps it was she who was being contrary. Addicts were just as trustworthy as runners.

She sighed and carefully folded Wife Five's silk dress and set it on the bed. The peasant homespun she now wore were so much more comfortable to move in—pants and a tunic jacket—but so much less sweet on the skin. Was it strange that she would prefer just being naked?

"Are you longing for opium?"

His voice flowed over her from the bedroom door. It soothed her nerves' jagged edges even as she felt her chin lift in challenge. "Yes," she lied. But she'd much rather have his *distraction*.

He obliged by stepping right to her side, but when she lifted her face to his mouth, he kept his lips just out of her reach. "What are you planning, Anna?"

She bit her lip, wondering if he was ready for the truth. Wondering if she was ready to tell him. "Why did you become the Emperor's Enforcer? It can't be what you intended."

He flinched, but his gaze remained steady. "I wanted to study Lao Tzu and debate Buddhism against Taoism against your Christianity."

"A scholar."

He nodded. "But then I grew up. I went to Peking. I learned more philosophy, more politics, more of everything."

"Study doesn't turn people into . . . *bullies*." She used

the English word, since she didn't know the Chinese for police officer. Well, no polite one.

He gave her a rueful smile. "I met a girl." Then he abruptly swooped down and claimed her lips. The kiss was swift, possessive, and stole her breath.

But then it was over. He pulled back and pressed their foreheads together, but he didn't speak.

"You met a girl," she prompted.

"She died," he agreed.

"The one who died from opium?" she guessed.

"Yes. I killed her supplier."

Anna shuddered. She couldn't help it. His voice was so final. This was the Enforcer's voice, and she had a flash of understanding. This was the man she toyed with. This was the killer with whom she had shared her bed. And this was the man she wanted.

She swallowed, then offered her lips to him again. But before they connected, she had one last question. "How old were you?"

"Seventeen." She felt his hands tighten where they gripped hers. "No one protects women in China, not even the parents. Girls are sold, women are addicted and abused." He looked into her eyes, pleading for her to understand. "I hate killing, Anna. I *hate* it. But these vermin prey on the girls. Who will stop them if I don't? Who will end it?"

She swallowed, feeling his anguish all the way through to her soul. "You, Zhi-Gang. You save them."

He shook his head. "Too little, too late."

"You are only one man," she whispered.

He took her mouth again, thrusting his tongue inside with all the brutality that was so integral to the Enforcer role he played. And perverse woman that she was, she loved it. She opened her mouth to his invasion, his ownership. She gave herself to him as completely as she had last night, and he took all she offered and then some. She resisted a bit, of course. She fought a little, but that didn't last long. He was too strong and she was too willing.

For a time, they both forgot themselves in the wonder of each other. But then he raised his head. She was bent backward over his arm. Her hands gripped his shoulders and burrowed into his hair. She thought for a moment that she could completely let go and he would still hold her, still support her. That thought alone made her smile.

"If we were in Peking," he murmured, "I would shut the house to everyone, claim some illness to keep even the servants away, then spend a month or more with you in my bed."

"If we were in Peking, I would agree," she murmured. "And I would not once think of opium or your job or anything but pleasing you."

They broke apart, thoughtful. He helped her adjust her peasant clothing while she darkened her face with ash. And when they were done, he stepped back with a frown. "You look like a boy. A poor, dirty, peasant boy."

She nodded. "Only you know what is underneath."

"No," he said with a grimace. "The others know. Your Halfy and his men."

She turned away from him, her mood soured. "They're not *my* men." Perversely, she wanted to burrow back into his arms, and so her tone became even more bitter. "I just know them."

"Because they're your father's men," he pressed.

She nodded. "Adopted father. And, yes. Halfy went with me on my first run." How she hated to say that bastard's name. "The others are new to me." She looked out the window, seeing a tree quiver in the wind. "Except for the straw soldiers. Those I know very well."

"Used that trick often, did you?" His tone was cold.

"Rarely." She turned to him, her expression open and honest as she explained, "We don't force opium on anyone. They come to us begging for it."

"Opium in exchange for girls."

She winced. "I didn't broker that deal."

"Would you?" he pressed, his face shifting into tortured lines. "Would you have ever done such a thing?"

"Never," she said vehemently. "Girls who have no choice, sold into prostitution?" She shuddered. "It's cruel, vicious, and . . ." She sighed, forced to admit the truth. "It's just bad business. There are enough people willing to hand over cash, jewels, even silk shot with gold thread. Why bother with a girl who has no choice, would fight you every step of the way, and may or may not be a virgin?" She took a deep breath, knowing now was the moment to lay her soul bare. "Well . . . that's what I told my adopted father. Do you know what he said to me?"

Zhi-Gang shook his head, his expression blank.

"That a pretty girl would pay off for years, whereas jewelry could only be sold once. And better yet, he got girls by the dozens for the price of a few yuan." She lay her hand lightly on his chest, anger lacing her tone. "He said the Chinese don't value their girls except for their ability to spread their legs. What matter was it in marriage or in prostitution? If the Chinese didn't care, then why should we?"

"I care," he said, his eyes dark with fury.

"I know," she answered, twisting and grabbing a watermelon cap to cover her hair. She believed. "That's why I want you to kill him."

228

He blinked, clearly startled. She pressed her advantage while he was still off balance, dropped a warm kiss full on his lips then smiled.

"Yes, Mr. Enforcer. I want you to kill my father."

His eyes narrowed. "Why?"

"Because he's a bastard. Isn't that enough?"

He waited a moment, clearly considering whether to delve deeper or not. She interrupted his thoughts, outlining everything clearly.

"You're the Imperial Enforcer. You track down opium dealers and destroy them. My adopted father has a bustling trade. Samuel sells girls to whorehouses, opium to governors, and does a little loan-sharking on the side. It's a booming business, and one you are sworn to end." She paused. "You *are* sworn to it, aren't you?"

He shrugged. "I swore to defend China and my Emperor."

"Good enough."

"No, it's not good enough," he snapped. "If you want him dead so badly, then why don't you kill him? Why didn't you?"

"Because he's a suspicious bastard. I can't get near enough without a good reason. Not now . . ." She cut herself off, but he filled in the gaps.

"Not after you fled with a shipment of opium."

She sighed. "I could claim that I had to run. That the Enforcer was after me." It wasn't a lie, though she'd twist the timing a bit. "But he'd still be suspicious. He'd still be on guard against me. With you there as a new buyer, we could get close, then *whoosh* . . ." She made a cutting motion with her hand. "You kill him with your knives."

He shook his head. "You say that so easily."

"It won't be easy. We'll still have to get out. But my father likes to celebrate new contracts. There will be an opportunity to do it and run. I know it."

Zhi-Gang folded his arms and sat down on the bed, watching her with narrowed eyes. "Why take the risk?"

"It's your sworn duty!" she snapped.

"Not me. You. Why not just board a boat to England and be done with this life forever? Wasn't that your original plan?"

She bit her lip and nodded. It *was* what she wanted, or thought she did. She wasn't exactly sure when her goal had changed, when her thoughts had turned from escape to revenge. "He gave me my first taste of opium," she said.

Zhi-Gang's eyebrows rose. "Why would he addict a runner? There's too much risk."

She shook her head. "It takes a year to addict. "He was showing me a good time, and I so desperately wanted that taste." How could she have ever been so naive? So stupid? "He was trying to win me over. He needed a sweet young girl to open up the territory. To work in the mission and sweet-talk the governor."

"That was you."

She nodded, self-loathing like a lead weight in her stomach. "The gamble paid off. I did good work for him for almost ten years."

"But now you want him dead."

She nodded.

"Killing is no cure. You'll still be an addict. You'll still crave—"

"I know what I am!" she snapped. She abruptly stomped up to him, challenging him eye to eye. "It seems to me that you're the one who has forgotten. Are you the Emperor's Enforcer or not?"

He didn't answer at first, merely held her angry gaze

with his own. Then he sighed, the sound world-weary enough to cut deep into her heart. "I was there that day in the Forbidden City."

"What?" She was startled as much by his sober tone as his change in topic.

"That day when the Empress imprisoned Guangxu, the Emperor. I wanted to see him. Right after the morning ceremonies, I intended to demand more men, more weapons, more . . ." He lifted his hands. "More power. As you said, I am only one man. I can only fight the tips of this monster. I cannot reach the heart." His hands dropped down, useless in his lap. "But it was already too late. Jing-Li and I tried, but . . ."

"The Empress had already taken control." Anna stepped forward. "But she supports your task. She hates the whites more than anyone. Surely she would give you want you want."

He shook his head. "All her attention is in Peking right now—on the threats against her and the politics between nations. She has no men to spare for me."

Anna slowly lowered to the bed as she thought what must have happened. "So your friend—the Emperor—was imprisoned, his mother busy consolidating her power, and that leaves you doing what? What you have always done?"

He nodded, but his eyes betrayed how useless he felt. She saw a desperation there, a need to do something more or nothing at all. She recognized the look and the feeling. It was what had finally led her to try to escape China. What little good she did at the mission did not make up for the damage she had caused. Better to leave all for good than do so little for Zhi-Gang's beleaguered country.

"Jing-Li and I needed to leave Peking, at least until the politics settled down."

"So the Enforcer went on another mission, this one to find a girl lost decades ago."

He nodded. "My sister."

Her breath froze in her throat. His *sister?* "She was sold . . ."

"Years ago. To pay for my education."

No wonder he held such anger, such raging fury at those who bartered opium for girls.

"Jing-Li and I would find her then leave China for good. All three of us."

"So you do not want to continue as the Enforcer," she realized.

"I wish to be done with the killing."

She shook her head, the knowledge crystalizing within her as she spoke. "No, That's not it. You wish to be done with *useless* killing. With striking at the runners and the buyers rather than the real problem—men like Samuel who set up the supply lines in the first place." She straightened in her enthusiasm, grabbing his hands as she tried to make him understand. "Finish what you started. Kill the head of this one monster. Kill Samuel and then run away with me. We can climb onto a boat and leave forever, you and me, your sister and Jing-Li."

She could see it all so clearly in her mind. But she had to finish things with Samuel. She had to end her ties to him forever or she would always be running from him. And Zhi-Gang would always feel as if his life as the Enforcer had been completely useless. She dropped down on her knees before him and pressed a kiss into his palms. "You need to keep fighting or you will end up like me: lost and alone with nothing to hold but opium dreams."

He remained silent a long time, his only comment in the gentle stroke of his thumb across her cheek. Then he leaned down and whispered into her ear. "I will do this, Anna. I will walk with you to meet this evil white man who so used you. I will pretend to be his buyer and then cut his heart out with all the skill in my arms."

Relief filled her body, but he did not let her speak. Instead, he stood up from the mattress to tower over her, his eyes dark, his expression intense. "But I will do this, Anna, not because it is my job or my sworn duty."

He fell silent, and Anna found she was holding her breath waiting for him to finish. In the end, she had to ask. "Then, why?" she whispered. "Why risk your life?"

"I do it for you, Anna. Because you asked, and because you think it will end your torment."

She lifted her chin, visions of spitting on her adopted father's dead body. "It will. It *will* bring me peace."

"No, little Anna. It will just bring you and me more blood." He sighed.

Anna would not to moved. "There is already blood, Zhi-Gang. With every shipment of opium, more of your people die. We will be ending the blood."

She could tell he didn't believe. He'd lost faith in what he did. And she of all people knew how helpless one man could be in stemming the opium tide. For every drug route he ended, five more would crop up in its place.

"One more death," she whispered, not even knowing if she spoke to him or to herself. "One more and then we can both be done. We can both leave this land and its stench behind."

He bent down and his lips claimed hers for a long, tender moment.

She changed the tenor of the kiss. She reached up and wrapped her arm around his neck; she opened her mouth to him and pressed her tongue against his teeth. He surrendered. He met her passion with fire. Soon they were wrapped around each other in a conflagration of hunger and desire.

It ended. They pulled apart with slow reluctance, but they did separate.

"I changed my mind," he said, as he dropped his forehead against hers. "I will kill your adopted father because it is my duty. And then I will put you on a boat to England. I will even wave from the dock as you leave my country forever."

"You won't come with me?" she asked in a small voice.

"No. I have a sworn duty, remember?"

"But you don't really believe in it anymore. It was odd, to know this man's thoughts and feelings. But she did. She always had. "You're tired, just like I am. You want it done with, just like I do."

He nodded. "But you are white and can leave. You should leave. This is not your country."

She felt her hands clench on his shoulders. She wanted to shake him, to make him see. "Why stay? Why fight against a foe you know will win—is winning? You can't fight this drug, Zhi-Gang. Not when everyone you try to protect works so hard against you."

He knew that. She could see it in his eyes, but he didn't say anything.

"Why, Zhi-Gang? Why do you feel so responsible for China? For the corruption that eats your country?"

His face was taut with a pain she did not understand. "You atone for your sins in your way, and I shall see to mine."

She pulled back. "I don't understand."

He abruptly stepped away from her. "At least Jing-Li has found his purpose. He remains here to govern the province. Without an opium route, it will be hard work, but he wants to try."

"But what about leaving China? What about running from the Empress—"

He dismissed his plans with a shrug. "An opium fantasy. The Empress is too busy to worry about this backwater province. With the right bribes, Jing-Li can establish himself simply because he is already here."

She nodded. It made sense, but . . . "What about you?"

He spun on his heel. "Jing-Li is remaining here," he said over his shoulder. "To run the province and protect the widows. You and I will leave with Halfy and his men as soon as you are ready." Then he disappeared down the hallway.

Anna stood a moment before her knees gave way, slowly sinking to the mattress. She was dressed to leave, had nothing to pack and no good-byes to say. And yet, she still sat. She felt as if she had always been ready to leave. From her earliest childhood memories, she had longed to escape her surroundings, to fly far, far away. And yet, just now, she couldn't do more than sit and look at this chamber.

What things she had done here with Zhi-Gang. Fully aware, fully willing, she had explored their bodies to the furthest sexual extent. Well, she thought with a soft smile, perhaps not the furthest, but quite far. Quite far indeed. If ever there were a place she would stay awhile, ever a home she might rest happily inside without once thinking of opium or England or murdering fathers, this would be it. This place, this home, this province.

Except, of course, it wasn't this place that held her, it was Zhi-Gang: his tenderness, his sudden passions, his equally surprising understanding. When he looked at her, he saw more than anyone ever had. And in turn, she told him more than anyone else. It was Zhi-Gang she wanted to stay with, not this place. And it was he that she would leave when the time came.

The thought created a physical ache in her chest. With that ache came an automatic response—the longing for opium and forgetfulness. She hardened her heart against it. Pushing to her feet, she walked steadily to the door.

"I won't do it," she said to no one in particular. "I won't give up just because he doesn't want me." She walked out into the hallway. "I have a family in England who loves me. They want to know me. I know they do. I know it."

So saying, she picked up speed and ended up running down the hall. She couldn't wait to get to Shanghai and finally aboard a boat headed far, far away.

From Anna Marie Thompson's journal:
June 3, 1886

Susanna is a bitch. A liar and a bitch! I didn't steal her necklace. I can have a dozen of them from Samuel if I want. Why would I want her stupid old crucifix? Or the chapel wine? I didn't take any of it, but they found it in my clothes. That, and dirty linen that smelled of wine. It's a lie, lie, lie! Created by that bitch, but no one will believe me. No one!

And so I left. I wasn't going to join Samuel just yet. I

wanted to wait until I was bigger because some of his men aren't as nice as him. The nuns said I could stay another year, but with this now . . . I couldn't.

So I just walked out. They were going to expel me anyway. I heard them talking, so I just packed my bags and left before they threw me out in front of everyone as an example. That's what Mother Francis said. Throw me out at dinner as an example to everyone else.

No, I left first. I just packed my bag and walked out, and now I am free, free, free! It was the easiest thing in the world! No fight, no tears. I said good-bye to no one, and no one said good-bye to me. Janie will cry, I think. And Sarah. But all the tears will dry when I come back with presents. With big, beautiful, wonderful presents for all of them. When I am rich.

I went straight to Father, and he has something arranged for me already. I am going on my first trip with Halfy, a simple run of only a couple days. And the funny thing is, I'm supposed to dress as a nun! Only missionaries are allowed inside China, so I will be a nun. And Halfy will be my acolyte, plus some other man who will protect the money. And we will visit a mandarin who is a regular, and I will be paid in gold!

Could I revive within me
Her symphony and song,
To such a deep delight 'twould win me,
That with music loud and long,
I would build that dome in air,
That sunny dome! those caves of ice!
                    —*Samuel Taylor Coleridge*
            from "Kubla Khan: Or, a Vision in a Dream. A
                                            Fragment"

CHAPTER FOURTEEN

"I have some extra. Want to share?"

Halfy's words floated through the air to where Anna was brushing down the horses. Since she was dressed as a peasant—much poorer than the others—Anna was supposed to act the servant boy to the group; that was the cover they often used whenever she travelled with her father's men. When she wasn't playing a nun.

Years ago, it hadn't bothered her. She liked being useful, was accustomed to hard labor from her childhood in the mission, and dressing as a boy kept her away from men who made jokes she didn't like. But it had also isolated her at times—like now—when she was alone rubbing down the horses after a long day's travel. That was Halfy's favorite time to catch her—then and now.

"Did you hear me, little Anna?" Halfy called again, his voice barely louder than a whisper. "I have fun to share."

He meant opium. Opium to share. And then, when she was so drugged she could barely move, he would do the moving for her. She didn't remember clearly, but he had made comments. And she knew he had done it to others. It was the only way Halfy could get women, and he seemed to find a perverse enjoyment out of them being unconscious.

"No, thank you," she answered aloud, disappointed that there wasn't more conviction in her voice. Truthfully, she did want the opium. It was just what happened afterward that she despised.

She swallowed and bent low to rub down the horse's belly. As she moved, she quickly scanned the little campsite. Zhi-Gang was nowhere to be seen. He'd been helping her all evening, despite Halfy's protest that it would look very strange to anyone who happened upon them.

It turned out that Zhi-Gang wasn't nearly as pampered as she'd once thought. He wasn't averse to gathering wood, was a skilled hand at making a fire, and even made a passable soup. True, his work with horses was rather ham-fisted, but he was smart and willing to learn, which is more than she could say for the others in their company.

Now he was gone to clean the pot, and that left her alone with the horses and Halfy, since the three other men had already settled in for their evening tobacco. Halfy was the only one offering opium, and he had sidled up behind her, his voice low as he bent over her.

She crouched even lower, slipping beneath the horse before rising up on the other side. Halfy didn't follow. He wasn't nearly as nimble as she, but his words had no problem reaching her.

"It's my pay, Little Anna. Not skimmed from Samuel, so he won't be angry. And besides, I'm an important man with him now. He doesn't begrudge me a little fun. I could protect you from him, you know. If you're nice to me."

240

"I *am* being nice to you," she answered, her mouth painfully dry. "I brought you the new governor. Don't think you could have managed that without me. And perhaps you should be nice to me. After all, one word from me and Zhi-Gang will give up on you and leave."

Halfy's response was a loud snort. "The Chinese will sell their own mother for opium." He slid around the horse's tail with a leering grin. "And I am trying to be nice to you. You just aren't being nice back."

Anna straightened to fully face Halfy. In her mind, she wondered how she could have ever thought his crude advances even remotely palatable. She sighed. It hadn't been Halfy that had been the temptation; it was the opium. It's what she'd wanted then, and what she still craved—though not nearly as desperately as before. Not now, not with Zhi-Gang by her side. Then she remembered Zhi-Gang wouldn't always be by her side. He would soon put her on a boat and wave good-bye to her from the dock. And with that thought came panic.

She swallowed, feeling her spirit weaken, the hunger beginning to fog her thoughts. She didn't want to remember what she had been before, what she had done. "I'm married, Halfy," she finally managed. "Go away."

It took all the strength inside her to turn away from him, but she did. She turned her back on Halfy and began scrubbing the horse's other side. But it was all a game. In her heart, she knew that Halfy would not give up so easily. And she knew that she would falter—again—because she always did. Her hands itched to cradle the pipe, her mouth was beginning to salivate in anticipation of the sweet smoke.

She couldn't. She didn't want to. But she always did, and that thought made her eyes tear.

He grabbed her. She'd known he would. Halfy did not like being denied. She felt his hands—small despite his large size, but painfully strong on her arms. Except . . . She frowned. The hands were large and not hurtful. They cupped and supported rather than forced.

She gasped in surprise, abruptly lifting her head. Zhi-Gang. He was studying her face, his eyes dark in the evening gloom, but she could feel the concern in his touch, in his breath, in every aspect of his body as he stood beside her.

"Are you all right?" he asked.

She had no words. Her gratitude cut them off. All she had was a welling of thanks that he could now stand between her and Halfy. And that for one more day, one more hour, he stood between her and the opium pipe.

"Anna?" His voice was sharp with worry.

"I'm fine," she managed. "Thank you. Stay here, please. Don't leave me alone."

"Of course not." He stayed a moment more, studying her face, and as he held her she grew stronger. Her spine straightened, though she barely realized she'd been slumping. Her shoulders stiffened and her chin lifted.

"I am almost done with the horses," she said. "If you could but wait, I will be able to help you with your boots afterward."

His expression eased. "I can handle my own boots, Anna. But I will happily help you finish this."

She was about to nod in thanks, but he gave her no opportunity. He had barely completed his sentence when he abruptly spun and slammed his fist into Halfy's jaw. The large man's head snapped backward and he lost his balance. It was like watching a tree fall as he slowly toppled backward to land in a pile of dung.

Anna was so startled she could only gasp, though a

smile quickly formed on her face. Not many people had ever laid Halfy out. Certainly no one had in years.

Unfortunately, Halfy was quick to recover. His fists were bunching and he drew breath to roar for his companions. But Zhi-Gang wasn't finished with him. Before Halfy could stand, Zhi-Gang leaped forward and pressed his boot hard into Halfy's throat.

"Speak to my wife again," Zhi-Gang growled, "and I will use my blades instead of my boot." Then he drew his deer-horn knives and clicked them lightly together for emphasis. The last of the sunlight flashed red along the expertly wrought steel.

Halfy was still furious. Anna could see the rage in the man's eyes, but he was in no position to fight—not with Zhi-Gang's boot on his throat and so many inches of curved steel hovering over him. "You are not nearly so weak as you pretend," Halfy hissed.

Zhi-Gang leaned down and spoke in an even lower tone, one that was all the more frightening because it was so soft-spoken. "If my wife becomes high in any way, if there is opium in her food or a pipe wends its way into her hands, then I will come to you and I will kill you. Do you understand? I have killed before, and I will kill again." He lifted one of his blades, shifting it back and forth in the light. "I can slice the skin off a mango in eight seconds. Imagine what I could do to you." He slowly straightened, but he did not lessen his pressure on Halfy's throat. "And, by the way, when I skin a man, I start with his genitals."

Halfy's eyes widened in horror. The last of his resistance fled. He didn't even try to speak when Zhi-Gang finally lifted his boot away; he just rolled onto his side then scrambled up. Anna watched with a mixture of awe and fear as he fled.

"He's getting suspicious, "she said." He might try to slit your throat while you are sleeping.

Zhi-Gang turned with a mischievous smile. "Then it is a good thing I don't plan to sleep tonight." The twinkle in his eyes left no doubt as to what he hoped to be doing instead, and with whom. Anna merely shook her head, shocked and a little stunned.

"No one has ever done that for me before." The words escaped without thought. In truth, she had no idea what she was doing until she heard her own voice.

Zhi-Gang's eyes sobered. "China is hard on women."

"Life is hard on women," she murmured as she looked away. Years ago she had wished and prayed and hoped for someone such as this to carry her away on a white steed. The nuns had read fairy tales to their charges, stories of princes and castles and great big dragons that had to be killed before the happily ever after. How she had dreamed of that.

Zhi-Gang gently touched her chin, lifting her face to look at him. "Do not wander from my side again. Not until this whole thing is done."

"I didn't wander away," she protested. "I am tending the horses. You went to wash the pot."

He nodded, but his expression did not soften. "Do not leave my side," he repeated firmly. "And I swear I will not leave yours."

The words reverberated in the air, a solemn vow. Nothing said in any church could have held more power. Anna felt a shiver skate down her spine.

"I won't," she answered. And at that moment, she felt as if she had really married him. As if they were bonded together. It was a lie, of course. It was definitely a lie, but the thought held such power that she couldn't help wishing, couldn't help praying that just this once it would be true.

"Good," he answered. "Now let us finish with this poor, smelly horse."

He bent to work with a genial smile and a willing hand. He even whistled as he brushed down the nag, and Anna was left to stare, her heart in her throat.

It's an illusion, she told herself; as great a temptation as the opium she craved, and just as big a lie in the morning. Even if he were offering what she desired, there was no future for a mixed couple in China. He was merely using her to destroy the opium route, just as she was using him to kill her dragon of an adopted father.

In short, it was a temporary lie, a pretend game, no more real than her life as Sister Marie. And yet she was seduced. She was tempted to believe one last time, to hope.

"Do you believe in love?" she asked, wondering if she sounded like a lost adolescent.

The gentle whooshing of his brush stilled and his head popped up from the opposite side of the horse. "Love? What kind of love? Love of family, of country, of politics?" He waggled his eyebrows. "Or the love we shared last night?"

She shrugged, trying to match his casual tone. "Was that love? I thought that was distraction."

He grinned. "It was fun."

"But not love," she pressed.

His face slowly sobered as he met her gaze across the horse's back. "No," he responded slowly. "That was not love."

She nodded and sternly ordered herself not to press the point. But then she heard herself ask again. "But do you believe in love? In romantic love between a man and a woman?"

"All scholars believe in love. Have you not heard our poetry?"

She had, actually. Doomed lovers, every one. Couples were separated by wars, gods, or malicious relatives. "So you don't really believe it is *possible*, do you? That a man and a woman can end happily together."

He looked at her, his eyes infinitely black. "No," he said honestly. "I don't believe it is possible."

"Neither do I," she said as she returned to the horse. Before she could make a single stroke, he touched her hand, stopping her motion.

"But tonight we will believe. Tonight we will have happiness beyond measure."

She blinked back tears. "And in the morning?"

He shook his head. "In the morning, we continue on to Shanghai where I will meet your father . . ."

And kill him. Those were the words he did not say. After all the soft kisses and tender caresses of a night, for him the morning always held drugs and deception and murder.

She pressed her lips tightly together as she toyed with the mud-caked brush in her hand. "I will go to my family in England," she said.

"Of course." His tone sounded light, but a quick glance at his face showed his skin to be white and his jaw clenched. "Where else would you go?"

She shook her head. "Nowhere." There was nowhere else to go.

Zhi-Gang was dreaming. He was standing in the middle of a Shanghai whorehouse, looking at the "flowers" and smelling the sweet opium stench that pervaded the air.

He heard a customer grunt in release and imagined the feel of a bawd's tears slipping unnoticed down her cheek. He knew it all with stark clarity, and yet he also knew this was a dream.

He stepped deeper into the darkness, surprised that he didn't choke in the foggy smoke. He peered through the blackness to the back room and saw exactly what he knew would be there: the madame buying a mulish, frightened little girl. It was his little sister, and she was being dragged away. Her screams echoed in his head, and he winced at their shrill power.

At this point in the dream, he usually pulled out his knives and rescued his sister. She ran gratefully into his arms and he carried her home. Except, they never made it. Instead, he carried her to another garden of delights where she was suddenly not in his arms anymore but being sold again. And again he rescued her only to end up at another house. And another. Until he woke bathed in his own sweat.

Not this time. He would not repeat that nightmare over and over. He decided to change the dream even as he dreamt it. But nothing changed as he planned.

This time, when he pulled out his knives to rescue his sister, he saw a second woman: Anna. She was dressed as a high-class whore, all silk elegance with bright red lips, taut full breasts and long, long legs. As he watched, she put an opium pipe to her lips and closed her eyes in ecstasy. The sight sickened him, and he gripped his knives tighter, preparing to kill everyone in the room except for the girls. He could hear his sister screaming, knew exactly where she was and how to rescue her. And it would be no problem at all to knock the pipe from Anna's hand, to smash it under his heels, then drag her out. Even in this dream state, he knew how easy it would be.

And yet, he didn't do it. His sister continued to scream, Anna continued to smoke, and he slowly put away his knives since they had become like bricks in his hands: too heavy to carry, too unwieldy to use. He put them away and turned, heading for the door.

"What are you doing?" bellowed his conscious mind. "Save them!"

His dream self simply shrugged and looked him in the eye. It made no sense, but that was the beauty and horror of a nightmare. His dream self pulled out his knives and dropped them on the ground in a pool of blood. "They're too heavy," he said.

"But they need your help!" Zhi-Gang cried back. "They need you."

His dream self had no answer. He simply pointed at the knives and repeated himself. "They're too heavy." Then he stepped over the knives, sloshed through the expanding pool of blood, and continued out of the pleasure garden.

Zhi-Gang's conscious mind remained behind, screaming, ordering, bellowing, doing anything he could think of to make his dream self turn around. But nothing worked. His dream self kept walking. Bit by bit, the Dream Enforcer climbed out of the blood, shucked his gore-soaked clothing, and hailed a rickshaw. In this pristine and naked state, Dream Zhi-Gang left Conscious Zhi-Gang behind. He didn't even look back to wave. Dream Zhi-Gang was focused completely ahead on an emerald green field of rice on the horizon. The baby shoots had just broken above the waterline, and both Zhi-Gangs grinned at the sight.

But then it faded. Everything disappeared: the green rice paddy, the bawdy house, even Anna and his sister's screams. All disappeared, leaving Conscious Zhi-Gang standing in the middle of nothing. He kept screaming, of course. He was still trying to bring Dream Zhi-Gang back. Then he was trying to return to the bawdy house to rescue his sister and Anna. Then he was simply screaming to be heard. But soon even his voice disappeared, then his thoughts, then the image of himself. It—he— faded into nothing. A huge expanse of gray nothing.

Gone.

He remained gone for a very, very, very long time.

"Zhi-Gang! Zhi-Gang!"

A voice came to him through the gray. He barely heard it except as an echo or perhaps a memory. It didn't matter. It was not nothing. It was something, and he ran for it with all his strength.

"Zhi-Gang!"

"Anna!"

He gasped awake, his body incredibly heavy as he struggled upright and into her arms. She caught him easily, which was fortunate because he hadn't the control to grab her. His arms were like blocks of black rock—heavy, dark, and completely useless. And yet he flung them around her and clung with all his strength.

She held him equally tight, equally strong, until feeling gradually returned. With her warmth, the rock softened, became fluid, and eventually he found hands instead of blocks, fingers instead of stone chips.

He held her. He breathed in her scent. And with one swift move, he pushed her on her back and spread her legs.

She gasped in surprise, but didn't resist. Her eyes held

tender sympathy as she spoke. "I don't think you're quite ready for that yet."

He wasn't. Her power hadn't reached his organ yet, but that was rapidly changing. In a moment he would have potency enough to bury himself inside of her. And when he was there, when she surrounded him completely with her sweet, sensuous beauty, then he could forget the dream and all it represented.

He looked down at her, relishing the pale luminescence of her skin in moonlight. Just outside their tent, he heard the soft snores of the other men in their party, and beyond that he heard the nighttime noises of locusts and crickets.

She quirked an eyebrow at him. "I don't suppose you want to talk about your nightmare instead of just wiping it away?"

In response, he abruptly pulled off the rough tunic that covered her body. She had not worn the pants to bed, and so with her shirt off, she was completely naked beneath him. He smiled as her breasts puckered in the sudden chill. Her hair tumbled wildly about her head and crackled as the fabric pulled away, but she was smiling as her head tumbled back down to the single pillow they shared.

"I guess that means no," she said, a smile softening her features. "But really, Zhi-Gang—" Her words ended on a gasp as he pulled a nipple into his mouth. It pebbled into a tiny peak that lengthened as he sucked then teased up and down with his tongue. Her legs went around his, tightening around his thighs, and her musky scent blew through his thoughts, clearing away other dream-smells and the memory of gray nothing.

"Only you," she gasped as she arched beneath him. "No one else has ever made me feel this way."

He gave her one last sucking kiss on her nipple before lifting his head. "What way?"

She met his gaze with wide, honest eyes. "Like I want it. Like I want you."

She gripped his hips and arched. He could not resist. Her words had sent a white-hot heat though his body, and he flexed his buttocks in answer to her pull. One full thrust and he was as deep as he could go inside her.

She groaned. "Yes!"

He grinned and allowed sensation to wash over him, obliterating everything else. Then he opened his eyes, wanting to see if she looked at him. She did, and he rapidly became mesmerized by the roundness of her eyes, the gentle upsweep of her cheekbones, the full red of her lips.

"You are beautiful," he whispered.

"You say that like you mean it," she said, awe coloring her tone.

"I do." Then he dropped a tender kiss on her nose. "This isn't just to forget," he said, surprised that he spoke, stunned by what he said. It was the complete truth. "I have wanted you since the first moment I saw you."

She frowned. "Why?"

"I don't know." He shifted his hand to tenderly brush the hair from her face. "I have never wanted a white woman before. But you challenge me, you interest me. You . . ." He shook his head, at a loss for words. "You are you. And I cannot be away from you—even in my dreams—without wanting to be back."

She blinked, and he saw the sheen of tears in her eyes. Then there were no more words as she squeezed him from deep inside. He had no idea if the movement was conscious or not, but it didn't matter. Heat boiled through his system and his body began to flex.

She arched beneath him, opening herself fully to his desires. He raised up enough to give himself room to move, then drove into her in long, powerful strokes. Again and again he lost himself in her while she gasped in delight.

He felt contractions roar through her, beginning deep inside around his organ, but it seemed to expand, taking her whole body into a shiver of joy. He wanted to watch. He wanted to see her beauty shimmer during her ecstasy, but his own needs drove him harder.

He felt the power grow deep in his belly. His masculine strength—his essence—hovered just at the threshold. Then with his conscious will, he released it. He gave it to her; he poured it into her so that he could reside there inside her long after the moment. So he could be with her forever.

And in that moment, he was completely, wholly happy.

Anna smiled, her body still in that weightless shimmering that came with fulfillment. She wondered how it was that this feeling only came with Zhi-Gang. She had experienced sexual release before. Chinese women whispered of such things in private, and she had learned then what to do.

But only Zhi-Gang gave her this feeling of flight. With him, the sweet contractions became a soaring joy. She rolled her head to look at where he had collapsed beside her. The light cotton tent muted the moonlight, but she could still see the chiseled shape of his face. And what she couldn't see, she remembered: his piercing, black eyes, the slight twist of his lips when he was amused, the anger that could suddenly cut through his features.

All of these things she saw as she looked at him now. And as she stroked the black silk hair from his face, she wondered why things were different with him. Why did he give her a feeling of such lightness when they were together, of such happiness well beyond what her body felt and did.

The answer hovered at the edge of her understanding. It teased her conscious mind but did not cross over into awareness. Not until she leaned forward and dropped a kiss on his lips. Not until she caressed his beard-roughened cheek as he slept.

She loved him. She loved that he cared enough to want to make her forget her need for opium. She loved that he knew who she was, what she had done, and still seemed to worship her. His eyes followed her wherever she went, and she felt his presence even when she couldn't see him. He touched her with reverence. Even better, he kissed her with need—raw, elemental need. For her. And that thought alone left her weak with lust. And love.

No, no one else had ever wanted her like he did. No one else had ever truly cared about *her*. Certainly, no one else would brave her father's organization and kill for her. She bit her lip to keep it from quivering. She would *not* cry. And yet, the knowledge of what this man would do for her made her eyes water with gratitude.

She struggled with these unfamiliar emotions, trying to convince herself that simple gratitude was not love. It couldn't be. Unfortunately, what she felt wasn't simple thanks. She was in love with the Enforcer, and that thought terrified her as much as it warmed her.

She thought about telling him. She thought about kissing him awake to share her most amazing news, but she couldn't make herself do it. The feeling was too raw. What would she do if he laughed at her? What was she going to do when he put her on a boat and waved good-bye?

A temptation to stay in China burned inside her. She desperately wanted to believe it was possible, that she could live with Zhi-Gang forever. That they could make a home, have children, be in love. She wanted to grab him and tell him and to make it true by sheer force of will.

But she didn't. She turned away from the temptation. She rolled onto her side and closed her eyes. She had almost convinced herself she had dreamt the emotions, pretended to feelings that weren't real, when she felt his hand. She doubted he even opened his eyes. Certainly the rhythm of his breath hadn't changed. But she felt his fingers slipping beneath her elbow to slide around her ribcage. Within moments, he had tugged her tight to his belly, and they rested like two spoons, her back against his chest, his nose tucked into her shoulder.

She nearly said it then. She nearly whispered, "I love you," into the darkness. But she held the thought in, only to find worse words slip out instead.

"What was your nightmare, Zhi-Gang?"

He sighed. She could almost hear the thoughts inside his head: keep quiet, pretend to sleep, and eventually the question will go away. But he surprised her. He spoke in a gravelly whisper that shivered into her skin.

"I dreamed I left China. I thought I left it all behind to start new somewhere else."

She bit her lip, barely daring to probe further. But she couldn't stop herself. "That was a nightmare?"

He nodded against her back. "The worst kind."

"I don't understand."

He took a deep breath and then exhaled in a sigh. She

felt his heat brush down her spine. "Would you give it all up?" he asked. "Would you stop everything you are, throw away everything you've been just to start over?"

She nodded. "In a heartbeat."

He pressed his lips into the space between shoulder and neck. "That is why you are leaving China. And why I cannot leave with you."

"You won't change your mind? Even to visit England with me? Just for—"

"I cannot." His voice was heavy with regret. "Anna. This is my home, my country. I need to stay and fight for it."

She didn't respond. Instead, she closed her eyes and visualized her love and her hopes. She poured all her emotions, all her strength into that image—a shining light that she cradled in her two hands. She held it gently, feeling its warmth even as she added her need to confess all to him. Indeed, she even added his image into her imagination. He stood before her, watching what she held, standing tall and proud as the emotionless Enforcer.

Then, with a sudden and abrupt resolve, she smashed her hands together. She crushed it all flat. She felt it shatter in her hands, disintegrating into a thousand tiny shards. Then she threw it away.

From Anna Marie Thompson's journal:
June 8, 1886

I have my gold. It is a necklace of little links that Samuel gave me as pay. It is beautiful and I am wearing it right now. I have never had anything so wonderful, and yet I want to throw it into the Shanghai mud. But that would be stupid. I chose this life. I don't want to be a nun. I don't want to.

I didn't want to do what I did, either.

Samuel told me that the mandarin might want to cel-ebrate. He said that after we got the money—if the mandarin wanted to share—that we could share. And that's what happened.

The mandarin wanted to celebrate. He boiled the opium and gave me a taste. It was like always. It was wonderful. And the world was beautiful, and Halfy was shy, just like before. Except, Halfy wasn't shy, and he was very strong. And the mandarin celebrated in his own way inside me while Halfy held me down. And I cried because it hurt. It hurt so bad, but Halfy was nice and gave me more opium because it hurt.

Then it was Halfy's turn. And the money man's. Maybe more, I don't know. I couldn't fight so I took the pipe instead and let them do as they would.

I don't want to be a nun, so I'm selling the necklace and keeping the money in a bank. And I'll never, ever do a run with Halfy again.

No drug, not even alcohol, causes the fundamental
ills of society. If we're looking for the sources of our
troubles, we shouldn't test people for drugs, we
should test them for stupidity, ignorance, greed and
love of power.

—P. J. O'Rourke

CHAPTER FIFTEEN

Shanghai had its own peculiar shape and scent, and
though Zhi-Gang curled his lip at the smell, it wasn't the
yellow mud that turned his stomach; it was Madame
Ting's Garden of Perfumed Flowers. That and the way
Halfy fondled every girl in the place.

Apparently, Halfy now ran the whorehouse, after the
mysterious disappearance of Madame Ting. He was therefore the best source of information on the girls who
might or might not have been brought here ten years ago.
Unfortunately, Zhi-Gang didn't think he could talk with
the man much longer without killing him. Yet he
couldn't very well pass the task on to Anna, and Jing-Li
was back in Jangsu.

Which meant he had to sit in a tiny back room with
this bastard he'd almost killed, smelling the man's sour
sweat as it mixed with the nauseating scents of old tobacco, opium, and sex. Anna was with a few of the "flowers," to clean up and get a fresh set of clothes. He worried

that she wouldn't be safe, that she would run, that if he left her alone for five minutes, he would never see her again.

But the fear was illogical. Over the last few days, her desire for revenge against her adopted father had taken on a life of its own. It was all she talked about now, in whispers in their bed, in veiled comments about a horse named Betrayer, even in idle doodles she made with a stick in the dirt. She seemed to believe that once Samuel was dead, her life would suddenly return to a sweet perfection where all was rainbows and flowers.

But that wouldn't happen. She must know. Even if she really were that naive, he had pointed out the truth often enough. No death—even a righteous one—could restore innocence. But the moment he tried to suggest such a thing, she began spinning a tale of what would happen when she arrived in England. Of the parties her family would throw on her behalf, the gifts she would receive, even the suitors that would vie for her hand.

The stories always set his teeth on edge, but he had allowed her to pretend. Better she let her mind remain in a fictional life in England than the ugly reality of what they planned for her adopted father. And so they had continued into Shanghai, and now here they were at Halfy's brothel. Zhi-Gang sat in the tiny back office listening to the half-white bastard brag about his privileges with the girls while chewing greasy dumplings with an open mouth.

"Did you run this place ten years ago?" Zhi-Gang asked, trying to bring Halfy back to the discussion at hand.

"I been here since I was born," he said as the door opened and a young girl of about sixteen years brought in a tea tray filled with teacups and a bottle of American whiskey. "Samuel thought I had potential and trained me. Now I'm what he calls his right-hand man."

A lie if there ever was one, but Zhi-Gang liked it when idiots bragged. They always let something key slip. "What about the new girls? Do they come directly to you?"

"Yeah." The man grinned. He watched as the girl set out the cups and poured the whiskey. Her hands were steady, her expression blank. For a moment, Zhi-Gang wondered if there were a real person inside or not, then Halfy abruptly demonstrated there was: Just as she turned to leave, he snatched her around the waist and pulled her back, hauling her onto his lap. She squeaked in alarm and tried to struggle, but he cuffed her on the head and she abruptly quieted. He hadn't even hit her hard, but she settled immediately, her eyes going eerily blank. Even her half-shed, shimmering seemed to dry up.

"What are you doing?" Zhi-Gang growled. "I can't drink with a woman sitting there."

"Aw, she won't say nothing. See, that's what I been telling you. I help in training all the girls. Have since I started outweighing them."

Zhi-Gang winced. "I'm interested in learning about a particular girl," he began, but Halfy wasn't paying attention.

"They're all the same. Just cunts needing to be opened up." So saying, he hauled the girl's legs apart.

"You'll rip the dress," she murmured—a small protest from a beaten woman.

"We got lots of dresses," Halfy returned, but he jostled her enough to tug her skirt up all the way, exposing a shaved and rouged bottom.

"I don't need to see—"

"They do whatever I say after they're trained. And if they don't, we got beds with chains. Opium to make 'em agreeable, and lots of customers who want to help with the initiation." Then he visibly preened. "But I get to use 'em early. It's part of the training. Gotta get used to a white man's cock. They're bigger, you know." He grinned and shoved a thick finger inside the girl. "They usually scream with me."

Zhi-Gang showed more reaction than the girl. She simply stared at the far wall, her body completely still as Halfy spread her legs even wider. Acid churned in Zhi-Gang's gut. Even knowing that Halfy was too young to have initiated his sister, he couldn't stop imagining it. In his mind's eye, Halfy became the bastard who had touched his sister, who had raped dozens of young and very frightened girls, who continued to abuse them every chance he got. The need to end the persecution burned through his body making his hands clench.

"Stop it," Zhi-Gang growled. "I don't enjoy watching." And when Halfy ignored him, he abruptly leaned forward and hauled on the man's arm. "You are disgusting," he spat.

"You'd rather enjoy her yourself? She's available. I'll even discount her for you."

Zhi-Gang didn't bother commenting. He hauled the girl to her feet and tugged down her skirt. The girl's eyes fastened on him her expression was still blank, but there was an edge of surprise in her eyes.

"Go find Anna," he snapped. "The white woman I came here with. Tell her where you were born."

The girl just stared at him, uncomprehending. Zhi-Gang had to physically turn her around and shove her out. Then, slamming the flimsy wood door, he spun back to Halfy. "How will you contact this Samuel?" he demanded. "When can I meet him?"

Halfy shrugged. "He's a regular here. He'll hear that I'm back and come to see me. Probably tomorrow night."

"Really?" Zhi-Gang drawled. "You don't send a message? He just appears at your door?"

"Yes." His eyes got a nasty gleam. "I initiated Anna, too," he said, obviously relishing the memory. "She was smaller then—young and tight. I was young, too, but still big enough to make her scream. A lot."

Then Halfy leaned forward and grabbed the teacup filled with whiskey, throwing his head back as he drank. It was the last thing he did. Zhi-Gang slammed his knife straight into Halfy's heart.

Five minutes later, Anna burst through the door. Zhi-Gang was leafing through what passed for the house's accounts, looking for a mention of his sister. Mrs. Ting had been quite meticulous, and he found a wealth of information on the running of a brothel. It was only when Halfy took over that things had become sloppy.

Zhi-Gang was on his feet, knives at the ready before Anna was more than halfway through the door. She abruptly stopped, her eyes flickering over Halfy's corpse. "I can't leave you alone for five minutes, can I?"

He shrugged. "I couldn't stand the pig anymore." He glanced down. "I'll clean up later—though another towel would be useful." He'd already found a grease-stained rag and a bucket. Between the two, he'd handled most of the blood.

Anna made a sound of disgust, then stepped back outside. She returned a moment later with many thick towels and two thick-armed waiters. "You know what to do?" she asked the men. They nodded, though they stood frozen to the spot, their minds obviously churning.

Zhi-Gang looked up from the accounts. "Spread the word: I'm in charge now." Then he flicked his gaze to Halfy. "Do your duty, and you will be amply rewarded."

As he'd guessed, they were merely wondering how Halfy's death affected their jobs. With the promise of continued employment, they leaped to it. Halfy was removed in record time.

"And tell the girls that we're closed today," Zhi-Gang called before they left. "For everyone except special customers."

They grunted in acknowledgment and were gone, hauling the body between them.

Anna watched the waiters leave, her expression unreadable. Then she nodded as if satisfied. "They've done this before. They didn't even spill any blood."

Zhi-Gang exhaled, the tight band around his chest releasing with her casual disinterest. "Shanghai brothels are the best and worst in all of China." He looked at her face. "Now, you don't mind that I killed—"

"I thank you for it." She caught his gaze. "You cannot know how he has tortured these women."

But he did know. He saw it in his nightmares. He sighed and admitted, "It could make things more complicated."

"I don't think so. Who's the 'special customer' you're waiting for? Samuel?"

He nodded, but his attention was suddenly riveted on something else: his sister's name, written in neat calligraphy, and the date she'd arrived here. Other notations followed, each like an ice pick to his heart. Names with dollar amounts. No less than seventeen men had apparently bought his sister's "virginity." And then came a final notation, years later, with an exorbitant number beside it.

"What does this mean?" he asked no one in particular. "What does it mean?"

Anna peered over his shoulder. When he gave her more room, she ran her finger like water down the page. It flowed over the men's names, the money exchanges, ending on the last dollar amount and two more words.

"Little Pearl," she read aloud. Then she lifted her gaze to him. "I think she was sold to Little Pearl."

His mind reeled with fury even as his heartbeat accelerated. After all this time, he finally had proof that his sister was close. That her time of horror might nearly be done.

"Who is this Little Pearl?"

Anna straightened. "That's what I came to tell you. I've been talking to the girls here. They say there's a teacher, a woman named Little Pearl who instructs whores in expensive techniques. If anyone would know where your sister is, she would."

He pushed to his feet. "Then we must find Little Pearl."

"And after we find her, are you going to kill her, too?"

"Very likely," he growled. The madames were often worse than Halfy, allowing—even promoting—the most vicious and depraved acts.

She sighed. "Then let's wait until the boys get back from dumping Halfy. They can come with us as drivers. I'm too tired to carry a dead body through Shanghai."

Little Pearl lived in Chinese Shanghai at a Tigress temple, whatever that was. Anna didn't really care, except that she was a white woman who wasn't supposed to leave the foreign territories. But Zhi-Gang wouldn't leave her in the brothel, and so they used the brothel's carriage. With the right bribes, no soldier would look inside the dark, closed interior, so she ought to be safe. But just in case, Zhi-Gang joined her inside after giving a great many coins to the driver.

"It will take at least a half hour," he said as he settled beside her.

She nodded, then gasped as the vehicle lurched into motion. He looked at her in surprise.

"You've never been in a closed carriage before?"

"Only a couple of times. With Samuel, a long, long time ago." She shrugged. "The missions all had open carts."

Zhi-Gang nodded. "The missions didn't need to transport screaming girls or bags of opium."

True enough. Anna relaxed back against the overstuffed squabs only to feel her belly tense again. She wasn't sure why she was so nervous. It was still daylight. The afternoon sun poured in through the lacy curtains. She could see outside if she wanted; the interior was warmer than the cutting wind outside, and Zhi-Gang was here beside her.

She turned to him, seeing him fidget with his knives, shifting them back and forth between his hands. He replaced a blade in its holster only to abruptly whip it out again. She narrowed her eyes. The anxiety she felt wasn't hers. It came from him.

"Trying to work up your nerve to kill me?" she asked. She'd meant the question as a light tease, but a part of her still worried. He was, after all, still the Enforcer. He had once calmly said that he intended to kill her as soon as it was convenient.

"What?" He jumped slightly, then abruptly slammed his blades away. "No! No. I'm just thinking about . . ." His voice trailed off, but she had no problem guessing the direction of his thoughts.

"About your sister?"

He nodded, his expression dark.

She hesitated a moment, then decided to make him face the truth. "You know that she is likely dead, don't you? Or untraceable. That last notation was a long time ago." The words were cruel, but it would be better if he were prepared for the worst. "We were lucky to learn this much."

He nodded. He knew. He'd always known, she realized, and yet something drove him to find this girl. Perhaps it was just their family bond—a brother searching for a betrayed sister—but she sensed there was something else behind his actions. Something more personal to Zhi-Gang himself.

"Did you care deeply for her? Were you two very close when she was taken away?"

He shrugged, shaking his head. "I was a year older. I found her irritating in the way of all little girls." He sighed and pulled out a blade again. "She cried a lot because of her feet. They were bound and hurt her badly." His gaze lifted off his knife to stare at the darkened wall opposite. "She used to run so fast—faster than me, I think. Or at least that's what my brothers used to say. That even little Xiao-Mei was faster than I was."

"But not on bound feet."

He sighed. "No. Not on bound feet."

"Then, what happened?" She wanted to keep him talking. She sensed that this was a rare moment for him: a time when he was vulnerable enough to share some of

265

the darkness that ate his soul. She had to learn now, before they saw this Little Pearl, or he would tuck it away again.

"My parents sold her. The slaver showed up in the middle of the night. They dickered over her price and then sold her. She was more valuable because of her feet, you know. Customers like tiny feet, but only the wealthy aristocrats bind their girls."

"So your family were aristocrats, if poor ones. You needed the money for food?"

He shook his head, his voice growing darker and thicker. "She was hiding under the table. My brothers were asleep, but I heard the slaver come. I crept to our bedroom door and saw her watching from the upper hallway."

"She watched her parents sell her?" Anna shuddered.

"She screamed. She kicked. She did everything she could to run, but she was just a little girl with bound feet."

Anna sighed. She could feel the anger coiling inside Zhi-Gang, knew here was the source of his anger. "You became the Enforcer to stop this from happening—to stop the trade in girls and opium? That's a good ending, you know. You may have lost a sister, but there are many girls who will live long and happy lives because of you."

He rounded on her, and the blade of his knife flashed. He wasn't even holding it, but she saw it in her mind and recoiled. He gripped her shoulders—not painfully, but with all the ancient hurt in his heart.

"Yes!" he snapped. "I became Enforcer because of her. But not how you think."

"Then tell me," she shot back. "Tell what makes you kill anyone who traffics in girls or opium."

He pushed away from her, his motion shoving her back into the cushions as he turned away. "I became the Enforcer because I am good at killing. Because my first lover was addicted to opium, and I killed her supplier. That had nothing to do with my sister."

She said nothing, knowing he would continue in his own time, in his own way. But he said nothing, and in the end she leaned forward, stroking her arm across his back. "You cannot think I would revile you for whatever happened, Zhi-Gang. Whatever it is, I have done worse. I am worse."

He shook his head. "You took the only life you had available to you. I cannot damn you for being tricked by this Samuel, for doing his business when you had little choice between that or starvation."

She gasped. She had not told him all of that. She had not talked about the temptations Samuel had offered or the threats he used. It was only after years of thought that she'd realized he had likely engineered the theft that expelled her from the mission. He had created the situation that left her destitute but for his beneficence.

She pressed a grateful kiss into Zhi-Gang's strong shoulder. "So you can forgive me?" she whispered, her heart filled with awe. "What is so awful that you cannot forgive yourself?"

He shuddered. It was a violent motion, but she held on nonetheless. She would not let go of this man now. "Tell me," she pressed.

"It was my idea!" he bellowed. Then he rounded on her, his entire body clenched with fury. He unleashed it not at her, but at himself, beating his fists down upon his legs as he spoke. "I had a friend. His sisters had been sold, too. Suddenly, his two annoying sisters were gone and he had food and a bright green plot of land to till."

She nodded. "It was the way of things in Jiangsu until you stopped it. Just a few days ago, you ended that."

He shook his head. "Too late. Too late. Xiao-Mei was crying. She wanted to see what I was reading. She wanted to play with her doll but couldn't walk easily to it. She was always there, always wanting. And we barely had enough to feed ourselves. There was no way we could afford the kind of tutor I wanted." He lifted his head, and she saw tears wet his cheeks.

"You weren't in Peking then, were you?" she asked.

He shook his head. "We were in Huai'an, but Father knew I was smart. He said with the right schooling I could take the examination. I could become powerful. I could advise the Emperor and be everything he himself wanted to be but was too stupid to achieve."

"Your father sold your sister. Not you."

Zhi-Gang growled, the sound like a pestle grinding ice shards. "It was my idea! She was crying—again. I don't even remember why, but I told her to shut up. That if she didn't be quiet we'd sell her like my friend's sisters. I started talking about the new life we'd have from all the money we'd get. I didn't know my father was listening. I never thought he'd actually do it."

"You were a child. You didn't understand what you were saying."

His eyes burned fever-bright, his gaze cutting. "Didn't you hear me? I was smart! I knew exactly how it could be done; I just didn't think they would." Tears shimmered in his eyes. "I tried to help her that night. I ran to her, but was thrown aside. He was too big. There was nothing I could do to stop it. And then she was gone.

We sold her and used the money to move to Peking, to make friends with the right people and hire the right tutor. Before long, I was best friends with Jing-Li and had the run of the Forbidden City. I played with the Emperor's son and then we had everything we ever wanted."

Anna sighed. "They couldn't have paid that much for her, even if she did have bound feet. And you can't buy your accomplishments, no matter how much money you have. You worked hard. You studied hard. You—"

"It all began that day. Because of Xiao-Mei. Because she was sold into . . . into . . . ." He couldn't finish his sentence, but then again, he didn't need to. They both knew the short, brutal life of a whore. "I started training with knives as soon as I could. That's why I use these small ones. I was too young to wield a heavy sword and I wanted to carry them all the time. I was never going to get caught unaware like that again."

There was nothing for Anna to say, no way to ease Zhi-Gang's pain. His life had begun when his sister's had ended. Did that make what he'd done with his life wrong? No. But it didn't end the guilt. Nor did it ease little Xiao-Mei's suffering.

"I'm so sorry," Anna whispered as she wrapped her arms around him. "I am sorry for your sister, sorry your family faced such a choice, and sorry that you bear the burden of supporting a family based on such a horrible thing. It is terrible, Zhi-Gang, but it doesn't make you irredeemable."

He didn't speak for a long time. If he cried, she couldn't tell, his body was so still. He remained tight and contained in her embrace until finally his body softened. He wrapped his arms around her and held her as tightly as she gripped him.

"I just want to find her," he whispered. "If she is dead, I will take her bones to Peking. I will bury them beside my mother and put a jade carving of her name on the family altar though she is a woman."

Anna swallowed, tears blurring her vision. She had a good idea how revolted his entire family would be at such a thing. To revere a prostitute? To put a woman's name in carved jade on the altar? Such things were not done except by a man like Zhi-Gang. A man who lived by his own strict code of honor and forced others to admit to their crimes. A carved slab of jade was a small price to pay for what his parents had done. And if he shamed them before their peers, then so be it. They should be shamed.

"But what if she is alive?" Anna asked. "What will you do then?"

"I will buy her freedom no matter the cost. Then she will live in her rightful place in my father's home. He will have to come home every day and look into his daughter's face. He will have to live with the daily reminder of what he did."

Fair enough. Zhi-Gang obviously lived with it. "But what of her?"

"I will shower her in silks and jewels. She will be honored for her sacrifice, treated better than any hero of China. I will make her life as beautiful as possible. That will be my thanks for what she did for me."

Anna smiled and pressed her lips to his neck. His skin was warm where she touched, if dry as parchment. On it she wrote her respect, her awe, and her love of him. She did it in kisses, in whispered caresses, and swift, sharp nips designed to inflame his senses. She did all these things, and together they discovered another use for a closed carriage beyond carting opium and bartered girls.

And when he was pressed deep inside her, she whispered words into his ears. She did not say what was in her heart, she did not speak of the love she had crushed a few nights before; what she said was simple and elegant and made him pour his seed into her like a great river gushing forward all its power.

Three words, but she knew from experience how wonderful they were. "I forgive you," she said. And then she repeated it as often as he allowed her the breath and space to say it. "I forgive you. I forgive you. I forgive you."

They arrived at the Tigress compound. Anna adjusted her clothing while Zhi-Gang resettled his knives. Then they stepped out of the carriage and prepared themselves to meet—and likely kill—the woman who taught whores as her part in this unholy business.

Whatever Zhi-Gang expected when he stepped into the Tan Tigress compound, it was not a white ship captain named Jonas Storm. The name fit, for Jones was a huge bear of a man with curling dark hair and turbulent gray eyes. But he was quiet and unassuming in his own way— like a poised thundercloud—and he greeted Zhi-Gang and Anna with perfect Chinese and equally polished manners.

Zhi-Gang gave the false name of Lan, and then the white man showed them to a receiving room. Tea arrived moments later, and the captain cut straight to the heart of the matter.

"How may the Tan home assist you, sir?" he asked.

"We search for a woman named Little Pearl," Zhi-Gang replied.

Captain Storm nodded. "So I was given to understand. May I ask why?"

"I come on behalf of the governor of the province of

Jiangsu. I mean her no harm," Zhi-Gang lied. "But I wish to speak with her about a girl she may know."

The man's eyes narrowed, but not with animosity. "What is the girl's name?"

"Please," Zhi-Gang countered. "This is a matter best discussed with Little Pearl."

"And not a white man?" the captain challenged. "And yet you come with a white woman." His gaze cut to Anna, and he switched to English. "Are you well, ma'am? Do you need any assistance?"

It took a moment for Zhi-Gang to process the English words. Though he was well versed in the language, the Captain spoke with his own accent and in words likely designed to confuse one who was not a native speaker.

Anna, too, frowned a moment before she answered. "I am well," she said in stilted English. "My apology. It long time since I use English. We tried to speak in Mandarin at mission." She blushed and looked at her hands. "I should speak better. I will be going to England. I need learn English better."

Zhi-Gang turned, touching her hand so that she looked directly at him. "He wants to know if I am hurting you," he said in Chinese. "If you are afraid of me and need his protection."

Anna blushed prettily and shook her head. "Oh no," she gasped. "I am quite safe."

In truth, Zhi-Gang could not tell if she was playing the innocent for Captain Storm's benefit or if she truly was embarrassed. Either way, his heart burned even brighter for her. Either she was extraordinarily skilled at manipulating others to her benefit, or she truly didn't understand how a white man might think her in danger from a Chinese.

The captain stared at her hard, and she returned his

scrutiny with equal measure, even going so far as to arch an eyebrow when his study became obvious. The moment stretched on and on until the man slowly relaxed.

"He is looking for his sister. Tau Xiao-Mei," Anna explained. "Really, we mean no harm."

The captain's eyes flickered a moment in recognition, then his gaze steadied. Zhi-Gang saw the movement and nearly leapt from his seat to demand an answer, but Anna gripped his arm to hold him steady and Zhi-Gang settled on a barely controlled question.

"What do you know of my sister?"

The captain pushed to his feet. "If you wait here," he said. "I will get Little Pearl. Perhaps she can answer your questions." He shot them a wry grimace. "But it might take a moment. She's touchy about when she leaves her steamed *bao*."

Zhi-Gang nodded, though his belly was tightening with every moment that passed. He would find his sister. He would not let some cook or displaced white captain deter him. He would not—

"Try to relax," Anna said. Her hand covered his fist.

It was her touch more than her words that broke his fury. But then she continued speaking, and he found himself flowing into her words, the sharp bite of his mood smoothing out with her logic.

"We are here to gather information. She may or may not have it. And it's possible that Little Pearl has been *helping* the women she meets."

He slanted her a disbelieving look, but she squeezed his hands.

"It's possible. This place is not what it seems. What home in Chinese Shanghai is run by a white man? Give the woman a chance."

"She teaches whores, Anna." He shoved out of his seat to pace the room. "What does that mean? She shows them how to pickpocket their customers? How to cut opium and water down wine? Or maybe how to bilk secrets out of viceroys?"

Anna followed his movements with a steady gaze. "Would that matter?"

He spun, a sharp rebuke on his lips. But she raised her hand, stopping his words.

"What does it matter what she teaches, so long as it gives power to the powerless? Hope to the hopeless?" Anna stood, crossing to his side. "Do not condemn her until you understand."

"Wise words, white woman," came a voice from behind.

Both Zhi-Gang and Anna spun around to see a small woman with bound feet standing in the doorway. She wore a simple blue silk gown, rather commonplace in appearance but that hugged her young curves the way only a favorite garment could. Behind her stood the captain, one hand resting casually on the woman's shoulder, but his alert gaze showed him to be anything but relaxed.

Anna dipped her head in greeting. "Little Pearl, I assume?"

The woman didn't speak. Neither did Zhi-Gang. He stared at her, seeing in her face the exact image of his mother from years ago. From before they left Huai'an. From a time that never was, when his mother had been young and beautiful and unburdened by the sale of a daughter.

Little Pearl was his sister. She was Xiao-Mei.

Zhi-Gang stared at her, and she at him, while a lifetime of loss and hope thickened the air between them. In the end, it was Zhi-Gang who moved. It wasn't by conscious thought; his knees simply gave out. He dropped bit by bit, then furthered the movement by pressing his face to the dirty floor.

He could feel Anna's surprise as she tried to catch him. She thought he had fallen, but as he completed his kowtow, she relaxed her hands and stepped back. All the while, Zhi-Gang tried to speak, but his throat was frozen. No sound emerged though he tried. He tried with all his heart, but nothing came out.

In a moment, he would wonder how a girl sold into whoring could appear so beautiful nearly two decades later. In a while, he would have breath to ask the questions that crowded together on his numb tongue. But for now, all he could do was press his forehead to the dirt and pray she understood.

In the stunned silence, he finally heard her speak. Her voice was surprisingly mature given the youthful cast to her features. "Well, brother," she drawled. "This is a change. Me standing and you on your knees."

He looked up, his eyes moist, his mouth still frozen. In his mind's eye, he remembered every moment of when he lay crumpled against a table while he watched her dragged screaming from the house.

She stepped forward, her expression soft. "As you can see, I have learned how to walk on my tiny feet. I can fetch my own dolls, even manage a large household." She reached out and pulled a crease out of his ragged clothing. "All in all, I believe I have done better than you."

He blinked, confusion warring with guilt in his thoughts. And still no sound emerged from his mouth.

His sister rolled her eyes then folded her arms. The gesture was so reminiscent of his mother, Zhi-Gang nearly choked. "Oh, get up. It strains my back to talk leaning over like this."

How many times had his mother snapped at him in just that tone? Enough that he responded without thinking, lifting up to settle back on his heels, his jaw slack with shock. Beside him, Anna muffled a laugh. He even saw amusement flicker in the white captain's eyes.

"How?" he finally managed.

"Aie-yah," his sister responded. "You haven't changed at all. No understanding of culture. Get up, brother. Drink your tea and eat a dumpling. They are excellent, you know," she said with clear pride. "And I will tell you everything."

From Anna Marie Thompson's journal:
January 10, 1890

They sell girls. They trade young girls for opium. Samuel was smart to hide that from me. I would never have agreed—years ago—if I knew. I would have never begun running. Or maybe I would, but I won't run girls.

I told him I'd work for someone else. That I was the best runner he had, and that I could easily work for someone else.

He took out his knife to stab me, just like on my sixteenth birthday. But I saw it coming. Samuel's older now, and I was faster. I won't do runs with girls, I said. It's gold or jewelry or nothing. No girls.

Samuel agreed. He had to with his own knife as his throat. But he kept the bargain when I put the knife away, and he even gave me a gram for being so clever.

*He suggested we use his needle. "The best time ever."
But I already knew how to use a hypodermic, and I
don't trust him like I used to. So I said no. Said I didn't
celebrate with the customers anymore.*

*He smiled at me then. He's a twisted bastard, smiling
like that at me. He was proud of who I was. Proud of
what I've become. And I'm twisted too, because I liked
it. It was like he was Father again.*

*Then he opened his book—the one where he writes
the accounts. And by my name, he wrote something
new. He doubled my pay.*

*I found a room and celebrated with my own hypoder-
mic.*

And all who heard should see them there,
And all should cry, Beware! Beware!
His flashing eyes, his floating hair!
                    —*Samuel Taylor Coleridge*
            from "Kubla Khan: or, A Vision in a Dream. A
                                    Fragment"

CHAPTER SIXTEEN

Zhi-Gang stared at his sister in amazement as she served them tea. Her skin was pure and clear; her body young. And most strange, her eyes had an inner clarity that defied explanation. "You're so . . . so . . ." He didn't know how to phrase it.

Captain Jonas spoke up, his eyes crinkling at the corners as he smiled. "Beautiful. So very beautiful."

"Yes," answered Zhi-Gang; except, that wasn't what he meant at all. "Happy," he finally blurted. "You look happy."

Xiao-Mei—Little Pearl—set down the teapot with practiced ease. She kept her eyes lowered as she spoke, but he heard the ring of truth in her words. "I was angry at you for a very long time, brother. At you and all the family."

"You look like Mama," he said. "Only better. She was very sad after . . . after you left. She never recovered."

Little Pearl blinked then folded her hands quietly into her lap. "I want to know more," she whispered. "But not now. Not until I have adjusted to having my brother again."

"Xiao-Mei, it was because of you that . . . ," he began, but she shook her head.

"Please. Just listen." He froze in silence. "A few months ago, I would have fed you poison instead of tea. I would have thrown your body in the sewer and prepared a feast in celebration."

He glanced at his empty teacup. "And now?" he asked.

She laughed—a delightful cascade of notes that sounded so free. "Now you get green tea and my best dumplings," she said. "Because I am no longer angry."

He studied her face. She had lifted her gaze to his with an openness that stunned him. It was even echoed in her qi. "How?" he whispered. How could she not revile him for what they had done to her?

"The past is gone, brother. Neither you nor I can change it."

"But you must have been . . . You were sold into . . ." He couldn't give voice to what she must have suffered. Beside him, Anna gripped his hand with hers, lending her strength.

On the other side, Little Pearl also touched his hand, her caress as gentle as it was strange. "It was awful," she said. "And it is over. Nearly ten years ago, I came to the Tan household." She leaned forward. "Do you know what is taught here?"

He shook his head. He did not want to call it lessons in whoring. She must have read his thoughts, though. She must have seen his discomfort, because she smiled.

"It is not whoring, brother. It is a way to find peace in the mind and ecstasy in the body. Have you heard of ti-gresses? Do you know what a dragon is?"

He nodded, but the movement was slow. "In the For-bidden City, the concubines whisper of a strange practice to promote beauty and immortality through sex. The women are tigresses, the men are dragons. They touch each other and call it heaven."

"I have tigress sisters in Peking," Little Pearl acknowledged. "And it is a great deal more than simple touching."

He pushed to his feet, unable to comprehend that she could believe such foolishness. "Women's gossip and ignorance."

"Really?" challenged Little Pearl. "Look at me, brother. I have become an Immortal. Can you find any other explanation for my beauty? My youth." She leaned forward. "My *joy?*"

He had no answer for her. Beauty could be explained by handsome clothing, restorative creams—or so many women claimed. But the happiness in Xiao Mei's heart, the joy that pervaded everything she did and said—that could only come from . . . He shook his head. "It cannot be." And yet the more he looked at her, the more he wondered.

"It's true," Captain Jonas said. "I didn't believe it either, but she has changed so much. We both have."

Anna shifted uncomfortably. "From sex?"

"And love." Captain Jonas's gaze drifted back to Little Pearl and she smiled in return.

"Yes," she said. "And love." Then her gaze came back to Zhi-Gang. "I could teach you, brother. If you would just listen." When he had no response, she arched her finely sculpted brow at him. "Do you not wish for peace, brother? Do you not long for an answer to so many questions." She smiled. "That is what I remember most about you. You always had questions. All the time."

Longing burst through him, a need to grasp the happiness his sister had found. If a girl sold into prostitution could now be so happy, surely there was hope for him.

Perhaps there could be truth in her strange religion. But it seemed so . . .

Anna abruptly stood, her movements agitated as she turned for the door.

"Anna? Where are you going?"

"I . . . I . . . I thought I'd look around a bit. Let you . . . And Little Pearl . . ."

He frowned, trying to understand her thoughts. Meanwhile, Captain Jones smoothly pushed to his feet. "Perhaps you'd like a place to rest."

Anna nodded gratefully. "That would be lovely. Thank you."

The white man extended his arm to her and she took it: two whites in absolute accord, looking like a perfect couple. Zhi-Gang shot up from his seat, gruffly interposing himself between them. He took her hand and turned to his sister.

"What are you doing?" Zhi-Gang demanded.

"I apologize. I did not formally introduce you. Xiao-Mei, I would like you to meet my wife, Anna."

"No," whispered Anna, clutching Zhi-Gang's arm. "Do not lie to her. Do not begin again like that."

He shifted, his hand gripping hers. "It is no lie. The papers were official, the marriage binding. We are married."

"But—"

"And therefore," he continued. "I would like you to remain here. I wish you to share in this most joyous moment of reunion with my lost sister."

Little Pearl stood to look with narrowed eyes at the two of them. "White and Chinese wed? How can this be? You cannot tell me that the family approved."

Zhi-Gang actually rolled his eyes, the motion comical

enough to break the tension. "They do not know. But I have ceased worrying about what they know and do not know of my actions."

He swallowed, forcing himself to bare himself before his sister. "Because of your sacrifice, I have done very well. Our other brothers have adequate government appointments, our father spends his days drinking expensive tea and commenting on politics, and I work for the Dragon Throne to destroy opium. I came to Shanghai looking for you, to save you from the life we had forced on you. I thought to bring you home in honor, but . . ." His voice trailed away as he indicated her stunning home. It was more luxurious than anything his family owned.

His sister smiled. "My living is adequate as well." She grinned. "And I have no wish to leave Shanghai." Her smile shifted to the white captain who turned to Zhi-Gang.

"Little Pearl and I are married as well—"

"In secret!" Little Pearl shot out. "Tell no one!"

Captain Jonas nodded and wrapped a large arm around his wife's shoulders. "She fears retribution," he said, "but it is possible. We have been very happy."

Little Pearl frowned, pretending to struggle against his all-encompassing arm then settling tight against his side with a happy sigh.

Beside Zhi-Gang, Anna made a soft sound of distress. "Our marriage is a fiction," she whispered, her voice growing in strength. "We pretend to it so that we can destroy an opium king." Then she looked at the couple before her. "I wish you the best of success. But then, I believe you already have that." So saying, she pulled away from Zhi-Gang and headed to the front garden.

Little Pearl grabbed his arm and drew him back, her

words audible despite her low tone. "Stupid brother! Let her go."

"But . . . Anna!" he called just as she slipped out of the room.

Anna made it to the front garden, her progress made all the harder as her vision was washed with tears. Stupid, stupid, stupid, to cry now when all was within her grasp. With Zhi-Gang's help she would not only end the evil propagated by her adoptive father, but she would finally be able to leave for England and the glorious reunion with her family. Except, it was all a lie. Her family in England didn't want her. Zhi-Gang didn't want her.

"Watch out!" Captain Jonas's voice rang clearly, but it was too late. Anna stumbled on a broken tile and crumpled to the ground.

He was beside her in a moment, though not before she had scraped her hands in the stony dirt and ripped her skirt at the seam.

"Come, come," he said in a surprisingly fatherly tone. "There's a bench here. I've told them to replace that walkway, but the gardeners do what they want sometimes and don't listen to the white man." He guided her to the bench, then stood back, his hands shoved awkwardly in his pockets. "For all that money talks, this is still a foreign land. Little Pearl rules the roost, and I'm just the hairy ape who hangs around."

"Not to me," she murmured. She looked up, if not all the way to his face. She couldn't manage to meet his eyes just yet, so she stared at a spot over his right shoulder.

"I beg your pardon?"

She took a breath and put a little more volume in her

voice. "This isn't a foreign land to me. I was born here. I've known anyplace but China."

"I see."

"But Zhi-Gang's going to send me to England," she added in a rush. "I have family there."

"Oh. Good. Good." Jonas's voice trailed away, and an awkward silence descended. After a bit, he spoke up again. "I have a ship. Foundered for a while. A long while, actually, but she's in port now and being stocked as we speak. Fred's a good man and a good captain. He'll look after you, if you like."

She blinked, her gaze finally meeting his. "I don't understand."

He smiled warmly down at her. "I am offering a berth on *The Auspicious Wind* when it sails back to England in two days. Would you like it?"

She hesitated, her thoughts spinning. "I have money saved. I could start fresh in England." She looked at him. He seemed honest enough, but she didn't trust anyone anymore.

He smiled, as if sensing her thoughts. "I'll send a note to Fred. The ship leaves in two days. You can board anytime before then."

She didn't understand at first. Then her eyes widened. "*Now?* As in right now?" Without Zhi-Gang. She could escape. She could leave China. She could get everything she wanted right then.

She glanced back to the interior of the house. Zhi-Gang didn't need her to meet with her adopted father. She had absolute faith that the Enforcer would do his duty for China and destroy the man who had so used her for the past decade. She would have her revenge and could begin her new life all in one quick and very safe stroke of luck. All that was needed was for her to act now without hesitation. She could seize her future with both hands and never, ever look back. Could she do it? Yes!

She pushed to her feet.

Except, she didn't turn toward the front gate. Her feet turned, but her head twisted the other way. She was looking back. She was thinking of Zhi-Gang and of leaving him forever. She was thinking about Little Pearl and Captain Jonas. How could a girl prostitute end up happily with a white ship captain? She wanted to know; she wanted to believe such miracles did occur. How would she ever learn the story if she left?

She stood still, poised with indecision. What to do? And in that moment, the possibility was lost. Zhi-Gang came out of the house, his gaze trapping her in place as securely as steel chains.

"Anna, are you well? You left so quickly."

She swallowed and nodded, wondering how to explain. "Everything is happening so fast," she said honestly. "I just needed time to think."

He glanced behind him as Little Pearl stood in the doorway. "We need to go back to the Ting . . . home. The special customers could arrive at any moment."

"For whom do you search?" Little Pearl asked. "Governor, viceroy, or businessman? Madame Ting's Garden caters to the most exclusive customers and they must be handled with care."

Zhi-Gang turned, his face changing color. As if they were words on parchment, Anna could read exactly what emotions were flowing through his mind. He and his sister had been talking about their past history, their brothers and parents. He had almost forgotten that she had been forced to be a whore. Now she brought that under-standing back, and he had trouble accepting.

Anna stepped forward, speaking without any thought beyond giving him time to adjust. "We are looking to end a drug route into China. Samuel Fitzpatrick is the king-pin we—"

"A right bastard, he is," Captain Jonas muttered.

"That, too," Anna concurred. "But to kill a serpent—"

"You have to cut off its head," Zhi-Gang finished. His gaze focused on his sister. "What do you know of him?"

Little Pearl shook her head. "Nothing firsthand. It has been many years since I was slave to Madame Ting." Then she smiled. "But I know he likes variety: anything new or different. He enjoys all the new girls, tries any new device or perversion, even searches the world over for something unusual." Her gaze sharpened. "Tempt him with some-thing no one has ever done, and he will risk a great deal."

"His life?" Anna pushed. "Will he risk his life?"

Little Pearl shrugged. "Twenty years ago, certainly. Now? In middle age, a man thinks a great deal of his health."

Zhi-Gang nodded, his manner once again that of the Enforcer. "Then we will give him something else to think about."

Anna glanced at his face, wondering what he meant. But the moment slipped away before she could under-stand, and all too soon, Zhi-Gang took her hand in his to lead her out of the garden to the carriage.

"Come back soon, brother," Little Pearl called before they reached the gate.

Zhi-Gang turned, and his gaze caught and held his sis-ter's in a long, silent communication. Then he bowed in a deep show of respect. "It would be my greatest honor to visit with you again."

Anna watched from just behind him, feeling a moment of joy at the obvious accord between brother and sister. She knew just how important that was to Zhi-Gang. But then her sight caught on the captain's. She looked over Zhi-Gang's shoulder to see the white man frown in concern.

He opened his mouth to speak, but she shook her head, stopping his words. She already knew what he offered, and with her gaze she answered. Yes, she would take the berth he offered. In two days, she would board *The Auspicious Wind* and finally set sail for England. In two days. But not now.

"Until then," she said.

He nodded in understanding. And then there was no more communication at all as Zhi-Gang drew her out the gate. They climbed into the carriage in silence and rode out of Chinese Shanghai.

Finally, Anna could stand the quiet no more. "What is your plan?" She didn't know if she was speaking to the Enforcer or to Zhi-Gang, her lover. Either would be fine, so long as one answered.

In the gloom, she could barely make out his form as he turned to stare at her. "What were you speaking about with the white captain?"

She swallowed, strangely nervous. "Captain Jonas? Nothing. Why?"

A muscle in his cheek twitched. It was a small movement, only discernable because his face was turned at the right angle for the light. So she saw him twitch and knew that he suspected. But how to answer?

"You want honesty between us," she said, forcing herself to think before she spoke. But the words poured out despite her best intention. "You have reconciled with your sister. Does that change your plans?"

He reached out and abruptly pushed open the curtains

so that the afternoon sunlight poured into the carriage. Apparently he, too, wanted to see her more clearly. Then he turned, his expression tight. "Why would that change anything?"

She sighed. Why did men never understand that all things were related, one to another? "When you set out from Peking, your plan was to find your sister, yes?"

He nodded.

"And you have found her. She is well and happy and better than you could have hoped possible."

"Yes, yes," he said, irritation lacing his voice. "But what does that—"

"So you have accomplished your goal. Do you still intend to meet with Samuel?"

"We are in the carriage, are we not? We are heading to the brothel, are we not? My duty to China has not changed. The man who engineered this trade—opium for girls—that man must pay for his crimes."

She nodded, unsure why they were arguing, uncertain what to do to repair the breach between them. She didn't even know where it had appeared or how.

"What did Captain Jonas speak to you about?" he repeated, his voice harsh. With sunlight flooding the interior, she could now see his hardened expression—his clenched jaw and flared nostrils.

"I have searched for my sister for years. I studied every whore, every addict, hoping and fearing to find her. And now that I can finally speak to her, to redeem all that was lost between us . . ." His voice trailed away.

"What?" Anna demanded. "What went wrong?"

He looked at her, his eyes hard with anger. "You," he accused. "You left and I could think of nothing else. Only that you were not with me."

She stared at him, unsure what to think. He seemed so angry, and she did not know how to explain her feelings. "They are so happy together—your sister and her captain. I . . . it was hard . . . I couldn't . . ." She sighed. "They have everything I want, Zhi-Gang. I couldn't stay there and see it without wanting it, too."

"So you ran away."

She nodded. "It is what runners do."

"No more!" he snapped. "You do not run opium anymore."

"No, I don't. But I don't know what to do now, Zhi-Gang."

He pressed his lips together, saying nothing. And once again Anna felt her hopes die. If only he would try, if only he would ask her to stay, then she would do it. She would remain with him for as long as possible. But he didn't want her. And truthfully, she could not blame him. Who would want a drug addict as a wife? And for all his scoffing about doing as he willed before his family and Empress, she knew a white wife would destroy any political ambitions. No mandarin truly had a white wife.

"The white captain offered you a berth on his boat." Zhi-Gang's voice was a harsh rasp.

"Yes," she answered.

"I told him yes, that I would leave on his boat in two days—after all is resolved between us."

He frowned, his gaze leaping back to hers. "Resolved?"

She understood his confusion. She even shared it. It seemed as if nothing would ever be resolved between them. They had started too badly, there were too many lies between them. And yet, it did not prevent her from hoping for a solution.

"What do you want, Zhi-Gang? Do you ask me to stay

in China? For what? Do you ask me to give up my family in England? Why? What are you planning?"

He looked at her in silence, his expression unreadable, his heart and mind closed off from her. When he spoke, it was in a distant way, and yet she wondered if his words were closer to his heart than he intended. "I plan to be with you tonight. I plan to kill your adopted father when I next see him. And I plan . . ."

His voice faded, but she wouldn't let him stop. She needed to know, so she leaned forward and dared to touch his clenched fists where they rested on top of his thighs. "What, Zhi-Gang?"

"To send you to England." His gaze dropped to where they touched. "White people belong in their own country, and a woman belongs with her family. There is no other option." So saying, he removed his hands from beneath hers.

Samuel had not yet visited. Nor had he sent word to reserve a girl for his pleasure. According to Yi-Li, the most senior "flower" in the garden, it wasn't unusual for the man to miss a night or two. Apparently, Samuel liked to keep Halfy waiting. But Zhi-Gang wasn't predisposed to patience. Not when everything—all his hopes and his plans—depended on finishing things with the white bastard.

He paced the tiny confines of Halfy's office while both Anna and Yi-Li watched with dark, silent expressions. In the end, he settled on the simplest lure of all. He began a rumor.

"Whisper to the customers of a secret girl. A technique imported from the Peking Tigresses. Tell them about a new flower who will sell for a thousand yuen a night."

Yi-Li's eyes widened at the amount, even as her gaze

cut to Anna. But she knew better than to question. Instead, she bowed to them both before scurrying away.

Anna sighed. "He will know that you lie."

"It's not a lie," he said quietly. "Did I not tell you I was a darling of the Forbidden City? There is much that bored concubines will teach an enterprising young man."

He watched closely as Anna's gaze dropped away from his to look out of Halfy's office door. She had no interest in what was in the hallway; she was simply was trying to hide her thoughts. But that he could not allow.

He stepped up to her, cupping her chin with the gentlest of touches. She looked up at him easily, but it took longer for her eyes to lose their wary anxiety. And the fluttering pulse beneath his fingers never truly steadied.

"Do you know what a tigress is?"

She blinked. "A large cat?"

He smiled, startled the gesture came easily. "Yes. It is also a woman who has studied the way of the tigress. It is similar to Tantric Buddhism from India."

There was no understanding in her gaze, and so he continued, wishing he had the words to make her see. "You heard what my sister said. You know she teaches a way to reach Heaven through sexual congress."

Anna frowed. "You don't really believe her, do you?"

He shrugged. "It is taught in Peking and here. It is about energy, about stimulating a person's energy enough to talk with angels." He paused, weighing his next words. "You saw her beauty, her serenity. Do you not want that for yourself? Forgiveness, Anna. And peace." We hungered for it.

"But through sex?" He could see the disbelief in her eyes, and he shared her doubt. But he had been taught the techniques as an adolescent, and he understood the theory behind the practice.

Anna pulled away from his touch, but he pursued her, stroking his hand down her arm. "Samuel will visit tomorrow. We can end this all tomorrow. But in the meantime, I wish to try something with you." He took a deep breath. "My sister believes you whites have something special, something that makes the transition to Heaven easier. She knows of three couples—all Chinese with a white partner—who have made the ascent."

"You cannot think that this is true," she said, but in her eyes he read curiosity.

He sighed and let his hand fall away. "I have questions," he said. "I would like to talk to the angels. I would like answers."

She threw up her hands. "I would, too—but through sex? You cannot be serious."

"I know the techniques. It is supposedly about intention." He caught her gaze. "And the willingness to try."

"Why?" she pressed. "What do you want to know? What is so important—"

He cut off her words with his mouth. He was across the room and pressing his lips to hers before either of them realized. Once met, their mouths fused, mated, and set their hearts to beating in sync.

He slowly drew away, saying, "We are matched, Anna. You fire my blood more than any woman ever has. When I look at you, my breath quickens. When I touch you, my heart beats with the same tempo as yours. When we join, you and I—"

"We will not go to Heaven," she said.

"We have not tried."

Her gaze moved as she searched his face. "You have a reason for this," she said. "What is the purpose? What do you want?"

He shook his head, finding it difficult to verbalize what he hoped. "I want to ask the angels for a path. For my path." To see if *she* was his path.

Anna stared at him. "But you have always chosen your own path. You are the Enforcer. You were the darling of the Forbidden City. You have chosen all that you are."

He nodded, unable to deny it. And yet, he was also not proud of his choices. Perhaps it was time to choose something else, to allow the angels to guide him. His own choices had brought him little but blood and pain.

"Will you help me?" he asked.

She nodded without hesitation, though he could tell she did not believe.

"We have one night," he said. "Whatever can be done in that time—"

"We will do together," she finished for him.

He smiled, taking her hand in his and drawing her to his side. "I have had a chamber prepared for us."

From Anna Marie Thompson's journal:
September 21, 1895

I can't stop. I have tried and tried, but I can't quit taking opium. The dreams haunt my nights, and I spend all my money on it. I am so afraid that one day the pain will get too much and I will steal from Samuel. I can't. He will kill me.

But the dreams come, and they're so real. They're not dreams. Dead men whose blood gushes hot into the dirt. Living men in an opium stupor. And I know I'm one of them, with dead eyes but a beating heart. And then, worst of all—the memories I can't remember except when I re-live them in dreams. The times with men and unspeakable things. The things I allowed. The things I did . . .

I'm not even a whore, because I wasn't paid.
I want to die.
I want to stop.
I have to stop or I will die.
I have to stop.

Suppose there were people from another country who carried opium for sale to England and seduced your people into buying and smoking it; certainly you would deeply hate it and be bitterly aroused . . . Formerly the number of opium smugglers was small; but now the vice has spread far and wide, and the poison penetrated deeper.

—*Lin Zexu, high commissioner of Canton,*
in a letter to Queen Victoria, 1839

CHAPTER SEVENTEEN

Anna wasn't sure what to expect. Enlightenment through sex seemed to be a silly, heathen idea. But Zhi-Gang was the best educated, smartest man she'd ever met. And more important, he didn't have to lie to get her into bed. Why fall back on an elaborate religion just to sleep with her? Because he believed it? He couldn't possibly think that he could commune with angels just from bed play?

Apparently, he did. His manner was excruciatingly serious as he escorted her into the best bedchamber in the brothel. The house was closed for the night, which meant most of the prostitutes were gone or taking a much needed rest. That left the large building eerily quiet. Fortunately, the room they were in had been cleaned, the bedding changed, and the window open enough to let a soft breeze ripple through the faded silk tapestries.

Anna stood in the middle, next to the massive bed, and felt the most bizarre urge to giggle. She ruthlessly suppressed it, but that only made the feeling worse. Like a held-down a jack-in-the-box, her mirth twisted and bubbled inside her, refusing to be denied.

"Are you hungry? I could have them bring up dumplings."

His statement wasn't funny, but she lost control anyway. A snort burst out of her mouth. He looked at her in startled surprise. She pressed her lips together and shook her head.

"Um, no," she finally managed with all seriousness. "I'm not hungry."

He nodded, his expression unreadable. Then he stepped closer and put a hand on her shoulder. The touch was electric, sending a shiver down her spine, but it also released another giggle. She tried to swallow it, but it slipped into her nose where she both snorted and choked at the same time. All in all, it was not an attractive moment. And yet, when she looked up at him, she saw humor in his eyes.

"You are nervous," he said.

"I . . ." The word came out as a high-pitched trill.

"I understand." He reached out to touch her face, but stopped just short. "It is a frightening thing, this attempt to speak to angels."

"It's . . ." She stopped just short of saying it was ridiculous. He knew her opinion, and she had agreed to try. So she adjusted her thoughts and her words. "It's a different thing," she said. "And I am not one who leaps easily into things that are different."

He frowned. "You left an orphanage to follow your adopted father. You ran opium up and down China. You tried to escape on the Grand Canal carrying that opium. I have never met a woman more different than you!"

She laughed, the sound coming easily now. "Nevertheless, there is different and then . . ." she dropped her voice. "There is *different*."

This time, his hand did touch her cheek. "There is no reason to fear. I am with you."

She closed her eyes, turning her face into his caress. She felt each of his calloused fingers as it curved across her cheek and under her chin. Then she felt his thumb roll over her lips and realized she was still smiling. How odd, that she would do such a thing as smile with the Enforcer. But she did. He made her smile, and she wasn't even sure why.

"I am not afraid," she whispered. Her words echoed through her heart and mind with more meaning than she expected. He kept her safe. Whatever else she felt around him—*for* him—she wasn't afraid, and that made all the difference.

She darted her tongue out to taste the pad of his thumb. Her eyes were closed, so she couldn't see his response, but she felt his thumb against her mouth. Then he exerted a slow pressure. Her lower lip pushed down and his thumb slipped inside. Again she tongued it, rolling the tip along and around, feeling the changing textures, tasting the faint echo of Little Pearl's soy dumplings and special tea.

But the memory of Zhi-Gang's sister recalled other things to mind—most especially, what they were attempting. She drew back, opening her eyes to see him staring mesmerized at his thumb.

"That's probably not the way we're supposed to begin," she said.

He blinked and shook his head. "There are techniques and exercises." He shrugged. "But my sister tells me that intention and presence are what matter."

Anna shook her head. "I don't understand."

"I intend to stimulate your yin, mix it with my yang, and use the combination as a force to launch me to Heaven."

She stared at him. His words meant less than nothing to her. They didn't even appear to mean much to him. His tone was flat, his words spoken quietly. She lifted her hands in a confused gesture. "What do you want me to do?"

"Let me touch your breasts."

Until he spoke the words, she hadn't been very aware of her breasts. Now she abruptly felt every inch of her chest constricted beneath the tight silk. She felt their weight, their lift and lowering with every breath. And though her nipples hadn't swollen, there was a slight tingling beneath, as if in preparation for what he intended.

"I . . ." She swallowed. "Of course." She looked down at her silk top, then began fumbling with the buttons at her neck. He extended his hand to help, but she shook her head. "No," she murmured, strangely reluctant to let him do this. "No. I can do it."

He nodded, his hands falling to his side. She was aware of him watching her, following the awkward movement of her fingers and seeing the slow drop of fabric away from her body. The frog clasps began high at her collar, then cut across the top of her shoulder before dropping down her side. As she undid the buttons, the silk dropped open across one breast. She wore no undergarment. There hadn't been any available. So as she worked, a triangular view of the top of her breast appeared. That exposed skin grew larger and larger until her whole left breast was revealed to both their eyes.

She glanced up, embarrassment heating her cheeks.

This was supposed to be a religious experience, a serious seduction, no matter how bizarre it felt. Yet, here she was, bungling the most basic of tasks. Shouldn't she be moving erotically or doing something enticing? She didn't know how, didn't understand what to do, and so she looked at Zhi-Gang hoping for an answer while simultaneously fearing to see his disappointment.

He didn't meet her eyes. His gaze was fastened on her breast. She was still trying to undo the last button above her hip. One arm was lifted awkwardly while the other stretched across her to fumble at her waist. There was nothing beautiful in the position, and yet he still appeared fascinated.

"Why?" she whispered. "Why is that one breast so interesting?"

He took a moment to answer, but his gaze never left it. "Your skin is so fine it is nearly transparent. I see the veins and the blood. It is like a tiny net just beneath the skin."

She couldn't tell if he was repulsed or fascinated. His words seemed clinical, and yet as he watched her breast in the fading sunlight she heard awe in his tone.

"This is very strange," she murmured.

He flashed her a grin. "I have never really looked at a woman's breast before," he said. "Well, of course as a boy I was fascinated by them. Small ones, big ones, fleshy ones, tight ones—all were intensely amazing. But only because they made my cock hard and my thoughts run to sex. Your breast is . . ."

"Just a breast?"

He shook his head no, but said, "Yes, just a breast. But it is also a thin net of blood and flesh, the source of milk for a child, and the place just above your heart." He shook his head. "It is just a breast, but it is amazing."

She looked down at her body and frowned, seeing nothing unusual in her shape or form. But in her heart, she felt an odd tremble of joy. She loved that he found her body fascinating. She *was* amazing, and as much as her mind discounted it as silly, her heart was warmed by the compliment.

"Is this part of the tigress ritual?" she asked, succeeding in unfastening the last of the buttons. She pulled her blouse off, finally exposing her entire upper body. The cool air felt wonderful on her skin, and she wondered if he would find her right side equally fascinating.

"We use no ritual," he answered. "Simple intention."

"The intent to go to Heaven," she said.

"The intent to stimulate your yin," he responded.

She didn't comment. In her experience, she could *intend* a great many things. She intended to go to England and rejoin her family. She'd intended that for nearly two decades now, and she was still here in China. And even if she made it there, her family didn't want to know her. Life took a great deal more than simple intention.

"Sit down on the bed." He gestured toward the headboard, but then he hurried around her to arrange the pillows.

She watched him work with a slight frown. "You do not want me to lie down?"

He shot her a rueful smile. "If you are on your back, there will be no time for intention. I will spread your legs and penetrate you within moments, no matter what I plan."

She looked down at his pants and noticed for the first time the tented fabric. The cloth was stretched tight.

"You want me that much?"

He nodded. "Did you ever doubt that? I have wanted you from the first moment in the boat. Even before you teased me in your bath, I wanted you. Why else would you think I was watching?"

She smiled and ducked her head, incredibly pleased that he desired her so much. "Then why not dispense with all this tigress—"

"No," he interrupted, his voice gentle but very, very clear. "I wish to try it."

She didn't comment except to climb onto the bed and tuck her legs beneath her as her back pressed against the cushions. She was very aware of her breasts bobbing before him, especially as his gaze remained locked on her chest.

"Your legs should not be underneath you," he said, his gaze unwavering. "Stretch one out this way and press the other tight to your groin."

She moved as he indicated, one leg spread to the side, the other with the heel pushed against her most intimate place. But her skirt was too tight, the position too awkward.

"I need to take off my skirt."

He nodded. "Perhaps we should both undress."

They said the words, but neither of them moved. Instead, they stared at each other, and Anna felt awkwardness creep into the air. He must have felt it too, because he glanced down at his body, his face darkening with a dull flush.

"Yes," she suddenly said. "Yes, we should both be undressed." Then she fitted action to her words. She straightened up on her knees and rapidly untied her skirt. Bizarre or not, this was something he wanted to do and so she would not stop now.

She was out of her skirt in moments, kneeling completely naked on the bed. He too pulled off all his clothes and stood before her. The last of the evening light flowed across the chiseled contours of his proud body. She noted muscles, bones, even the raised bumps of scars, and she found herself thinking the same thing he had said about her breast: Amazing. Each muscle was perfection. The breadth of his shoulders, the narrowness of his waist—his body was honed by hours of practice with his knives. And yet he was a scholar, with long fingers well suited to wield a brush over parchment.

She saw no "netting of blood and flesh," but she saw a man of determination with the strength to effect his will upon the world. And as she watched, he knelt down on one knee before her as if laying down his very essence as a gift.

"What are you doing?" she whispered, mesmerized by the sight of his silky black queue slipping over his shoulder as he bowed his head.

He glanced up. "Removing my boots."

She nodded, laughing at her fanciful thoughts. He was no more laying his essence before her than she was devoting herself to him. They were simply two people about to engage in the most carnal of acts.

And yet, as she watched him work the laces on his boots, she struggled with scornful thoughts. Was that truly all she was doing? Was she simply engaging in a sexual act with him, appropriately set in a brothel? No. As much as she feared to admit the truth, she knew there was more between them than simple sex.

She loved this man. She had known it for awhile, had admitted it to herself some time ago. But tonight's act held much more significance. Tonight was about . . .

He stood before her, interrupting her thoughts as her eyes focused on his sex. It was full and proud, stretching toward her. In truth, she found it a rather strange-looking thing: the tip wet, the head smooth, the sides soft and veiny. Her gaze lifted past his flat abdomen, up the smooth expanse of his chest to his darkened chin and face. All of this was Zhi-Gang, tall and proud. The man she loved. The man she would leave behind with all of China.

She reached out and touched him. Too far away to stroke his chest, she caressed his narrow belly. His muscles rippled and his sex bobbed in reaction. She would do anything for this man. She would gave not only her body, but her spirit to him. And if he wanted to try to use her to talk with angels, she would gladly allow it. Because she loved him.

Also, because she was leaving him. Tonight was about their love, but it was also about saying good-bye. He had made it clear that there was no place in his heart or country for a white woman. So for the time that they had left together, she would give him all she had and hope that would be enough. If nothing else, it would be one last memory to sustain her on the long voyage to England. And during the rest of her life.

She lifted her gaze and smiled at him. "What should I do now?"

"Arrange your legs."

She did as he directed, extending her right leg to the side while tucking the left in tight. It was strange having her heel pressed there. Her muscles couldn't relax in the position, and she didn't like the feel of her foot, but if this was what he wanted, she would comply.

She was still trying to settle into position when she felt his hands on her breasts. He cupped her, lifting higher as he thumbed her nipples. He stood beside the bed, his gaze on her breasts as if he couldn't stop himself from touching her. Then he abruptly froze and frowned. "I'm supposed to make circles or something. I . . . I don't remember."

"Is it significant?" she asked.

He didn't answer, but his hands began caressing again. There was no pattern to his touch, no circles or other shapes, just a focused obsession in his gaze. She didn't know if it was his total attention to her or the erotic brush of his fingertips, but her body began to tingle.

She gasped, and her hands twitched. She wanted to touch him, to feel his body, to give him the same pleasure he gave to her. She reached forward, stroking her hand across his hip. He trembled beneath her touch, and when she looked into his eyes, the color seemed to darken and intensify.

He pulled away. "I am stimulating your yang and combining it with your yin," he intoned.

She hesitated, her hand hovering in the air. "I thought I had yin, and you had yang."

He blinked and cursed under his breath. His hands stopped moving to flatten over her chest. Then he began slow circles that made her belly shiver, even if it all felt rather strange.

"I stimulate your yin and combine it with my yang."

Unable to resist, she cupped his organ and slowly slid her hand upward. "Can't I stimulate your yang and combine it with my yin?"

"No!" he growled, and he moved his hips back out of her reach.

"Why not?"

"Because it's supposed to be done this way." He paused. "At least that's what my sister said. I think . . ." He sighed, and his hands abruptly dropped to his hips. "Am I being completely ridiculous?"

She arched an eyebrow at him. "Your sister swears this is how she did it?"

He nodded.

"Then we will too." She folded her hands in her lap. "What should I do next?"

He looked at her, his eyes unfathomably dark. A slow smile curled across his lips. "Look at me. Hold my gaze, no matter what I do. No matter what happens."

She blinked, suddenly nervous. "What do you intend?"

His smile expanded into a grin. "We have never had any trouble stimulating our energies. I think it is simply the connection we lack. And so we will look at one another; we will join visually and let our eyes be the energy bridge."

None of what he said made any sense, but she had made her choice. She met his gaze with her own, even as he reached behind her and adjusted the pillows.

"You can lie back now. Move your hips this way."

She did. She reclined on the pillows while he arranged her legs to dangle over the edge. Then he stood above her, the inside of her knees resting at the tops of his thighs. She wanted to open to him then; she wanted to grip his thighs while he plunged into her. She also wanted to change position and turn away.

It was their gazes, she realized. They had never before watched each other so closely. It felt as if he would see her every thought, her every emotion, and she his. Now she understood what he meant by an energy bridge. This connected gaze revealed more of herself than she'd thought possible, though she'd many times laid naked and open before him.

She stared at him, her emotions welling up inside. She wanted to say she loved him, wanted to give voice to her thoughts, but instead swallowed them. He could surely see her devotion, but she couldn't bring herself to say it aloud. Not yet.

He dipped his head. She was raised up enough that she could watch his eyes, and he tilted his head enough to keep the connection. Then he used his hands to shape her breast, to lift it to his mouth. He caught her nipple with his lips, swirled around it with his tongue, then sucked it wholly into his mouth. Sensation shivered through her body and she reflexively let her eyelids drop.

He released her to snap a command: "Watch me!"

Her eyes flew open and she met his gaze even as her breath shortened. She watched his eyes though her back began to arch, pushing her breasts deeper into his mouth. He used his other hand to pull and stroke her nipple, while below she began running her knees up and down the outsides of his thighs.

She did none of these things with conscious intention; her only thought was to watch his eyes, to tell him with her gaze what she felt, what she wanted. And somehow, it seemed like he understood. He let her nipple slide from his mouth and rose higher above her. His eyes were wide, his breath as shallow as her own. And he seemed to look so deeply into her.

"I'm drowning in you," he murmured. Then he released a short laugh, like a burst of air and emotion. "How can I speak with angels when all I see is you?"

She had no answer. She could only raise her legs to coil them about his hips. Without breaking eye contact, he grabbed her by the waist and slid her down to the edge of the bed. She was spread wide to him, her belly tightening in anticipation. But he did not penetrate her.

Instead, he took a moment to roll his thumbs over the

top of her thighs, pressing deep into the flesh where belly and leg met. Then he slid lower, to her most intimate flesh. He used his thumbs to open her, to curl above and around her most sensitive spot, and to dip into her wetness.

She gasped as he worked, and her body shivered in wonder. But she never lost the connection with his eyes. "Fill me," she whispered.

His thumbs dipped in again before sliding upward, gliding with heavy pressure to her favorite spot. Her eyelids began to droop, but she kept them open with an effort of will. This experience was about them together, not herself in ecstasy alone.

He filled her. She had seen his intention in the slight flare of his nostrils, felt it as he tightened his buttocks beneath her calves, so she had been prepared for his penetration—and yet, nothing was like she anticipated.

He filled her. Not only with his organ, but his whole soul. She felt his spirit in his gaze, his touch, even in his gasp of wonder. In his eyes she read desperation and hunger existing side by side with the same miracle she felt shiver through her.

It was different this way: watching each other, being present for every thought, every caress as a shared experience. And in that moment, she realized she had to bare all. She had to share with him the total of her heart, because she could not hide from him. In truth, she had no wish to hide. She was his and always would be.

"I love you," she whispered.

His fingers spasmed slightly where he clutched her hips, but that was nothing compared to the reaction in his eyes. She couldn't even define it, except to say that all of him expanded. His eyes widened and their dark color shimmered—likely just a flicker of the candlelight. And yet, she felt as if he grew out of himself to engulf the whole of her. He surrounded her, he infused her, he *became* her.

It was more potent than any drug, more wonderful than any simple contraction of muscle and body; his soul leapt out of his eyes to join her. She felt a rush of warmth, a total immersion in love, and then a wonderful soaring. She was a bird in flight—except the bird was them together, expanding over oceans and soaring through clouds into sunlight.

She was dimly aware of her inner muscles contracting, of his repeated thrusting, even his abrupt roar of power as he released his seed. She knew these things, and yet only as an echo of the more powerful dance of souls. They were merged together in glory. And in the expansive sky, she felt love—total and abundant love.

"Did it work?" Anna struggled to form words. Her body was completely satiated, her mind still floating, but she had to know if his experiment worked, even if she could only do so without opening her eyes. "Did you talk to the angels?"

He didn't answer. He had collapsed beside her, and she felt his body as a boneless mass half covering her, half motionless. She felt his furnacelike heat and the slow, nearly imperceptible movement of his chest as he breathed.

She raised her hand and blindly stroked her fingers across his back. She couldn't reach much of him, not without lifting more than just her hand, but it was enough just to touch him, to remember and adore him with her fingertips.

"Did it work?" she asked again, finally opening her eyes.

It was dark in the room, well into the deepest part of the night. She could see little of Zhi-Gang except a vague outline of his body, the shadowy gray reflection of his skin and the movement of his lashes as he blinked. He was awake, and they were once again locking gazes.

"Did you see an angel?"

He nodded, the movement felt more than seen.

"Really?" she whispered, stunned. Yet, was she truly surprised? The experience had been extraordinary for her as well. "Did you ask your question? Where is your path?"

She felt him inhale, a deep breath that shifted his entire body. His hips adjusted a little more to the side, then most of his legs followed, sliding to the mattress. She welcomed the lessening of weight on her body, but mourned the separation.

She raised her arm, tightening her hold to try and keep them together, but she hadn't the strength and in the end he was fully on the mattress. She adjusted herself to rest on her side and look directly at him.

"Zhi-Gang," she whispered. "What is your path?"

He smiled, the expression both tender and mocking. "You don't understand," he said, his voice raspy with exhaustion. He blinked, momentarily breaking their connection.

She squinted, wishing there was more light. "What—"

"I saw *you*. The whole time. Only you."

From Anna Marie Thompson's journal:
December 9, 1899

I saw him again. The Emperor's Enforcer. He's becoming very well known in the northern villages. I saw him kill. I saw him cut open Governor Wan without so much as a blink or a twitch in his expression. He killed the governor's eldest son too, because he was an addict.

311

JADE LEE

And he killed other men because they were too drugged to move out of the way. He walked into the house and killed them all.

I saw it. I was watching from the women's room where he didn't come. He could have, but he has a softness for crying women, and so we are alive.

He cut the men's throats. He called them indolent wastrels and said their wives were better off without them smoking away their money. He killed them, I think, because he knew they were all distributors—like the governor—or runners like me. He just didn't want to believe a woman could be part of such unholy commerce.

I could have laughed at that. Women have always been the lifeblood of this unholy commerce. Some by choice, some forced into the life.

I hate it. I hate it. I hate it!

I couldn't quit. I didn't have the strength. I had the hate, but not the strength.

But I can now, and for the silliest reasons. I saw him. I saw the Emperor's Enforcer cut out the heart of the governor. The threat wasn't in the man's hands—that's where everyone watched: the two deer-horn blades he wields—but that's not were the danger is.

It's in his eyes. It's the darkness in his eyes.

I can't escape them. Every time I reach for opium or the pipe or the flame—anytime I even think of it—I remember his eyes.

He is the angel of death to any who deal opium. As long as I remember his eyes, I can quit.

It's already been a week and I haven't touched a drop. My hands shake, my belly twists and burns, but I haven't touched it. And I won't ever again.

Because of the Enforcer's eyes.

Weave a circle round him thrice,
And close your eyes with holy dread,
For he on honey-dew hath fed,
And drunk the milk of Paradise.
                              —*Samuel Taylor Coleridge*
                    from "Kubla Khan: or, A Vision in a Dream. A
                                                      Fragment"

CHAPTER EIGHTEEN

"So, this is my new son-in-law."

Zhi-Gang bolted upright in bed. Beneath him Anna gasped as well, the sound ending on a shortened squeal of alarm.

Where were his knives?

He blinked even as he kicked a leg out of bed. Then he froze, his vision clearing into a fuzzy and unfortunate tableau. It was morning. He and Anna were naked. And standing around the bed were, in order, a large Chinese man holding both of Zhi-Gang's deer-horn knives, a middle-aged white man with a long salt-and-pepper moustache, and a wiry Chinese man holding a pistol in lax hands. How had he not heard them enter? And where were his glasses?

Zhi-Gang sized up the nearest man, who smiled and taunted him with his own knives. The bastard was pretending not to know how to hold or manage the blades, but his fingers betrayed him. Though his grip was off center, his fingertips were settled in just the right way to quickly readjust. Zhi-Gang suppressed a grimace of frustration. The man knew how to wield the knives and would not be disarmed easily.

"So, what number wife are you, Anna?" the white man drawled. "Six? Seven?"

In his peripheral vision, he saw Anna lift her chin. "I am his only woman," she said. Zhi-Gang winced. That wasn't exactly true, but he didn't have time to explain. Meanwhile, her adopted father—Samuel—barked a mocking laugh.

"I doubt that, daughter. I most sincerely doubt that."

Zhi-Gang pushed up, ignoring his nakedness. Though he was tall for a Chinese, he only matched the white man's height, and he was clearly shorter than the man with his knives. "You will leave our bedchamber," he said with the arrogance he'd learned from the Emperor himself. Then he grabbed a corner of the blanket and threw it over Anna. She wrapped it tightly around her torso, covering herself but leaving her arms free.

Odd, how the sight warmed him. When other women might be screaming in hysterics, his wife did not act the fool. She was already shifting her legs beneath her, readying herself to fight. Except, there would be no fight. Zhi-Gang stepped forward to eye the white man. He was now close enough to focus. Now he could see signs of age: wrinkles around the mouth, a slight stoop to the shoulders. That was something.

"You will wait outside while we dress," Zhi-Gang ordered. "Call for tea and dumplings."

Samuel leaned back on his heels and crossed his arms over his massive chest. "I assure you, my daughter is well used to men in her bedchamber."

"That's not true!" Anna cried, though her cheeks flushed with shame.

Zhi-Gang waved his hand in dismissal. "I care not for the past," he said. "What concerns me is the present. And the future." His voice dropped to a lower register. "Leave now, or I will take my business elsewhere despite my wife's urging."

Samuel's lips curved in a sneer. "Or I could kill you for killing Halfy."

"Halfy was—," Anna began, but Zhi-Gang cut her off.

"The idiot touched my wife," he said, real fury darkening his tone. "And if you cared for his life, I would already be dead." He folded his arms, echoing Samuel's posture. "Leave now or never see your daughter—and my business—again."

Samuel's eyes darted around before finally coming to rest on Anna's face. "This is not new business. I already control Jiangsu province."

"Bai is dead!" Anna snapped. "Killed because of gambling debts." She jerked her head at Zhi-Gang. "*He* is the new governor. You must negotiate a new deal with him."

Samuel took an angry step forward. "You dare challenge me? After disappearing with an entire shipment?"

Anna swallowed and nodded, clearly anxious. "I had to run. The Enforcer was coming."

Samuel cursed and spit onto the floor.

"But I would never return to you empty handed," she continued. "You know that." Her voice dropped to an almost inaudible whisper. "*I* know that."

Samuel pursed his lips. "A husband with a new province. Hmph. We shall see." His gaze flicked back to Zhi-Gang. "I'll be in the office. Don't make me wait." Then, with a clenching of his thick jaw, he turned and walked out. His men followed, the one with the knives leaving last.

Zhi-Gang waited until the door shut behind them before turning to his wife. "Are you all right?"

She nodded, already reaching for her clothing. "You?"

"I don't know how I didn't hear them." He said the words, but he did know. Last night's experience had been so overwhelming, so exhausting, he had lost all sense of the world. All that seemed real to him was her. Even now, with the threat of the men gone from their room, his eyes traveled to her body as she pulled on her skirt. His gaze followed the curve of her hip and the bounce of her breasts while his memory recalled her scent, her taste, her joy.

Their joy.

Their *love*.

He sat down on the bed, covering his shock by pulling on his trousers. Had he truly fallen in love with a white woman? An opium runner and the adopted daughter of one of the worst of her kind? It was insane. And yet, was it a surprise?

"Are you all right?" Anna asked, her voice slipping into his thoughts as easily as every other aspect of her had infiltrated his body and mind.

He nodded, pulling on his boots without comment. He had to focus on the situation at hand. He was the Emperor's Enforcer, which needed his attention. Both their lives depended on it.

And yet, his mind was still soft with the memories of last night. Never had he thought he would live a Chinese love story, one of doomed lovers and tragic death. He had worked hard, his whole family had sacrificed everything—including his sister—so that he would gain the status and power he now enjoyed. He had his choice of brides. Why ever would he pick a white drug-runner?

He wrapped his tunic about him, leaving it just tight

enough to keep him warm but loose enough to allow him to fight. He could not allow Samuel to continue to ply his hideous trade. He would do better to establish an agreement with Samuel, then return later with a battalion of men. That would be safer for him. Safer for Anna. But would be get a better opportunity?

"Almost done," she said as she offered him his glasses.

He frowned as he looked at her. She was fully dressed. Even her hair was pinned up out of her way. At his confused expression, she smiled and continued. "You are almost done with me," she said softly. "We need only finish with this, then all will be over. We can both move on."

She meant she could board Captain Jonas's boat and head for her family in England. Which was as it should be. He nodded, though the motion felt as though it tore his chest open. The pain was almost unbearable.

"It would be safer to delay," he said, slipping on his glasses. Anna abruptly became that much more beautiful. "We are vulnerable this way."

She stared at him, her expression unreadable. Then she slowly stepped up to him. He spread his arms, welcoming her into his embrace without hesitation. And just that easily, his heart sealed, the pain faded. He pressed his face into her hair, closing his eyes as he gripped her tightly. She lifted her face, and he drew back, thinking she meant to kiss him. But before their mouths met, she whispered into his ear.

"You cannot maintain this fiction long. Someone will recognize you and you will never get close to Samuel again. We must end it now."

He swallowed, feeling a surge of anger that she could think so clearly. This was his job, and yet she was the one who focused on the task, who spoke logically while he was still trapped in the mists of last night's wonder. Was she truly as unmoved as she appeared? Or . . .

He drew back, searching her eyes. "Last night you said you loved me."

He saw a momentary panic swirl through her eyes before her gaze steadied. She did not hide from him, merely met his eyes with an open sorrow. "I did," she finally whispered. "I do." Then she glanced toward the door. "He will not wait much longer."

Zhi-Gang nodded, knowing she was acting exactly as she ought: putting away the past to concentrate on the present. And how easy it seemed for her. He ought to be following her example, and yet his belly churned with doubt. Had he misjudged everything? Did she truly love him? And did that matter?

"I have other wives," he said, stunned that he would speak of it now. "Some dead, another a political alliance. They mean nothing to me, but I *am* marrie—"

She pressed her fingers to his lips, stopping his words. "I don't care." She closed her eyes and dropped her forehead against his. "It's the truth: I love you the same whether you have no wives or a million."

"Only one," he whispered. "Only you."

He would have kissed her then. He would have tried to express what was in his heart, but he didn't have time. Only one thing was clear: nothing could be decided by hiding in this room. To move forward, he had to deal with Samuel. He had to be the Enforcer. As soon as that was done . . .

She would leave for England and it would be done for good.

He nodded, taking one last moment to breathe in her

scent. "So be it," he finally intoned. Then he set her away from him and turned to face one of China's darkest enemies.

The office smelled something like burnt tea. It took a moment for Anna to recognize the scent, but then she closed her eyes in memory. Her real father had loved Turkish café. That Samuel enjoyed the same brew was one of the ties that had bound her to him in the first place.

Beside her, Zhi-Gang frowned as he sniffed the air, and so she explained. He would not likely know the smell.

"Turkish café," she said, her eyes sliding from Zhi-Gang to the men framing the doorway just inside the office. The pistol and the deer-horn knives were out, but not aimed. They were there as warning, and Anna's back prickled with awareness as she and Zhi-Gang stepped into the room. Samuel sat at Halfy's desk, his eyes half lidded as he sipped from a cup.

"Welcome, daughter." He set his cup down and eyed Zhi-Gang. "Welcome, Mandarin."

Zhi-Gang nodded briefly, his gaze canting to the thugs. "Are they truly necessary?"

"Yes." Samuel flicked his gaze to Anna. "Do I not deserve a kiss from my daughter?"

Anna felt her face flush. "Of course," she said, ducking around the desk. But as she moved, she wondered at her actions. This man was not her father. This man had used her affection for his own ends. This man . . .

Had given her exactly what she'd asked for, and a great deal more. She wanted him dead for what he'd done to her, for what he was doing to China. And yet, she still felt a tie between them. He was, after all, her last link to her real father.

All these thoughts spun through her mind as she bent over to place a kiss on his cheek. He lifted his face, and she smelled the familiar scents: tobacco, perfume, opium. He rarely used himself, but he was always prepared to offer. He even carried a needle for his favorite customers.

She eyed his clothing, guessing that the wooden box would be in his left jacket pocket. She straightened, knowing he watched her closely. Was there any affection, as she'd once believed? Or suspicion? What did he feel for her?

"So, this is your new husband," he drawled. "Tell me how that came about."

"Oh, yes, well," Anna began breathlessly, slipping easily into the fairy tale. "I was running, you know, from the Enforcer . . ." The words flowed sweetly from her lips. In truth she had retold the story to herself a dozen times since that night she'd fabricated it for the governor's widows. It had become magical for her, a talisman, this idea that she and Zhi-Gang were desperately in love and could never be parted.

"You made it alone all the way to the Grand Canal?" Samuel asked, clearly skeptical.

She stiffened. Of all the things to doubt, he chose that? "I can be quite resourceful when I need to."

"That, I believe," Samuel said.

Zhi-Gang stepped forward, his irritation a palpable force in the room. "Women's tales are for the women's room. Wife, you will stand by my side now."

Anna blinked, startled by his tone. Gone was last night's lover. Back indeed was the Enforcer. She moved immediately to obey, but was stopped by her father's hand on her wrist. Samuel held her tight to his side, and no matter how hard she twisted her wrist, she could not escape.

"Father," she admonished softly, "I am married now. My place is at his side."

"He is a Chinaman," Samuel retorted. "And perhaps I do not recognize any wedding not performed in a Christian manner." He smiled up at her. "Stay here. Convince me of this marriage."

Anna blinked, thrown. How many times had he looked at her in just that way, his heart in his eyes, love pouring off him in waves? She knew it must be a lie. He could not have true feelings for her and still push her into the dangerous life of a runner. And yet, his love felt real.

Or it would have, if she had not known Zhi-Gang's attention, Zhi-Gang's love. Samuel was a liar and a manipulator. So she smiled sweetly—stupidly—down at her adopted father, and her heart remained with Zhi-Gang.

"Acknowledged or not," she said, "Zhi-Gang and I are—"

"He does not care," Zhi-Gang interrupted. "He cares only about the truth of the business you bring." He looked hard at Anna. "He thinks I have fooled you."

"To what end?" Anna asked, lost.

"To the end that all runners are disposable," answered Zhi-Gang. "I only needed you to meet with him. Now it is time for you to leave while I make arrangements with your father."

Anna narrowed her eyes, trying to read Zhi-Gang's expression. Was it true? Could he truly have used her just to meet with Samuel? Of course not. They had shared so much more. He intended to get her out of the way so he could kill Samuel without danger to her. She knew that. Her heart even warmed at the thought. But she could not be dismissed. Not yet. She had to see this through to the end.

Zhi-Gang continued, his voice as curt and cold as any of Samuel's mercenaries. The Chinese were never this openly derisive. Politeness was practically a religion, and yet Zhi-Gang's emotion seemed to darken the entire room.

"You want girls," he said. "I want opium. As the new governor of Jiangsu, I can supply you with what you need. You must prove that you can get me opium."

Samuel arched a bushy eyebrow. "You doubt that a *white man* can supply opium?"

"He doubts everything," Anna said with a shrug, using the movement to try to dislodge her father's grip. It didn't work. His fingers were strong, and he kept her tight at his side. So she turned to Zhi-Gang, staying with the pretend game of negotiation. "He has it," she said firmly.

Samuel spoke to Anna. "Does he have the girls? Young pretty ones?"

Anna wrinkled her nose. "It's a poor province. But as long as the peasants keep having babies, they'll keep selling the girls. That's how it works in China."

Samuel sneered, curling his lip as he took a sip of café. "Heathens."

"And yet you profit from it," Zhi-Gang growled from across the table.

Anna twisted to glare at him. What was he doing? He could not kill Samuel from across the desk, and he would never cross it without some show of congeniality.

"What else would these girls do?" Samuel sighed and shook his head. "How many starve to death or spread their legs as eighth concubine to some old man? At least this way they're getting paid for their work." Samuel pinned Zhi-Gang with a hard gaze. "And you get your opium."

Zhi-Gang didn't answer. He was, after all, pretending to be a buyer. But Anna could feel the anger that radiated out of him. Luckily, no change appeared on his face. In the end, he simply nodded, as if acknowledging Samuel's point. Then he stared pointedly at where Samuel still gripped Anna's arm.

"Release my wife," he ordered. "She has no place here."

"Oh, but she does," Samuel drawled. "She is my best runner. Or she was until she started tasting the product." He leaned back in his seat as he eyed her. "Is that why you married him? Because you knew I wouldn't give you any more? Not after you left the real buyer high and dry—"

"He was dead, father," Anna snapped. "Sliced open like a side of beef right before my eyes."

"Who was the buyer?" Zhi-Gang asked, his voice casual.

"Governor Wan," Anna answered softly. She remembered the night all too well, despite the opium haze. And sometimes when she looked at Zhi-Gang—moments like now, when his eyes were hard, his lips set in an angry grimace—she feared who he was and what he could do.

Zhi-Gang simply shrugged. "An idiot with even more idiotic wives." He shook his head. "A man can be forgiven for marrying a stupid woman, but only if he keeps her out of public view, away from ears that report to the Enforcer."

Samuel turned. "Is that what happened with Wan?"

Yes, realized Anna.

"I have no idea," answered Zhi-Gang. "But if *I* knew he and his friends ate opium—lots of opium—then how hard could it be for the Enforcer to know?"

Samuel slowly reached for his teacup, his eyes narrowed. "And you would avoid this fate?"

Zhi-Gang released a sharp bark of laughter. "I have not married an idiot."

The white man's eyebrows shot up in surprise. "Really?" he drawled. "She takes opium. Loves it. Craves it. Isn't that right, Anna?"

Anna had been momentarily lost in her memories of Governor Wan's death. She had been thinking of her husband and wondering when he would finally act, finally be done with this game and kill Samuel. But at her father's words, she felt her face heat with shame. "You gave me my first taste!" she cried.

"How much did you eat?" her father replied. "How much even of what was meant for Wan ended up in your stomach?"

"None," she whispered. "None at all." It was the truth, but she could see by Samuel's smirk that he didn't believe her. She looked to Zhi-Gang. *He* believed her. She could see it in the gentling of his mouth, the twist of his lips, and most especially in the fathomless darkness of his eyes. He saw she had given up the drug, that she had continued to resist despite the cravings that plagued her. He believed in her, and in his eyes she found the strength to play her role.

"Maybe just a little," she said with a cringe.

Samuel barked with laughter. "See!" he bellowed. "See what you have married."

"I'm careful!" Anna cried. "I only celebrate with the customer. Just like you taught me!" She dropped her voice. "I'm not an addict," she lied, knowing in her heart the magnitude of the lie. She was an opium addict, she would always crave the sweet heaven that it offered. But more than even that wonderful oblivion, she respected Zhi-Gang. His touch, his caress, his love—all were a hundred times more fulfilling.

She glanced at her lover, wanting him to see the truth in her eyes. She needed him to know that she wasn't lying, that she wasn't the fool her father suggested. But when she looked up, he wasn't there; He had crossed to her side. He enfolded her in his arms and dropped his face to her hair, He simply held her; and she closed her eyes, feeling his warmth, his acceptance, and his love.

In the background, she heard the guards shift in worry. But Samuel released her hand—probably to defend himself in case of a problem—and nothing happened except a husband hugging his wife. All the room settled into silence.

Anna lifted her gaze to meet Zhi-Gang's. "I'm sorry," she whispered, staying with the role she had adopted. "I don't long for it like I did before—"

"I know," he answered, and by the look in his eyes, she knew he did know—both the truth and the lie of what she said. "Now, go to the room while I finish with your father."

She knew what he meant. He was on the near side of the desk now. He would kill Samuel when she was out of the way. So she nodded, acquiescing. It was time she allowed him to do his job. She bowed her head in acceptance, but before she left she turned one last time to her pretend father.

"All I wanted was a father who loved me. You turned me into an addict for your own ends."

Samuel shook his head, his sneer all the uglier for the

way it tilted his moustache. "Do not blame me, little girl. You've been running from the day I met you—from the orphanage, from Shanghai, from wherever you are to something else." He looked at Zhi-Gang, his expression clearly indicating the marriage was just another of her way stops. "I just gave you a direction, that's all."

Shock hit Anna. At first it was a simple recoil in her gut even as her head began to shake, denying his words. But nothing she said or did could change the truth of his statement.

Her gaze leapt to Zhi-Gang, looking for strength and comfort. "It's not true," she said. "He created the situation. He manipulated . . ."

Zhi-Gang frowned, but not in the way of a man who believed her, who was outraged on her behalf. He was confused by her denial. "I have always known you are a runner," he said.

It was the simple, bald truth.

Her breath shuddered in her chest. She *was* a runner. She had always run—from her nurse, from the orphanage, from Shanghai, and over from her entire life, every time she ate opium. Her hands clenched at her sides, and she shuddered from the stark reality.

"It doesn't matter," Zhi-Gang said softly. "Go upstairs. I will follow soon."

She looked at him, and the truth hit her even harder. Her lover was offering her exactly what she most wanted: another escape. She would run while Zhi-Gang avenged her. Then she would run to England. She might as well light up a pipe.

"No," she murmured, anger stiffening her spine. It was time she stopped running away. It was time she finished something.

Where she found such strength of character was beyond her. A scant few weeks ago, such thoughts would have sent her scurrying for her opium pipe. But now, looking at the breadth of Zhi-Gang's shoulders, the dark slashes of his eyebrows, and the kind understanding in his eyes, she knew she couldn't release her burden onto him. He was more than willing to take it, but she knew the darkness in his soul. She knew the pain he suffered for decisions he had made as a boy, and as the Emperor's Enforcer. She knew, and she would not add to his burden. She would not be another soul for him to carry. It was time she took responsibility for her own life, her own decisions.

She straightened, squaring her shoulders though her heart beat in her throat. "You know, this business always made my head ache," she lied. "The truth is, you will both end up at the same place no matter how much you dicker." She stepped easily into the role of bargainer. She knew better than anyone the terms Samuel would accept.

"Three girls a month," she suggested to Zhi-Gang. "Agreed?"

Zhi-Gang nodded. It was a curt dip of his chin, and in his eyes she read fear for her safety. He did not want her in the middle of the coming fight.

She smiled in reassurance at him. For the first time in her life, she was going to fight for herself rather than run. The thought was terrifying, but it was also heartening. She might die in the next few moments, but she would at least die after having been fully alive.

She turned to her adopted father. "Where do the girls go? Which brothels?"

"He can bring them—"

"No," she interrupted. "Which brothels, Father? Write

down the names. I will ensure that the girls get where they need to be."

Her father narrowed his eyes at her. "Since when do you want to run girls?"

Anna let her gaze drop to the floor. "I have come to accept the world as it is. And I wish to please my new husband."

Samuel released a sharp bark of laughter. "You mean you are not so high and mighty about running girls when your opium supply is at stake."

She looked up with pretend insult. "I will take better care of them than Halfy! I will see that their life is tolerable, that all profit from their sacrifice." She could see that he didn't completely believe her, so she pushed on as quickly as possible.

"Halfy's gone, Father. We can make this a partnership, and you keep your profits. Who else knows your ways, who can run the brothels? Who else do you trust to oversee them?" She wrinkled her nose in disgust. "And I won't sample *this* merchandise."

Her father frowned. Zhi-Gang did, too. He didn't understand what she intended. But that didn't matter; he would understand as soon as she handed him the list of all her father's brothels. He would then know the names of all the hellholes that tortured girls, drugging them into prostitution. And he—the Enforcer—could decide what to do so that no one else suffered like his sister had.

Meanwhile, Samuel was obviously thinking hard. "I thought you were a married woman now. That you had no interest—"

She sighed loudly. "Enough, father. My husband understands that I have no wish to spend all my time in backwater Jiangsu. And we both want the money that can be made in Shanghai. Do you not trust me to do this? To let me take Halfy's place?" She waited, her breath held as Samuel judged her worth—or lack thereof. And then he followed where she was leading.

"You are rushing to get to the celebration," he said.

She flushed, her eyes dropping to his left jacket pocket. "I'm not rushing," she said.

He reached into his jacket and pulled out the wooden case. In it lay the glass hypodermic. It landed on the desk with a muted thunk. From his other pocket he drew out a small bag that held opium. She could smell it in the air, taste the smoke on her tongue, even feel the sweet drug as it slipped into her bloodstream. She had just resolved to stand strong against her father, to act instead of run, and yet here she was, already weakening at the sight of a bag—a simple velvet bag.

"Should we start?" Samuel asked. "Do you want to celebrate now while your husband and I finish the last of the negotiations?"

"Yes." *No!* She took a deep breath and spoke a truth she had never voiced. "As long as you control the opium, father, you control me." She glanced sideways at Zhi-Gang. "And him. Therefore, let me run your trade in girls. Pay me in opium." She allowed herself to stretch her hand forward toward the velvet bag. "We can both get rich off the trade."

Samuel's hand shot out to grip her wrist. The bag contained a great deal of opium. He would not allow her to get to it. Not yet. Not until he had the deal he wanted. Beside her, Zhi-Gang stiffened. He wanted to protect her; She could feel his need like a wave that surrounded and supported her. With him here, she felt strong enough to face her father, to do what needed to be done.

"How many brothels? How will I run your trade?" she pressed.

"How much opium do you want?" Samuel asked.

She shrugged. "We can sell thirty pounds a month." An exorbitant amount, and it was roundly scoffed at by all in the room but Zhi-Gang. She had expected no less, even hoped for the reaction, as the two guards visibly relaxed with their laughter. They knew the rhythm of dicker, then celebration. Their services would not be needed, and so they relaxed, thinking they would simply be observers.

"Not so ridiculous an amount," Anna began. But Zhi-Gang stepped forward.

"For three beautiful girls? Twenty-five pounds a month. No less. There is a great hunger for opium in Jiangsu."

Samuel relaxed his grip on Anna's wrist and turned to Zhi-Gang. The two men engaged in a heated back and forth, apparently both enjoying the exercise. And as the negotiation continued, Samuel relaxed even more. He allowed Anna to take the velvet bag and the wood box.

She wasted no time. It only took her a moment to find the other necessary implements in the cabinet behind the desk. Then she was heating the opium and filling the needle with practiced movements. Behind her, Zhi-Gang had stepped closer, but not close enough to strike—she still stood somewhat between him and Samuel. There simply wasn't a lot of room behind the desk.

"I need the list, father," she muttered as if fully entranced with what she was doing. "The list of all your suppliers of girls. Not just the brothels. I might as well run all your shipments."

Samuel glanced at her. She barely noticed, so careful

was she being with the flame as she heated the opium. But she realized he was checking the steadiness of her hands. If she trembled at all, he would believe she was untrustworthy, still an addict.

But she had been weeks off of the drug now, thanks to Zhi-Gang. Her hands were rock steady. She glanced at Samuel. "Did you want the first taste?"

It was a calculated choice. No addict would offer that; they would say there was enough for both of them, then would take that first taste. She was proving she was not the fool he'd believed. In truth, the words were unnervingly difficult to say, but she forced them out with a smile.

Samuel shook his head, seemingly pleased. "Give it to your husband first."

Zhi-Gang declined.

"More for me," Anna said—and at that point her hand did tremble, for the hunger hit hard. Would it be so bad to just take a little? For show? It might even help their cause.

She deftly maneuvered the hypodermic needle, drawing up the potent liquid. Pure opium injected directly into the veins gave joy like no other. Then she glanced at Samuel, her words off-hand: "I need all of Halfy's records, father. I have to go over them to understand who brings girls for how much opium."

"Of course, of course," Samuel said with a casual wave. "All in good time."

Anna set the bag of opium back on the table. She tossed aside the stick that had heated the spoon that melted the powder. She set everything down except for the needle, which she kept gripped and aimed for her arm.

"Have I ever done something you didn't expect, Samuel? Ever?"

He blinked, surprised. A slow smile slid over his features. "You have been an excellent daughter."

"I assume that means no. I have always done as you expected, always performed up to expectations. Even beyond, I think."

His smile grew. "Of course. I was nervous when you ran off, but . . . you have done very well for yourself."

"For you," she corrected.

He nodded. "Yes."

"Then let me do this now. Let me show you how valuable I can be. You can supervise everything I do, but let me show you how profitable running girls can be. Tell me where Halfy's records are."

Samuel glanced at Zhi-Gang, then back to her. "You searched but couldn't find them?"

She nodded.

"That's because I have them. Here." He pointed to a leather satchel beneath his feet. "Halfy couldn't write worth a damn. Kept it all in that idiot brain of his."

Anna nodded. "So you had to keep his records. I will be a much better manager."

Samuel smiled. "Yes," he said as he bent down. Anna watched him haul the satchel up and flip open the cover. Inside were the thick books she remembered from a day long ago. She remembered Samuel writing her name in that book, and how proud she had been at the time. These indeed were the records Zhi-Gang needed. The books held enough information to end a large chunk of illicit trade—drugs, child prostitutes. Which meant it was finally time to end Samuel's hold on her for good.

It took an act of will. In the end, killing the man—even an evil man—was still damn hard. But she remembered all the lies he had told her, the families his opium had destroyed, and the girls he had bought and sold. Most of all, she knew that he wouldn't stop unless someone ended his reign. Someone like her. Right now.

While Samuel was bent over, she slammed the hypodermic down, straight into his neck. He reared up in shock, but not before she squeezed down, shooting a massive dose of pure opium into his body.

It was enough to kill him three times over. It certainly would be if it had been shot into his veins. But she hadn't hit his vein. While he would die, it would not be as fast.

The room erupted into chaos. Samuel roared, his massive hand going to his neck to pull out the needle. His movements were supposed to be slowing, his fingers fumbling from the drug. They weren't. His arms were very strong as he knocked her backward against the wall with one hand and dragged out the needle with the other.

"Kill them!" he bellowed.

The guards hadn't needed the order. They were already readying their weapons. But Zhi-Gang didn't given them the chance. As soon as she struck Samuel with the needle, he had dived for the bag of opium and whipped it at the face of the guard who held the pistol. The bag exploded, powder erupting into the air around him, fouling his grip and his vision.

But that didn't stop the other man, the one with Zhi-Gang's knives. He attacked with the speed of a monkey. He barreled forward without subtlety, going for Zhi-Gang, raising the blades with a roar of fury. Zhi-Gang took a step backward, reaching for Anna as Samuel straightened, his eyes blazing with fury.

"I'll handle Samuel!" she cried. Her voice rang out loud and strong, despite the fact that she felt slightly dazed from striking her head on the wall, and she couldn't understand why Samuel hadn't fallen to the ground dead.

Zhi-Gang meant to argue. She could tell by his expression, but the guard with the blades was swinging wildly across the wood expanse of the desk, and so he backed up with her nearly to the wall. The only one truly in danger from the blades was Samuel, who was heading for Anna, barely keeping himself out of range of the blades.

Samuel was breathing hard and his movements were erratic. "You whore!" he spat. "Bitch whore!"

He raised his massive fists, probably to strike her. But Anna had learned a few fighting tricks—some of them from Samuel himself. She ducked and slammed her shoulder into his chest. He gasped, and she felt the heavy impacts of his fists on her back. The first was a glancing blow that numbed her shoulder. The other landed like a hammer on her lower back. She cried out and dropped to her knees.

She barely had the strength to draw breath, much less tense for the coming rain of blows. But it didn't matter, she told herself; all she was doing was buying time for the opium to take effect.

The shower of blows never arrived. Out of the corner of her eye, Anna saw Zhi-Gang step over her and slam his fists into Samuel. She heard her adopted father grunt in surprise and watched as his feet stumbled over his satchel that lay open and abandoned on the floor. She looked up in time to see Zhi-Gang throw her adopted father backward over the desk and into the man swinging the deer-horn knives.

With a gasp of surprise, the guard tried to recover. Samuel, too, stretched forward to grab at Zhi-Gang. Neither succeeded. A blade sliced across Samuel's shoulder and bit into his neck. Blood spurted everywhere and both the guard and Anna's father screamed.

Anna straightened. She needed to see what she had wrought. She would not spare herself the consequences of her actions. But before she could size, Zhi-Gang slammed his open hand on her shoulder and pushed her back down. A second later, a pistol shot sounded. The other man.

Zhi-Gang leaped across the desk, slamming his fist into the face of the horrified guard with the knife embedded in Samuel's neck. Anna heard two, maybe three blows land—flesh hitting flesh, a grunt of pain and then a tell-tale gurgle. She prayed it was the man with the knives who was dead. It couldn't be Zhi-Gang . . .

She lifted her head far enough to see over the desk just as another pistol shot deafened her, and dropped back down with a squeak of terror. But not before she had seen Zhi-Gang, one of his knives back in his hand, leaping for the guard with the pistol.

Anna cringed and half crouched, half crawled around the desk. She had to help if she could. She had created this situation; she couldn't allow Zhi-Gang to face it alone.

But she was too late. She rounded the corner in time to see that both Samuel and the first guard were dead. And as she looked up, the one with the pistol was slowly sinking to the floor, a deer-horn knife sticking out of his chest.

She gaped. She was no stranger to blood or death, but it still took a moment for her to absorb the sight. Her gaze went to Zhi-Gang. He was spinning around, his black queue coiling around him as he moved. His eyes were fierce, his grip strong as he pulled his blade out of the last guard and scanned the room.

"Are you hurt?" she asked.

"Are you all right?" he said at the same time.

Both answers came equally fast.

"Fine."

"No injury."

Then there was a long moment of silence as both of them stared at each other, at the room, and processed the knowledge of what they had done.

"It's finished," Anna said quietly. "I'm free."

"I would have done it," he answered, equally softly. "You didn't need to—"

"I did. You have enough of a burden. This was mine." She straightened to her full height. "I am not running anymore."

He paused then nodded, his eyes grave as he looked at her, looked at the dead men around them and then, as if a cord holding him back abruptly snapped, he closed the space between them. She was enfolded in his arms before she had a chance to draw breath. His arms surrounded her, she buried her face in his chest, and then she wrapped her arms around him, gripping him with all her strength.

"You have his records," she murmured into his chest. "You can trace all the girls coming into his brothels—not just from Jiangsu, but all over. You can stop it now. You can—"

He stopped her words with a kiss. His mouth landed on hers with a fierceness that sent a thrill of delight through her body. He was marking her with his tongue, was claiming her as his own as he thrust against her own, stroked her teeth, even teased the roof of her mouth. She opened herself fully to him. More; she filled herself with him, allowing his brand to sear her.

She was his. Body and soul, she gave herself to him. And in the moment when he at last pulled back, his breath coming in aching gasps, she looked into his eyes and realized the truth: she was still going to run—this time from herself. She could go all the way to England, but her life in China would always be part of her, would always break her heart.

From Anna Marie Thompson's journal:
January 1, 1900

A new year, a new century, a new decision: I'm leaving China. The Enforcer follows me wherever I go, whatever I do. I feel him looking for me, searching. It can't be true. He doesn't know about me, but I still feel it. And I can't live like this anymore.

So, I'm leaving. I'll board a boat and escape. I don't even care where. Maybe England. Maybe my grandparents will change their minds once they meet me. I'll be like the Prodigal Son. They'll hug me and throw a party. Maybe . . .

It doesn't matter. I'm leaving because the Enforcer is coming. If he finds me, I'll never escape. . . .

I am in dread of the judgment of God upon England for our national iniquity towards China.
—*William Gladstone, 1842*

The cure for all ills and wrongs, the cares, the sorrows and the crimes of humanity, all lie in the one word "love." It is the divine vitality that everywhere produces and restores life.
—*Lydia Maria Child*

CHAPTER NINETEEN

Anna said nothing. The bodies were cleared, the walls scrubbed clean, and her hands were raw from washing. And yet, she felt right somehow. This was like the end of a disease, like moments after a surgery. The tumor had been removed, the patient was now recovering, and all would be well.

She stood in the doorway and watched Zhi-Gang work behind the desk, his glasses slipping to the end of his nose. His expression was tight, his attention fully focused on ledgers before him. And in that moment, her heart broke again as it had been breaking every moment of the last few hours.

It was time to leave, to face whatever fate handed her in England. Zhi-Gang had no need for a white wife, and she had no desire to remain in a country so filled with sorrow. Or so she told herself.

Unwilling to get dwell on what her future held, she

stepped fully into the room, saying the first words that came to mind. "Can you read English?"

"Some," he answered from the desk. Then he lifted his face to focus on her, his expression unreadable. "You are packed to leave."

She glanced down at the bundle in her hands. She held very little: two dresses of serviceable cotton tied together inside a shawl. It was hardly respectable—not by British standards—but would be enough for the boat ride. And once she landed, she would find something appropriately English to wear.

"I have some money in a Shanghai bank. I will withdraw it and be on the boat by evening."

"A good plan—if it is enough money."

She nodded that it was: She had adequate funds to establish herself wherever she choose. "What about you?" she asked. She took another step into the room, needing to close the distance between them one last time. "You'll be dealing with both Chinese and white men. Will you be able to keep up the fiction for long?"

He blinked. "What fiction?"

"That Samuel is alive. That you're in charge." She knew what he intended. He hoped to keep Samuel's network alive long enough for him to learn of others—opium smugglers, slavers, anyone involved in the man's unholy business.

He shook his head slowly. "Not likely."

"But you're going to try, aren't you? You're going to—"

He abruptly stiffened. "I am the Emperor's Enforcer. I will do my duty." His words were a vow. But it was a dark vow, one filled with frustration and pain. And yet the words and their force were integral to who he was, giving him purpose even as it exposed his heart.

At least she had lightened his load. At least she had done something good for this tortured man. If only . . .

"What will you do in England?" he asked. He stood with a weary sigh.

She blinked, thrown. "Well, I will find my family," she said. "They will welcome me with open arms—throw me a party, no doubt—and I shall eat tea and crumpets until I burst."

He nodded, his expression still blank, and stepped around the desk. "Do you like tea and crumpets?"

"Oh, yes," she lied. She'd never had them.

"And what of our marriage?" he suddenly said, his voice low enough to send a shiver up her spine. "What will you tell them of that?"

She twisted to face him. "I don't know. They will want me to marry, I suppose. That seems to be the way of things in England. I . . . uh . . . I shall tell them I am a widow, I suppose. That will explain my reluctance to wed again."

"But I am not dead." He stepped even closer. She did not shy backward, though the impulse surged through her. He was in a strange mood, wore the mask of neither Enforcer nor lover but a dark combination of both.

Yet she was trying to not run anymore—not from anyone, including Zhi-Gang. So she stiffened her legs and faced him. "You married me so you could kill me legally," she reminded him.

He nodded. "Yes, that is what I told you."

She lifted her chin. "It wasn't true?"

He was towering over her now, his eyes dark, his expression enigmatic. "Certainly not. I believe I wished to *bed* you legally." He shrugged. "My motivation was never truly clear—at least, not to myself."

She looked at him, really studied his expression. She saw the darkness inside. He would carry that with him always—because he was the Enforcer, because of what was done to Little Pearl on his behalf. That stain would color him forever. And yet, she saw something else too, something brighter that brought a shimmer of light to his eyes and a quirk to his lips.

"You know what you want now," she said softly. It wasn't a question. She could see the truth of it in his calm.

"I have always known. I wish to end the slave trade—especially whenever it is tied to opium."

True enough. "But there is more." She reached out to him, setting her palm flat against his chest. She needed to feel connected to him, wanted to know how his heart beat in his chest.

Quickly. It beat quickly.

She looked up at him. "What do you want *now?*"

"You have given me the tools to fight. If I stay in Shanghai, I will pretend to be Samuel. To have taken over—"

"Yes, yes," she interrupted. "I know this."

"It will work much better—I can maintain the fiction for longer—if . . . if you do it with me." He gestured to Samuel's books. "Some of that is in code."

She stared at him, and this time she did take a step back—but only to prevent herself from leaping into his arms. She needed to understand exactly what he wanted. "You want me to translate Samuel's books?"

"And trace the runners. And get me into the brothels, so I can catch the slavers."

Her heartbeat accelerated, the mythology of England fading into the very real, very exciting possibilities of a life in Shanghai. She could indeed be of enormous help to Zhi-Gang.

"I want to," she said, the words expelled without thought. She desperately wanted this with the same kind of hunger she had once reserved for opium.

"Then do so," he pressed.

"I . . ." Her voice trailed away as she struggled with her thoughts. "Don't you understand? I want to be done with my old life. I don't want to run opium or girls. I don't want to be a stranger in a terrible land." She dared to look up at him and voice her deepest longing. "I want to be a respectable woman. To have a husband and children."

He didn't answer with words. Instead, he reached out and stroked her shoulders. His touch was warm and gentle, but when she would have swayed close to him, he held her apart. And with excruciating slowness, he let one hand slip down to her belly.

"It may already be happening, you know. You could already be with child."

Her hands began to tremble with his words, and she tightened them into fists rather than allow him to see how much she'd thought about that possibility. The idea brought equal parts ecstasy and fear. A half-English, half-Chinese child? Terrible! And yet, the thought of a boy with Zhi-Gang's fierce determination or a girl with his dark, intense eyes—these things thrilled her. She longed for such a possibility, and yet—if it were true, if she were pregnant—what would she do?

"I can't," she gasped. "I couldn't manage that by myself. I wouldn't know what to do. I couldn't . . ."

"Not in England," he agreed. "You'd be alone there."

She didn't respond. He obviously believed as little of her family in England as she did.

"Stay with me, Anna. We can live with my sister. You can help me end the poisoning of China." His hand stroked her belly with a kind of reverence. "And our children will have a father and protector." He looked into her eyes. "What more could you want?"

"Nothing," she lied.

"Anna . . ." His hand left her belly to stroke under her chin, forcing her gaze to his.

"Do you love me?" she abruptly blurted. Her eyes filled with tears, shocked and appalled by what she had just said but unable to stop. "I have loved you for so long," she whispered. "That story I told to the widows, it wasn't just a clever lie. It's what I wanted, what I felt." She swallowed. "Zhi-Gang, I love you. And I want you to love me back. But I'm white. I'm a runner. And I'm an addict. You hate everything I am, everything I've done. You—"

He kissed her. He crushed her mouth to his and plunged his tongue into her, branding her again and again. And just like before, she surrendered herself, gave up completely to him. He was her salvation, her love, though she would wither and die if he didn't love her back. If he didn't need her as desperately as she needed him.

She broke the kiss. She pulled away, expecting to see regret in his eyes, a wish for something that could never be. But . . .

"I love you, Anna," he said. His words were simple and direct, and so unexpected she stared stupidly at him.

"But . . . But I'm . . ."

"Yes, you've been many terrible things. But Anna, I already married you, a white runner. Why else would I do that if I did not hunger for you?"

"Hunger," she whispered. "That's not love—"

"But it *is*," he said. "I love you. I have always loved you. Long before you made up fancy stories about our romance. Long before I searched through Jiangsu for you. I think I loved you the moment you cursed me from the side of the Grand Canal."

"But why?" she whispered. "How could you love me back then?"

He shrugged, completely uninterested in the details. "Who understands the workings of the heart? It goes where it will when it will. My heart chose you."

She thought about that, felt the truth of his words in his solid presence around her. Then she suddenly hit him in the chest. "You threatened to kill me!"

He nodded. "That too happens sometimes when a man falls in love. I was not happy to be so ensnared. Not by a white drug-runner."

"*I* didn't trap *you*," she objected. "*You* held *me* captive!"

He smiled as he dropped his forehead to hers. "Will you stay in China, sweet Anna? Will you help me stop the evil that continues to destroy us? Will you—"

"Raise our children together, enjoy your bed every night, and wake to your solid, strong presence every day?"

"Yes," he said.

"Yes," she answered.

The rest came easily. Before she could draw another breath, he lifted her in his arms. Her satchel dropped to the floor as he carried her to the bedroom. Then they shared kisses and caresses, the sweet ecstasy of joining that was all the more potent because it the two of them mated in love.

Ecstasy. With him.

Much later, when she lay languidly against him and his contentment filled the room, he dropped a kiss on her forehead. "We could study my sister's religion as well. We could learn what she teaches, maybe reach Heaven itself."

She nodded, though the motion took most of her strength. Truly, Zhi-Gang was a thoroughly wonderful, completely exhausting lover. "Heaven would be nice," she murmured. Then she tilted to look into his eyes. "Tell me again how it is different from what we have right here, right now?"

He thought for a moment, or perhaps he simply looked down at her, his gaze comforting even as his arms tightened about her. "You're right," he finally said. "We have already found heaven."

She grinned. "Then I'm staying right here. Forever."

For those who love the
Carpathian novels of Christine Feehan,
here is a preview of a sweeping tale of
encroaching darkness and healing
light by an exciting new author.

C. L. WILSON

Lord of the Fading Lands

AVAILABLE OCTOBER 2007

PROLOGUE

Loudly, proudly, tairen sing,
As they soar on mighty wings
Softly, sadly, mothers cry
To sing a tairen's lullabye.
                    —*The Tairen's Lament, Fey Nursery Rhyme*

The tairen were dying.

Rain Tairen Soul, king of the Fey, could no longer deny the truth. Nor, despite all his vast power and centuries of trying, could he figure a way to save either the creatures that were his soul-kin or the people who depended upon him to lead and defend them.

The tairen—those magnificent, magical, winged cats of the Fading Lands—had only one fertile female left in their pride, and she grew weaker by the day as she fed her strength to her six unhatched kitlings. With those tiny, unborn lives rested the last hope of a future for the tairen, and the last hope of a future for Rain's people, the Fey.

But today, the painful truth had become clear. The mysterious, deadly wasting disease that had decimated the tairen over the last millennium had sunk its evil, invisible claws into yet another clutch of unhatched kits.

When the tairen died, so too would the Fey. The fates of the two species were forever intertwined, and had been since the misty time before memory.

Rain looked around the wide, empty expanse of the Hall of Tairen. Indeed, he thought grimly, the death of the immortal Fey had begun centuries ago.

Once, in a time he could still remember, the Hall had rung with the sound of hundreds of Fey Lords, warriors, *shei'dalins* and Tairen Souls arguing politics and debating treaties. Those days had long passed. The Hall was silent now, as silent as the long-abandoned cities of the Fey, as silent as Fey nurseries, as silent as the graves of all those Fey who had died in the Mage Wars a thousand years ago.

Now the last hope for both the tairen and the Fey was dying, and Rain sensed a growing darkness in the east, in the land of his ancient enemies, the Mages of Eld. He couldn't help believing the two events were somehow connected.

He turned to face the huge priceless globe of magical Tairen's Eye crystal called the Eye of Truth, which occupied the center of the room. Displayed on the wings of a man-high stand fashioned from three golden tairen, the Eye was an oracle in which a trained seer could search for answers in the past, the present, and the infinite possibilities of the future. The globe was ominously dark and murky now, the future a dim, forbidding shadow. If there was a way to halt the relentless extermination of his peoples, the answer lay there, within the Eye.

The Eye of Truth had been guarding its secrets, showing shadows but no clear visions. It had resisted the probes of even the most talented of the Fey's still living seers, played coy with even their most beguiling of magic weaves. The Eye was, after all, tairen-made. By its very nature, it combined pride with cunning, passion with often-wicked playfulness. Seers approached it with respect, humbly asked it for a viewing, courted its favor with their minds and their magic but never their touch.

The Eye of Truth was never to be touched.

It was a golden rule of childhood, drummed into the head of every Fey from infant to ancient.

The Eye held the concentrated magic of ages, power so pure and undiluted that laying hands upon the Eye would be like laying hands upon the Great Sun.

But the Eye was keeping secrets, and Rain Tairen Soul was a desperate king with no time to waste and no patience for protocol. The Eye of Truth *would* be touched. He was the king, and he would have his answers. He would wrest them from the oracle by force, if necessary.

His hands rose. He summoned power effortlessly and wove it with consummate skill. Silvery white Air formed magical webs that he laid upon the doors, walls, floor, and ceiling. A spidery network of lavender Spirit joined the Air, then Earth to seal all entrances to the Hall. None would enter to disturb him. No scream, no whisper, no mental cry could pass those shields. Come good or ill, he would wrest his answers from the Eye without interruption—and if it demanded a life for his impertinence, it would be unable to claim any but his.

He closed his eyes and cleared his mind of every thought not centered on his current purpose. His breathing became deep and even, going in and out of his lungs in a slow rhythm that kept time with the beat of his heart. His entire being contracted into a single shining blade of determination.

His eyes flashed open, and Rain Tairen Soul reached out both hands to grasp the Eye of Truth.

"Aaahh!" Power—immeasurable, immutable—arced through him. His head was flung back beneath its onslaught, his teeth bared, his throat straining with a scream of agony. Pain drilled his body like a thousand *sel'dor* blades, and despite twelve hundred years of learning to absorb pain, to embrace it and mute it, Rainier writhed in torment.

This pain was unlike any he had ever known.

This pain refused to be contained.

Fire seared his veins and scorched his skin. He felt his soul splinter and his bones melt. The Eye was angry at his daring affront. He had assaulted it with his bare hands and bare power, and such was not to be borne. Its fury screeched along his bones, vibrating down his spine, slashing at every nerve in his body until tears spilled from his eyes and blood dripped from his mouth where he bit his lip to keep from screaming.

"*Nei*," he gasped. "I am the Tairen Soul, and I will have my answer."

If the Eye wished to cement the extinction of both tairen and Fey, it would claim Rain's life. He was not afraid of death; rather he longed for it.

He surrendered himself to the Eye and forced his tortured body to relax. Power and pain flowed into him, through him, claiming him without resistance. And when the violent rush of power had invaded his every cell, when the pain filled his entire being, a strange calm settled over him. The agony was there, extreme and nearly overwhelming, but without resistance he was able to distance his mind from his body's torture, to disassociate the agony of the physical from the determination of the mental. He forced his lips to move, his voice a hoarse, cracked whisper of sound that spoke ancient words of power to capture the Eye's immense magic in flows of Air, Water, Fire, Earth, and Spirit.

His eyes opened, glowing bright as twin moons in the dark reflection of the Eye, burning like coals in a face bone white with pain.

With voice and mind combined, Rain Tairen Soul asked his question: "How can I save the tairen and the Fey?"

Relentlessly, absorbing the agony of direct contact with the Eye, he searched its raging depths for answers. Millions of possibilities flashed before his eyes, countless variations on possible futures, countless retellings of past events. Millennia passed in an instant, visions so rapid his physical sight could never have hoped to discern them, yet his mind, steadily commanding the threads of magic, absorbed the images and processed them with brutal clarity. He stood witness to the deaths of billions, the rise and fall of entire civilizations. Angry, unfettered magic grew wild in the world and Mages worked their evil deeds. Tairen shrieked in pain, immolating the world in their agony. Fey women wept oceans of tears, and Fey warriors fell helpless to their knees, as weak as infants. Rain's mind screamed to reject the visions, yet still his hands gripped the Eye of Truth, and still he voiced his question, demanding an answer.

"How can I save the tairen and the Fey?"

He saw himself in tairen form, raining death indiscriminately upon unarmed masses, his own tairen claws impaling Fey warriors.

"How can I save the tairen and the Fey?"

Sariel lay bloody and broken at his feet, pierced by hundreds of knives, half her face scorched black by Mage fire. She reached out to him, her burned and bloodied mouth forming his name. He watched in helpless paralysis as the flashing arc of an Elden Mage's black *sel'dor* blade sliced down across her neck. Bright red blood fountained. . . .

The unutterable pain of Sariel's death—tempered by centuries of life without her—surged back to life with soul-shredding rawness. Rage and bloodlust exploded within him, mindless, visceral, unstoppable. It was the Fey Wilding rage, fueled by a tairen's primal fury, unfettered emotions backed by lethal fangs, incinerating fire, and access to unimaginable power.

They would die! They had slain his mate, and they would all die for their crime! His shrieking soul grasped eagerly for the madness, the power to kill without remorse, to scorch the earth and leave nothing but smoldering ruins and death.

"Nei!" Rain yanked his hands from the Eye and flung up his arms to cover his face. His breath came in harsh pants as he battled to control his fury. Once before, in a moment of madness and unendurable pain, he had unleashed the beast in his soul and rained death upon the world. He had slain thousands in mere moments, laid waste to half a continent within a few bells. It had taken the combined will of every still-living tairen and Fey to cage his madness.

"Nei! Please," he begged, clawing for self-possession. He released the weaves connecting him to the Eye in a frantic hope that shearing the tie would stop the rage fighting to claim him.

Instead, it was as if he had called Fire in an oil vault.

The world was suddenly bathed in blood as his vision turned red. The tairen in him shrieked for release. To his horror, he felt his body begin to dissolve, saw the black fur form, the lethal curve of tairen claws spear the air.

For the first time in twelve hundred years of life, Rainier vel'En Daris knew absolute terror.

The magic he'd woven throughout the Hall would never hold a Tairen Soul caught up in a Fey Wilding rage. All would die. The world would die.

The Tairen-Change moved over him in horrible slow motion, creeping up his limbs, taunting him with his inability to stop it. The small sane part of his mind watched like a stunned, helpless spectator, seeing his own death hurtling towards him and realizing with detached horror that he was going to die and there was nothing he could do to prevent it.

He had overestimated his own power and utterly underestimated that of the Eye of Truth.

"Stop," he shouted. "I beg you. Stop! Don't do this." Without pride or shame, he fell to his knees before the ancient oracle.

The rage left him as suddenly as it had come.

In a flash of light, his tairen-form disappeared. Flesh, sinew, and bone reformed into the lean, muscular lines of his Fey body. He collapsed face down on the floor, gasping for breath, the sweat of terror streaming from his pores, his muscles shaking uncontrollably.

Faint laughter whispered across the stone floor and danced on the intricately carved columns that lined either side of the Hall of Tairen.

The Eye mocked him for his arrogance.

"Aiyah," he whispered, his eyes closed. "I deserve it. But

I am desperate. Our people—mine and yours both—face extinction. And now dark magic is rising again in Eld. Would you not also have dared any wrath to save our people?"

The laughter faded, and silence fell over the Hall, broken only by the wordless noises coming from Rain himself, the sobbing gasp of his breath, the quiet groans of pain he didn't have the strength to hold back. In the silence, power gathered. The fine hairs on his arms and the back of his neck stood on end. He became aware of light, a kaleidoscope of color bathing the Hall, flickering through the thin veil of his eyelids.

His eyes opened—then went wide with wonder.

There, from its perch atop the wings of three golden tairen, the Eye of Truth shone with resplendent clarity, a crystalline globe blazing with light. Prisms of radiant color beamed out in undulating waves.

Stunned, he struggled to his knees and reached out instinctively towards the Eye. It wasn't until his fingers were close enough to draw tiny stinging arcs of power from the stone that he came to his senses and snatched his hands back without touching the oracle's polished surface.

There had been something in the Eye's radiant depths—an image of what looked like a woman's face—but all he could make out were fading sparkles of lush green surrounded by orange flame. A fine mist formed in the center of the Eye, then slowly cleared as another vision formed. This image he saw clearly as it came into focus, and he recognized it instantly. It was a city he knew well, a city he despised. The second image faded and the Eye dimmed, but it was enough. Rain Tairen Soul had his answer. He knew his path.

With a groan, he rose slowly to his feet. His knees trembled, and he staggered back against the throne to collapse on the cushioned seat.

Rain gazed at the Eye of Truth with newfound respect. He was the Tairen Soul, the most powerful Fey alive, and yet the Eye had reduced him to a weeping infant in mere moments. If it had not decided to release him, it could have used him to destroy the world. Instead, once it had beaten the arrogance out of him, it had given up at least one of the secrets it was hiding.

He reached out to the Eye with a lightly woven stream of Air, Fire and Water and whisked away the faint smudges left behind by the fingers he had dared to place upon it.

«*Sieks'ta. Thank you.*» He filled his mental tone with genuine respect and was rewarded by the instant muting of his body's pain. With a bow to the Eye of Truth, he strode towards the massive carved wooden doors at the end of the Hall of Tairen and tore down his weaves.

«*Marissya.*» He sent the call to the Fey's strongest living *shei'dalin* even as he reached out with Air to swing open the Hall's heavy doors before him. The Fey warriors guarding the door to the Hall of Tairen nodded in response to the orders he issued with swift, flashing motions of his hands as he strode by, and the flurry of movement behind him assured him his orders were being carried out.

«*Rain?*» Marissya's mental voice was as soothing as her physical one, her curiosity mild and patient.

«*A change of plans. I'm for Celieria in the morning and I'm doubling your guard. Let your kindred know the Feyreisen is coming with you.*»

Even across the city, he could feel her shocked surprise, and it almost made him smile.

Half a continent away, in the mortal city of Celieria, Ellysetta Baristani huddled in the corner of her tiny bedroom room, tears running freely down her face, her body trembling uncontrollably.

The nightmare had been so real, the agony so intense. Dozens of angry, stinging welts scored her skin . . . self-inflicted claw marks that might have been worse had her fingernails been longer. But worse than the pain of the nightmare had been the helpless rage and the soul-shredding sense of loss, the raw animal fury of a mortally wounded heart. Her own soul had cried out in empathetic sorrow, feeling the tortured emotions as if they had been her own.

And then she'd sensed something else. Something dark and eager and evil. A crouching malevolent presence that had ripped her out of sleep, bringing her bolt upright in her bed, a smothered cry of familiar terror on her lips.

She covered her eyes with shaking hands. *Please, gods, not again.*